DAMAGED LIVES

Nico Swaan

RETHINK PRESS

First published in Great Britain 2015
by Rethink Press (www.rethinkpress.com)

© Copyright Nico Swaan

All rights reserved. No part of this publication may be reproduced, stored in or introduced into a retrieval system, or transmitted, in any form, or by any means (electronic, mechanical, photocopying, recording or otherwise) without the prior written permission of the publisher.

The right of Nico Swaan to be identified as the author of this work has been asserted by him in accordance with the Copyright, Designs and Patents Act 1988.

This book is sold subject to the condition that it shall not, by way of trade or otherwise, be lent, resold, hired out, or otherwise circulated without the publisher's prior consent in any form of binding or cover other than that in which it is published and without a similar condition including this condition being imposed on the subsequent purchaser.

This is a work of fiction. All characters in this book are fictitious. Any resemblance to real persons, either living or dead, is entirely coincidental.

Cover images © Shutterstock/Adrian Pluskota/Sean Gladwell/Peshkova/Anelina

This novel is dedicated to Barbara and Ellionna, who helped me to discover the sweet as well as the bitter complexities of human relationships.

PROLOGUE

1983

'Hey, Thomas. Aren't you going to invite me to dance?'

'Of course, my… um, Saoirse.'

'You almost said something else, didn't you?' she asked, smiling teasingly.

'I'm guilty. But I'm doing my best to behave.'

'I've said it before and I'll say it again: I really am so very happy that you're here. It means so much to me. Thank you.'

'So am I.' He spoke only a half-truth. Since his arrival in Dublin he had been unable to stop the fruitless current of 'if-onlys' in his head. Saoirse [*Seersha*] looked radiantly happy so he had to be happy for her.

She gave him a peck on the cheek. They shared a secret probably nobody else knew about… or did they? Thomas didn't know whether Saoirse had ever revealed to Brian the true extent of their former relationship.

She looked stunning in her long cream-coloured wedding dress. The contrasting memory of Saoirse in her shiny wet jeans in County Clare four years earlier flashed through his mind.

'And what are you smiling about now?' she asked as they stepped onto the dance floor.

'I had a sudden flashback to the beach near Spanish Point. Sorry. I probably shouldn't be going back there now, should I?' He tried to look repentant but couldn't quite manage it.

'Do. Those are our memories. Treasure them as I do.'

They danced to a slow waltz, Thomas wondering whether this might be the last time he would be able to feel her so close to him. When the music stopped Saoirse placed her hands on his shoulders and looked into his eyes. He was astonished to see that her wonderful grey-green eyes were covered with a film of moisture.

'Saoirse?'

'Write, Thomas. Stay in touch, please,' she said softly.

He fought off the urge to throw his arms around her and searched for an adequate response to replace the 'Goodbye, Saoirse, and be happy' which he had thought would be more appropriate.

'I will, I promise.'

She gave him a quick hug and another kiss on the cheek before moving away from him, from his life, perhaps forever, like a beautiful princess lured away in a sad children's story. She blended into what looked like a tank full of colourful, exotic fish swimming in random directions while avoiding contact – until the band struck up the next number and the fish paired off, moving in rhythm, as if in a mating dance.

He wondered what Saoirse had meant. Why that look on what was supposed to be the most joyous day of her life?

He fought a desire to get away as quickly as possible and stayed for another half hour, chatting politely with several guests. After saying his farewells to Saoirse's mother, brother — and of course Briana — he retreated from the elegant ballroom. Memories played through his mind, memories of when he had first met Saoirse five years earlier.

Should I be here at all? Am I in a dream – or in a nightmare?, he wondered.

Images of both Saoirse and Briana drifted through his mind as he fell into a sleep filled with strange, unsettling and dark dreams of which only feelings of separation and loss survived his waking.

CHAPTER I

1978

On a Friday evening in early September, a week after arriving in Belfast, Thomas walked through a depressing drizzle to Foyle's Bar. His fellow journalist Rupert had recommended it as a friendly and relaxed place, in contrast to Daly's pub, where he had spent an unusual evening six days earlier.

Foyle's was brightly lit and filled with the noise of conversation and laughter. A row of beer taps and a short row of whiskey bottles on a shelf behind the bar gave a clue to the popular drinks. The walls were covered with faded photographs, prints, bric-a-brac and antique agricultural tools. The long bar was on the left; tables and chairs filled the area to the right and at the back. At one table, three men and a woman repeatedly burst forth in gales of laughter. Two men just down the bar were engaged in earnest conversation. Whether about philosophy, religion, or politics, they spoke earnestly and respectfully, occasionally touching each other's arm or shoulder in apparent friendship when making a point.

'Hi there. What can I get you?'

Thomas turned towards the sparkling voice and saw a very attractive woman in her mid to late twenties. Auburn hair fell in a fringe over her forehead and flowed evenly over her shoulders. She had sparkling grey-green eyes, even features and a clear complexion with just a hint of freckles. She wore a dark blue shirt, knotted at the waist.

The contrast between her and the tired, desperate mothers or Sarah could not have been greater. Seeing such an attractive woman came as a surprise. Her expression and eyes radiated an extraordinary intelligence.

'What can I get you?' she repeated, with just a hint of impatience.

'Umm, sorry, I'd like a pint please.'

'Aye, and what sort of pint might that be?' She looked at him directly, holding his eyes.

His mind went blank. 'What would you recommend?'

She nodded and stepped towards one of the taps, to return two minutes later. 'Try this then.'

He looked at the glass with its almost black liquid topped by thick creamy foam.

'Thank you.'

She winked at him and quickly moved off to another customer, her bright eyes lingering in his memory.

The cheerfulness all around lifted his spirits. Maybe this was where people came to stay sane. His eyes followed the young woman behind the bar. Suddenly he felt an awkward teenager again, forced to go to a dance, seeing a pretty girl and being too shy to even say hello.

Thomas broke out of his reverie and joined a group of three welcoming older men standing further down the bar. One, with a red, bulbous nose, introduced himself as Bernard. After a few minutes of small talk Thomas asked, 'Bernard, how would you explain to an American what's going on here in Northern Ireland?'

Bernard looked surprised by the question. He glanced at his companions and they all laughed.

'You Americans get to the point quickly, don't you? But let me try to give you an answer. Now, to understand it properly you'd have to be going back to the 12th century. Henry the Second was the first English king to give himself the title "King of Ireland".'

A companion with bushy sideburns interjected with a laugh, 'No, Bernard, it started when the English brought all them Scottish Protestants into Ulster in the 17th century, after the Irish were betrayed by the Spaniards and lost the Battle of Kinsale.'

A wiry man entered the discussion. 'What are ye all on about?

Don't be confusing this gentleman now. All he needs to know is that in 1690, as any school-boy will tell you, King Billy sent King James and his Papists running off with their tails between their legs. The Papists were poor losers.'

Thomas laughed. 'Gentlemen, you're sure succeeding in confusing me. And I don't sense much agreement amongst you here.'

'Disagreeing is so much more fun,' said Bernard, and they all laughed. Thomas was surprised by the light-hearted way they talked about disagreeing in a country where disagreement had led to so much bloodshed.

'Okay, now whether you go back to the 12th or the 17th century,' Thomas persisted, 'how does that explain what's going on in Belfast and the rest of the North today?'

'We're still defending our country against the Papists.'

'Ah, such a predictable comment from you, Fred. But you've got it all wrong again. It's really about what it's always been about in Ireland: land and power. And the politicians are still fighting centuries-old battles over the bodies of our young men, from both sides.'

'I'd say it's all down to discrimination against the Catholics by the Protestants.'

And so the discussion went back and forth, with each taking his turn to buy a round of beer, even as they disagreed.

'Is there anything you can agree about here in Northern Ireland then?' Thomas asked.

'No, probably not,' Bernard replied, laughing. 'We'll disagree with anyone about anything. It's a way of life for us. But not all of us reach for a gun to settle the argument.'

'Bernard, tell me. I know there has been and is a lot of misery and suffering here, and I've seen some myself in just a week. But you fellows all seem to be of good cheer. How do you do it?'

'Ah now, it's not always easy, to be sure, and sometimes you have to pretend, or it'll all drive you quite mad.'

Thomas' eyes continued to follow the young woman behind the

bar and he wondered whether she was pretending too. Twenty minutes later she appeared before him again.

'How are you getting on with that pint?' Her eyes seemed to look at him in a mocking, yet friendly way. Though he found the beer smooth it was treacly and too warm for his taste. 'Yes, fine, thank you.'

She leaned towards him over the bar and looked directly into his eyes again. 'You know what now? I don't think you really like that Guinness at all. Let me take that from you and let you try something else.'

'How did you know...?'

'Ah now, I'll only warn you once. I read minds, and yours is an open book.'

He felt caught out and embarrassed.

She laughed and turned away, to return after a few moments with a lighter beer.

'You're American?'

'I am, but I try to play that down. I've already understood that Americans are not universally popular here in the North.'

'I guess that's wise. But what brings you here then?'

'I'm a journalist.'

'Then you'll probably be staying in the Europa.'

He nodded.

'We get folks from there from time to time, usually in pairs or small groups, and they spend their time talking with each other. But you came in alone.'

'Yes, well, I didn't come to Belfast to meet fellow journalists.'

'Don't go away. I'll be back,' she promised, as she moved several yards down the bar to attend to another customer.

'She's lovely, isn't she?' Bernard asked, rhetorically.

'Yes, yes, she certainly is.'

'Shauna knows how to treat people real well, so they keep coming back. She's very sweet – but if someone steps out of line she'll let him have it. Has a temper too.'

'I can believe it.'

She returned. 'Shauna', she announced, stretching her right hand out towards him.

'Thomas, Thomas Cassidy.'

Her hand felt warm in his.

'How are you then, Thomas?'

'Thanks, great.'

Thomas had the feeling that she was able to look straight through him. Had he met someone from whom he could hide nothing? A scary thought.

Shauna went off again to pour a couple of pints. Two older men with wizened faces who had come in earlier unpacked cases and took chairs at the back, armed with a fiddle and a whistle. They started to warm up. Thomas had noticed a sign announcing 'live music' beside the door but had assumed that it had been hanging there since before the Troubles began. The two musicians played a tune and were soon joined by three others, one with a banjo, one with a concertina and one with another fiddle. They chatted over their pints before embarking on a couple of cheerful airs. Foot tapping, applause and verbal encouragement greeted their performance. One of the musicians called out, 'Shauna, will ye join us?'

Shauna said something to the man who was apparently her boss. He smiled and nodded. When she had finished drawing another pint Shauna stepped towards the musicians. They consulted one another briefly. After some opening chords, Shauna joined them with a clear, beautiful voice. The words were familiar to Thomas:

Down by the salley gardens my love and I did meet;
She passed the salley gardens with little snow-white feet.
She bid me take love easy, as the leaves grow on the tree;
But I, being young and foolish, with her did not agree.

The song was greeted with cries of 'More, Shauna, more!'

'Maybe later, lads. Have to work, ye know.'

When Shauna came back to check on him Thomas said, 'William Butler Yeats'.

'Yes, I'm impressed.'

'I studied and loved Yeats when I was at college. It's an early, simple poem, and you made it sound absolutely wonderful.'

'Thank you, Thomas,' she responded brightly, before hurrying back to work.

Thomas was smitten. He felt that he had left the pain and darkness of Belfast behind and found a little bit of Irish heaven. At the same time he was dismayed by his unexpected feelings towards Shauna. He had hoped that he would stay well clear of anything like this while in Belfast.

The music went on, with a short break, for well over an hour. Thomas shared his surprise at finding music in Belfast at all.

'It's the only pub in the centre with music these days, sadly enough,' was Bernard's answer.

Thomas thought he should be getting back to the hotel, but couldn't tear himself away. Shauna returned once to the musicians. When she sang, the pub went very quiet and, if Thomas wasn't mistaken, some eyes misted over as their owners listened.

At the next opportunity, Thomas said, 'That was a very beautiful and sad song. What was it?'

'It's called "Steal Away", written by a fellow from Derry. It's about two young lovers who want to get out of Belfast and go away somewhere together to find a new life.'

'Do you? Want to go away, I mean,' Thomas asked, surprising himself with this forward question.

'Yes, someday… but not yet. I have to stay for now. But hey, do you read minds as well then?'

Thomas, at a loss again, just smiled.

The crowd was thinning, returning to the rain, the cold, and the empty streets. It was time for him to leave too. He caught Shauna's eye and settled up, leaving a generous tip, and said he would be back.

'I hope so,' she said brightly.

With what afterwards seemed like someone else's voice, he added, 'I really enjoyed your songs, Shauna, and I couldn't take my eyes off you all night.'

Before he had time to get embarrassed, she replied, with a twinkle in her eyes, 'I know. Take care, now.'

He walked back to the hotel, oblivious to the wind and the cold drizzle in his face. Back in his room, as he lay in bed, he kept hearing Shauna's voice and her songs. The contrast between Shauna and Sarah passed through his mind. Had Sarah ever been like Shauna?

David, his boss and editor at the *Boston Tribune*, had offered Thomas an assignment in Belfast, providing him with a welcome opportunity to find his own way, without having to respond to daily assignments, while becoming better acquainted with Irish culture. Also, nobody there would bug him about finding a new girlfriend. Nobody there would push him to connect with others – or himself – at an emotional level. Maybe, though, that had been a naïve idea and Rupert had been right. 'Stay in Belfast long enough,' he had said, 'and you'll meet yourself whether you want to or not.'

Now he had met Shauna. Shauna with the alluring smile, the wonderful voice and, above all, the amazing eyes. First Sarah, then Owen, and now a totally different person, Shauna. He felt he was falling in love and couldn't wait to see her again.

Or should I avoid going to Foyle's ever again? he wondered. A girl in a bar. Jesus, Thomas, what are you doing?

CHAPTER 2

The afternoon after his arrival in Belfast Thomas emerged from the hotel to explore the area. He passed through the security fence and turned left, crossed at the first intersection, headed down Howard Street and lost himself in the busy streets, which looked grey and cheerless. He was reminded of photographs of Boston and other American cities during the great depression. It was Saturday and shoppers filled the sidewalks. He tried to study the people as they walked by, and saw pale, freckled, unsmiling faces that reflected few signs of happiness. These are the people I have come here to meet, he thought. These are the people whose stories I want to write about. For the moment he just looked, unnoticed by anyone, as they rushed by. Most were dressed in drab, well-worn clothing. Thomas wondered what was going through their minds and what had happened in their personal lives. What opportunities would present themselves or would he be able to create to find out about them?

He wandered into a couple of shops and listened to the shoppers and shopkeepers, husbands and wives, mothers and children interact. It would be a challenge to get used to the way these people spoke English; sometimes he couldn't begin to make out what they were saying, with their heavy accents.

Some shops were boarded up, the plywood covered with graffiti. He passed what had once been a restaurant, but was now a mass of rubble behind a chain-link fence. He recalled the heavy 'boom' he had had heard the previous evening. 'That was a bomb,' Rupert, an English journalist from Manchester, had explained laconically, going on to add that the Europa had the dubious reputation of being the most-bombed hotel in the world.

Heavily armed police surveyed the scene warily from street corners. He had occasionally encountered a strong police presence before, like during the bussing riots in South Boston, but here it was apparently quite normal.

Nevertheless Thomas felt a great excitement. For two months or so this would be his territory to explore — perhaps occasionally guided by Henry in London or David in Boston, but he would decide about whom and what he would write. It was these people whose stories he would try to tell. The challenge was daunting but the sense of freedom to pursue whatever he wanted was exhilarating.

He recalled what Rupert had said during dinner the previous evening:

'In my experience, what you write will say as much about you as it does about the people or events you write about.' That had given him pause because he had not thought of it that way. He had jumped at the opportunity to 'cover' Belfast in order to get away from himself. It offered an escape from a series of unhappy months in Boston. His last girlfriend, Jennifer, had walked out three months earlier after an angry scene.

'You're so damned stuck in your head, Thomas. Eight months, and I still haven't got a clue who you really are. I never know how you're really feeling. Or don't you have any fucking feelings? Where's the connection, the passion? Even when we make love you're somewhere else.'

That had cut deeply because he liked Jennifer. He had enjoyed their trips to theatres and museums, their dinners out and their evenings reading and talking about poetry. He missed her, but he understood her point. In bed, he couldn't deny, he wasn't able to be 'all there' with his partner. He had not talked about himself, nor had he inquired in depth about her. Before Jennifer it had always been short affairs, casual sex, and it didn't matter. He had hoped for a deeper relationship with her, and now wondered whether a deeper and truly open relationship would ever be possible for him. Sometimes he thought it was due to his upbringing. His parents didn't talk about personal things; 'love' was neither mentioned nor displayed. He had never felt free to talk about his feelings or anxieties, and certainly not about his big secret. After he moved to Boston to study he returned to his parents' house near Philadelphia as little as possible.

Thomas caught himself. 'Damn,' he thought. Here he was in the middle of Belfast and he had just covered two city blocks while turned inward rather than outward. He refocused on his surroundings. Shop names were quite different from the familiar names and brands in Boston. The produce in a grocery store bore different labels. Even the cuts of meat in a butcher shop had largely unfamiliar names. He was a foreigner here, and it felt truly exciting.

Rupert had suggested he visit Daly's Pub if he wanted to get an impression from the Loyalist, Protestant perspective. When asked 'Why Daly's?', Rupert had simply smiled and replied, 'You'll see. But mind yourself, old chap!'

After a simple dinner of boiled ham, cabbage and mashed potatoes in an unpretentious restaurant, Thomas found the pub. Daly's exterior was a dark, dirty green. The interior looked as if it had not been painted or washed down in a century. The men leaning over the bar or seated at small tables ranged from their twenties to their sixties. Most wore frayed jackets or sweaters and corduroy trousers. Thomas felt conspicuous in his American-style light blue, buttoned-down shirt and khaki trousers. The air was heavy with cigarette smoke, most facial expressions were tight and grim, and conversations were generally subdued. There was only one woman, seated alone in a far corner.

Thomas ordered a pint and tried to take in what was going on. Though intensely curious, he didn't want to be intrusive. A few pairs of eyes glanced up briefly. He smiled and nodded whenever he noticed someone looking at him, probably sizing him up. He wondered how obvious it was that he was a visitor, a foreigner, an American.

After only five minutes a man of about 50, sporting bushy, greying sideburns, sat down beside him.

'You're new here, aren't you? You sounded like an American when you ordered your beer. Am I right?'

'Yes, you are, on both counts. I'm a journalist for the *Boston Tribune* and in fact just arrived yesterday.'

'Then I should say, welcome to Belfast. But the way we hear it, American reporters like to make the IRA out for a bunch of heroes,' the man said. 'Are you going to be writing more of that same shite?'

'You're right that news coverage in the States has frequently been one-sided. That's something I'd like to help correct.'

The small talk developed politely and Thomas hoped the man was sizing him up before opening up. Eventually he introduced himself as David and offered another pint.

'Seriously now, you Americans tend to glorify the IRA gunmen as freedom fighters. Well, the truth is different. It's we Protestants who've been fighting for our freedom, for more than 300 years. The IRA? They're a band of thugs and murderers, agents of the Papists who run the show in Dublin.'

Thomas nodded, hoping to encourage David to keep talking. David waved an index finger in front of Thomas' face to emphasise each point he made.

'We'll not have our country ruled by the bishops. We're fighting to keep our freedom. We don't want violence, but the IRA and the Catholics are forcing it on us.'

He nodded. David had worked himself up and kept on talking, interrupting himself only long enough to slake his thirst. It was difficult to cut in with a comment or a question.

'Sure, in Dublin they have their president, their prime minister and their parliament. But they never pass a law that's not been approved by the bishops and the bishops don't approve of anything that's not been approved by the Pope.'

'David, as I understand it, there's a growing resentment in the South as well at what they call the rule of the bishops. Doesn't that ...'

David interrupted. 'Well, it's about bloody time, but that just makes my point, doesn't it? Just a month or two ago the fuckin' archbishop had the nerve to come up here to visit the prisoners in the Maze and liken it to a Calcutta slum. Well, what do they expect, that we build them a friggin' Hilton Hotel? Last February the IRA firebombed a small hotel and killed 12 Protestants. For what? For attending a dinner and dance sponsored by the Collie Club, for chrissake!'

David paused to drain the rest of his pint and order another.

'We're defending our way of life, Thomas. Now you tell that to your readers.'

'I will, David.'

David went off to the men's room and Thomas felt himself relaxing into this unusual environment. Just then a younger man, noticeably drunk, staggered up and stood beside Thomas, swaying, his mouth twisted aggressively.

'So ye're a fuckin' American, are ye?'

Thomas nodded.

'Ye Americans might as well come over here and shoot our women and children yerselves.'

'What do you mean?' Thomas asked, taken aback.

'Ye've been buyin' guns for the IRA for years, haven't ye?'

He had heard doubts about the true motives behind the Irish Northern Aid Committee's campaign, supposedly to raise money for widows and orphans and support the peace process. But this strong anti-American feeling surprised him and he couldn't immediately think of what to say in reply. He looked down into his glass while considering an appropriate response.

The man raised his voice. 'Hey, I'm talkin' to ye. Are ye ignorin' me now?'

The man took a step forward and pushed against Thomas's shoulders aggressively with both hands. He retained his balance on the bar stool, but the man stepped forward again, his arms raised. In his drunkenness he was slow and Thomas reacted quickly. He grabbed the man's left arm with his right hand, twisted it towards the man's back and, sweeping his right leg across the man's legs while pushing him forward, had him on the floor. With one knee on the ground, he held the left arm firmly. The man swore. Thomas let go and started to get up in time to see another man step towards him.

'Stop! Dan, stop right there, Jamie started this.' It was the man behind the bar asserting his authority, and Dan backed off. Thomas offered Jamie a hand.

'I'm sorry, I hope I didn't hurt you,' he apologised.

Jamie looked more shocked than hurt.

'Fuckin' hell! Are ye a commando or something?'

Thomas was still breathing heavily. 'No, I'm just a journalist. I'm sorry.'

Jamie muttered in slurred syllables at the bartender. 'Can't even have a quiet drink anymore. Fuck this.'

He staggered towards the door and left.

Thomas was still waiting for the adrenaline to subside. He wondered whether Rupert had foreseen that this might happen when suggesting the place. The publican turned to Thomas.

'I'm sorry about Jamie there. He's a dear lad, usually. Y'see, his brother was killed by the IRA four years back now. He loses it sometimes. It's what all this shite does to people, you know.'

Thomas thanked the publican and made to leave.

'I'm sorry about causing a disturbance.'

'I'm Ian. Stay, and have another pint on the house.'

'Oh... well, thank you very much, Ian. I'm Thomas, and sorry again about causing a problem.'

'You didn't start it. You're very welcome. I picked up enough to understand that you came here to find out about what the Troubles are doing to people. Well, you saw a bit of it for yourself. There is a lot of anger, a lot of fear. It's sad. Jamie and others like him were – and are – really very good people. But where did you learn that move you put on Jamie? Never seen anything like it.'

Thomas played it down. 'Oh, I spent a number of years learning some martial arts.'

'Well, you learned something pretty well. And I wouldn't take you for a tough guy.'

That, Thomas reflected, was exactly why he had taken up taekwondo and, later, judo. As a teenager he had what people called a baby-face; he was regarded as being 'bookish', did not engage in team sports and had sometimes been picked on mercilessly by classmates. He had learned how to survive.

Thomas took a draught from the pint Ian had offered him, and, gradually calming down, returned to his reason for being there.

'Ian, I'm just a naïve Yank. So help me out. What's going on here in Northern Ireland, for the ordinary folk just trying to have a life?'

'Protestants are afraid that a growing Catholic population will tip the balance of power and result in a united Ireland, run by Catholics and the Pope. They're afraid of losing their identity as part of the United Kingdom. The Catholics, well, I suppose they're afraid of what they see as continuing repression by a majority that waves the union flag. And today: well, most everyone's afraid of the other side's paramilitaries.'

David returned and Ian, deftly changing the subject, told a local joke, shifting into an exaggerated Belfast accent.

'Now did ye hear 'bout yer man from Belfast who, bein' 'shamed of his accent, went to England to learn the Queen's English?'

'No, I haven't.'

'Well now, he was there for three years and learned to speak like an English gentleman. He came back here, went into the first establishment he could find, and said "I say, old chap, perhaps you could furnish me with a large gin and tonic?" "No, I can't," said the proprietor. "Well why the fuck not?" says the man, reverting to his Belfast accent. "Now you see, this here's not a pub, it's a butcher shop."'

Thomas joined Ian and David in their laughter. It was the first Irish joke he had heard, and he was pleased with what he experienced as a certain measure of acceptance in this, in some ways such an alien, environment.

He looked again at the woman sitting alone in the corner, half hidden behind a dense haze of cigarette smoke. She looked to be in her early thirties but might have been younger. Her face was an expressionless mask, though it could once have been quite attractive. No makeup, tightly drawn mouth, carelessly brushed blond hair half covering her face. She wore a dark brown dress under a grey cardigan and stared fixedly ahead over her beer.

'Ian, do you know anything about the woman in the corner?' Thomas asked.

Ian shrugged his shoulders.

'Not much. She used to come in here a lot with her fella. All lovey-dovey they were too, and kept to themselves. She looked, well, real pretty then. But then she started to come in by herself, always sitting at the same table, looking… well, whatever. Never talks to no one.'

'I wonder what happened,' Thomas said more to himself than to Ian.

'Terrible things happen to people every day here.'

Thomas carried his glass across to her table.

'May I sit down?'

'Ah, go fuck yerself, will ye.' She didn't so much as glance at him.

Deciding not to retreat immediately, he drew a business card identifying himself as a journalist from the *Boston Tribune* from his pocket and slid it over the table towards her.

'I'm not trying to pick you up.'

She glanced at the card and looked up at him briefly.

'Ye act more like some kung-fu master than a journalist, but what the fuck do ye want with me then?'

'I'm here to find out more about what the situation in this country is doing to people's lives. You look like you have story to tell.'

'So ye can score with yer fuckin' editor?'

'No, I'm just trying to understand.'

Thomas slowly pulled out a chair and sat down. She lit a cigarette and drew on it angrily, her wide eyes looking past him. He expected her to get up and walk, but she remained seated.

'Your glass is almost empty. Would you like a refill?'

A long silence ensued. He waited quietly, if not comfortably.

Finally she said, 'Yeah, sure.' Her shoulders and face relaxed ever so slightly and she added, 'Ye're lookin' to understand? How do ye understand insanity?'

He stepped over to the bar and asked for what the woman had been drinking. Ian raised an eyebrow, and pulled a half pint of Harp.

Placing the drink in front of her, he lifted his and said 'Cheers' quietly.

She didn't return his toast, but killed her cigarette, picked up her glass and took a deep swallow. She looked at him closely for the first time. He looked back at her dark, solemn eyes. Thomas wondered whether he had been right to confront the woman. He slowly pushed back his chair and started to get up, saying, 'I'm sorry for intruding.'

'No, wait,' she said, with an urgency that surprised him.

He sat down again as she studied his face.

'I killed a man,' she said, almost in a whisper, her face betraying nothing.

Thomas looked at her, wondering why she should make such an open confession to a stranger. Or was a stranger the only person she could tell this to?

'I'll do it again, too.'

'I'm Thomas. What's your name?'

'Ye can call me Sarah.'

'Why, Sarah? Why did you kill a man?' Thomas enquired gently.

She looked directly at him. He tried to interpret the look in her eyes. Did he see hatred, or anger, or grief? All three?

'They killed me husband, that's why. The fuckin' IRA killed me husband.' Without raising her voice, she spat those last words out.

'I'm very sorry, Sarah.'

'They shot him outside a pub three months ago. He never done nuthin' to no one.'

Her eyes took on a pleading expression, as if seeking understanding or even forgiveness.

'So you killed the person who was responsible?'

'They're all responsible, aren't they?' she exclaimed, with venom in her voice. 'I know where those Provos hang out. I just chose one, followed him, and shot him in the head when no one was around. Pinned a note to his jacket saying "Greetings from Fergal". His mates is probably still wondrin' who the fuck Fergal is.'

'Fergal was your husband?'

'Yeah. Married just over a year we were, just a year…'

Thomas tried again to look behind her eyes, to discover what lay hidden there.

'The RUC must have investigated that shooting, I mean your husband's. Did they…'

'The RUC are a useless fuckin' bunch of eejits. Think they've done their job when they've rounded up another dozen or so RAs and sent them to the Maze. They'll never find who killed Fergal.'

She paused for a quick drink and then continued in a hushed tone. 'The bastards killed me that night too.'

He tried to imagine her as she might have been four months ago: laughing, singing, dancing, loving? A part of her certainly seemed dead now.

'Can I get you another beer?' he asked.

'No, but I'll have a Bushmills if ye're offrin'.'

He walked to the bar and asked for two Bushmills. Ian gave him a quizzical look but was quick to pour two shots.

'Sarah's not your real name, is it?'

'I don't have a name anymore. "Sarah" will do.'

'Okay, Sarah… Thank you for telling me what you have.'

When she looked up he thought he saw a hint of tears in her eyes.

'Ye're the first person I've told me story to, d'ye know that? I'm not even sure why.'

She lapsed back into silence and downed the rest of her whiskey in one go.

'Enjoy Belfast, and thanks for the whiskey,' were her last words before she stood up abruptly and stepped towards the door.

He remained where he was for a couple of minutes, digesting the woman's story, before returning to the bar.

Ian quickly appeared in front of him.

'You're the first person she's spoken more than two words to for months. What's your secret?'

'I really don't know, Ian.'

'I'm guessing she and her man broke up.'

'Yeah, or something…'

Thomas downed his whiskey, thanked Ian and bade him farewell.

Her question, 'How do you understand insanity?' reverberated through his head as he walked back to the hotel. He was glad to see Rupert, reading a book and having a drink, in the downstairs bar.

'I took your advice and dropped by Daly's this evening. Strange place.'

'For someone just in from Boston, I'm sure it is. How did you get on?'

'I almost got into a brawl and had an amazing conversation. It's given me a couple of things to write about, for sure.'

Rupert smiled. 'You don't look like the brawling sort. What happened?'

Thomas played back his encounters with David, Jamie, Ian and Sarah.

'You're off to a good start then, mate.'

Rupert was athletically built and had a lined face with bags under his eyes though he was probably not over 40 years old. His unruly head of dark hair looked in need of a trim. Thomas had taken an immediate liking to his openness and directness. Rupert said he came from a well-off Surrey family, had studied political science at Oxford, had enjoyed rugby and debating, and had been working for the Manchester *Guardian* for almost four years. Thomas told him about his Irish roots, his favourite grandfather having emigrated from Country Clare seventy years earlier, and about the love for Irish literature he had developed while an undergraduate at Northeastern University. They argued for a while about the pros and cons of reporting on the activities of the politicians (Rupert's choice) and the impact of events on the average citizen (Thomas's choice).

Back in his room, he stared at the typewriter. Though too tired to write, he knew he had experienced something he must write about in the morning. Sarah had told a part of her story and it was stories like hers that he had come to write about. But he had also become a part of her story. He was the first person she had trusted enough to tell what she had done. He had intervened in her life. Though always priding himself on being the objective outsider, in Sarah's case he had become an insider. He felt involved with her and an obligation towards her, in return for her trust in him.

Images of Sarah and echoes of her words played through his mind before he fell asleep.

CHAPTER 3

On Sunday afternoon Thomas sat in on a meeting of Concerned Parents for Children. He had seen a short article in the *Belfast Telegraph* announcing a start-up meeting for parents of any persuasion to share stories about children who were severely troubled by what they had experienced, and to offer mutual support.

The two organisers expressed their surprise at seeing an American journalist but welcomed him cautiously. He listened to numerous mothers, all looking distraught and anxious, talk about children fearful of going to school, bed-wetting, crying, and throwing temper-tantrums. Some talked about the terror etched on little faces when they heard gunshots or police or army vehicles on their streets. Most children would not talk openly about their fears.

One woman hesitatingly told about her seventeen year old son, who had been badly beaten a year earlier. He refused to talk about it so she had no idea why he had been attacked, but her beautiful, fun-loving son had been transformed and was now locked deep inside himself.

During a break for tea, Thomas approached the woman. Her eyes looked sad and tired and the corners of her mouth were turned down. Her eyes darted about when he addressed her.

'Hello. Your name is Margaret, right? May I ask you a couple of questions?'

'Um, well, I didn't expect to be talking with journalists here. I…' Her voice tailed off as she looked at him with a questioning expression.

'I can imagine that it's a surprise to see someone like me here. I just hope to be able to convey to my readers what life here in Northern Ireland is like for the average citizen, like yourself. But of course if you'd rather not speak with me I'll respect that.'

'It's a nightmare.' He sensed that she was prepared to engage with him.

'Yes, that was a terrible story you told. It must be very difficult for you.'

She nodded.

'Margaret, why did you decide to attend this meeting and how do you hope to benefit?'

'I know that no one here can solve my problem, or my son's problem, but it does feel good to share and to hear others tell their stories. It makes me feel less alone.'

'You feel alone?'

'Yes. My husband left me a few years ago and Owen sees very little of him. And, you see, there is really no one I can turn to. I just don't know how to help my son.'

'How is your son now?'

'He can walk again, with the help of crutches. They beat him up badly and then struck him with an iron bar. They broke two ribs and shattered a kneecap. Inside the house he manages without the crutches now, but he limps and sometimes it hurts badly, he says.'

'Is your son at school?'

'No, he dropped out. He was in his final year. For the first months he stayed at home, mostly. That was difficult for me because he refused to talk. Now he works part time at a music shop, but…'

Margaret bit her lower lip and looked away for a moment.

'…but twice now I've dropped in on the shop when I thought he would be there, and he wasn't. The owner couldn't or wouldn't tell me where he was. I don't know what Owen is up to, what he's doing.'

She pulled a handkerchief from her handbag and wiped her eyes.

'What are you afraid he might be doing?'

'I… I'm afraid he might be involved with drugs.'

'Why do you think that?'

'The shop specialises in punk rock and what they call heavy metal music. I've heard that drugs are part of that scene. And sometimes when he's home he… he just seems to be a totally different boy compared to what he used to be. He's off in his own world.'

'Is there anything you can think of which might help him?'

'Maybe he needs a man he respects, who can draw him out, get him to talk. And I think it would do him the world of good to get away from Belfast, out of the North, at least for a while.'

'Why?'

'The climate here now is so poisoned, especially for young people. I wish I could get away too, but I'd have nowhere to go.'

She dabbed at her eyes again.

An idea flashed through his mind, one that he would give more thought.

'Thank you for talking with me, Margaret. I do wish you all the best.'

She smiled timidly and nodded.

As he returned to the hotel he struggled with himself, and with his role. The lives of Margaret and Owen, like the life of Sarah, were none of his business. He was a journalist and he would write stories based on what he had heard and observed. But as had been the case the previous evening with Sarah, he felt involved. It would be a dereliction of some form of moral duty to simply write them up and forget about them. Should he have become a social worker instead of a journalist? He smiled at the ridiculous idea but acknowledged that in both cases he felt genuine concern and a perhaps foolish wish to make a difference.

Two days later, hoping to find young Owen, he asked at the hotel about a music store specialising in punk rock and heavy metal. The concierge gave him a surprised look but after making a few enquiries suggested he try McAfee's on Dublin Road.

Records were stacked on dusty shelves and in cardboard boxes set out on narrow tables. A young girl with purple spiky hair was thumbing through them. What served as a counter was cluttered with papers. An unshaven man of about Thomas' age came from the back, responding to the bell attached to the door.

'Yeah, what can I do for you?'

'Hi. I'm visiting from the States and my nephew asked me if I would look for an Irish punk band and maybe bring back a record or cassette. I don't know anything about that music though.'

'Okay. Well, the best we have in the North is a group called The Undertones.' The man picked a record off a shelf. 'This includes "Teenage Kicks", which was played a lot by the BBC. No cassette, just this EP. There's four tracks on it.'

A telephone rang in the back room. The man excused himself. Thomas heard him say, 'Owen, look after the gentleman out front, will you?'

Owen appeared wearing ripped jeans and a black T-shirt with an image of the Sex Pistols. His dark hair had been gelled into sagging spikes and he limped noticeably.

'Hi,' said Thomas. 'Your man was telling me that this is a really good group. I'm looking for something for my nephew in the States. What can you tell me about The Undertones?'

'Yeah, they're great,' Owen replied, with little apparent enthusiasm. 'Influenced a lot by the Ramones and the Sex Pistols. Know them?'

Owen's eyes had a vacant look.

'I've heard of the Sex Pistols, but not the Ramones.'

'Do you want to hear a track?' Owen asked dutifully.

Though Thomas couldn't imagine himself liking punk rock of any description, he said, 'Sure.'

Owen put the record on. 'This is "Teenage Kicks".'

Much to his surprise Thomas liked it. The lyrics were clearly understandable above the driving rhythm of guitars and drums and seemed to reflect no more than normal adolescent rebelliousness.

When the song finished, he said, 'Never thought I'd say it about punk music, but I do like this.'

Owen broke out in a shy smile. 'Oh yeah?'

'So this group is from the North. Belfast?'

'No, they're from Derry. Here's a picture of them. Owen pulled a grainy black and white photograph from a drawer, showing five smiling young men posing in front of a large mural with the words "You Are Now Entering Free Derry".

'They look like pretty normal young men,' Thomas ventured.

'Yeah, they don't go in for weird outfits like some punk groups.'

'Have they turned out any music related to the Troubles?' Thomas asked.

'No, but I heard they're working on some ideas for that.'

'Well, I'll certainly take this record.'

Owen limped towards the cash register.

'I just mentioned the Troubles. Is your limp a result of that in some way?'

'I fell off my bicycle,' Owen mumbled in reply.

Thomas laughed. 'I've heard of a lot of ways folks get hurt in Belfast, but not by falling off a bicycle.'

Owen tried to laugh too. Thomas added, 'Tell you why I'm asking. I'm a journalist trying to discover what I can about the effect of the Troubles on the people of Northern Ireland.'

'O yeah?' Owen glanced around and after a pause and in a lowered voice confided, 'Well, actually, I was beaten up.'

Thomas looked at him gently. 'Hey, it's lunchtime by my watch. If I treat you to lunch would you be willing to tell me something about that – in absolute confidence?'

Owen looked around uncertainly. He overcame his hesitation and called into the backroom, 'Dan, okay if I go out and get a bite?'

'Yeah, okay,' was the muffled reply.

Owen grabbed his coat and a crutch. 'There's a burger joint a few doors down.'

It looked like a run-down American diner, red vinyl-covered benches in a long row of booths down the left side. Thomas suggested one at the back, and they ordered.

'My name's Thomas. I heard Dan call you Owen. Is that right?'
'Yeah.'
'Well, hi, Owen. Thanks for giving me some of your time. What do you feel like telling me about being beaten? You're what, nineteen or so?'
'Seventeen. Well, I got mixed up with this group, said they was IRA, said I should join them to help the cause of freedom. I agreed.' He paused.
'So you joined.'
'Yeah, sort of.' Owen's eyes wandered around the restaurant.
'Are you okay talking about it, Owen?' Thomas asked.
'Yeah, I guess so. I… I haven't really talked about what happened to anyone.'
'It's up to you.'
Owen looked around again and then seemed to make up his mind. He looked at Thomas, took a deep breath, and carried on.
'Well, a couple of months later one of them handed me a gun and said we were going to do in some Prod. I asked who. They said I didn't need to know, said he was an enemy. So I was in this car with two guys, a driver and another guy a few years older than me. We parked on a street and waited for the target to come home. Then this man walks up the street carrying a big bag of groceries or something. Looked as old as my da. "That's him," one of the guys said. "Here's your chance, Owen."'
He paused to take a long drink from his milkshake.
'I couldn't do it.'
'Then what happened?'
'The other guy shot him. The man collapsed by his front door. We sped off. … I was shaking. Never seen a man get shot before.'
'It must have been terrible to see.'
'Yeah. Well, later the driver pulled into an empty alley somewhere. They dragged me out of the car. Said I'd betrayed them, betrayed the cause. They shouted at me, callin' me a fuckin' coward and traitor. Then they started to punch and kick me, like really hard. One of them

got an iron bar out of the car. He hit me across the chest. I fell on my back and then he whacked the bar across my left knee. Told me they'd be back with a gun if I ratted on them. They drove off. I was screamin' with pain.'

Owen was struggling to stay composed but his face twisted as he relived the memories.

'You must have been terrified, as well as in agony. Then what happened?'

'Somebody must have heard me screamin' because after a while an ambulance came and I was taken to the Royal Victoria. My mam came down, all hysterical she was. They operated on my knee and put a tight bandage on my chest. A couple of days later I was sent home, my leg in a cast. My mam just stayed hysterical. I couldn't tell her anything. It was terrible at home.'

'What about your dad, Owen?' Thomas asked.

Owen's face hardened. 'I haven't seen the bugger in almost two years.'

'So your mother is alone; I can well imagine she must have been very upset.'

'Yeah, well, I guess. But I just couldn't handle all her frettin' and fussin'. As soon as I could get around a bit I found this job, because I've always liked that kind of music. Doesn't pay me shit, but it's better than sitting at home.'

'What's next for you, Owen? Any idea?'

'No. … I'd just like to get out of this fuckin' country, that's for sure. Maybe to England. I don't know.'

Owen had finished his burger. 'What time is it?'

Thomas looked at his watch. 'It's a quarter past one.'

'I'd better be gettin' back then. … Thanks for the lunch.'

'Hey. One more question. Somebody told me that drugs are part of the punk music scene these days. Is that right?'

'I wouldn't know. Would never touch the stuff anyway.'

Thomas guessed from the shifting eyes that he was being less than honest, but let it be.

'Okay, well, thanks for talking with me, Owen. And thanks for the help with the music.'

Owen smiled again. 'You're welcome.'

'Hey, Owen,' Thomas added as an afterthought, 'if you'd like to talk again, contact me at the Europa Hotel. I mean it.'

He pulled out a hotel card and wrote his name and room number on the back.

Owen looked at it uncertainly, but stuffed it into a back pocket.

'Okay, thanks.'

They shook hands and Owen made his way back to the shop.

Thomas was left feeling frustrated. Owen's mother had shared her sorrow and now he had met Owen and felt his pain and sense of hopelessness. Once again he wished he could make a difference. But that was not his role and maybe he had overstepped the mark even by giving away his contact information. On the other hand, he thought, just maybe he had helped Owen by providing a place where he felt free to talk. As he had, just maybe, helped Sarah. Someone reaching out was what he himself had missed twenty years earlier. But was that reason enough to start playing the role of an amateur social worker? On the other hand, nobody else seemed to be bothering and that stirred his anger.

Thomas submitted two articles, in one of which he hinted at the idea of offering breaks of six months or a year in the United States to youths struggling to cope with their traumatic experiences.

CHAPTER 4

While continuing his work productively and quite happily, with a few interviews as well as miscellaneous chance encounters, Thomas was frequently assaulted during quiet evenings by his own memories and thoughts. Jennifer would not leave him alone. Or, more accurately, perhaps, he couldn't leave his memories of Jennifer alone.

When not thinking back on his time with Jennifer, he thought of Shauna. At the most unexpected moments he saw her eyes and heard her voice. He longed to know more about her, to get closer to her. At the same time, his old fears haunted him. He tried to rationalise: even if she were the least bit interested in him other than as a customer, what hope in hell did he have of creating a serious relationship? He'd be gone in a couple of months and he couldn't imagine Shauna engaging in a brief affair, assuming she wasn't already in a relationship. He convinced himself that she would be above that, too good for that. He had put her on a pedestal after seeing her once. Why?

As for Sarah and Owen: their stories stayed with him. What could he do for them, or should he let them go?

After a day of writing and an interesting meeting with a Queen's University professor he returned to Foyle's on Thursday evening. Shauna was there. It was quiet and there were no musicians.

'They usually come in on Fridays and Saturdays', she explained. 'What have you been up to?'

'Quite busy, talking to people and writing,' Thomas replied. 'Just standard journalists' work, but I've met a few very interesting people who opened up more than I had any right to expect.'

'People here have learned to be pretty guarded about what they say, you know. It's hard to know who to trust. You're not from here and I'm sure that helps.'

He nodded. 'Yeah. One woman even confessed that she had killed a man, and a young lad told me more about the trouble he had gotten into than his mother knew.'

Shauna looked at him as if sizing him up. 'Well, you do have a way of gaining trust, I'd say. There's something of the air of a priest about you, do you know that?'

Shauna's remark felt like a blow to the stomach. He looked away and grimaced.

'Did I say something wrong?'

'No, no,' he stammered. 'It's just that priests and I have not always gotten along.'

Shauna looked at him quizzically but then laughed out loud.

'Sure, you're not the only person I've ever heard say that. What I meant was, you have very warm eyes and a gentle expression. But I haven't even offered you a pint yet. What will you be having? A Harp?'

'No, give me a Guinness. I'm developing the taste.'

Shauna carefully tapped a pint, leaving just the right amount of foam on top.

'Thomas, you might be interested in meeting some young children. See if you can work your magic on them.'

'Do you have something in mind?'

'I do indeed. I work at a child care centre by day. We usually have a dozen or so children from five to eight years old and try to provide a safe place where they are well looked after. We offer a space where they can be the children they are. It's been very difficult for many of them.'

'In what way do you mean?'

'Nightmares, anxiety, withdrawal, and so on.'

'Yes, I've heard about that. It sounds like you do difficult but also important work.'

'I think it is. Would you like to visit and see for yourself?'

'Yes, I would. In fact I'd been wondering if anything is being done to help the children of the Troubles.'

'Not enough. We'll fix a day.'

Shauna went off to attend to a group of talkative customers who obviously knew her well. He watched her engage in easy banter and firmly deflect the attentions of a well-lubricated man.

After about ten minutes she returned.

'Shauna, I've a question for you. The other night Bernard… do you know him? He seems to be a regular. In fact he's over there now.' He nodded in the general direction.

'Oh yes, we see Bernard and his pals in here a lot.'

'Well, Bernard said that people in the North sometimes have to *pretend* to be of good cheer even when they're not, when they're carrying around the burdens inflicted by the Troubles. He said they do that to remain sane.'

'Yes, that sounds pretty true, I'd say.'

'Then let me risk asking a very direct question. Do you, Shauna, ever pretend? I mean, you're always smiling and outgoing and I can't help wondering…' His voice trailed off when he saw her eyes boring into him.

After a significant pause she replied. 'Yes, I sometimes have to pretend too. And now let me ask you the same. Do you sometimes pretend, Thomas?'

'I admit it. I do.'

She looked at him, waiting for him to continue.

'I admit to sometimes pretending to be a self-confident, experienced journalist when I'm feeling very unsure of myself, when I'm mainly aware of searching for the right question, the right approach, the best way of writing something appealing to the readers.'

'That sounds like pretty normal professional humility to me. Let me ask you a very direct question. Do you ever pretend when it comes to women?'

The question caught him completely off guard. Shauna slowly broke into a wide grin.

'Sorry, that was nasty of me, wasn't it? You don't have to give an answer. But think about that for a few minutes while I go and see to that lot down there.'

When she returned she picked up the conversation. 'So, Thomas, aside from being a university graduate, not on good terms with priests, not always honest and easily embarrassed, tell me something about yourself.'

'Well... er... I'm... Well, I enjoy my work, at university I played squash and trained in martial arts. I'm intrigued by Irish culture and I love some Irish literature and poetry.'

'That's not about *you*! I didn't ask what you do or did.'

He felt totally flustered and frustrated with himself. Shauna wouldn't be asking if she weren't in some way interested in him. He searched desperately for an answer.

'The other night, when I said I couldn't take my eyes off you, I couldn't believe I'd said that. But it was true, and saying it wasn't easy... at least it wouldn't have been if I'd stopped to think about it first.'

'And I said I knew you'd been watching. It was okay. I liked you, and still do, in spite of your being such an enigma. Why is that?'

Thomas stared silently into his pint.

'Have I embarrassed you again?'

He laughed. 'Yes!'

'Colin is giving me a look, but I'll be back.' It was getting busier. She went down the bar, drew a few pints and rinsed some glasses. Fifteen minutes later he saw Shauna and Colin exchange a few words, Colin laughing and nodding. She returned to Thomas and urged him to move down to the end of the bar where it was still quiet.

'Will you tell me something about yourself, Shauna?'

'Well, I finished secondary school and did quite well. I wanted to study psychology, but had to help look after my family. I worked in a restaurant for two years before the child care thing came up, as well as the opportunity to work evenings here.'

'Look after your family? You mean you have children?'

She laughed. 'Good lord no. My da lost his job as a bookkeeper about six years ago. That was because we're Catholic. Now he only does very occasional odd jobs. My mam worked as a seamstress and later in a shop, but she's usually at home too. They... they live off the dole, basically.'

He looked into her eyes, momentarily sad. He guessed this was not something she would normally share with guests.

'I have a...' Shauna hesitated. 'I have a younger brother, Kevin, but... he is, he has changed. He's withdrawn into himself. He's sixteen, but sometimes behaves as if he were ten. He's very unsure of himself, very dependent on mam and me.'

Thomas looked at Shauna carefully. Her eyes darted back and forth, and she seemed about to say more, or perhaps she regretted having said what she had.

Finally he said quietly, 'So you too have had to deal with a lot of difficulty, and that's where you find yourself sometimes needing to pretend.'

'Yes. But you turned the tables by asking me about myself without revealing anything about yourself. I'll get something out of you yet. Be warned!' And off she went, pouring pints, washing glasses and wiping the counter top.

When he was about to leave he managed to tell Shauna he was happy to have talked with her and apologised if he had pushed her too far.

'You're a good listener, Thomas. I don't talk like that often.' She took a deep breath and added, 'What I didn't tell you is that I had an older brother, by two years. But he was shot nearly three years ago.'

A mask descended over Shauna's bright features.

Not knowing what to say, he impulsively placed his hand on hers, on the counter, and then quickly withdrew it, though Shauna had made no move to remove hers. He wondered whether he had overstepped again, but Shauna gave no sign to that effect. Feeling awkward, not knowing what he should say next and battling a wish to give Shauna a hug, he said, 'I'm very sad for you, Shauna, but thank you for telling me.'

She nodded at him.

'See you again soon.'

They smiled at each other and he left.

As he walked back the short distance to the hotel Thomas felt like kicking himself for his awkwardness, his inability to say or do anything that felt appropriate. She had reached out to him by giving him an insight into her life, and all he had managed was 'See you again soon.'

In his room, he wondered and doubted. He was amazed that Shauna too had told him, a stranger, so much. Not yet two weeks into his stay in Belfast, and he felt himself to be on an incredible ride. Where it was taking him he couldn't even begin to guess.

CHAPTER 5

One evening Rupert introduced him to Ben Anderson, an amiable fellow-American on assignment for the *Washington Post*. Ben was a few years older than Thomas, tough-looking but with a warm smile.

'I'm finding it a bit boring here,' Ben confessed at one point.

Thomas was surprised. 'How so?'

'I like it when things are hot. Four years ago I was in Vietnam.'

He looked carefully at Ben and decided that he was not boasting. Ben added that he was definitely anti-war but felt that the best way to give expression to that was to report on the horrors of conflict from the front line.

'I can understand that, Ben,' Thomas responded. 'But I don't need to see blood and guts. I've already seen how the conflict here is fucking with people's minds, and lives. There's horror here too.'

Two evenings later Ben challenged him. 'You want to know what's going on in the streets with average people. Let's go out and see for ourselves, at the front line.'

They set off as darkness was falling for an area where there were frequent clashes between youthful gangs and the British army. Soon they found themselves in narrow, gloomy streets amongst piles of rubble and shards of glass, and occasional boarded-up homes. At an intersection they came across the burned-out carcass of a bus. Many streetlights had been shattered. A dozen or so distant shots echoed in the darkness.

'Don't worry; that was far away,' Ben commented.

Few lights were to be seen in the homes and most curtains were drawn tight. Hardly anyone was out and those who were, were hurrying to get somewhere. They encountered a British army checkpoint. Ben showed his press card and explained to the sergeant, flanked by two nervous-looking young soldiers, who they were and what they were doing. They were allowed to continue.

After half an hour, having come across nothing and with a light drizzle carried by brisk gusts of wind blowing in their faces, they were about to turn and go back.

'Hang on. I hear something,' said Ben.

The approaching vehicle sounded more like a tank than a car. A six-wheeled armoured personnel carrier slowly emerged from around a corner.

'That's an Army Saracen.'

Whatever it was called, Thomas thought it looked sinister.

Out of nowhere a dozen youths appeared, teenagers, possibly even younger. Some had their faces covered. Shouting abuse, they started hurling bricks, broken paving stones and bottles in the direction of the Saracen.

The missiles clanged off the vehicle's steel hide. The back doors opened and six soldiers spilled out, waving their rifles.

A few youths disappeared but most continued to provoke the soldiers, who advanced towards them. The boys ran down the street, directly towards Thomas and Ben who, with nowhere to hide, had pressed themselves up against the wall of the nearest house. Stopping their flight just in front of them, the youths picked up rubble again and flung it in the direction of the troops before continuing down the street. The troops ran after them, the Saracen following in reverse.

The boys hurled another volley of rocks at the soldiers, who were then within spitting distance of Thomas and Ben. 'Duck!' yelled Ben. It was too late. Thomas felt a stinging blow to the forehead. Dazed, he struggled to remain upright, leaning against the wall and supported by Ben's quickly outstretched arm. He felt blood trickle down his face and pulled out a handkerchief.

'We'd better get that seen to,' said Ben in a concerned tone.

Meanwhile, the skirmish between the soldiers and the kids had ended. One of the soldiers approached.

'Let me have a look at that.'

After a brief inspection he returned to the Saracen and came back with a first-aid kit. He wrapped Thomas's head in a long bandage and said, 'You'd better take that to the Royal Victoria. Sorry we can't give you a lift.'

'Thanks, mate,' said Ben, and the two of them walked in the direction the soldier had indicated.

'Shit, that hurt. But at least I've got something to write about,' said Thomas with a weak smile, recovering his equilibrium after the initial shock.

In the busy emergency unit of the Royal Victoria Hospital a nurse greeted Thomas cheerily, took a look at his forehead and brought him to a curtained-off cubicle. She removed the blood-soaked bandage.

'That's messy but it's hardly life threatening. What have you been up to?'

'Just in the wrong place at the wrong time.'

'You and at least a dozen others every night. But you're the first American I've seen in here. It is American, isn't it?'

'Yes, that's right.'

The nurse sighed. 'We've become a tourist attraction now, have we?'

After fifteen minutes or so a young doctor came in, took a look, gave a few instructions, and left. The nurse cleaned the wound, applied a disinfectant spray, deftly inserted three stitches and bandaged the head expertly. She gave him a tube of ointment and some large plasters to apply from the next morning.

'You'll be fine. Just try to stay out of trouble, will you? We have enough to do here without nursing tourists.'

He smiled and thanked her, then he and Ben headed back to the Europa by taxi.

Thomas was greeted in the hotel by stares and a solicitous question from the concierge, who knew most of the long-term journalists by name.

'Are you all right, Mr Cassidy?'

'Yes, I'm grand now. Thank you, Darcy. Just feeling rather conspicuous.'

Darcy smiled. 'You do stand out, Mr Cassidy.'

Ben asked, 'Like a drink after all that?'

'Sure. Meet you upstairs in about fifteen minutes.'

Thomas went to his room to change into dry and clean clothes. His head was still throbbing, but he also felt strangely energised by the evening's events.

Self-consciously he walked into the 12th floor bar, sporting his white turban. Eyes turned towards him. Laughing comments flew fast and furious:

'Rough day?'

'Did you lose?'

'A door get in the way?'

A Poppet was more solicitous. 'Poppets' was the name given to the attractive young hostesses, dressed incongruously a little like Playboy Club bunnies.

'Oh dear. What happened to you?'

'I got in the way of a brick.'

'Well you'd better let me get you something.'

He ordered a whiskey and asked her to take Ben's order as well. He told a curious Rupert what had happened. A couple of colleagues offered moral support by muttering abusive comments about the 'no-good kids' who had hurled the missiles, but Thomas couldn't feel that way about them. He felt concern for them, and wondered what drove them to do the sometimes dangerous things they did.

Thomas woke up groggy, whether from his last double whiskey or the bruise he wasn't sure. He removed the bandage and, after showering, applied the ointment and a large plaster. After breakfast he sat down behind his typewriter. He had another story to tell.

In mid-afternoon he headed back into the area of the previous night's skirmish. The rain had passed and occasional rays of sunshine broke through the clouds. He found the street where the incident had taken place; it was empty. He continued walking and went around several blocks. It occurred to him that he might look suspicious to someone peering through curtained windows.

During his second walk down the street a woman in her early forties emerged from her home.

'Are you looking for something? May I help you?'

She looked intelligent – and suspicious.

'Yes. I… um, I was here last night when there was an incident. I got in the way and was hit. I'm a journalist.'

'It's dangerous to be walking about here at night.'

'I was hoping to find the boys involved. Simply to talk with them, about why they go out on the streets to confront the army.'

'People here are not generally very talkative, you know.'

'I understand that. And I'm certainly not here to seek revenge or to blame anyone.'

The woman's expression softened.

'I heard that a stranger had been hit. That was you, then. How are you?'

'Thank you, I'm fine. No serious damage.'

'Would you like to come in for a cup of tea?'

'Thank you, ma'am. I'd be delighted, if it's not too much trouble for you.'

'No trouble.'

'I'm Thomas Cassidy, here for the *Boston Tribune*.'

'Anne, Anne McEwan. Please come in.'

He followed her into a small, tidy, sparsely furnished sitting room. Family photographs were the only decoration other than a crucifix. Even though it was afternoon, heavy brown curtains were drawn closed.

Anne brought in a tray with cups and a teapot.

'We'll just let that rest for a few minutes. So you're American? We don't see many of you in Belfast any more.'

'There are several of us journalists, but if you're referring to tourists, I guess not.'

'And what have you discovered, Thomas? I may call you Thomas?'

'Yes of course. Well, I get a sense of deep sadness and hopelessness. I know that there are fewer deaths now than two years ago, but there seems to be little optimism about the future.'

'I think you're right.' Anne looked down at her lap for a few moments before continuing. 'When the British arrived we thought they were here to protect us from the Protestants, the gangs and the RUC. But now it feels like they have taken the Protestant side and patrol our neighbourhoods like an occupying force.'

She spoke in a soft, gentle manner.

'It must be very difficult for people like yourself.'

'Sometimes, yes. But we, I, have to trust in God and in the many good people on the Protestant side too. It is true that we Catholics feel we have been discriminated against ever since 1921 and, Lord knows, long before that. But that's the politicians' doing.'

'Do the Protestant paramilitaries come into your streets often?'

'Less now than a couple of years back. But yes, they are a threat. When they do come it usually means a shooting or a burning. They target anyone they suspect of being involved with the Provisionals.'

'What's your most fervent hope, Anne?'

'I just want to feel like a real citizen, I want to feel safe when I go into town, I want my children to be safe and I want my husband to have a fair chance of getting and keeping a good job.'

'How many children do you have?'

'We have three, a boy and two girls.'

The conversation was full of pauses, which they filled with sips of tea.

'Our oldest, Ryan, was out on the street yesterday evening. He was probably in the group you met. I hate it when Ryan goes out to provoke the soldiers. It's a game to him, but it's dangerous – maybe that's what makes it exciting. Lord knows, he and his sisters are often very bored, and being out there is more fun than sitting at home watching the telly.'

'Anne, what needs to happen so that all of you can get your lives back the way you want them?'

'A miracle?' She smiled ruefully, but went on. 'I think it's up to all of us, we can't just trust in the politicians. What has to come from all of us is respect, acceptance, Christian love. But ...' Anne looked down again, wringing her hands in her lap. 'Will I see if Ryan will speak to you? He's upstairs.'

'Thank you.'

Thomas was struck by Anne's warmth and, after nine years of Troubles, her despair at the politicians' inability to resolve anything. The only hope lay with the people, like herself, working to bridge the gulf between the two communities.

Two or three minutes passed before Anne came downstairs, followed by Ryan. Ryan looked to be about sixteen. He had an unruly head of wavy reddish hair and was dressed in a sloppy sweatshirt and faded jeans. He slouched into the living room and stuck out his hand without looking Thomas in the eyes.

'How are you?' he mumbled.

'Hello, Ryan. I'm Thomas. I'm glad you're willing to talk with me.'

'Uh huh, okay.'

Thomas watched Ryan struggling to find the right balance between a macho bearing and his feelings of uncertainty.

'I'd like to talk to you about last night.'

Ryan looked briefly at the plaster on Thomas' forehead.

'I'm sorry sir. We didn't mean for you to get hit.'

'I know it was an accident. And please call me Thomas.'

Anne moved into the kitchen.

Ryan spoke slowly at first but grew more animated as he realised that Thomas was not there to blame or punish. He described his gang's activities as being 'good sport' and the only excitement they ever had.

'How do you feel about having the troops in your street?'

'I wish they'd go home.'

'Why don't they, do you think?'

'They need to show us every day that we're under British rule.'
'How do you feel about that?'
'They shouldn't be here. But I've never really known anything else. Not much we can do but accept it, like the weather, I guess.'
'How do you feel about the Protestants?'
'I had a couple of good Prod friends once, but I never see them anymore. They moved into their own neighbourhoods. Now the Prods have become our enemies. Some have probably joined the UVF, the Ulster Volunteer Force.'
'Would you ever think of joining the IRA, the Provos?'
'I hope not. I don't know. Maybe I will. But I want to go to college and study. I'd like to become a doctor.'
As he said this he shrugged his shoulders, suggesting that he did not believe it would ever be possible.
'You said "maybe" about joining the IRA. What did you mean?'
'Well, maybe I'll just have to. Somebody has to protect the Catholics. I mean, it's not like we all want to fight, but what has to be done has to be done.'
'I don't mean to sound stupid, but – to use your own words – protect the Catholics from what?'
'A friend's dad was shot by the UVF. Several homes around here have been torched by petrol bombs. Nobody is protecting us, certainly not the army, so we have to do it ourselves.'
'I think I understand, Ryan. But you'd rather just get on with your life and study, right?'
'Yeah.'
There was a pause.
'Mam said you're from Boston. What's it like there?'
Thomas thought he heard a longing to be elsewhere.
'I've always liked it there. It is a lovely city, busy, lots of parks and universities, and lots of Irish too. But there are parts of Boston that are pretty dangerous as well.'
'Maybe I can move there someday.'
'If that's what you want, I hope you make it.'

'Thanks.'

'I'd also like to talk with a couple of the guys you were out with last night. Can you put me in touch with one or two?'

'Nah, I won't do that.'

'Okay. I understand. That's okay.'

Their talk seemed to have come to an end. 'Well, I really appreciate your talking with me, Ryan. Thanks. And best of luck to you.'

Ryan looked straight at Thomas this time when he extended his hand.

'Thanks. And, uh, I hope your head gets better soon.'

Ryan walked slowly back up the stairs.

Thomas called out 'Anne' softly and when she appeared he thanked her for the tea and the hospitality.

'You have a nice son, Anne. I wish you both, and the rest of your family, the very best.'

'Thank you, Thomas, for coming by. Do so again if you're around here, now.'

Thomas felt that she meant it, and hoped to take her up on the invitation.

'Thank you, Anne.'

'God bless.'

Thomas walked back towards the hotel. He had heard Anne and Ryan share something of their dreams, and understood their fear that those dreams might never come true. He had heard them, listened to them – and, somehow, felt he had connected to them. He wondered once again how he might be able to help in some small way, besides telling their stories to his readers. Might Ryan, like Owen, be helped by a number of months in the relative peace and safety of the United States? Could that ever be arranged?

CHAPTER 6

Shauna gasped when she saw the large plaster on Thomas' forehead when he entered Foyle's on Saturday evening.

'What happened to you?'

'I ran into something unexpected,' he replied, trying to make light of it.

'Colin, I'm taking a minute,' she called, while guiding him over to a corner table.

'Seriously now, what have you been up to? What happened?'

'I was hit by a piece of brick that a boy had aimed at British troops.'

She touched his forehead lightly.

'Does it hurt?'

'No, not anymore.'

'Well, how did you get into that kind of situation?'

He told her about his evening walk with Ben and his subsequent conversation with Ryan and Anne.

'I'm glad you went back. Most of those kids are okay. They don't really mean to hurt people…'

'Are you thinking of your older brother? Is that what happened to him?'

'No… not that way.'

'What did happen to him, Shauna? Will you tell me?'

She took his hand and squeezed it gently.

'Yes, but not now.'

He felt a little current of electricity pass from her hand to his.

She sat up straight and combed her hair back with her fingers. Smiling again, she asked, 'What other trouble have you been getting into?'

'None really. I've been a good boy. I even went to church last Sunday,' he added with a smile.

Shauna's reply was neutral. 'That's nice.'

'It was Ian Paisley's Free Presbyterian Church.'

She looked shocked.

'I just went as a journalist. It was, well, frightening. When people hear the kind of poison that man pours out… it's just brainwashing.'

Shauna agreed. 'And there are some on the Catholic side who aren't much better. That's what's wrong with Northern Ireland.'

'How about you, then? You don't seem to have bought into all that stuff.'

'No… at least not anymore. I don't let anyone tell me what to think and do,' she replied firmly.

'You said "not anymore".'

'I did.' Shauna looked Thomas directly in the eyes, making it clear that she was not about to elaborate, so Thomas let it go.

'Shauna, when may I visit the child care centre?'

'Why don't you come up mid-afternoon on Monday?'

Thomas nodded.

'But you won't see Shauna there,' she said through a mysterious smile.

'Okay, now I'm confused. Who will I see? I mean I'd rather visit when you're there.'

Shauna smiled.

'Oh, I'll be there. But…' and she leaned in close and in a conspiratorial whisper said, 'My real name is Saoirse. I'm only Shauna when I work here.'

'But why?'

The noise level in the pub was increasing. She glanced towards Colin.

'I'll tell you. But I'd better get to work now.'

'Okay, Shau – er, *Seersha*.'

'Just remember: here it's "Shauna",' she whispered.

They both got up and to his surprise she gave him a quick hug before returning to the bar. He followed.

'What can I pour for you today?' she asked, back in her barmaid role.

Before he left he asked where he should go on Monday.

'It's the Springfield Community Centre. Here, I'll write it down for you.'

'That's okay, I've been there.'

She was surprised, so Thomas told her he had been there three weeks earlier for the Concerned Parents meeting.

Thomas was happy that he didn't have to wear a plaster any more when he visited the centre. There was a visible bruise and the stitches showed, but it was not conspicuous enough, he hoped, to attract undue attention.

Saoirse greeted him with a warm smile and a handshake as he entered the room where about 15 children were busy drawing or painting. They sat at little tables with crayons or brightly coloured water paints in small plastic cups. On one table a cup had tipped over and a young woman was mopping the paint up with paper towel while reassuring the child.

Thomas noticed that Saoirse was wearing jeans, a reasonable precaution around children messing with paints. They also emphasised her attractive figure.

He was moved by what he saw and heard over the next two hours. He watched as Saoirse and her assistant, Carol, moved among the children. They looked at what they were drawing and painting and urged them to talk about the images they had created. He was taken by the gentle way in which Saoirse talked with the children, holding them close whenever emotions spilled over. He sensed the warmth and empathy that she showed towards each child with whom she spent a few minutes. This was an entirely different Saoirse from the one he had found so attractive, in all her spirited sassiness, in the bar.

He also experienced himself as two different persons. At a personal, emotional level he felt himself being drawn more and more to Saoirse; indeed, he was falling in love. Simultaneously, the professional journalist was composing an article that would take form in the next day or two.

Children of the Troubles

A six-year-old girl works with concentration to depict her family: mother, father, two siblings and herself, with watercolors. The figures are all brightly colored, except for the tallest one. It is painted grey. Asked why, she explains that it is her dad. Why grey? Because he is not here any more, she explains with tears in her eyes. She doesn't know why. Perhaps wisely, nobody had told her that her dad died in a pub bombing.

The setting is a rundown building on the edge of Belfast, where two young women devote their days to helping young children deal with the traumas inflicted by the on-going conflict. The 12 to 15 children present at any one time, aged between five and eight, cannot get the help they need in normal schools or at home. They spend half days, sometimes whole days, in the child care centre, run by the women with remarkable warmth and caring, attentive to each child's personal story.

A five-year-old boy is reluctant to talk about what he has experienced, and cries a lot at home. For now he seeks succor and support from a remarkably empathetic Golden Retriever named Socrates, who wags his tail enthusiastically and offers wet licks to the boy's face. Two years ago the lad was a lively and outgoing three-year-old. The women offer him their love and attention and wait patiently for him to talk – when he is ready to – about witnessing an exchange of gunfire during which a neighbor was killed.

Another boy paints a house in black, with red and yellow streaks issuing from it. When asked about it, he explains in a very matter of fact tone of voice that his house burned down. Somebody had thrown in a 'bottle of fire' after the family had been told to get out. Totally composed, he tells this story – until he admits that what he misses most is his teddy bear, his friend. The teddy bear was lost in the flames. He starts to cry.

When we read about Northern Ireland, we do not usually hear about the thousands of traumatised children who spend their days in fear, in silence or in tears, and their nights with recurring nightmares.

To end the afternoon Saoirse led the children in a simple song. As she and Carol picked up the drawings and paintings and pinned them to the wall the first parents came in. Most children gave Saoirse a kiss on the way out. Socrates walked out, wagging his tail, with one of the parents and her child. Twenty minutes later, Saoirse and Carol had everything tidied away and Carol took her leave.

Saoirse turned to him. 'Well then, how would you like to invite me out for dinner?'

Though surprised by the forthright proposal, he quickly replied 'I'd be delighted.' This undoubtedly meant that she was not currently in a relationship. Perhaps there was some hope for him, or for them.

As they waited for a taxi, she asked for his impressions of the afternoon.

'You do wonderful work here, Saoirse. I was very touched, listening to the children talk.'

'You seemed to be doing very well too. I saw you talking with Ross.'

'Yes, he is very upset at having lost his teddy bear when his family's home was burned down.'

Her expression turned more serious. 'I'm just working by intuition. I wish I knew more about child psychology. I'm never sure if I'm doing the best, or right, thing.'

'I didn't study psychology either, but it looked and felt as if you were doing the perfect thing. I thought you were wonderful, and the kids, well they seem to trust you and love you.'

'I think that's what they need most: to know that they're loved, and to be able to trust.'

He asked about the Golden Retriever. She explained that they borrowed Socrates from one of the parents because while some children weren't willing to talk much, they could often relate easily to the dog.

'Socrates senses when a child is particularly upset, and will go to that child and nuzzle up. They always respond, and it's wonderful. I couldn't manage the place without him, he's beautiful.'

When the taxi arrived, he asked the driver to take them to the hotel.

'…If that's all right with you?'

'That's fine. I've never been inside.'

'You haven't?'

'No, now what would I be doing in a grand place like that?'

He wondered at the fact that she was going to that 'grand place' now, with him, and what it meant.

'Good evening, Madam, Mr Cassidy.' Darcy greeted them as was his custom.

'Hello Darcy. How are you?'

Saoirse hooked an arm around his. 'I'm impressed already, Mr Cassidy.'

Her eyes scanned the bright, comfortable lobby and took in the smiling receptionist.

'It does all look very grand.'

The waiter was his usual dour self when presenting the menu and asking if they would care for something to drink.

When they had made their choices, Thomas said, 'Now I'm dying to know: who is Shauna and who is "Seersha"? Did I pronounce it right?'

She smiled. 'You did. Let me write it down.'

She signalled to the waiter and asked if she might borrow his pen and a page of his order pad. She gave him a lovely smile and Thomas saw the dour expression melt away as he smiled in return. Poor guy, hardly ever sees a lovely woman or a smile in here, Thomas thought.

She wrote down her name and he puzzled over the strange spelling. 'Saoirse is my real name. It's a very Nationalist, Irish name. The word means "freedom" in Irish. Colin wants Foyle's to be a non-sectarian pub, so we agreed that guests would know me by a neutral name. I used "Shauna" at the restaurant as well, for the same reason.'

'Incredible, that you can't just use your own name.'

'I know it sounds stupid, but that's the way it is.'

Their waiter brought the first course and topped up their wine. Saoirse gave him another smile with her 'thank you' and once again the man beamed. She then looked at the plate.

'It's beautiful,' she exclaimed, before gingerly attacking the smoked salmon and shrimp. Thomas hardly looked at his plate, he was so enchanted by this third side of Saoirse: not the quick and charming barmaid, not the caring, gentle person from the Centre, but the spontaneous, girlish side, delighting in a new experience. He had fallen in love with all three and looked at her dreamily.

Saoirse's voice drew him back to the present. 'Hey, aren't you going to eat? It's delicious.'

'Yeah, sure. I was just … I was just enjoying looking at you.'

After a few bites, Saoirse looked at him enquiringly and said, 'You still haven't told me anything about yourself, Thomas, aside from the fact that you're from Boston and studied there. When I asked about you, you avoided the question.'

'There's not much to tell, really. I was born and raised near Philadelphia and have no brothers or sisters.'

Saoirse smiled at him. 'I know it's difficult to get the Irish to open up; you're even worse. What are your interests, your passions?'

Thomas looked down at his plate. 'Well, I like good literature and poetry…'

'Yes, that much you told me,' she said as her remarkable eyes bored into his.

'I enjoy going to the theatre, and I like music. Classical/romantic, jazz, like Dave Brubeck, and some modern balladeers like Leonard Cohen and Kris Kristofferson.'

Saoirse shook her head but kept smiling. 'God, you are hard work. *What* do you like about Cohen or Brubeck, or the theatre, or Yeats' poetry? At least I've seen that you have a lovely way with children.'

'Sorry, I guess I'm totally unaccustomed to talking about myself. Maybe also because I'm so rarely asked.'

'That's sad, but maybe it's something for you to work on then.'

He returned to something that lingered in his memory. 'Saoirse, the last time at the pub, you said "not anymore" when I asked whether you got caught up by all the propaganda and rhetoric. What did you mean?'

She put down her knife and fork and, after a pause, replied. 'You have a real gift for avoiding questions. But to answer yours: five years ago I did get involved. I was stupid and my age then is my only excuse.'

He remained silent as he looked at her.

'For a while I was a sort of courier, carrying small arms – pistols – from someone to someone else. They said a young woman was unlikely to be caught. I was stupid because I ran a huge risk, but at that point I was still caught up in the fervour.'

'And you were not caught?'

'No, I wasn't. But… some time later I learned that one of those weapons had been used to kill someone, an RUC constable, I heard. I felt… I felt terrible, and…'

Thomas placed his hand on hers.

'…and I decided then that I would have nothing more to do with this insanity. I felt complicit in someone's murder, and that was – and is – very hard to live with.'

Surprising himself, he got out of his chair, leaned forward and kissed her forehead lightly.

'What happened when you told whoever you carried guns for that you were quitting, getting out?'

Something changed in Saoirse's eyes; if it weren't so completely out of character, he thought, it would have looked like deep-seated anger, even hatred, smouldering there. He reached out for her hand again, which now felt cold, and held it, keeping his eyes fixed on hers.

Her voice was equally cold and hard when she spoke again.

'They stopped me in the street one evening and tried to change my mind and when that didn't work they threatened to rape me. One of them groped me. I crunched my knee into his crotch. The other slapped me hard on the face and the two of them called me names I won't repeat. They said I'd be sorry, and left.'

She turned her hand over and grasped his, but her face remained set.

'Two of them came to the restaurant where I worked and called me a bitch and a Catholic whore so the dozen or so patrons could hear. They walked out and with a can of spray paint wrote "whore inside" on the front window.'

Unable to find any appropriate words, he squeezed her hand.

'I never worked in that restaurant again.'

Silence followed. All he could think to say was, 'I'm shocked, Saoirse, I really am.'

She excused herself to go to the ladies' room. He was stunned. Anne had said that hope lay with the people. But here was a story illustrating the cruelty and barbarism of which people were capable.

When she came back five minutes later her face had softened again.

'I only ever told my brother about that before.'

'Kevin?'

'No, Niall, my older brother.'

'Thank you then for trusting me, Saoirse.'

They finished their starters quietly, and when their plates had been cleared he said, 'I might as well disclose something too.'

'What's that then?'

He paused, looked at her, and took her hand again.

'I've fallen in love with you, and I really don't know what to do with that.'

She stared at him and remained silent for what felt like a long time. Then she smiled gently at him. For the first time, he saw her blush a little.

'Well, I guess you finally opened up a little bit about your feelings.'
They both laughed.

Her expression suddenly became serious again. She took a sip of wine and her eyes darted back and forth before settling on him.

'Now that we're telling all anyway, I'd like to tell you what happened to Niall.'

She paused, as if mustering the courage to continue.

'Niall had occasionally been a rock-thrower. Later we didn't know what he got up to; he wouldn't say where he'd been. We were afraid that he was getting tied up with the IRA, because he was outspoken in his anti-British sentiments. He had a job by day in a carpentry and woodworking business, but after hours… we just rarely knew. There wasn't much mam and da could do. I know, though, that mam rarely slept if he was away late into the night, sometimes all night.'

'You have no idea what he was up to?'

'It's possible that he was in some way involved with the IRA. I just don't know.'

The waiter came by and refilled their glasses, unnecessarily, Thomas thought. He wanted to hear what Saoirse was going to say next. But the waiter claimed her attention.

'Excuse me, ma'am. But is it possible that I have seen you in Foyle's Bar?'

'Why yes. In fact, I thought I recognised you.'

'I only come in some Wednesdays because I work here the other evenings.'

'Well, I look forward to seeing you there on a Wednesday then.'

'Thank you, ma'am.' Once again, he walked off with a big smile.

'Anyway, to continue,' Saoirse went on, 'one evening, just about three years ago, three masked men came to our door. We were all frightened. Niall wasn't home. One of the men said that we had to move out of the house within a week. We wouldn't be welcome after that.'

'What…?' Thomas interjected.

'We lived in a mixed neighbourhood, but a lot of Catholic families had already moved out. We knew these kinds of threats were being made. My father went very quiet and my mother started to cry. Then the man said that Niall was on a death-list and would be removed from it only if we moved out. My mother almost fainted and my father grew very pale. But I…'

She stopped her story and he saw her eyes fill while she struggled to keep her face from collapsing.

'That's incredible. I can't imagine…'

'No, I suppose you can't.'

After a minute or so she took a deep breath and continued.

'I was furious. I shouted at the men that we would never be forced to move by their blackmail. I might have hit the one who had done the talking but my da held me back. I told my parents they must never give in. I shouted at the men to go back to their caves and leave decent citizens alone. Finally they disappeared into the night. One shouted "stupid Catholic bitch" at me, but I thought I'd scared them off.'

Again she paused. She took several deep breaths to regain control. 'Eight days later Niall was found shot dead a half mile from our home.' Very quietly, she went on, 'It was my fault, Thomas. He was my older brother, we were very close and it was my fault.'

A tear trickled down one cheek. He said nothing, but folded her left hand in both of his and held it tight. He wished he could move to sit beside her and wrap his arms around her.

She withdrew her hand and wiped her eyes discreetly before continuing.

'We did move. We were offered another house by the authorities. With some help from friends we moved everything we could, but had to leave some stuff behind because the new house was smaller. So small, that now I have my own tiny room around the corner from them. My da seemed to give up on everything and retreated into silence. He doesn't even go out to his pub with his friends. My younger brother, Kevin, also retreated into himself.'

This story of door-to-door terror went beyond anything Thomas could have imagined.

'My God, this is unbelievable. I'm so sorry for you, and for your family. And I understand why you said that you can't leave Belfast yet.'

'No, I can't. But I hate it here, I really hate it.'

They were both silent, and the waiter used the break in conversation to place their main courses in front of them before withdrawing discreetly. They both looked at their plates with little interest.

'Are you all right now, Saoirse?' Thomas asked quietly.

She managed a wan smile and a subdued 'Yes'. She continued, 'But I do have a temper and I lost it that night. Now Niall is dead.'

They picked at their food for a few minutes in silence before putting down their knives and forks. They just looked at each other. The waiter sensed that there was no interest any more in the food.

'Do you wish me to remove the plates, sir?' he asked.

Thomas nodded.

Saoirse said, 'When we've finished our wine I'd like to see your room.'

He tried to hide his surprise. He took a sip and almost choked on it.

She laughed. 'I just want to see where you live.'

'Yes, sure, okay…'

He desperately looked for something else to say while she smiled at his discomfort.

'If you're okay with that, of course.'

'Yes. Just surprised. As you said, let's finish the wine first.'

'I like surprising people.'

'I've noticed.' Awkwardly changing the subject he said, 'Well… you're great with children, Saoirse. Ever thought about children of your own?'

'Is that a proposal?' She laughed as his embarrassment grew. 'Of course I have. I was even engaged, and marriage and having children was part of my dream. But…'

'What happened?'

'I was actually engaged to a man called Dermot, about four years ago. We thought we would be married and be very happy together. That only lasted about a year. Then Dermot, like Niall, took to disappearing and staying away for days at a time. By the time Niall was shot I was hardly seeing him – and when I did he was very withdrawn. He never came around to speak to the family about it. I saw him once or twice and all he ever said once was "Sorry about Niall." He has disappeared from my life. I don't know where he lives now. Maybe he still hangs around the Grange. It's a seedy pub on the Falls Road. I don't know… I won't go there. Can we go to your room now?'

He opened the door, switched on the light, and said, 'Well, this is it. Sorry it's not very tidy, I wasn't…'

She didn't look around, but flung her coat onto the bed, threw her arms around him and held him in a long, tight embrace, burying her head in his shoulder. They stood in silence.

Slowly, she loosened her hold. With her hands on his shoulders she smiled at him again.

'I do like you, Thomas, very much. I trust you, you're gentle, and I've seen how well you get on with children. And you're also very shy. Where does that come from?'

'Um… I don't know.'

'Sometimes you're as closed off as some of the children, you know. But let's see if we can do something about that. I've wanted to put my arms around you all evening, maybe all afternoon. I don't usually ask men to take me out for dinner and then show me their hotel rooms, just to be clear.'

There was a mischievous smile on her face and a twinkle in her eye.

'I've fallen in love with you, Saoirse.'

'I'm not sure what I feel, but it scares me,' she whispered.

Their lips drew closer. They kissed gently, searchingly.

'I don't usually kiss men in their hotel rooms either.'
'I hope not.'

They stood there, looking at each other, with longing and with a strange anxiety, on the brink of a large new step in their young relationship.

Suddenly she broke away.

'But I really have to go, Thomas,' she said softly. 'Thanks for coming to the centre, thanks for dinner and thank you for listening. I've dumped an awful lot on you tonight.'

Her expression had changed suddenly, so he asked, 'Are you all right?'

'Yes... I'm fine. I... I just have to go now.'

He had the impression she was hiding, or not saying, something, but simply asked, 'May I see you again soon?'

'I'm counting on it. By the way, I'm working at Foyle's tomorrow evening as well. It's only Tuesday but Colin asked me to come in because someone else can't make it.'

She reached for her coat. He helped her into it, and escorted her out of the room, down in the lift, and towards the entrance of the hotel.

'Bye.'
'Bye.'

Thomas stayed in the downstairs bar and ordered a drink. He didn't want to talk with anyone, he wanted to be alone with his thoughts and his memories of a magical evening and then a rather sudden departure.

What was happening? He was being drawn into human dramas, he was suddenly in love and emotions he had hoped to avoid were overwhelming him. He felt inexplicably certain that somehow Saoirse would always be a part of his life. But how and in what capacity? He had no idea, and perhaps it was only an idle dream. What was it Rupert had said? That spending two months in Belfast would change him? He had not really believed it, but Rupert had been right. He had come to report on the impact of the Troubles on the people. He had done that, but also been unexpectedly moved by what he had heard from so many people, and wished he could make a difference. And now Saoirse. He wished he could take her away from all this, make her forget the horrors she had been through. He felt certain that he loved her. He also understood clearly why she could not even think about leaving Belfast. But even if she could, he wondered, would he be able to give her the happiness and love and freedom she needed and deserved? What if he failed... again? Would she end up hating him?

When he went to bed images of Saoirse drifted through his mind, together with an internal debate that became less coherent as the clock ticked on. Eventually sleep took over. He dreamed more than usual – an odd mixture. Dreams that were warm, soothing and even erotic, but there were nightmarish elements as well. He saw the dark figure of a priest laughing at him; something was being taken away from him, he was struggling to get it back – but he didn't know what 'it' was. He woke up in a sweat, wishing that Saoirse were beside him.

CHAPTER 7

1983

In the early summer Saoirse wrote that the wedding date had been set for Saturday 4th September. Thomas congratulated her and promised to do his very best to attend, though he continued to struggle with feelings. Saoirse was still the love of his life and now she was marrying Brian, but he knew he could not turn her down.

A relationship with another woman had ended after eighteen months. He knew that there could never be anyone to replace Saoirse in his heart, so he had covered his loneliness by immersing himself in his work and the occasional brief affair. He had gotten very good at 'pretending', he realised.

Three weeks before the wedding Saoirse wrote that she had graduated *cum laude* and provided details about the plans.

Thomas arrived in Dublin from Boston two days before the wedding. While delighted to have been invited, he wasn't looking forward to the hours he would have to spend alone, yet so close to her.

An airport coach dropped him off five minutes' walk from Buswells Hotel, where he found flowers and a card in his room.

'Welcome to Dublin, dear Thomas! Give us a call if you can; I should be home most of the day.' The card was signed: Saoirse and Brian.

Thomas dialled.

'Hello, this is Brian.'

'Hello Brian, this is Thomas.'

'Thomas, good to hear your voice. You made it in okay, then?'

'Yes, it was a smooth flight. I'm looking forward to meeting you tomorrow.'

'Likewise. Hang on, I'll get Saoirse for you.'

Thomas could hear him calling her and felt his heart pounding. He heard footsteps walking away from the phone and within seconds, her lighter steps coming closer.

'Thomas, I'm so happy that you're here. How are you?' she asked with an unchanged, sparkling voice.

'As you say here in Ireland, I'm grand! But it feels very strange to be back in Dublin.'

'It has been a while, hasn't it? But we'll have a chance to catch up. Have you any plans for this evening?'

'No. Thought I'd walk around a bit, if the rain stops, and explore the bookshop around the corner.'

'If you're not too tired, go to Devitt's Pub on Camden Street this evening. It's the best music pub in Dublin. A session starts there around 9:30. I can't promise but Brian and I will try to come by. Okay?'

'Yes, sounds good. How do I find it?'

'Just take a taxi. Brian and I can drop you back afterwards, if we make it of course.'

'Okay, Saoirse. I'll hope to see you there.'

He was dropped off in front of a plain, green-painted pub. Inside was equally plain: dark wood panelling with a few prints on the walls. He was directed towards a staircase leading to the upper room where the session would take place.

With a pint of Smithwicks in hand he watched as people trickled in and the first musicians arrived.

When half a dozen musicians had gathered and ordered their drinks, one of them struck up a tune on his fiddle. The rest joined in, with a button accordion, a whistle, another fiddle and a bodhrán. More musicians joined them, until there were about a dozen, including two more fiddles, a banjo, a guitar and an elderly man who played the 'spoons'. There were two youngish women and the men were of all ages. Meanwhile the public streamed in and it quickly became very crowded. People chatted noisily even as the music played, but the rhythm was reflected in tapping feet and bobbing heads and shoulders. Occasionally a couple of musicians would skip a number and chat between themselves. Thomas was so absorbed by the exuberant music and the infectious rhythms that he almost forgot that Saoirse and Brian might drop by. They did, around a quarter past ten. Saoirse edged her way through the crowd and she and Thomas hugged each other tightly.

'It's so good to see you, Thomas.'

'Just over four years since the last time, and you look more beautiful than ever. Hi, my darling – oh oh, I shouldn't say that anymore, should I?'

'Just this one time, then.'

Meanwhile Brian, tall and strongly built, had shouldered his way through the crowd.

'Thomas, I'd like you to meet Brian. Brian, this is Thomas.'

Brian had a handsome face and long wavy brown hair.

'A pleasure to meet you, Thomas. We're really honoured that you could come over.'

'The honour is mine, believe me. You're going to make a very special person your bride.'

Saoirse intervened, laughing.

'Brian, see if you can find us a couple of chairs or stools.'

Brian managed with some difficulty and squeezed them into the already crowded space.

Saoirse briefly took Thomas's hands in both of hers.

'I'm truly delighted that you were able to come.'

They turned to give their full attention to the musicians.

To Thomas it felt almost surreal to be sitting so close to the woman he loved, surrounded by cheerful music, less than two days before she would wed Brian.

They stayed until about 11:30, laughing and chatting through the music when that was possible. Saoirse had to remind Brian that there were two big days ahead of them. They left while the musicians were still going strong and Brian and Saoirse drove Thomas back to his hotel. He ordered a stiff nightcap in the bar.

He spent a good part of the next day exploring Phoenix Park, cycling and looking at the animals in the zoo. The activity distracted him and he enjoyed the afternoon.

At nine in the evening he entered the luxurious Shelbourne Hotel for the pre-wedding party. Saoirse spotted him immediately and came over, looking lovelier than ever in a shimmering maroon dress with straps over bare shoulders. She led the way to her mother and brother Kevin, who expressed their pleasure at seeing him again. She then took him over to meet Brian's parents.

'Dad, Mum, I'd like you meet my very good friend, Thomas Cassidy, from Boston.'

'How do you do, Mrs O'Donnell, Mr O'Donnell.'

They looked every inch as if they belonged in a place like the Shelbourne, very handsome and distinguished. He wondered how comfortable Saoirse's mother was; this would certainly not be the type of setting she was used to.

Mr O'Donnell engaged Thomas in brief polite conversation.

'I understand that you're a journalist and met Saoirse in Belfast. Five years ago was it?'

'Yes, almost to the day in fact.'

'Well, she must have made quite an impression on you, for you to come all the way over for their wedding.'

'Yes sir, she did.'

'Enjoy yourself this evening then, son.'

He flinched at O'Donnell's use of the word 'son'. He had taken an immediate dislike to Saoirse's soon-to-be father in law. O'Donnell reminded him of a politician or a banker, which, for all he knew, he was. He was clearly extremely well off. Thomas wondered whether Brian would take after his father and, for Saoirse's sake, he hoped not.

Drink in hand, he made his way back to Saoirse's mother, who indeed appeared to be overwhelmed. They chatted pleasantly enough, though he felt awkward. He had no idea whether she knew the true extent of his former relationship with Saoirse.

'Saoirse must have become very fond of you and you of her.'

Part of him wanted to blurt out 'Fond is an understatement. We were deeply in love with one another,' but of course he accepted the role into which he had been cast and replied, 'She's a lovely young woman. You must be very proud of her, Mrs Kelly, with her Trinity degree and now getting married.'

It was somewhat of a relief when Saoirse whisked her mother off to meet someone else. He renewed his drink from a passing tray and moved off to the sidelines.

A young woman approached him with a radiant smile. 'Hi! I'm Briana. You must be Thomas.'

'That's right.'

'Saoirse has told me so much about you.'

Thomas extended a hand. 'It's a pleasure to meet you Briana. Saoirse mentioned you several times in her letters and said you were to be her maid of honour.'

'We became very good friends at Trinity.'

Briana was just a little shorter than Saoirse, with black hair, dark flashing eyes and a slim figure under an attractive black cocktail dress falling high enough to reveal a pair of very shapely legs.

'And you're a journalist, getting into some television now.'

'Yes, gradually. I'm starting to enjoy that.'

'You have a wonderful voice.'

'Thank you, but it takes more than voice, you know.'

'Of course it does, but I'd say you have that too.' She looked at him from head to toe, nodding.

It felt like Briana was hustling him and Thomas didn't know whether to play along or retreat. She was certainly very sexy.

'Are you going to see any more of Ireland on this trip? Saoirse once said you had a lovely time in County Clare a few years ago.'

Thomas coughed and wondered whether he was blushing.

'Yes, it was a wonderful week.'

She laughed at him and in spite of himself he felt drawn towards this appealing young woman. He didn't know whether he was relieved or disappointed when someone came by and called out, 'Briana, I'd like you to meet someone.' She excused herself and said, 'I'll be back,' before disappearing among the other guests.

Saoirse sailed by. 'I see you met Briana. She's lovely, and a live one.'

'Yes, I noticed.'

Thomas was approached by a man who introduced himself as Herbert Reilly, a colleague of Brian's father at the Irish Allied Bank. He confided that Ireland was about to see an unprecedented economic boom, with property prices set to go through the roof. Thomas didn't know what to do with that information, so he thanked the man for the tip, made an excuse and drew away.

He had taken an instant dislike to Reilly, just as he had to O'Donnell. He retreated to the hotel entrance for a while and watched people come and go.

When he returned to the event room he spotted Kevin, also looking a little lost.

'So how's it going, Kevin? It's good to see you.'

'Very well, thanks, Thomas. I'm assistant manager for a small warehousing and trucking business now.'

'Good for you. And what's life like in Belfast?'

'It's better than it used to be. We still have shootings and other troubles. You get used to that, eventually. We've had a couple of lorries hijacked. That's all.'

'Hijacked?'

'Yeah, you know, a gang pulls a gun on the driver, tells him to get lost and then plunders whatever's inside.'

'That sounds bad.'

'Yeah, well, it's the price of doing business. Nothing to do with the Troubles. It's just gangsterism.'

A small band had set themselves up on a stage at one end of the room and was starting to warm up. They soon struck up a waltz.

Briana appeared again.

'May I have the first dance, Thomas?'

'I'm not a good dancer at all, Briana.'

'I don't believe you. Come on.' She dragged him onto the floor.

He soon found the rhythm of the music and managed, even starting to enjoy it. When the music ended she held him by the elbow.

'How long are you staying?'

'I'm flying back Monday morning.'

'That soon, huh? Where are you staying? Here?'

'No, this is well above my means. I'm in Buswells, just down the road.'

'Any good?'

'It's very comfortable.'

'Nice. I've never stayed in a Dublin hotel.'

Briana's flirtatious manner gave him the distinct impression that she was leading up to something. Saoirse suddenly came by.

'Hey guys. Am I interrupting? Actually I don't care if I am. Just saw you two dancing and that's something we've never done. Thomas, may I have the next one?'

'Of course.'

With Briana's smile following them, they took to the floor as the band launched into a foxtrot, immediately followed by a slower number.

'One more, Thomas.'

It happened to be 'Dancing Cheek to Cheek'. It felt wonderful to be so close again, picking up familiar scents. But he felt awkward.

'Hey, loosen up!' Saoirse admonished.

When the number was over she said, "Thank you, Thomas' and smiled warmly. 'I think Briana is waiting for you.'

He wondered when he could graciously make an exit, but Briana cut that thought short.

'Will you give me a second dance, Thomas?'

'Well, I was just about to go, but sure.'

He led her onto the floor as the band started another slow number. Briana moved in close and placed her head against his chest. Thomas caught whiffs of an enchanting perfume and enjoyed the feel of her taut body pressing against his. If she was trying to seduce him she was doing a grand job. He could feel himself getting aroused and wondered whether she could sense that.

When the number ended she put an end to any doubts he might have had about her intentions.

'I'm ready to go too, actually. How about a nightcap somewhere quiet?'

'Where do you have in mind? There doesn't seem to be a quiet spot anywhere in the Shelbourne.'

'How about Buswells? Don't they have a bar?'

Thomas hesitated and then decided to go with it.

'Yes, they do. Okay then. Let's say goodnight to some folks and get our coats.'

The bar was very quiet and they took a candle-lit table in a dark corner. Soft background music filled the air. Briana and the romantic atmosphere wove a spell around him.

'Saoirse told me you were a bit reserved at first. But I've noticed you're not made of stone.' She smiled at him with apparent innocence.

So she had noticed! *Che sera, sera*, he thought. He placed an arm over her shoulders and she responded immediately by moving in close against him. The bartender brought over their drinks. They clinked glasses.

'To first acquaintance,' Briana said.

'To first acquaintance.'

'Saoirse told me that you were coming and she was very excited about that.'

'It was a long-standing promise. I couldn't let her down. I'm delighted to be here,' he said, not quite honestly.

'She asked me to take care of you a bit, you know. She realised that being here might be a little difficult for you and she didn't want you to feel lonely.'

'So you're my carer, huh?'

'If you want to put it that way, yes. Of course, only if I want to be and if you want that too. I'm quite happy in the role and I'm not in any relationship at the moment,' she said, smiling seductively again. 'Are you comfortable with it?' Dropping any hint of innocence, she moved in even closer and placed a hand high on his thigh.

'Yes, certainly, but I'm feeling a little overwhelmed.'

'You find me overwhelming, do you?'

'As a matter of fact, yes.'

'Let's see if I can overwhelm you even more then.' She laughed brightly and slowly moved her face towards his to place a light kiss on his lips. It felt good and Thomas felt himself responding again. The tip of her tongue slid into his mouth. Her hand moved further up his thigh until it found the bulge in his trousers.

'That's better. Hmmm, I think I'd better stay,' she murmured into his ear.

'You're taking your carer role very seriously,' he whispered back.

'Only because I want to.'

'Would the priests approve?'

'Fuck the priests,' she whispered into his ear.

They finished their drinks and headed towards the lift.

Thomas flicked on the light and closed the door quietly.

'Briana, I…'

Briana placed a finger on his lips. 'Let's see if I can make you relax completely.' She folded her arms around him and pressed her body and her lips against his. He felt her tongue explore the inside of his mouth. She drew back, pulled the jacket off his shoulders and started to loosen his necktie.

'Hey, but just a second, I don't have a…'

Briana released him long enough to step over to her purse and withdraw a condom.

'But I do.'

'I thought they were illegal in Ireland.'

'They are, but if you know where to look, you can find.'

She waved it in front of his face, grinning. He had never experienced a situation like this before and didn't know what to do next. She obviously did.

Her smile left no doubt that she was a woman who was confident of success. Thomas abandoned any thoughts of resistance as he felt the shirt being slipped off his shoulders and his belt being undone. He found the zipper of her dress and pulled it down.

The dress and the trousers lay in little heaps on the floor. She stood before him in a very sexy red slip and bra. Thomas stopped thinking entirely. Briana pulled down his shorts and gently kissed his erection, taking the tip into her mouth and massaging it with her tongue.

He drew her back on her feet and led her to the bed, where they wrapped their arms and legs around each other.

He unclipped her bra and kissed her nipples, then moved down to her belly and, after sliding off her lacy slip, moved down further into the moist warmth he found there. His tongue found her clitoris and Briana, uttering cries and moans, clutched his head. When he was afraid she was done, uttering a loud cry, she abruptly changed positions, drew his penis full into her mouth and sucked hard while somehow managing to tickle his balls. Thomas lost awareness of anything except the sensations of the moment. When he felt he couldn't hold himself back any longer she paused and expertly slipped the condom into place. With her guidance he thrust himself into her, felt the urgent rhythm of his loins, heard Briana's ever-louder moans. The inevitable explosion followed. Briana cried out loudly, and his own voice uttered primitive cries of pleasure.

After a minute he withdrew, and they lay side by side, panting – and, after a couple of minutes, smiling.

Briana was the first to speak. 'I knew I detected something under that reserved exterior.'

She placed her head on his chest, while her fingers ran all over whatever parts of his body they could reach.

'Briana, you are amazing.'

'And you sure know how to satisfy a woman. Do you feel happier about being in Dublin now?' she teased.

They cuddled and chatted about nothing until they fell into untroubled sleep.

Thomas woke up and felt around him, but the other half of the bed was empty. He looked up and saw that Briana was dressed.

'Hi, sleepy.'

'Hey, Briana. What time is it?'

'It's half nine. I need to get home. Got a wedding to go to.'

'Don't you want breakfast first?'

'No. I'm fine.'

'But what will I do without my carer?'

She laughed. 'Don't get lost. I'll see you this afternoon at church.'

'What a strange thought. Yes, okay.'

She pulled on her coat, opened the door and walked out, throwing him a wicked smile as she did.

Thomas groaned, turned over, and tried unsuccessfully to catch a few more winks. He got up, showered and dressed, and went down for breakfast with memories of the night going round in his head. He could never have foreseen the surprise that this short trip to Dublin would have in store for him. And Saoirse had helped to set it up. He wondered whether she had any idea how far Briana would take her role. Briana had certainly filled the emptiness and had seduced him so easily. Or had he so easily and willingly let himself be seduced? Was this a plot to help him leave Saoirse behind? What the hell, did it matter? One thing was certain: he had never engaged in such uninhibited, wild, exuberant sex before. He also felt a niggle of guilt; had he 'betrayed' Saoirse?

CHAPTER 8

1978

Thomas spent most of the morning after his intense evening with Saoirse writing.

Teenagers on the Brink
Larry is a sixteen-year-old living in a poor Belfast neighborhood. He is bored. The most exciting thing in Larry's life, and that of many of his friends, is throwing bricks and bottles at the British army patrols that roll through regularly. It's 'good sport', he explains. Provoking soldiers provides an adrenaline rush. Will he trade in the rocks for a gun and join the IRA when he is a year or two older? He might, he admits, out of a sense of duty to his community. But he would prefer to go to medical school.

Jimmy was a normal young teenager until three years ago. His older brother was shot dead by a paramilitary group. Why? Only because his family refused to move out of their home, out of a 'mixed neighborhood' where Protestants and Catholics had lived in peace with each other for decades. Jimmy's father, unable to find employment because of his religion, retreated into depressed solitude. Jimmy withdrew into himself and became as dependent as a ten-year-old on his mother and older sister.

Fred was viciously beaten by two paramilitaries when he was seventeen. He had refused to shoot someone. But his mother does not know why he was beaten and now fears that her son has turned to drugs. He is withdrawn and sullen.

These three young men and no doubt hundreds like them are

not included in the casualty statistics and they are not receiving any form of professional help.

He wasn't terribly pleased with his pieces. They missed something. He couldn't express his own anger, his sympathy, his empathy without breaking a cardinal rule of journalism. Personal comments or judgments were not permitted.

Thomas also made numerous phone calls to set up appointments. Following up on a tip from Rupert, he was particularly pleased to have arranged to meet Sean McCann, one of the organisers of the Derry Civil Rights March in January 1972, a day which had become infamous as Bloody Sunday. McCann had first said he refused to talk about that day, but Thomas was able to sway him by saying he was reporting on the impact of the Troubles on average citizens and did not want to question McCann about his specific role on that tragic day. One thing was certain: 'Bloody Sunday' had had a huge impact on the people of Derry, well beyond the 27 who were killed or wounded. McCann finally agreed and said he would show Thomas around the area where the shootings had taken place.

He looked forward to seeing Saoirse again in the evening. Mixed with the longing, though, was the recurring tension.

To take his mind off these thoughts he spent a couple of hours reading Maire O'Shaunnessey's *A Different Place*. He enjoyed the informal account of her travels through Northern Ireland on a bicycle and was grateful to Rupert for having loaned it to him.

He set out for Foyle's in lashing rain. When he arrived Saoirse had not appeared yet so Colin drew him a pint.

Shortly afterwards Saoirse came in, shaking the water off her coat.

'Hiya! Glad you're here.' She held his eyes for longer than a normal greeting required.

'Hi Shauna. Didn't think I'd miss it, did you?' He was glad he remembered to use her bar name.

'Nope. Not unless you were out getting into trouble again today.'

She hung up her coat and stepped behind the bar, consulted with Colin and set about rinsing glasses. She greeted clients, poured a few beers, and engaged in chat. His eyes followed her.

Saoirse replenished his glass but was too busy for conversation.

After an hour, Saoirse stepped into the vacant musicians' corner. Her move caused a lull in conversation as eyes turned expectantly towards her. It was not a regular music night.

'There's a special song I'd like to sing this evening,' she announced. 'It's called "Help Me Make It through the Night"' and added, 'I'm sure a lot of us feel that way from time to time.'

Without any accompaniment, she broke into the song. Thomas knew it well, but it had never before touched him as it did now.

And it's sad to be alone. Help me make it through the night.
I don't wanna be alone. Help me make it through the night.

After the last note she dropped her eyes towards the floor to a burst of applause.

As she walked by, she tweaked his nose and said, quietly, 'That was for you.'

'Thank you. You remembered that Kristofferson is one of my favourites.'

'Aye, I did.'

It was a good half hour later when Saoirse came around for a brief chat.

'How are you?' she asked.

'I'm okay I guess. And yourself?'

'Ah, I'm grand!'

'Thank you for that song.'

'"Okay, I guess" doesn't sound very convincing.'

'I guess it doesn't. I'm not pleased with some of my writing. Shauna, I'm going to Derry tomorrow; I've arranged to meet someone there. I'll be renting a car and can keep it over the weekend so if you have time I'd like you to come with me, into the countryside, somewhere around Belfast. Will you show me a bit of Northern Ireland – if it's not still lashing rain?'

Saoirse thought this over for just a moment.

'I'd like that very much. Are you okay about driving on the left, though?'

'I think I can manage. Just following the car ahead of me should do it.'

'How about Sunday? I can be down at the hotel about ten o'clock.'

'Terrific!'

He walked out into the rain, keeping his head down. He was totally preoccupied by his forthcoming 'date' with Saoirse. It was dark and there wasn't a soul to be seen on the street. As he walked past a dark alleyway he heard his name being called. Surprised and thinking he might have imagined it, he stopped and looked around but saw nothing.

'Cassidy. In here.'

The voice came from the alley. Looking through the gloom he saw a man standing in the darkness. His first instinct was to walk on quickly, but he stepped into the alley, his body preparing itself for anything – except a gun. The figure waved him on about fifteen feet to a sort of loading bay where they could stand protected from the rain.

'Thank you,' the man said as he reached into an inside pocket of his coat and withdrew a small white envelope.

'I'd like you to give this to Saoirse.'

'Who are you, and why don't you give it to her yourself?'

'I can't risk Saoirse being seen with me. You shouldn't be seen with me either. Will you give her this?'

Thomas stretched out his hand to take the envelope.

'Okay, I'll give it to her. But who are you?'

'Thanks, Cassidy.'

The man turned to head further down the alley.

'Who…?' Thomas started to ask again.

'Dermot.'

In a few seconds he was out of sight.

Thomas was unnerved by the fact that apparently both he and Saoirse were being watched. How did the man know his name? Was it really Dermot? What was the message for Saoirse?

With a sense of relief he entered the hotel and nodded to Darcy. He pushed the 12th floor button in the lift; he needed a drink and to talk to someone.

'Hey, Thomas, come on over and sit down,' Rupert called out to him as he entered the bar. 'You look wet and upset. Where have you been?' He looked towards one of the Poppets. 'Sally, come here and take my friend's order. He needs a strong one, I think.'

'Rupert, someone stopped me, drew me into an alley and gave me an envelope to pass on.'

'That's weird. What do you think that's all about? Any idea?'

'Yea, well, the person I'm supposed to pass the envelope on to is in fact the woman you saw me with in the dining room last night.'

'I remember. She's very attractive.'

He told Rupert something about his connection to Saoirse, and the fact that she had been engaged to a guy who might be mixed up with the Provos now.

'And that might have been the man who gave me the envelope. What spooks me is how this Dermot, if that's who it was, knew my name, where to find me, and that I've been seeing Saoirse.'

Rupert pondered this and then suggested, not very helpfully, 'Belfast is full of eyes and ears. That's why so many people keep their heads down and their mouths shut.'

After a night of fitful sleep Thomas was, by mid-morning, navigating his way cautiously to the Antrim Road and then up the A6 towards Derry. As he relaxed with the right-hand drive he started to enjoy the countryside, the green rolling hills flecked with patches of sunlight. Approaching Derry, the hills grew higher and were dotted with sheep.

He found the City Hotel beside the River Foyle and waited for Sean

McCann. It was an old hotel, with narrow corridors and dark panelling throughout. Not attractive, but okay for a night.

McCann had been a close associate of Ivan Cooper in the Civil Rights Movement. He showed up at the agreed 2 o'clock. He was about 40 and had a lined face, haunted eyes, unruly black hair and scruffy sideburns. He greeted Thomas with a firm handshake.

'This is the hotel where the final preparations for the march were made. There was an incredible buzz that day. There was some tension but above all excitement and confidence. We would change history. We did, but not as we had planned. But as I suggested, let's walk.'

It was only a short distance to William Street, lined by the familiar, simple redbrick terraced housing

'This is where the march came down, from up there.' McCann pointed west. 'The plan had originally been to continue down William Street towards the Guildhall for a rally but we had to change that. The army had built a barrier down there.'

He pointed down William Street in the other direction.

'There were two other barriers up to the right. The paras were behind that wall at first, with regular army units and the RUC at the barriers.'

'What was the mood among the marchers, with so much military presence?'

'There was defiance and self-confidence. Everyone knew that this was a peaceful march. We were all sure that justice was on our side. But we hadn't expected so many soldiers, so the tension mounted. The trouble started here, at the intersection with Rossville Street that we're standing on now. Some of the marchers ignored our calls and went straight on towards the army barrier, along with a bunch of young people who started to throw rocks and things at the troops.'

They turned to walk down Rossville Street, which featured three large, bleak apartment blocks to the left and a cluster of lower apartment buildings to the right. McCann reconstructed the day as best he could, pointing out where people had been shot and wounded and where bodies were found. Thomas was amazed that McCann could recall the names of the dead and in many cases where they had fallen. They had ranged in age from 17 to 41.

Thomas saw a large mural on the side of a building depicting a scene from that day and another mural with the inscription 'You Are Entering Free Derry', the same as on the photo he had seen in the little music shop.

'This is difficult for you, isn't it, Sean?'

'Yes, it is. It's a day I'll never be able to forget. It was an unimaginable horror. I rarely walk these streets because the memories are still so vivid.'

'Will you let me buy you a drink? It looks to me as if you'd rather get away from here.'

'Sure. I know a place.'

They walked back to William Street and turned in the direction of the river, to Peadar O'Donnell's pub. It looked welcoming, with yellow stuccoed walls and dark brown frames around the large windows flanking the entrance.

'How did it get so out of hand, Sean?'

'We knew the paratroopers were a ruthless bunch, yet we didn't consider carefully enough the possibility that they would act the way they did. And we weren't able to control the couple of hundred young lads who were out for a confrontation.'

'Should the march have taken place?'

'Ivan was in a difficult situation. If he had called off the march it would have meant the end of the civil rights movement to which we were committed. As it turned out, the movement died that day anyway.'

'Why is that?'

'After that nobody believed that non-violence was going to prove successful. The IRA, which had never been strong in Derry, recruited many dozens of young men. The path of violence was chosen.'

'The impact of that day on Derry must have been devastating.'

'It was and is, and will be for generations. Most people here are

Catholic. Hundreds of families had relatives or friends killed or wounded, or lost loved ones as a result of later violence and internment.'

'Are the paratroopers the villains of the piece?'

'Yes, they are. But even more so is the British Government's whitewash of the whole event. The dead and wounded were swept into the dustbin of history with words like "regrettable". As for the paras: the officers are to blame. They lost control of a situation they should have been able to manage. We had made it amply clear that it was to be a non-violent demonstration. The officers should have been punished rather than honoured. A number of paras reported hearing shots fired from "the other side" and seeing rifles pointed at them. That was simply untrue. I think they believed the IRA was about to attack them and they panicked. It's not what you expect from professional soldiers, but I'm pretty sure some of them are suffering from their personal memories of that day.'

Sean stood up and started to button up his coat. 'Thomas, I have to be off, so I hope you'll excuse me. You know how to get in touch with me if you think of anything else.'

'Sean, I'm very grateful for your time.'

They shook hands and Thomas remained where he was, digesting what he had seen and heard. British troops shooting unarmed British citizens? It was mindboggling, and he remembered the shock and disbelief he had felt when he heard about National Guardsmen killing four students at Kent State University in Ohio in 1970. McCann and Cooper, idealistic civil rights leaders, organising an event that ended in such mayhem – what had it done to them? He had seen the pain on McCann's face as he recited the names of the dead and felt very sad for him.

A man in his mid-thirties who had been sitting at the bar stood up and, with the help of crutches, approached Thomas.

'Hello. My name's Peter. I saw you talking with Sean and heard your American accent. May I join you?'

'Of course, please do. I'm Thomas.'

Peter had a pleasant face and a warm smile. Thomas also noticed that he was missing his left leg.

'What brings an American to Derry?'

'I'm a journalist for the *Boston Tribune*, writing some articles on the effects of the Troubles on… the "normal" folk, for want of a better word.'

Peter smiled and said, pointing to his missing leg, 'Here you see one of the effects.'

'Yes, I noticed. I'm finding the whole situation very hard to get my head around.'

'You have to know that we grow up here thinking in terms of "sides", of *us* and *them*: Unionist, Nationalist; Protestant, Catholic – but we're all just people trying to get on with our lives. To me the conflict is, in the end, about as significant as the conflict between Celtic and Rangers. Like, who really gives a shite – or should give a shite?'

Thomas was glad he knew just enough to recognise that Peter had referred to the arch-rival Glasgow soccer clubs.

'Do many people share your views?'

Peter looked down and shook his head.

'Probably not. Too many people are still looking for ways to fight the battle between Kings James and William all over, and that was almost 300 years ago. Who cares? I mean, why do we have to fight the same war over and over again? But we do, and with every battle more lives are lost. That's the tragedy of Northern Ireland.'

Glancing down at the missing leg, Thomas ventured: 'But you haven't always thought of it this way, I take it.'

'No,' Peter replied. 'That's why I got into trouble. I was there on Bloody Sunday. I was one of the yobbos throwing rocks at the paras. And after that I joined the IRA.'

Thomas asked, 'Would you have another pint?'

'A half would be grand, thanks.'

Thomas ordered, adding a couple of bags of crisps.

'Peter, why were you and others throwing rocks during what McCann said was supposed to be a peaceful march?'

'The troops, and the paras in particular, provoked it by being there, with their hostile attitude towards everyone, marchers included. But I never imagined what the result would be. It was a nightmare.'

'So then you joined the IRA?'

'Many of us did. Stupid, but such was the anger and the hatred many of us felt that armed struggle seemed to be the only remaining option.'

'And you paid a price,' said Thomas, glancing towards the missing leg.

'I did.'

'What do you do now?'

'I have an administrative job and study accountancy. I married a year ago and we're expecting a child in about six months. All I want to do now is ensure a good future for all of us. And talk about that, it's time for me to head home.'

They shook hands and Peter hobbled out the door, leaving Thomas admiring his resilience. He had lost a leg, but it sounded as if he had laid a firm claim to his life and future.

He walked along the river, enjoying the peaceful view, and particularly the old city walls, with cannons that stood as silent sentinels, guarding over the secrets of previous conflicts. What a strange, tragic country he thought. Small wonder that Saoirse wished to leave.

The next morning he decided to see some more of the countryside. He detoured along narrow B-roads to villages the names of which he couldn't always pronounce, like Dunnamanagh, Ballynamallaght, Plumbridge (that was easy) and Cranagh. The road wove through peaceful farming country, and occasionally he caught whiffs of peat smoke curling up from cottage chimneys. He was reminded that all was not as peaceful as it appeared when he was stopped briefly at a police checkpoint.

He arrived in Magherafelt, which felt more like a real town. If it had had to endure the Troubles, it was not immediately visible, and the town centre was pleasing to the eye. Walking down the main street he again picked up the sweet scent of a peat fire burning somewhere. People were going about their daily business, greeting each other cheerfully.

He found a small inviting restaurant with an old-style exterior. Inside, the atmosphere was cosy and welcoming, with only a couple of customers. A heavy-set woman looking like a friendly farmer's wife came to his table, welcomed him, and offered him a menu. After he had ordered he asked her about the town.

'Well, we used to have quite a few tourists. It's a lovely area, so close to Lough Neagh. It's a market town for all the farmers around here. And we're very proud of Seamus Heaney, the poet. He's from these parts, you know.'

'Really? I've read some of his poetry.'

'Of course he lives in Dublin now, but we do see him around here from time to time. Very nice man. That gentleman sitting over there could tell you more about him.'

She pointed towards a middle-aged man wearing a greenish tweed jacket and a trimmed moustache. He had a cup of coffee in front of him and was reading a newspaper. Thomas walked over and introduced himself. The man folded his newspaper away.

'Paul O'Connor. What brings a young American to this town?'

Thomas explained and added that he was pleasantly surprised that he had landed in 'Heaney country'.

'Heaney is a wonderful writer; I'm sure he will go far. He has written a volume of poetry inspired by the Troubles and his hope for the future. Have you read *Wintering Out*?'

'No, I haven't,' Thomas admitted.

'Well, you must lay your hands on it. I think Grant's bookshop, opposite the church down the road, will be having it in stock.'

'*Wintering Out*… thank you. I'll go down after lunch. I would associate the term with what people might attempt in the snowy winters of the north-eastern United States. But does it have another meaning here?'

'It surely does,' Paul smiled. 'In Northern Ireland "to winter out" means "to see through and survive a crisis". What Heaney expressed is his wish that we survive the Troubles and his hope that we can all look forward to a brighter future.'

Thomas thought of Peter, and how he seemed to have survived his personal troubles and was building towards a brighter future. It flashed through his mind that Heaney's collection might just have a personal meaning for him, too.

'Do you believe that Northern Ireland has a brighter future to look forward to, Paul?'

'I don't like to say it,' Paul replied, slowly, 'but I'm afraid it will not be in my lifetime. When I read about and listen to the politicians, or should I say, most politicians, I can't be optimistic. There's not the collective will and wisdom in Belfast, and London and Dublin hope the problem will just go away. However, I do think that the citizens of Northern Ireland could create a brighter future for themselves and for each other. Sure, some people still think the gun and the bomb, the march and the demonstration, will help them achieve what they want. But there are others who see it as a step-by-step moving forward, by individuals, driven by their own spirit, their own commitment, and their own courage.'

Paul stood to leave; Thomas shook his hand and thanked him. As he savoured his tasty sausage and potato, he reflected that almost everyone he spoke to said the same thing: it was not the politicians but the people who would have to bring about change.

Thomas decided to stay over in Magherafelt rather than drive on to Belfast. He walked to the bookshop and found a copy of *Wintering Out*. A small hotel called the Temple looked clean, despite a slightly down-at-heel air and a sheet of plywood in place of one large window. The receptionist was welcoming and said there was a room available, which turned out to be immaculately clean and bright. Thomas settled into a comfortable chair in the lobby-bar and opened his new book. It was almost five o'clock and his only companion was a man preparing the bar for business.

He skimmed through the eighty or so short poems and found them difficult reading. They were filled with metaphors and imagery, written in dense language full of Irish words and expressions. Starting a second read-through, he silently spoke the words and started to feel the magic of Heaney's style.

The silence was broken when a woman entered. Thomas looked up. Thin, with sharp features and long grey hair that flowed wildly over her shoulders, her age was hard to judge. Her eyes, clear and wide, caught Thomas's attention. Her style was eccentric: a brown dress down to her ankles, covered to below the waist by a colourful cape.

'Hello, Mary! Your usual cuppa then?' asked the man behind the bar.

'I was dandering by and says I, I might as well call.'

'Well, Mary, you're always very welcome,' the man replied.

'Cloudburst and steady downpour now for days,' she said.

'Yes, could well be that we're in for a wet spell, Mary,' he replied, as he set a cup of tea in front of her.

She stirred in some milk.

'Soft voices of the dead are whispering by the shore… what do I say if they wheel out their dead?'

Intrigued, Thomas put the book down on the table and listened. The woman spoke in a clear voice with a thick accent.

After a pause to sip her tea, Mary went on, 'It's twenty to four on one of the last afternoons of reasonable light.'

'Aye, the days are getting shorter, Mary.'

It didn't appear to be a real conversation, but the words Mary spoke fitted the context in a strange way. They also sounded familiar. Thomas realised he had just read some of them in the little book in front of him. She was quoting Seamus Heaney.

'Fishermen at Ballyshannon netted an infant last night along with the salmon,' she went on, addressing the man as if sharing the latest news. The man nodded. Thomas noted the sympathetic and even protective manner in which he played along with Mary.

Two well-dressed men entered. As the barman drew their pints Mary looked around the room, taking in Thomas and the book on the table.

'Seamus,' she said, apparently recognising the little book. 'I knew his family, from a farm down the road. It's poor as Lazarus, that ground.'

Thomas smiled, and nodded.

'Riverback, the long rigs ending in broad docken and a canopied pad down to the ford.'

Unable to reply, Thomas nodded again.

Mary took another sip of tea, then turned back to Thomas and said, sadly, 'My brain is a whitewashed kitchen hung with texts. ... Ireland, I was born here. Ireland.'

Thomas responded to this by saying, 'I'm American.'

But this was of little interest to Mary. 'I am wintering out the back end of a bad year,' she continued, turning back to the man behind the bar. 'Rain on the roof tonight.'

She wrapped the cape around herself, picked up her large bag and headed towards the door.

'Good night, Mary, mind yourself now!' the man called out.

'My hide stays warm in the wind. My wide eyes read nothing. The semaphores of hurt swaddle and flap on a bush,' was Mary's parting line.

The two men who had come in for a beer also called out, 'Good night, Mary.' And she was gone.

Thomas stepped up to the bar and ordered a pint. He asked the barman, 'Who is that woman, if you don't mind telling me?'

'Ah, poor Mary. She is a dear, kind soul. She used to teach English at the local school, you know. She was very bright.' He paused before going on. 'Her husband was killed by a bomb two years ago. In County Armagh. He was a contractor doing work for the RUC at a new station down there when the IRA attacked it. He was just unlucky. And Mary, well, Mary never recovered from the shock.'

Thomas shook his head. 'The poor woman.'

'Yes, we all do our best,' he gestured towards the other men, 'to look after her. She comes in here often for a cup of tea, looking for some company. It is very sad.'

A small group of men came in and the man behind the bar was busy. Thomas went back to his table but found he couldn't read any further; his mind was still going over Mary's strange utterances. Perhaps they could provide a partial key to his understanding of Heaney's poetry. If the poetry formed a commentary on the pain and suffering in Northern Ireland, maybe Mary found consolation in the lines.

After a quick dinner and another pint, Thomas went to his room. He read some more, then let images from the poetry drift through his mind. He thought about Saoirse, about their 'date' on Sunday. Again he imagined himself taking her away from this sometimes insufferably sad country. He felt himself becoming infected by the pain and despair surrounding him, and questioned the usefulness of his journalistic mission. Did his readers care? What, in the end, could they do about it? What was the point of reading daily stories about how societies in various parts of the world tore themselves apart? Wasn't the only healthy reaction to take brief notice and then move on to those small daily activities by which individuals try to make a difference to their lives, the lives of family and friends, the lives of colleagues?

A Heaney line came to mind: 'My serenades have been the broken voice of a crow.'

Sadness swept through him as he recalled Saoirse's gentle admonition that he disclosed so little about himself. Eventually, he dozed off to sleep, listening to the rain on the roof.

CHAPTER 9

When Thomas returned to the Europa the next afternoon there was a message asking him to call Henry Farmington, his direct chief in London.

Henry asked whether he could come to London for a few days the next week but was vague about his reasons other than to say that he wished to discuss Thomas' immediate future.

He agreed, and then asked, 'Henry, is there any chance your contacts at *The Times* might be able to find a former member of the British Paratroopers who was present during the Bloody Sunday shootings and who would be willing to talk with me?'

'I obviously can't promise anything. But I'll see what I can do.'

He dropped in briefly to a busy Foyle's, heard Saoirse sing several songs and confirmed that she would be at the hotel at ten on Sunday morning. He did not mention his encounter in the alley and the envelope yet. Wanting to be fresh in the morning, he wished Saoirse goodnight and headed back to the hotel, imagining her walking beside him.

He rose early on Saturday and wrote an article on his trip to Derry. It included:

Catherine teaches no more. Her personal loss and tragedy have tipped her over the edge. Dishevelled and lonely, she wanders around the town in a world of her own. In a restaurant she is greeted kindly and offered a cup of tea. She does not converse but she does speak: in lines drawn from the work of poet Seamus

Heaney. Some of the lines make sense in an uncanny way. But no words are her own.

She wanders like a lonely ghost, seeking only tea and sympathy, another victim of the years of sectarian violence in Northern Ireland.

He wrote a separate, reflective piece about the profound sense of loneliness that afflicted so many who had suffered traumatic experiences they were unable to discuss with others. He thought of Owen, Mary, Saoirse's brother and the children in Saoirse's care. He wondered to what extent Saoirse too suffered, given her feelings of guilt about her older brother and whoever had been shot with the pistol that she had delivered. Of course he realised that he was also writing about himself: how painful it was to be haunted by events twenty years earlier at the summer camp and never being able to talk about them.

In the afternoon Thomas set out for a short walk to catch some fresh air. His thoughts went to the day with Saoirse, which he both looked forward to and worried about. How would she respond to whatever Dermot had written? After the warm embrace and gentle kiss in his room the other night, the next step was obvious and he longed to take it. He yearned for true intimacy. But would she? If yes, would he be as ineffectual as he had been with Jennifer? Nagging doubts assailed him. He recalled some lines by Rainer Maria Rilke. Thinking hard, he reconstructed them from memory:

> 'For one human being to love another, that is the most difficult of all tasks, the ultimate test, the work for which all other work is but preparation.'

He asked himself whether he was really up to the task. Self-doubt almost got the better of him. He briefly considered cancelling tomorrow, making some excuses and leaving her to get on with her life. But wouldn't walking out on her and on himself be the ultimate act of cowardice and a betrayal of both of them?

He became so caught up in his own thoughts and feelings that the noise and bustle of the city streets were totally wiped from his awareness. When he focused on his surroundings again he found himself near Daly's pub. He walked in, hoping he might see Sarah again and feeling guilty about not having followed up on her earlier.

Ian greeted him. 'Good to see you back. Uh… Thomas, isn't it?'

'Yes it is, and a good afternoon, Ian.'

It felt comforting to be recognised. Belfast was starting to feel like 'his town'. Thomas and Ian chatted as Ian drew a pint of Guinness before telling another Irish joke. Thomas was happy to laugh again.

'Ian, remember the woman I was talking to a few weeks ago?'

'Yes, sure.'

'Does she still come in often?'

'No, well, not anymore. She was in once a few days after you spoke with her and asked the same about you: did you come in often. I said no, just that once. She looked disappointed, as if she was hoping to continue the conversation.'

Thomas had missed out on something – and he was worried. He had a strange feeling that something terrible had happened but couldn't figure out why.

He became aware of Jamie standing beside him, looking friendly and pleasant. What had Ian called him? 'A dear lad.' He looked it now.

'Thomas?'

'Yes. How are you Jamie?'

'I'm glad you came in because I want to apologise.'

Thomas stuck out his hand.

'That's okay, Jamie. I came here to learn about the Northern Irish, and you taught me something that evening – and you're doing the same again now.'

Thomas told Jamie about some of his encounters and added that he found it difficult to understand why there was so much killing.

'It's not as if we understand it either, you know.' Jamie stared into his beer.

'I heard that your brother was killed, Jamie. I'm very sorry about that.'

'Aye.' Jamie continued to stare into his pint. 'About four years ago now, in Bangor, and I still have no idea why. But the shooting was claimed by the IRA.'

'Some of the money to buy weapons has come from the United States. I understand why you took it out on me that night.'

'Yeah well, but it wasn't right.'

'Jamie, may I get you another pint?'

Jamie accepted but was reluctant to speak any more about his brother, so Thomas switched to small talk. Someone else joined them and a lively conversation followed, mainly disparaging comments about the politicians, but it was mixed with friendly laughter.

Eventually he thanked them both and walked back to the Europa in a much better mood than when he had entered the pub two hours earlier.

Saoirse appeared at ten o'clock sharp, looking wonderful in a green sweater, tight jeans, a sturdy outdoor jacket and a bright smile. He gave her a big hug.

'Let's decide where we're going first,' gesturing to her to take a seat. 'I've had recommendations to drive north to the Giant's Causeway and south to Newcastle. But they seem a little far away, especially given the weather.'

'You're right. I don't have a deadline for getting back, but we don't want to spend the day sitting in the car. How about Bangor, and there's a lovely little park near Helen's Bay where Belfast Lough opens out into the Irish Sea. That's all just ten miles or so away.'

'Sounds great. Let's go.'

As they drove northeast along the A2, Thomas told her about his trip to Derry, his meeting with McCann, his encounter with poor deranged Mary. He also admitted to getting depressed on Thursday evening in his hotel room; depressed by what he heard almost every day and questioning the usefulness of writing about all the misery.

'Do you know, this is almost the first time you have told me about your feelings? I think I understand, and thank you, Thomas.'

Saoirse related a few touching anecdotes from the past week at the centre, but added that her younger brother Kevin had been having a bad week.

He felt a wave of warmth and affection for her, glanced over at her and wished he could play a positive part in her life.

'Saoirse, I'd like to meet your family one day – just as a journalist you happen to have met,' he added, when she didn't immediately reply.

'Okay, I'll ask them.'

Before he knew it they were entering Bangor.

'Turn left here and follow the road to the marina. Let's stop off at the Salty Dog – it's right beside the yachting harbour. I didn't have time for breakfast and need something before we walk.'

The Salty Dog was located in a redbrick Victorian townhouse. The restaurant was bright and welcoming, and they were able to claim a table by a window.

Once they had placed their orders Thomas said, 'There is something I need to tell you about and give to you.'

Saoirse looked at him inquiringly.

He told about the strange meeting in the dark alley with a man who said he was Dermot, and withdrew the envelope from his pocket.

'He asked me to give you this. He said it would be risky for you to be seen with him, but obviously he has seen you, and you and me together. He also knew my name, Lord only knows how.'

Saoirse remained silent for a few moments when he had finished. She rummaged in her bag and pulled out a slightly wrinkled photograph.

'This is Dermot. Was it him?'

Thomas looked at the smiling, rugged face of a young man in his mid- twenties.

'Yes, that's him.'

Saoirse took the envelope, opened it, withdrew a piece of paper and read. Thomas saw her eyes growing damp and waited for her to speak.

'Dermot says he's sorry he had to break off our relationship, that he still cares about me, that it's best for me not to be seen with him, and…' She paused. 'He says not to worry about him… But I do, Thomas. What's he up to? He's probably involved with the IRA, but how deeply? And why is he apparently keeping an eye on me, and on you. I just don't understand.'

Thomas saw her struggling to keep her tears back, and placed a hand on hers.

'I'm going to write a note in reply. But how will I get it to him?'

'Saoirse, you once mentioned that he frequented a pub, on the Falls Road I think it was. If you think he still goes there I might be able to figure out a way to get it to him without being conspicuous about it.'

'Okay, thank you.'

'But it won't be next week. I have to go to London for a few days.'

'All right. Let's eat now,' Saoirse suggested.

Somewhat subdued, she dug into her pancakes while Thomas enjoyed his bacon, sausages, fried egg and beans.

As they left, Saoirse, apparently recovered, said brightly, 'Let's walk up to Castle Park. It's only about a mile. I see some blue sky so maybe it'll be a fine afternoon.'

Hand in hand they set off through the centre of town. It was quiet on a Sunday morning.

'Do the Troubles ever come to a place like this?' Thomas asked.

'Oh yes, there were two terrible bombings, but that was at least four years ago.'

Thomas remembered that it was in Bangor that Jamie had lost his brother.

They walked past a formal garden in front of the castle, and admired autumn flowers in a well-tended walled garden. When the sun broke through they sat on a bench and soaked up its warmth. She took his hand.

'Thomas, last week in the hotel you said you loved me. I said, "I don't know how I feel, and it scares me." I have thought about it.' She paused, as if hesitant about what she would say next.

He found the suspense almost unbearable.

'I think I love you, Thomas.'

He threw his arms around her. She moved her face towards his, their lips met, and they kissed each other with feeling. When they broke away Saoirse was smiling.

'And it still scares me,' she added.

'I love you, Saoirse, and that scares me too.'

She laughed. 'That makes us two scaredy-cats then, doesn't it?'

He drew her close again and she rested her head on his shoulder.

'Do you think scaredy-cats can purr?'

'I think they purr especially hard. But come on, I'm going to take you to the other park, by the sea.'

She led him back onto the streets of Bangor and towards the car.

In only a few minutes they reached the park, even lovelier than the one in Bangor. The sun was shining brightly and it was surprisingly mild. They left their coats in the car.

'Let's go down to the beach,' Saoirse proposed, as she pulled him down a path. The water in the Lough was deep blue; several pleasure boats dotted the water and a ferry headed out to sea. Hand in hand they walked along the beach. Where the beach ended at a rocky outcrop they took a path that led them to the top. They watched the surf slapping rhythmically against the rocks below.

'Saoirse, a few days ago you told me about the two men who had threatened you and verbally abused you after you gave up being a gun-courier.'

'Yes?'

'Did you ever see them again after that incident in the restaurant?'

'No, I never did.'

'Well, that's good, but it also strikes me as a bit strange... I mean that they should stop so quickly with their sick game of "punishing" you.'

Saoirse looked thoughtful. 'I see your point. I was just happy that they had decided to leave me alone.'

'And you said that I was the only person you had ever told about that.'

'No, I said I had also told Niall about it. I was happy to have a big brother I could confide in once in a while. He was absolutely furious. I had seldom seen him so angry, and, in a way, that made me feel better.'

'I can imagine.'

Saoirse looked at him quizzically. 'Why are you asking? It feels a bit like you're being an investigative journalist now.'

'I'm sorry; I'm far from that. I guess I just want to try to understand how things work in this strange country.'

'Good luck with that. Now come on, let's go back down.'

For a minute or so Thomas wondered whether there was a link: Niall had been furious, and Saoirse's tormenters had disappeared. But he also knew it would be virtually impossible to find out if there was even a grain of truth to his suspicions.

They walked back down into a small sandy cove nestled between the rocks. They sat down and wrapped their arms around each other.

She looked up at him. 'You know, this feels almost unreal. We've known each other only a few weeks, but I feel so close to you. That started on your second visit to the pub. Unbelievable – particularly as I still know so little about you. I have to admit that in part it was simply you being American, and not Irish.'

'What you see is what you get,' Thomas replied with a silly grin.

'No, there's more than that. You've never mentioned your family, for instance, other than that you have no siblings.'

This was not what Thomas hoped to be talking about. 'I guess that's because I don't really know my parents.'

Saoirse looked puzzled. 'What on earth do you mean?'

'I mean that while my parents provided me with a very comfortable home they were never able to relate to me and therefore I couldn't relate to them. They were always full of praise for my achievements, mainly at school, but never asked me about my life. And they never talked about theirs. In a way we were strangers who happened to live in the same house.'

'That's very sad. You must have felt terribly lonely sometimes.'

'Yes, I did.'

'I can't easily imagine a home like that. But thank you for telling me. And, you know what? I still love you.'

Thomas placed his lips on hers. They enjoyed the intense, quiet moment.

Saoirse's face lit up with an impish grin.

'Okay, come on now. Off with your shoes.'

He followed instructions while she unlaced hers. She tried in vain to roll up her tight jeans, then pulled him up and led him down to the water's edge.

'I love the feeling of sand and water between my toes!'

Together they stepped gingerly into the sea, the cold water washing over their feet. A little wave rolled up to their ankles and they both stood there laughing as the bottoms of their jeans turned dark blue.

'I always loved water, but when I was little my parents always called out to me, "Careful you don't get wet now." Of course I was naughty and did anyway. I'd blame it on a big wave or a hole in the sand.' Saoirse laughed and took another step forward. Thomas followed. He pulled her around to face him and looked into her sparkling eyes, which laughed back at him. They walked slowly through the shallow water.

'You're lucky it's not a warm summer's day,' she said.

'Oh, why's that?'

'Well, I'd be guiding you out that way,' and she pointed into the Lough, smiling mischievously. 'Would you be ready to go really deep with me?'

'Literally or figuratively?'

'Both.'

'I'll go anywhere with you, Saoirse.'

'I'll hold you to that.'

They returned to where they had left their shoes. The spot was now falling into the shade of the trees on the rocky outcrop. They picked up their shoes and headed onto an expansive grassy area. The sun still shone on a bench, where they sat down to dry off.

They turned towards each other and Thomas thought he saw colours and a warmth in her pupils he had not noticed before. He slowly ran a finger over her nose, with its slight turn-up at the end, over her forehead, around her eyes, to her ears and neck.

'You're turning me on, Thomas.' She was giggling like a little girl being tickled.

He dropped his hand and she ran the fingers of her right hand over his face and his lips.

'Now who's doing the turning on?'

'Do you know what I want to do – someday?' she asked.

'No, what's that?'

'I want to make love in the grass, under the sun!'

Thomas laughed. 'What a lovely thought.'

'But not today. Let's go back to the car. I'm starting to feel peckish.'

They walked over the grass in bare feet.

It was less than a mile into the village, where they found a pretty seafood restaurant decorated outside and in with fishing nets and related gear.

They both ordered John Dory and a glass of white wine.

'Saoirse, a personal question. Have you ever made love, in a bed or elsewhere?'

'No, I haven't. Ridiculous, I guess, if it weren't for my upbringing as a good Catholic girl.'

Their eyes met and the colour rose in both their faces. They looked away as the waitress brought their meals.

As they ate they exchanged stories of life at school or, in his case, university, what they had enjoyed and what not. They discovered many similarities in taste: English and Irish literature, psychology, and history.

'Can we go back now?' asked Saoirse as they laid down their knives and forks.

'Oh, I thought you didn't have a deadline.'

'I don't.'

'Well, then why do you want to get back?'

'You silly man. I just want to get back to the hotel of course.'

She unbuttoned his shirt carefully. He watched her eyes and face closely and let her set the pace. An important moment in his life was unfolding but it was no doubt an even bigger moment in hers. Stupidly, he had not given precautions a thought and was surprised when Saoirse briefly interrupted events to withdraw a condom from her purse.

'You are prepared,' he laughed.

'Yes. At least in this regard I am. Make love to me, Thomas, but gently, and slowly. We have the whole evening, the whole night. And I am nervous, as well as excited.'

'Tell me to stop or slow down anytime, dear Saoirse.'

They let their hands slide over each other's bodies, which responded eagerly to the exploring touch. He felt her firm, warm breasts and erect nipples and her hands moving down his body to his legs. His erection brushed between her legs, sensing the warm moisture. She moaned softly as his hands moved down to her legs, onto her buttocks. They moved against each other seeking ever-greater contact.

Saoirse sat back and grasped his penis firmly, clumsily trying to slip on the condom.

Feeling her hands on him, something else took possession of his mind, a dark current of anxiety and guilt. He fought to stop it, to stay here, now, with Saoirse. But the dark force overwhelmed him. His erection wilted. Shame swept through him and he rolled away, staring at the ceiling, searching for words. He felt a surge of panic; he had lost Jennifer; he just couldn't lose Saoirse in the same way.

'What happened, Thomas? Was it something I did?'

'No, no. It was nothing you did. I, I'm sorry,' he stammered.

'Doesn't it just happen sometimes? Don't worry about it.'

'It wasn't just "something that happens". I …'

She placed her arms around him.

'Just relax. Breathe.'

After a few moments he spoke again.

'I want to make love so much. But…'

'What's going on?'

'I, I… It wasn't you. It's about something that happened a long, long time ago. I couldn't…' He couldn't continue; a dam burst and sobs shook his body while she continued to hold him close. 'Oh fuck.'

She let the surge of emotions exhaust itself.

As the sobbing ebbed, he managed a weak smile and kissed her lips.

'Tell me. Don't drown in whatever's going on.'

'I'll try.'

He got up, staggered to the bathroom, splashed water on his face and returned with two bathrobes. Wrapped up in those, they sat up in the bed.

He searched for first words, a place to begin.

'Just start,' she encouraged, as she held onto his arm and looked at him.

He took a deep breath.

'Okay. What I'm going to tell you now, I've never ever told anyone before. But I'll try to tell you.'

'I'm a good listener. Tell me.' She stroked his arm encouragingly.

'This goes back twenty years. I was thirteen, attending summer camp. Priests ran it, an order of brothers…'

He told her about his time at camp as he gazed at the wall, reluctantly projecting himself back twenty years.

'It was a lovely camp, nestled in the woods beside a big lake 150 miles north of Philadelphia. There were about 120 boys there between the ages of 12 and 16. We slept in tents with wooden floors, four to a tent, and the tents were arranged in clusters of three, each with a young priest as counsellor. Ours was called Father Donald, in his mid-twenties. I thought he was wonderful; a sort of older brother. He was always cheerful. Everyone found it really easy to talk with him and he seemed to care about each of us. He was also in charge of sailing, which we practised in little dinghies. He also played the guitar and led us in many singsongs.'

Thomas hoped he wasn't rambling on but when he looked at Saoirse he saw that she was still giving him her undivided attention.

'I loved it there and made some great friends during those two weeks. I especially liked swimming and canoeing, and even learned to dive. We were taken on hikes in the woods and learned about the trees, plants and flowers, and in the evenings there was usually a campfire where we sat around and sang fun songs. But there was also free time to just horse around or to be by yourself and read, or write letters home. On Sundays there was a service, outdoors, in what we called our "cathedral in the woods". They were two of the happiest weeks I can remember from my childhood, until the second-last evening.'

He paused. He had been staring straight ahead. He looked at Saoirse again and saw that she was still with him. He took a deep breath.

'Father Donald asked me to follow him, which of course I did. He led me into a secluded area in the woods and asked me to sit down beside him on a big log. Then he started to tell me that I was very special and how much he liked me. He asked if I trusted him, he kept talking, quietly, nicely, and put his hand on my leg.'

Thomas faltered, and Saoirse kissed him lightly. 'Go on, Thomas.'

'Then his hand started to move up and down my leg. It didn't feel bad to me, just strange. I didn't know what it meant. He kept talking – I don't know what about anymore. Then his hand stopped, at my crotch.'

He stopped, trying to hold back the emotions that recalling the episode released.

'Go on, Thomas' she said gently. 'Go on.'

'I knew that something was wrong. But, but… under the warmth of his hand I was getting a hard-on. Then he unzipped my shorts and his hand went inside, stroking my erect penis. I just sat there like a statue. But… while I knew that it was very wrong, it was also strangely pleasurable. He just kept talking, very quietly, saying things like "Trust me, Thomas, it's okay." But I broke away in a panic, was off the log, zipping myself up, and crying. He got up too and stepped towards me, trying to console me. But I was terrified and ashamed and ran off through the woods back towards the camp buildings.'

Thomas started to choke up and turned away.

'Come here,' Saoirse said quietly, and drew him towards her again.

He gradually pulled himself together.

'I know how wrong it was, what he did. But what shamed me and still shames me is the fact that I got an erection. Some part of me actually liked what he did.'

She looked at him gently.

'Anyway, I stayed away from Father Donald the last two days. He spoke to me once, to say that I must never tell anyone what happened. I was too afraid and confused to even consider it. I certainly didn't dare tell my parents. My parents never, ever spoke with me about sex. Besides, I felt it was my fault that it had ever happened. The shame never left me and it still hasn't, irrational as that may sound.'

He stopped, breathing hard. She watched him settle down before she responded.

'My love, there is nothing to be ashamed of. What would you be saying now if a young boy was telling you this story? I love you.'

She drew his face towards hers and gave him a long kiss. The tension in his body flowed away. When they drew back she was still looking at him, and repeated, 'I love you. And I'm glad you told me. But you told your parents nothing at all?'

'No. Of course they asked how the two weeks had been. I think I just said "fine", but not talking about anything was part of the way our family worked, or didn't work. The next year when they said they were going to allow me to go to camp again, I said "no". They were perplexed, I guess, and tried to force the issue but I rebelled and they eventually gave up.'

He got out of bed and poured two glasses of wine.

'At least it's no longer a hidden secret is it?' she said, with a twinkle in her eye again.

'Nope, I guess not. But it's so ridiculous. Why should I have suddenly remembered Father Donald when I desperately wanted to make love to you?'

'I think you know from all the people you've talked to that leaving old shit behind is not easy, especially when you can't talk about it. What do you think I try to do with the children every day? In one way or other I try to get them to talk about things, with me and with one another.'

'You're right,' he replied, gradually feeling back in control of himself. 'But the story isn't quite over yet. For a couple of years I thought I must be homosexual. It was the time at school when homosexuality seemed to be on everyone's minds and they made lots of jokes about it, sometimes at the expense of boys who were for one reason or another suspect. I felt no physical attraction to boys, but my response to Father Donald stuck in my memory. I decided not to have anything to do with sex, which remained a big mystery to me for a long time. I just stuck to what I knew I was good at, and that was school and being "academic".'

'Have you ever slept with a woman?' Saoirse asked gently.

'Yes, at university, a number of times, and after that too. But it was never serious and to be honest I was most often stoned at the time.'

She smiled.

'But what just happened has sort of happened several times before. With a girl I really liked, Jennifer, almost the same thing happened. I mean, we did have sex, the memories didn't entirely stop me, but she was right when she said I wasn't "all there" with her. That eventually meant the end of the relationship. I couldn't tell her my story and my excuses didn't help. She walked out on me. I was so afraid that all that would happen again.'

'I'm not walking out on you and it's not all going to happen again.'

'Saoirse, I built a wall around myself. It's so bloody lonely inside that wall.'

He couldn't hold back a few more tears, which trickled down his cheeks. She handed him his glass of wine. Her hands slipped under the bathrobe and gently moved up and down his chest, over his face and then down his legs. He felt himself relaxing as he accepted her caresses.

They snuggled together, talking gently, until he felt himself becoming drowsy. The emotional half hour had drained him. With Saoirse's arms wrapped tightly around him he fell asleep.

Light was peeping into the room from behind the curtains when he opened his eyes. Her hands were again roaming over his body. Light kisses descended on his face, his eyes, his ears.

She smiled at him. 'Are you up for a little morning exercise, my love?'

'Yes, I think so.'

He let his eyes, his hands and his tongue explore the length of her body.

Saoirse talked to him softly, reminding him constantly that it was she beside him, as she responded to his touch with a hunger of her own.

Awareness of time faded and caution gave way to passion, interrupted briefly when he, this time, took charge of slipping on the condom.

He entered her gently. Arching her back, Saoirse moaned and cried out. He tried to slow things down, to make the sensations last as long as possible. But that wasn't to be for long. Feeling his climax approaching, his thrusts became stronger, until, at the climactic moment, they both screamed.

Reluctantly he withdrew. They were both panting deeply, as their hands massaged the sweat on each other's bodies.

Eventually they lay quietly in each other's arms.

Saoirse was the first to speak.

'I think you just did go deep with me, my love'.

'I said I would go anywhere with you'.

'Yes you did, and it was wonderful. You were certainly all here with me.'

'I sure wasn't anywhere else. I've never had an experience like it.'

'Neither have I. And you did make me purr.'

'But I was the big scaredy-cat last night,' he remarked with a pained smile.

'Are you all right now?' she asked.

'I've never been better.'

'Good. Me too.'

They lay side by side for a little while longer, and then stood together in the bathtub watering each other down with the handheld shower and lathering each other with soap.

CHAPTER 10

1983

Following his incredible night with Briana, Thomas walked around St Stephen's Green. It was a mild and sunny day, just as Saoirse had hoped for. His thoughts flashed back and forth between Saoirse and Briana. He still felt an immense love for Saoirse, and here he was about to go to her wedding – with someone else. It shamed him to have to acknowledge jealousy. And then there was Briana. He had never in his life experienced such uninhibited and exuberant sex. He was smitten with her; that was perhaps the right word. Or was it 'infatuated'? That word made him feel like a teenager, a teenager he had never been.

After an hour of wandering and trying to put everything in its place he returned to the hotel, changed into a crisply ironed shirt and his best suit, and set off again, across the Liffey, up O'Connell Street and to the Pro Cathedral. It looked more like a Roman temple than a church, with six heavy columns holding up the grey portico. He entered through the massive oak doors. The interior was white and light, with a high cupola directly above the altar. A young lad of about ten, looking uncomfortably self-conscious in a formal dark blue suit and tie, escorted him to a pew. The organ played quietly as a small Irish harp waited to the right of the altar.

The sound of people entering and talking with each other increased in volume. The groom and his attendants took their places, handsome in their dark blue tuxedos. The organ struck up the Wedding March and all eyes turned to the rear. Saoirse, stunning in a long cream-coloured wedding gown, walked slowly down the aisle, escorted by Kevin, also in a dark blue tuxedo, and followed by Briana in a sleek dress matching the colour of Saoirse's.

When Saoirse had taken her place beside Brian and the priest had said a few opening words a young woman behind the harp and another standing beside her launched into Schubert's 'Ave Maria'. The pure and harmonious sounds they created were enhanced and amplified by the wonderful acoustics.

The priest took over and led the ceremony through readings, a homily, prayers and the formal words to which the guests could hear the 'I do' responses. Brian and Saoirse were declared man and wife and permitted to kiss.

To a joyous burst of organ music the newly-weds walked back down the aisle, waving and smiling happily, pausing every now and then to receive the congratulations of someone seated nearby.

Outside the cathedral there was a throng of smiling faces, with cameras everywhere aimed at the happy couple.

Colin appeared at his side. 'Thomas. Do you remember me?'

'Of course, Colin. How are you?'

'I'm grand. Saoirse asked if I would drive you to Killiney. May I offer you a ride?'

'Terrific, thank you, Colin. I was just wondering about finding a taxi.'

'No need for that. You're very welcome.'

Briana had edged towards him with an enquiring look. Thomas looked at her and at Colin, then asked whether Colin had room for one more.

They waited with the crowd until a white limousine had whisked Saoirse and Brian away.

Killiney Castle Hotel was impressively situated on a hill overlooking Dublin Bay a short distance south of the city. The wedding party was already in the garden, where a photographer was capturing memories.

Saoirse spotted Briana and waved her over. She called out to Thomas. 'Hey, get over here.'

When he had walked over she said, 'I want you in a couple of pictures too.'

While still feeling uncomfortably like an outsider he did his best to smile warmly.

In the grand ballroom, a couple of hundred people milled about. Thomas found Saoirse's mother and congratulated her on her daughter's marriage.

'Thank you Thomas. It was lovely. I do hope so much that the two of them have a wonderful life together.'

There was something in her tone that suggested some doubt. Or perhaps he was just projecting.

The harpist who played at the church was now seated in the middle of the stage and fingered a number of enchanting melodies. He watched her pluck the strings, fascinated.

'That's by Turlough O'Carolan,' said Saoirse's voice from beside him. 'Wonderful, isn't it? Now let me show you to your place at the head table.'

'Head table? But…'

'Oh shut up. You're my special guest. Consider yourself my own "best man".'

She led him forward, placing him between her mother and Briana. With a wide smile she added, 'I'm going to ask you to say a few words. So be prepared.'

'What? Without notes or a teleprompter?'

She laughed. 'Go on with you.'

When everyone had found his or her designated place, Brian's Best Man struck a glass with a knife.

He gave the first word to Kevin. Though obviously uncomfortable, Kevin did his best, keeping it short and, speaking also on behalf of his mother, wished his sister and Brian a blessed life together.

Brian's father spoke his obligatory words about being happy to welcome Saoirse into the family in a very self-assured manner. Thomas thought he spoke in a tone he might use to address the board of his bank. Saoirse whispered something to the Best Man, who then turned to Thomas. Searching for words, he did his best to keep his remarks light-hearted.:

Many years ago I met a very attractive and sassy young woman disguised as a barmaid in Belfast. Little did I know then that she would become a dear friend, nor that one day I would be present on her wedding day. Brian, you are an extremely fortunate man, and I congratulate you.

However, I still secretly harbour my own hopes. That will sound like a strange thing to say, so let me explain. I met a young lad the other day and asked him how often an Irish woman might marry. 'Sixteen,' he replied. Astonished as I was, I begged him to explain. 'Easy,' he said. 'Four richer, four poorer, four better and four worse.'

There was a burst of laughter from the guests, but Thomas noticed that the humour seemed less appreciated by Brian's parents and Brian himself. He ended by saying, rather conventionally,

Now I would like to do what I came here to do today: to wish Saoirse, and Brian a life filled with love, happiness and good health. I invite you all to raise your glasses in another toast to this wonderful couple.

He gave Saoirse a kiss on the cheek and shook Brian's hand before sitting down, uncertain whether he had struck the right note.

A few more speeches and toasts followed. The staff worked hard to keep glasses filled. When the speeches were over the guests were served with a fine three-course dinner. Between courses everyone got up and moved around. Briana soon found her way to Thomas.

'Great speech, Thomas. You choose your words well and you have such a wonderful, sexy voice.'

'Thanks, Briana.'

'Are you back in Buswells this evening?'

'No, they've booked a room for me here.'

'That's nice.' She wrapped an arm around his waist. 'Would you like company?'

Though tempted, he replied, 'Sadly enough I don't think that would be appropriate here.'

'Oh, I guess not. What are you doing tomorrow?'

All sorts of thoughts flashed through his head. He felt incredibly attracted to Briana. But: did he want a 'two-night stand'? He knew next to nothing about her, and what if he really were to fall in love? Once again there would be three thousand miles between them. Another hopeless relationship with an Irish woman. And though she must be physically attracted to him, good as that made him feel, what would she think of him if she ever really got to know him?

'You seem to be thinking over your answer very carefully,' Briana threw in. 'It was a simple question: What are you doing tomorrow?' She looked at him with an amused smile.

Struggling with his conflicting feelings, he lied.

'I'm having dinner with a journalist friend.'

'What about lunch then?'

Briana did not give up easily.

'Uh, sure, I guess that will work. Where do you suggest?'

'Anywhere. I'll call by your hotel – is around one o'clock okay for you?'

'Yes, that would be fine. I look forward to it.'

'Good.'

Briana skipped off to speak to someone else, leaving Thomas wondering whether he was more sorry about having agreed to lunch or for having lied about his evening. Maybe lunch would provide an opportunity to learn who she really was, and it felt safer than agreeing to dinner.

He went outside for some fresh air and some quiet, accompanied by a handful of smokers. Walking around the gardens in the falling darkness, he took in the view over Dublin Bay and the city lights beyond, but inner turmoil threatened to overwhelm him as his thoughts returned to Saoirse. Had he been alone in a remote wood he might have screamed out, 'Saoirse, no!' For a moment he wished he had not come to Dublin and regretted his stupid joke. He picked up a pebble from a gravel path and hurled it as hard as he could into the darkness.

When he returned to the ballroom a small band with a piano, drums, a guitar and a saxophone had replaced the harp. Brian and Saoirse had the first dance. It almost pained him to see how radiant and happy Saoirse looked. But of course, he thought, hadn't he just wished them both much happiness?

It was then Brian's father's turn to dance with Saoirse. Her smile looked slightly forced. Brian asked for the hand of Saoirse's mother. Both looked uncomfortable, while Brian's mother looked on with a plastic smile.

He went to the bar and picked up another glass of wine. Saoirse invited him to dance. There followed the moment he would never forget, when her eyes moistened and she urged – or pleaded? – that he stay in touch, write.

He was down for breakfast early. Saoirse and Brian were nowhere to be seen. He accepted an offer for a drive back into town, and was back at Buswells before noon.

Dressed in casual clothes, he awaited Briana's arrival in the lobby, still wondering whether he was looking forward to the lunch or not.

She arrived just after one, smiling brightly, now dressed in tight jeans decorated with eye-catching glitters on the pockets and an equally tight dusty pink sweater, covered by a black jacket on which a few drops of rain glittered like sequins. She pecked him on the lips and sat down beside him, a little breathless. Thomas was unexpectedly delighted to see her again. For a few hours he might be able to get Saoirse out of his mind.

'You look incredibly sexy, Briana.'

'I do my best for special occasions,' she replied with that same devastating smile.

They chose Milano on Dawson Street.

'I'm really glad you have time, Thomas. I did want to see you again. We got to know each other very... intimately. But I don't know much about you and you don't know much about me.'

'That had certainly occurred to me too,' he replied, already more relaxed now that he sensed what this luncheon meeting would be about.

'So shall I start by simply asking, "Tell me something about yourself, Briana"?'

'That's as good a way as any. But let's make a choice first. I'm starving.'

After they had chosen pasta salads, Briana started.

'Well, first of all, I want you to know that I don't fling myself at all men the way I came onto you. Maybe I came on too strong. But I do find you very attractive. I was not simply playing the role Saoirse had asked of me.'

'That's a relief, and the attraction is mutual,' Thomas replied. 'Only I wouldn't have had the guts to be as forward about it as you were. It was a fantastic night.'

Briana raised her eyebrows and smiled.

'Well, that's one thing you'll remember me by. But I'd like there to be more.'

He silently encouraged her to go on.

'First of all, people have described me as being spontaneous, impulsive and sometimes even reckless.'

'Why doesn't that surprise me?'

'But I have a serious side too. I graduated in psychology, though Saoirse and I took many different courses. My direction became organisational psychology.'

'Why that?'

'Like Saoirse, I want to work with people. But I prefer adults to children. And I believe there is a lot to be done in organisations. Another thing: I do not necessarily want to stay in Ireland. I would love to go to the United States or Canada at some point, perhaps even soon, for a Masters and maybe even a Ph.D. Now, what about you?'

He told her about his current work and his hopes for the future. Briana listened and asked intelligent questions as Thomas went on to describe his dream of writing fiction as a way of exploring the lives of ordinary people in extraordinary circumstances.

'Have you ever had any contacts in the North, Briana?'

'Hardly, except that I dated a guy from Belfast for a few months during my third year at Trinity. That was fun at first, but after a few drinks he'd go off into rants against the "papists". I got totally fed up with that and broke it off.'

'Are you Catholic?'

'Lapsed Catholic. But that's not the point. The whole mess, both sides, disgusts me. I just didn't want to listen to any more of his tirades. So that was it.'

They skipped dessert and over coffees talked about books they had read and movies they had seen. Thomas felt very relaxed and was delighted he had agreed to lunch.

'What time are you meeting your journalist friend?' Briana asked as they prepared to leave.

'There's something else you need to know about me, Briana. I'm a liar. I have no meeting.'

Briana looked at him sternly, betrayed by a twinkle in her eyes. 'Didn't think so. I really did frighten you, didn't I?'

'I don't know whether it was you frightening me or me frightening myself.'

'Are you still frightened, or shall we spend some more time together?'

'I can't think of anything I'd rather do. And that's the truth.'

'We could do a museum or art gallery, or catch a movie.'

'If it's not raining, let's just walk for a while and see where our footsteps take us.'

'Good, I was hoping you'd say that.'

Grafton Street was a pedestrian thoroughfare, and in Catholic Ireland on a Sunday afternoon, it was bustling. Most shops were open.

Briana led him into a men's casual wear shop, searched the racks, and came up with a slightly stretchy slim-fit pair of deep blue jeans with silver decorative stitching the likes of which he had never seen.

'You seem to approve of my jeans and think them sexy. I think these will look great on you. Try them on.'

When he came out of the changing room, Briana immediately said 'Yes! Much better than those baggy khakis.'

'Aren't I a bit too old for this style?'

'Not at all. You look terrific.'

Thomas paid and was then led to the men's department in the basement of the Brown Thomas department store. 'Let's see if we can get you a nice shirt here, instead of the boring pale blue one you're wearing.'

She suggested a fanciful print with various shades of red and purple.

Twenty minutes later he had another bag to carry.

'Are we done, Briana?'

'I think that'll do for now. Get you into that gear and you'll look great. So let's celebrate with a drink.'

Once settled into a bar and with drinks in hand, he confessed, 'I've never been taken out shopping by a woman before. But I enjoyed it. The jeans are a bit un-American: we have pretty conservative tastes over there, you know. But for you…'

She leaned over and kissed him.

'Yes, also for me, and besides I think we'll be seeing each other again soon, anyway.'

'Okay, mystery woman: what do you mean by that?'

'I want to visit Boston – and you.'

She reached out and took his left hand in hers. Thomas looked into her sparkling dark eyes and felt like he was being swept forward, out of control, on some strange ride.

'Well, great, but what about your work, whatever you're doing right now, and the courses you wish to follow?'

'I can start the courses in January, if I decide to stay here, and I don't have a job right now. So I was thinking, soon. If you have time, of course.'

'Wow. You are full of surprises.'

He felt as if he was 20 again, except that when he had actually been 20 he had not experienced anybody like Briana.

'How do they feel?' she asked when he had changed into the new jeans and shirt.

'The jeans are very comfortable but they do make me feel self-conscious.'

'Oh, come on. I think you look brilliant. Now, let me discover how they feel.' She nudged him over to the bed. Her hands moved slowly up and down his legs. 'Oh yes, they feel very nice indeed. And I'll bet they would look absolutely incredible soaking wet.'

'Like in the bath or shower?'

'Well, that might work, but I was thinking of the ocean.'

Thomas gave her a questioning look.

'Yes, as in your little adventure on the beach with Saoirse.'

'She told you, huh?'

'Yes. I thought it was hilarious. Of course, I would have dived right in headfirst and insisted that you follow.'

'No secrets between girlfriends, are there?'

'Sometimes not. Does it bother you?'

'I guess not.'

They dined at the Café en Seine. Meal orders placed, Briana carried on.

'Now, to get back to Boston: I'd like to visit in about four weeks. To see you and to see Boston and to see whether I can find the degree course I want to follow there. I know this is all a bit quick, considering we only met two days ago.'

'Sure, great. Make it six weeks and I can take you up into New England to see the autumn colours. They're usually incredible.'

'Brilliant. But I'd like to spend three or four weeks, to give me time to scout around. Is that too long for you?'

'Not at all. But I'll have to work while you're there.'

'I'll find my way around. I'm a big girl.'

He talked about some of the places he would like to take Briana to.

'Most of downtown Boston has a charming old-world feel about it. I think you'll like it. Cambridge is just, well, so peaceful and academic. And a couple of hours' drive north takes you into the beautiful New England mountains.'

'I do think I will love it, Thomas.'

She spoke more about her dreams for the future.

'I'd like to get at least a master's degree and work in a consulting firm.'

'What do you see yourself doing in such a firm?' Thomas asked.

'I think I'd like to focus on team development. From what I have read and heard there is a lot of future in that field. And also personal coaching.'

'I know nothing about that field, but it sounds good. Good luck to you, Briana.'

As they finished their meal, small talk became interlaced with sexy talk.

On the way back to Buswells, Briana stopped in a late-night store and bought a bottle of wine.

In his room Thomas filled two glasses.

'I do have to catch the bus to the airport at 8:30.'

'Don't worry. I'll make sure you catch it. Let's make the most of tonight and you can sleep on the plane.'

They embraced and slowly their hands started to explore each other's bodies.

Hers moved teasingly over his shirt, his jeans, up to his face, his ears, his lips, his eyes. He caressed her, loving the way the tight jeans fitted snugly over her shapely legs and buttocks.

'Too bad you can't come with me tomorrow,' he murmured.

'We'll just have to be patient for a few weeks, won't we?'

Clothing was discarded; stroking and kissing became more intimate until neither could maintain the slow pace.

Afterwards, it took about ten minutes before either could speak a word.

Turning towards him Briana said, 'You do know how to treat a woman, Thomas.'

'With you it comes naturally, if you'll excuse the expression.'

The alarm was a rude awakening at 7:30. Thomas struggled out of bed and into the shower. There was no time for breakfast. At the bus stop, waiting in the grey dawn under a Dublin drizzle, Briana spoke.

'I think I've fallen in love with you, Thomas. See you in a few weeks.'

'I'm looking forward to it. Take care of yourself in the meantime, Briana. Nothing reckless now!'

She laughed. 'I promise.'

When the bus pulled up they gave each other a final embrace.

Thomas boarded and waved through the window as the bus pulled away. Briana waved back and blew a kiss.

CHAPTER 11

1978

'Breakfast?' Thomas asked when they had dressed after their joyous lovemaking.

Saoirse pondered her response before replying. 'Yes, but not here. There's a little place down the road which does a good breakfast.'

'Why not here?'

'I just don't want all your – oh, never mind. Come on.'

He caught on that she didn't want his colleagues to see him with a woman who had obviously spent the night so he let her lead him to the restaurant, where they played back their memories of the previous evening, and the morning.

'I guess I've said "goodbye" to Father Donald,' Thomas threw in with a happy smile.

She didn't answer the smile. 'You've taken a big first step, my love. But you've been carrying him around for so long, he may not disappear immediately.'

He frowned.

'I'm just being realistic. Traumas don't lose their grip on a person overnight. But…' and she reached over for his hand, 'talk about it anytime he comes back to haunt you. Okay?'

'Thank you, my darling. I will… But damn it, I've waited twenty years for someone I felt safe enough with to talk about it. Why did it have to be that way? Why does it have to be that way for so many other people, including here in Ulster?'

He told her what he knew about what he was going to do in London, which wasn't much, except that it had something to do with his immediate future.

'And, well… at some point we'll also have to talk about the fact that sooner or later I will be called back to Boston.'

She put down her cutlery and stared at him, eyes both angry and sad.

'Don't you think I know that? But why the fuck do you raise that now? I've just slept with a man for the first time in my life, knowing but trying not to think about the fact that the relationship can't last. Why do you think I said I was afraid?'

She stared disconsolately at her food and he wished the ground would open up beneath his feet.

'I'm really sorry, Saoirse. I just wanted to…'

'What did you want to? What?' she hissed. 'Do you have any idea how important and wonderful this morning was for me? Why pick now to talk about… that?'

He sat there feeling like a chastened little boy. Gradually the storm subsided, but Saoirse's face betrayed her deep upset. Both had lost their appetites.

After a minute or so, she spoke again.

'I'm sorry, Thomas. Your timing was terrible, but I shouldn't have reacted like that. Sometimes I… I understand that we need to be open about all this. I love you, and that's what makes all this so difficult.'

'Let's try to forget how this breakfast ended. Come on, my darling. I'll walk you to the taxi.'

He put his arm around her and she put her head on his shoulder as they walked slowly down the street.

'You have my telephone number at home and at Foyle's. Will you call me?'

'I will. I promise.'

She stepped into the taxi and disappeared. Thomas returned to the hotel, still angry with himself.

That evening he had dinner with Ben. When they had finished he said, 'Ben, you keep track of reported incidents, don't you?'

'Yes, I try to.'

'Can you have a look to see if anything was reported about a woman, late twenties, blond hair, between about roughly the 15th and the 25th?'

'Yes, sure. Now?'

'I'd be grateful.'

Half an hour later Ben returned.

'I found something which may fit. A young, blond woman was found shot dead in a Catholic area of West Belfast on the 22nd. The RUC identified her as Sheila McCartney, 28 years old, a widow.'

'Fuck. That was her. I spoke with her one night at Daly's and apparently she was back there a few days later looking for me. Anything else?'

'Yeah. She was armed and is said to have fired a shot before being killed.

You wonder what she was doing there, don't you?'

'I think I know.'

Thomas told Ben what he had learned, and feared. She had apparently been out looking for another victim.

'I was probably the last person she reached out to, if only a little bit. If only I had… Shit.' He pounded his fist on the table and stared into his empty glass.

'You can't save the world, Thomas. Another drink?'

'No thanks, Ben. I'd better get going. Flying to London in the morning.'

He spent a restless couple of hours before falling asleep. 'How do you understand insanity?' kept running through his head. The feeling that he had let her down didn't leave him.

He was on his way to the airport by nine o'clock. When he had arrived in Belfast he had wondered how long he would last there. Now it felt like his only home.

By early afternoon he was in Henry's office, still unclear about the real reason for his trip. Henry didn't waste much time before enlightening him.

'Thomas, David and I have both been very happy with the articles you have submitted. We have received some very positive reactions from readers – here, read them for yourself.'

He pushed over a file folder.

'Thank you, Henry.' As he had been wondering about the usefulness of his writings, here was perhaps a welcome confirmation.

'There has also been a positive response to your idea of searching out appropriate American homes for young people from Northern Ireland. David has someone working on that now.'

'That's really terrific. Thank you.'

'But, Thomas,' and here Henry's tone suddenly resembled that of a schoolmaster, 'try not to get too emotionally involved. You're a journalist, not a social worker. Stick to the story – and your job.'

Thomas felt and no doubt looked taken aback by this reprimand.

Henry stared at him sternly for a few moments to let his message sink in, before going on to something else.

'It's not only ordinary readers who have responded. International News Network, INN, wants to interview you here in London, Thursday afternoon.'

This caught Thomas totally by surprise.

'But I've never been on TV, never even been interviewed. My workplace is behind a typewriter, not in front of a camera. I don't know if I can…'

Henry interrupted.

'You won't have to go in cold. They'll prepare you, let you get used to the surroundings and give you tips. They've also provided a list of possible questions so you can prepare yourself. The interviewer will be Susan Sheridan. She's a lovely woman; very good at putting people at ease and letting them tell their own story. See this is an opportunity.'

Thomas still felt doubtful, but his reflexive resistance was crumbling.

'Well, okay. At least it won't be a live telecast, I assume, and if it's a grand failure they can always find something else to fill the time.'

Henry smiled. 'It won't be a failure. You'll go down to their improvised studio Thursday morning around ten. That'll give you time to prep.'

Henry wasn't finished. 'Now, there is a second reason for wanting to talk with you. We, meaning David and I, want you to expand the scope of your reporting to cover political developments. This will mean talking with politicians in London and Dublin, as the need arises, as well as in Northern Ireland.'

'But I've only superficially been following political developments, Henry. It's not my field.'

'Your field just got bigger. You'll have to do some reading up of course; we have prepared material for you. The point is, I'm shifting my attention to the rest of Europe and the Middle East. You'll be the key man when it comes to the Irish question. But it won't happen overnight. You'll be joining me for a couple of talks with people over the next weeks, starting tomorrow morning, as a matter of fact. I'm picking you up from the Savoy at 9:30 and we'll have an hour with Airey Neave.'

'That is the second surprise you've thrown at me. Any more?'

'I've saved the best for almost last. We'd like you to think about moving to London or possibly to Dublin.'

'No, Henry, I don't want that. I want to stay in Belfast. I don't want to lose touch with the people there. I want to continue doing the type of reporting that I've been doing.'

Henry looked surprised by the determination with which Thomas had spoken.

'We thought you would jump at the chance to get away from that dismal city.'

'I'm not finding it a dismal city at all; the people are really lovely.'

'The people are lovely, or do you have a specific lovely person in mind?'

Thomas's silence confirmed Henry's suspicion.

'Never mind. It's none of my business. But I want you to think about it seriously. Now, my final surprise: You asked if we could find a former paratrooper for you to interview. Well, we did, a man called Reginald Adderley. He lives in Slough, near Heathrow, and has agreed to meet you in the lobby of the Holiday Inn at Heathrow at ten o'clock on Friday morning. Your flight to Belfast is at two, so you'll have plenty of time.'

It was eight o'clock when Thomas arrived at the Savoy, carrying a considerable bundle of photocopied articles. The first thing he did was call Saoirse.

'Hi darling. How are you?'

'I'm grand, especially now that you've called. What's your news?'

'They asked me whether I'd like to move to Dublin or London and I said no.'

'Good. I know you will have to leave at some point. I just don't want it to be now.'

'And the good news is that they want me to broaden the scope of my reporting. That would mean that I won't be asked to return to Boston any time soon.'

'That's brilliant!'

He told her about the television interview – 'Oh, I'm so proud of you!' she interjected – and about his Friday interview with the paratrooper and finally, that he expected to be back at the Europa by late afternoon.

'And what are you doing Friday evening?'

'Well, I thought I might drop by Foyle's for a pint.'

'You'd better.'

'And I'm sorry again about my insensitivity yesterday.'

'I'll forgive you this time. No news from here. I plan to go to bed early before another four nights at Foyle's.'

'I'll be thinking of you, my love.'

Over breakfast Thomas read the file he had been given on Airey Neave again: Margaret Thatcher's opposition spokesman on Northern Ireland and a probable cabinet member if the Conservatives managed to unseat the Labour government during the next election. Eton; Oxford; Second World War – first escapee from Colditz; Military Cross; Nuremberg trials; in politics since 1950, a hardliner. It was an impressive resumé but he couldn't get excited. What had any politician done in nine years for the people in Belfast, and the rest of Northern Ireland?

During the interview, which took place in Neave's comfortable panelled office in the Palace of Westminster, he kept quiet, making occasional notes. He listened to Neave's support for strong action against all paramilitary groups and his opposition to a devolved government for Northern Ireland. He told how Conservative policies would differ from and improve upon Labour policies and about the continuing need for a strong British armed presence.

Thomas heard no mention of the people of Northern Ireland. He heard nothing about the causes for which the Peace People and the followers of Ivan Cooper had fought: civil rights, equality with regard to housing and work, one man one vote. Neave's perceptions and interpretations were solely political and strategic. Sitting at the heart of the British establishment, the everyday realities on the ground seemed very far away.

When they were back in the car Thomas shared his thoughts with Henry.

'You're right,' Henry confirmed. 'Neave looks at Northern Ireland as if he were flying 30,000 feet above it. He takes in the political and military landscape, but he's far removed from the people. For all that, he's not an evil man. He's limited by his position and his own life experience, which you read about. When you listen to the people who matter from a political point of view, your job is not to like them, agree with them or disagree with them. Your job is to ensure that the readers gain a balanced understanding of the forces that are making a solution to the Irish question so intractable.'

They lunched together, Henry sharing some of his experiences. Thomas realised that he would have to change his mindset when taking on this new side of his assignment. He might not enjoy it as much as what he had been doing, but it would allow him to gain a broader understanding of the Troubles. He could try to connect that with his other work. He would have to learn to create his own helicopter, allowing him to move quickly between the 'view on the ground' and the view from 30,000 feet. There would be no Yeats and no Heaney at 30,000 feet. Mary, Jamie, Ian, Ryan, Owen, Sean, Peter – and Saoirse – would be invisible specks on the terrain.

The next morning a taxi took him to the Dorchester Hotel, where he was directed to a suite equipped with lighting, recording equipment, two video cameras, a control panel, and three technicians. Susan Sheridan put him at ease quickly. She was attractive, about 40, American, smartly dressed in a grey suit and very professional. She took him through a brief dry run, invited him to see himself on a small monitor and offered suggestions, pointing out the moments at which he had been concrete and specific, and when he had become vague.

'Be as vivid as you can be when you are describing people and what they told you, Thomas. Now, how are you feeling about doing this? We want to shoot right after lunch. Care to join me?'

'I think I'll be okay, and yes to lunch.'

By one o'clock they were back upstairs, where a young woman applied anti-glare powder to Thomas's forehead.

They took their places and after a final 'Just relax, Thomas,' Susan gave a nod towards the technicians.

'Good evening, ladies and gentlemen. This is Susan Sheridan talking to you today from London, England. With me is Thomas Cassidy, who has been reporting from Belfast and other places in Northern Ireland for the *Boston Tribune* for the last month. Welcome, Thomas, and thank you for joining me.'

'It's a pleasure, Susan.'

'Thomas, you have been focusing on the citizens of Northern Ireland, and how the Troubles have impacted on their lives. Tell us what impressions you have gained.'

The interview had started.

Guided by Susan's practised questioning and attentive listening Thomas found it easy to tell her about Peter, Ryan, Ross, Sarah, Sean McCann, and the concerned parents, without mentioning names.

Twice Susan said 'Let me just interrupt you there,' and followed up with another question. She was very much in charge of the interview, and he was happy to be led. He lost track of time and, before he knew it, she was saying, 'Thomas, is there a final thought you would like to leave with our viewers?'

He had expected this question, and said, 'All of us who have followed events in Northern Ireland know that over 2000 people have lost their lives there since 1969. I have come to realise over the last month that the casualty numbers have been far higher. Thousands more have lost their lives in a figurative sense. They have lost their loved ones, their homes, their jobs, their dignity. Some are recovering; many others are not. They need help they are not getting and, if I may add a personal comment, I find that shameful.'

'We'll have to leave it there. Thank you very much for joining me, Thomas.' Turning to the camera, she wrapped it up. 'I'll be back again at the same time next week. I hope you will all be watching. Good night from London.'

A technician's thumbs up told them the recording had gone well. Susan thanked Thomas for his time and assured him that the interview had gone just fine.

After a relaxed dinner with Henry, he took a taxi to Heathrow and started to think about how he would handle his interview with Reginald Adderley.

At a quarter to ten the next morning, he positioned himself in the lobby. A few minutes after ten, a man entered and looked around uncertainly. Thomas got up, walked over and enquired, 'Reginald Adderley?'

'Yes.'

'Thomas Cassidy. It's a pleasure to meet you, and thanks for agreeing to talk.'

Adderley looked relieved at being spotted, but nervous. Thomas sensed that he would have to take it slowly. He led Adderley to a relatively secluded corner of the coffee shop.

'Coffee?'

'Uh, yes, please.' Adderley lit a cigarette with shaky fingers.

Thomas caught a waitress's eye.

'Reginald, do you feel comfortable talking with me about that January day more than six years ago?'

'Well, no. Not really. Or maybe I am, I dunno. But I think someone's got to do it. The press covered the events and the official enquiries and all that, but there's been nothing said or written about what it was like for us.'

'Let me assure you that your name will not be used. So tell me what you want, please, in your own time and in your own way.'

Reginald sipped his coffee and lit another cigarette while the first still smouldered in the ashtray.

'Okay. Well, I'd never been in combat, you know, but that's what they told us to prepare for. They said we were at war with the IRA, that the IRA would be there, they would be armed and would try to pick us off.'

Thomas interrupted. 'By "they" you mean your officers?'

'Yeah, that's right.

'Most of us couldn't see a thing from behind the wall. We just stood around and waited, while a few guys who had climbed up to the top of the wall called down, telling about the shouting masses on the other side. The officers were edgy as well.

'We were – I was – bloody terrified. For all I knew it might as well have been a regiment of battle-hardened soldiers out there.'

Reginald painted a vivid picture of the scene, the mounting

tension, and how they had to abandon their position and move behind a barricade. 'There were hundreds of yobbos hurling rocks and bricks and whatever they could lay their hands on. We were told to fire rubber bullets, and a water cannon came in to drive the mob away. But it all just escalated so fast…'

Reginald stopped, perspiration glistening on his forehead, and asked if he could have a glass of water. Thomas signalled to a waitress.

'I never saw any weapons on their side, and if there were Molotov cocktails or nail bombs like some guys said, I never saw or heard them. Most of the kids were, like, in their teens, seventeen to nineteen, I guess.'

He gulped down the water and continued. 'The barrier was removed on an order and we went after them with four or five vehicles. When we were in the middle of them we got out and rounded up as many as we could. There was a lot of shouting and confusion and, well, some of my mates weren't exactly gentle. Kids were being knocked about by rifle butts and pushed roughly up against walls. Others ran away from us, and that's when they met the marchers.'

Reginald shifted in his chair.

Thomas felt sorry for the man. 'Would you like to take a brief break, Reginald?'

'No, no. I'd best carry on now. Anyway, all hell broke loose. I don't remember an order, but suddenly real bullets were being fired and people started dropping. Someone shouted that we were being fired at, but I didn't see that. I did see an old man falling to the ground. There was lots of shooting and shouting, and bodies were all over the place.'

Reginald paused for some water and tried to light another cigarette, but his hand was shaking too much. He wasn't looking at Thomas anymore and looked like he was reliving the experience.

'It was like a scene from hell. From bloody hell.' He stopped again.

'Reginald, did you fire any shots yourself?'

'Yes, three or four rounds.'

'Did you hit anyone?'

'I, I don't know for sure, I don't think so... I hope to God I didn't. We were not fighting enemy troops, we were shooting at British citizens.'

'Did you, at any point, see anyone firing at you?'

'No, I didn't. But some of my mates swore they did. At some point the order came to cease fire. We stood there for a little while as people tended to the dead and wounded. I'll never forget that scene. I just kept thinking, God, what have we done?'

He put his head in his hands and shook it. Reginald continued. 'Anyway, shortly afterwards we were instructed to pull back. I don't know what happened there after that. Later we heard there were thirteen dead and fourteen injured, with no casualties on our side.'

'Is it correct that no weapons belonging to the mob or the IRA were ever found, and no shell casings that weren't your own?'

Adderley paused, and in a very quiet voice answered, 'That's right. We shot 27 unarmed civilians, God help us.'

Thomas waited until Reginald had regained some kind of composure, then asked how Adderley had dealt with the experience afterwards. Adderley told about frequent nightmares, taking to drink and losing his girlfriend. A year or so on, somebody recommended he seek help from an organisation called Combat Stress. That had helped a bit, and eventually he was able to go back to part-time work, but he still drank too much.

'It has obviously been extremely difficult for you to talk about it again. How do you feel now that you have done so?'

'Even two years ago I don't think I could have. But now, yeah, it feels all right I guess. I know how your paper got my name by the way. They contacted Combat Stress. The person I'd seen there for a while called me and asked whether they had my permission to pass my name on to the press. I said sure, why not. But... I didn't think it would be this difficult.'

He wiped his brow with a handkerchief.

Thomas got up and extended his hand. 'Thanks, Reginald. I really appreciate your coming in. And all the best of luck to you.'

'Okay, well, goodbye then.'

For the first time since he had come in Reginald smiled a bit as he shook Thomas' hand.

Thomas hastily wrote a few notes before taking the hotel's minibus to the terminal. His mind kept returning to the interview with Adderley. It had been six and a half years since his traumatic experience, and he had now finally talked about it with someone other than a professional counsellor. He hoped that the morning would in some small way ease Adderley's burden.

He grabbed something from a sandwich bar and strolled through the terminal, looking in the shops. In a toy store he saw some teddy bears. He picked up a cheerful-looking one and thought, 'For Ross.'

He wondered if there wasn't an adult version of a teddy bear, one that could give Adderley some comfort.

Four hours later he was in the taxi heading back to the Europa, glad to be 'going home' after four tiring days in London. During the journey he had wrestled with the dilemma with which Henry had confronted him: take on the politicians and be reasonably assured of a longer stay in Belfast, or refuse, knowing that that would probably lead to an early recall to Boston. The Neaves of this world and more time with Saoirse, or refuse the Neaves and… The more he recalled the hour with Neave, the less qualified or motivated he felt for that kind of interview, yet he desperately wanted to stay near Saoirse.

CHAPTER 12

Saoirse was uncharacteristically subdued that evening. She told Thomas that her father was not well and she would have to return home immediately after work. She did want to hear about his London trip but not tonight and hoped that the next evening things would be better.

He left after a single pint, sympathetic yet disappointed.

In the 12th floor bar he found Ben sitting at his usual spot and told him about his meeting with Adderley.

'The fucking authorities in the States have no idea how serious the problem with shell shock or battle fatigue, or whatever you want to call it, is among soldiers returning from Vietnam,' Ben said angrily. 'I read that they're using the term PTSD, post-traumatic stress disorder, now. But it's all the same thing. They give them heroes' welcomes and a parade and expect them to pick up their lives where they left off. But it just doesn't fucking work that way, not for hundreds of thousands of them. And the UK is just as irresponsible.'

Ben's anger resonated with Thomas.

He spent Saturday writing, and pondering a question stirred by Adderley's account. He devoted a brief paragraph to Adderley and Bloody Sunday:

Calvin is a 33-year-old former member of the British paratroop regiment that carried out the shootings. He is racked by emotion as he recalls that terrible day six and a half years ago, reliving the fear, the panic and the pain. He had been led to believe that they could expect a direct, armed assault by the IRA. In fact, no evidence of an armed IRA presence was ever found. Now he 'hopes to God' that none of the three or four rounds he fired hit anyone. Damaged for life, he is yet another victim of the conflict – one we never read about.

Did believing result in seeing? The paratroopers 'saw' weapons and indeed 'heard' shots being fired at them. No evidence of that was ever found. What they saw and heard is what they had been led to believe they would see and hear.

If Catholics are taught to believe that Protestants are violent, power-hungry and bent on the oppression of Catholics, surely that is what they will see around them. If Protestants are taught to believe that Catholics are mindless papists, lazy and murderous, that is what they will see around them. It was not a stupendous insight; it was just another way of looking at the immense power of propaganda.

From Rupert and Ben he picked up some ideas about political leaders he might interview: leading members of local political parties of course, but the big prize would be Britain's Northern Ireland secretary Roy Mason, a controversial figure because of his support for the dubious tactics used by the RUC to interrogate prisoners. However, Thomas' heart remained firmly on the side of talking with ordinary people.

Foyle's was packed when he arrived. Five musicians sat in the corner taking a break. Saoirse was behind the bar, and both she and Colin were pumping pints as quickly as they could. She signalled that she had seen him and, when he had taken up a position at the far corner of the bar, standing because the stools were all occupied, she placed a pint of his usual in front of him without asking and threw in a hurried 'Hiya!'

The musicians played several tunes before Saoirse was asked to join them. She sang 'Whiskey in the Jar', a highly appropriate song for a pub. He thought she must be in a better mood because she followed up with 'Galway Bay'.

When she finally came by she said, 'Sorry I haven't had any time to talk so far. But Colin will let me go in about half an hour. Would you like another pint or a whiskey while you wait?'

'No thanks, Shauna, I'll hold. I'm fine.'

It was a quarter to twelve when they left the pub.

'Will you stay?' he asked when they had reached the room.

'I was planning to.'

She flung her arms around him, drew him close and kissed him hungrily.

They relaxed into the two armchairs on either side of a small round table.

'How is your father?'

'He's a bit better. And I did ask my parents if it would be okay to introduce them to a charming journalist from Boston. I told them what you were doing here. My da just said, "I'll leave that to your mother." I reassured them that there would be no difficult questions and that the journalist was a lovely man simply out to meet people in Belfast. Finally she agreed. I'm glad, because maybe, just maybe, my father and Kevin will, if you give them time, say more to you than they do to mam or me. I think it's worth a try.'

'I'd be delighted to meet them. When might be best?'

'Well, if you're free, how about tomorrow afternoon? Could you come around half four?'

'Okay, half four it is.'

She wrote the address on a little notepad beside the telephone.

'Now I've got something for you to think about,' Thomas started. ' How do you think Kevin, and your parents, would feel about Kevin spending at least six months with an American family in Boston, attending an American high school for a term?'

Saoirse looked at him in wide-eyed surprise and disbelief.

'You know there is no way we could…'

'All costs would be covered.'

'How?'

He told her about the suggestion he had made in an article, and how a group called the Irish-American Association had picked it up. There were funds to support families in Northern Ireland and some members had started to think about how children or young people could be matched with appropriate American families for a break, away from the Troubles. Someone at the *Tribune* was liaising with them and was confident about the integrity of the people involved.

'I don't know what to say, Thomas. I can see how it might be an incredible opportunity for Kevin, but I have no idea how my parents, or Kevin, will respond.'

'Just think about it. Don't say anything to them yet; let's talk about it again after my visit tomorrow.'

'Okay. Have you got a glass of wine for me before we go on?'

She tossed her hair back and ran her fingers through it.

'How are the kids doing? What about Ross?'

'He's doing pretty well.'

'I bought him something at Heathrow. He told me his teddy bear had been lost in the fire, remember? I bought him a new one. I hope he'll like it. Will you give it to him?'

'No, certainly not. You'll have to give it to him yourself. And you're very sweet. Come here.'

Saoirse pulled him out of his chair, folded her arms around him, and nibbled playfully at the tip of his nose.

'Now, I want you to tell me about London. But let's do that in bed.'

As they stripped, pulled back the duvet and propped up extra pillows against the headboard, Thomas told her about the television interview and how, after his initial nervousness, he had rather enjoyed it.

'Maybe I'll switch from newspaper work to television myself some day,' he joked.

'You never know, Thomas. I think you might be great.'

He told her about the strange experience of sitting in on an interview with Airey Neave.

'Well, if you're going to interview politicians then you'd better learn to like it, my dear.'

'You know what was really great? Henry gave me a folder full of readers' responses to what I had written. It was mostly super-positive. I told you I was beginning to doubt the use of my writing, but apparently it's working well to raise awareness and even some action, like more pressure on Noraid to disclose exactly what they've been doing with the funds they collect.'

'Good. I'm delighted for you.'

He leaned over and plucked at her earlobes with his teeth; she giggled. He moved down to suck and play-bite her nipples. Conversation stopped but sounds did not, as they lost – and found – themselves in each other.

At 4:30 a taxi dropped Thomas off at Saoirse's parents' address. It was a small, two-storey redbrick house in the middle of a long terrace. Paint peeled from the window frames and the front door, which opened directly onto the pavement. Potholes scarred the road in front.

He rang the doorbell, but as it did not work, he knocked. He heard Saoirse's muffled voice call out, 'I'll get it.'

She opened the door, smiled, and very politely said, 'Hello, Thomas. Please come in.'

He replied, also in a neutral voice, 'Hello Saoirse. How are you?'

In front of him was a narrow flight of stairs; straight ahead he could see a small kitchen. To the right was the living room, into which Saoirse guided him.

'Mam, Da, I'd like to introduce Thomas Cassidy.'

'You're very welcome, Mr Cassidy,' said Mrs Kelly as she shook his hand while managing a warm smile.

'How do you do, Mrs Kelly.'

He turned to Saoirse's father, who looked to be a tired 70-year-old, though he was probably considerably younger.

'How do you do, Mr Kelly.'

'You can call me Bill, Thomas. Please, sit down.'

'Thank you, Bill.' Thomas sat down were he had indicated, in an armchair covered by a dark blue blanket.

Mrs Kelly suggested a cup of tea.

'Let me fix that now, Mam. You sit down.'

The living room was small, tidy and not uncomfortable, though it lacked any signs of luxury. There were a few faded, framed prints and a crucifix just over a low cupboard. Beside the crucifix was a photograph of a young man Thomas guessed to be Niall. A votive light burned in front of the photograph. In the corner opposite Bill was a small black and white television set.

Behind the living room was a small dining area with a window facing out onto a tiny patio, and beyond that a six-foot wooden fence with peeling paint and a gate that led, presumably, to an alley running behind the houses.

'Well, Thomas, Saoirse tells us that you are a reporter from Boston, that you have been here for more than a month now. What do you think of our tortured country?' Mrs Kelly asked.

The conversation didn't provide any new insights for Thomas, but he was happy to become acquainted with Saoirse's parents, whose comments revealed a great deal of weariness and resignation.

Saoirse came in balancing a tray with cups and a milk jug. Her mother fetched the teapot, calling upstairs, 'Kevin, will you have a nice cup of tea, son?' There was a muffled response.

'What makes me sad,' remarked Mrs Kelly, 'is that the community doesn't belong to the people anymore. Nobody can go wherever they please. Only Saoirse seems to go where she likes. She's a strong-willed girl, but… but it can be so dangerous.'

Thomas smiled.

'Now, I think the tea should be done. Will you pour, Saoirse, dear? Thomas, how do you take your tea, with milk?'

'No, just sugar please.'

'Oh dear, I'm so sorry. I'm afraid we don't have any.'

'No problem at all, Mrs Kelly.'

Saoirse poured four cups and passed them around.

It was clear from the way they looked at her that both parents adored their daughter.

'Saoirse, will you see if you can get Kevin to come downstairs?' Mrs Kelly asked.

'Sure.'

Thomas's eyes strayed back to the photograph on the wall.

Bill was the first to speak.

'That is our son, Niall. They shot him. They took away our oldest son, they took away our home, and they took away my job. There's not much left then, is there?' Bill spoke in a resigned, flat voice.

'Saoirse told me about Niall,' Thomas replied. 'I am very sorry for your loss. I can't even begin to imagine how painful that must have been.' He suddenly realised he had never said 'sorry' so many times in his life before arriving in Northern Ireland.

Mrs Kelly's eyes moistened as she looked at the photograph.

'He was such a fine lad. We miss him every day and will never forget him.'

Thomas looked at her gently as she went on, struggling to keep her emotions under control.

'What could the men who did this possibly hope to gain? Our priest reminds us that it is Christian to forgive. I try… but it is so difficult when it's impossible to understand. Why did they do this?' She dabbed at her eyes with a small handkerchief.

Bill gave his wife a warm look but his slouching posture was that of a defeated man.

Saoirse came back into the room with Kevin, who looked like an average awkward teenager. Sensing what was going on she quickly took her place beside her mother and held her hand, while Kevin stood by uncomfortably.

Saoirse put an arm around her mother and gave Thomas a desperate look. Bill stared at the floor in front of him.

When her mother had regained her composure Saoirse introduced Kevin and Thomas to each other. Kevin fetched a chair from the dining area.

A minute or so of grief-filled silence filled the room, with Saoirse still holding an arm around her mother.

Faced with such intense emotion, the whole family seeking to cope with their own tragedy yet again, Thomas searched for something positive to say.

'There is something which has impressed me deeply over the last weeks. That's the spirit of the people in Northern Ireland. Many have suffered a terrible loss, as you have. There have been so many people senselessly killed and injured. But I've met many who have shown immense courage in picking up their lives again, and in helping others to do so. It's that spirit in which I see hope for the people of Northern Ireland, and it has affected me deeply.'

He had their attention; everyone was looking at him.

'I honestly get the feeling that there are a lot of people who are trying to help others, to reach out, to bring about healing and reconciliation. It's one of the things I've been writing about: telling the readers in the States that Northern Ireland is not only about shootings and bombings.'

'I'm so glad you have seen a positive side, Thomas,' Mrs Kelly replied, while Bill shook his head ever so slightly, either not understanding or not agreeing.

Thomas asked Kevin about his interests, which were few. Those he did profess he spoke about in a very subdued way. He seemed very shy, giving never more than a glance in Thomas' direction. He certainly looked normal and healthy but was very closed off.

Then Kevin asked a question.

'What's Boston like?'

Thomas saw an opening, and described the city as best he could in glowing terms.

'Does that sound like a place you'd like to visit, Kevin?'

'Yeah sure. But not much hope of that, is there?'

Saoirse and Thomas exchanged glances.

'You never know, Kevin.'

By six o'clock Thomas felt he had taken up enough of the family's time. He thanked Saoirse's parents for their hospitality and asked Saoirse to call a taxi.

'I can do that, but we don't have a phone. I'll pop by my place. Be back in a moment.'

Mrs. Kelly gathered the teacups and took them to the kitchen; Bill wandered into the dining area.

Thomas tried to get Kevin to open up some more.

'What do you hope for, Kevin, for yourself?'

'I'd like to know that I can mean something, that I matter,' was Kevin's surprising answer. 'But with all this' – he gestured out towards the street – 'going on, all roads are blocked. I can't see a future for myself. Nothing to do, nowhere to go.'

'You'll find your way, Kevin. I'm sure of it.'

Saoirse came back in. 'The taxi will be here shortly.'

Thomas thanked everyone and shook hands. Saoirse retrieved his coat from a peg in the hall and grabbed her own. The two of them waited just outside the door, standing in a light but cold drizzle.

'Kevin seems like a good kid, but very withdrawn, as you said. Do you know what he said to me?'

He told her Kevin's comments about lacking purpose and meaning.

'Well that's amazing! He's never said anything like that to us. I take that as a good sign.'

'I do hope so. And maybe Boston?'

'Let's see. I'll find a moment to suggest it. Thanks very much for coming, Thomas.'

'I was really happy to. When may I visit the centre again? Teddy bear, remember?'

'How about Wednesday? Oh, before I forget…' Saoirse drew a white envelope out of her coat. 'If you get a chance and think this might get to Dermot, I'd be very grateful.'

Thomas accepted the note just as the taxi drove up. She gave him a sad look and a gentle stroke on the cheek. He mouthed the words 'I love you', she blew him a silent kiss, and the taxi drove off.

Saoirse's father and Kevin had spoken very little; the walls within which they had enclosed themselves were almost tangible. Without speaking a word about it all three had communicated how immensely dependent on Saoirse they were. Thomas understood much more clearly why she was such an important person in that depressed family and wondered how she kept it up. He wished there was more that he could do to support her, besides giving her his love as best he could. There would be no way he could do that from Boston, of course.

Over dinner with Ben and Rupert Thomas put a 'hypothetical' case to them: 'A young Catholic woman is harassed by a couple of Catholic guys because she refuses to continue to work for them as a sort of gun-runner. She confides in her older brother, who is furious. He is away from home a lot; his family have no idea what he gets up to. The two thugs disappear. I see a possible connection – or am I crazy?'

Ben and Rupert looked at each other.

'I can see a possible connection too. Where is the older brother now?' Rupert asked.

'He's dead. Shot, a couple of years later.'

'Does she know the names of the guys who harassed her?'

'No.'

'That gives you very little to go on indeed,' Ben offered. 'But it sounds as if this case is of interest to you.'

'Yes, it is.'

'What is… was, the brother's name?' Ben asked.

'Niall Kelly. Why?'

Ben noted the name in a small notepad and simply said, 'Leave it with me.'

CHAPTER 13

The next day Thomas received a call from the front desk just before noon. 'There's a young man here to see you, Mr Cassidy. He says his name is Owen.'

Thomas hurried downstairs. Owen looked slightly better dressed than on the previous occasion, and nervous.

'I have another record your nephew might like, Mr Cassidy.'

'Why thank you Owen. It's almost lunchtime again. Care to go out for a burger?'

'Yeah, sure. Thanks.'

Thomas led him down to the little restaurant where he and Saoirse had had their disrupted breakfast. Though limping, Owen leaned only lightly on his crutch from time to time. Once they had settled at a table, Thomas said, 'The record wasn't the real reason for your visit, was it?'

Owen smiled sheepishly. 'No, it wasn't.'

Thomas slid the record back across the table.

They ordered and when the waitress had left them Owen spoke hesitatingly.

'Mr Cassidy, last time you asked about drugs. Well…' Owen lowered his voice to almost a whisper. 'Dan does sell marihuana to people he knows, and he sends me out sometimes to collect it from a supplier.'

Thomas tried to reassure him by saying that he had used the stuff occasionally during university, that it was no big deal.

'Maybe not,' Owen replied, 'but I'm scared.'

Gently, he asked, 'of what or who, Owen?'

Slowly, as if trying to decide carefully about each word, Owen went on.

'There are big men around town who are into drugs, as a way of making money for the UVF or the IRA or whatever – they say. And, well... some of the shootings over the last months have been drugs-related, nothing to do with the Troubles. I'm scared, just scared.'

The waitress appeared with their orders and Owen started into his burger hungrily.

After a few bites Thomas said, 'I remember you told me that you would like to get out of this fucking country, to use your own words.'

Owen looked surprised by this turn in the conversation.

'Yeah, but how?'

'Owen, what would you say to an opportunity to spend a few months with an American family in the Boston area and maybe even finish your schooling there?'

Owen looked up in surprise. 'Are you having me on, Mr Cassidy?'

'No, I'm not. Let me explain.'

Thomas outlined what he saw as a real possibility. He also confessed to having met Owen's mother before looking him up at the shop. Of course he would have to speak to Owen's mother again, and would be happy to visit them in their home as soon as possible. Owen would have to acquire a passport; a visa for the United States could then probably be arranged quickly through the Irish-American Association.

'Fucking hell, I can't believe it!' Owen exclaimed, his face lighting up.

'Owen, I can't promise anything yet, but I'll send a fax to Boston this afternoon. I should have a reply by Thursday at the latest. Can you drop by the hotel again then, in the afternoon?'

'Yeah, sure.'

'Tell your mother about our conversation. Maybe we can all meet during the weekend. And, regarding the thing you mentioned: can you tell Dan that your knee is hurting badly again and either take some days off or at least get relieved of your job of walking great distances carrying marihuana?'

'Yeah, maybe.'

Owen looked almost euphoric. Thomas hoped that he'd be able to get things moving quickly and wouldn't end up disappointing the boy.

When they left Owen seemed to have a spring in his step. He caught himself, smiled, and started to limp along painfully, supporting his left leg heavily with the crutch.

It was late afternoon the next day when Thomas set foot inside the Royal Victoria hospital for the second time. He met clinical psychologist Herbert Clancy, a man in his forties, balding, wearing rimless glasses and a serious expression, but with a gentle voice and friendly demeanour, who expressed himself deliberately and thoughtfully.

Clancy talked about the people he saw regularly who were in a state of shock, understandable after a traumatic event.

'There is, however, a category which increasingly concerns us. Some individuals do not to have the ability to leave their traumas behind within a reasonable time. What we're dealing with here is clinically very similar to what the Americans are encountering in returning Vietnam War veterans.'

Clancy described common symptoms, most of which Thomas recognised from his encounters over the last month, as well as from his own experience. Chief among those was cutting oneself off from the outside world and consequently suffering a profound sense of loneliness. Clancy said there were no effective pharmaceutical cures; helping victims to rebuild trust and gradually getting them to talk about their experiences was the only proven treatment. But there were far too few qualified individuals in Northern Ireland to meet the demand. Animals, most often dogs, were also proving useful in terms of being able to offer unconditional love, allowing victims to relax and thereby relieving their acute anxiety symptoms.

'Why is there such a shortage of people qualified to help those who are so obviously in need of help?' Thomas asked.

Clancy sighed. 'There is simply a lack of awareness of, or interest in, the disorder, and the health authorities are unable to persuade the politicians to give it a higher priority when it comes to releasing finances.'

'How do you personally feel about that, Dr Clancy?'

'It makes me angry.'

Thomas had been heartened to learn that what Saoirse was doing at the centre was spot-on. He also felt increasingly certain that Kevin was suffering from a clinical disorder. Thomas checked out whether a period of time in peaceful and caring surroundings could help to pull victims out of their distress. Clancy said it could certainly help in some cases, but that the people in those peaceful surroundings should be aware of the problem and be able to encourage victims to tell their stories. Otherwise it would just offer an opportunity for victims to paper over their traumatic memories temporarily. Thomas presented the cases of Mary and Reginald. Clancy concluded that Reginald had a 'classic case' but would probably be all right, if given enough support. Mary would require professional diagnosis and possibly long-term therapy. Instances such as hers were rare but not unheard of.

The politicians, Thomas thought as he left. The politicians, remarkable only for not doing anything for the people who elect them. So what would be the point in interviewing them? Thomas also wondered why local journalists weren't doing more to raise popular awareness of the crisis and wake up the politicians. But he didn't feel he could criticise; conditions were clearly no better in the United States.

Back at the child care centre Thomas recognised most of the children and was happy to see that Ross was among them. There were also some new faces, so Saoirse introduced him much as she had the first time. This time most children, in pairs, were doing puzzles, while a couple of boys played with a meccano set. A little girl was keeping Socrates company.

Saoirse and Carol moved about, talking with and encouraging the children. Many of the children went on with what they were doing, but Ross broke away from his puzzle and approached Thomas.

'Hi Mr Cassidy.'

'Hiya, Ross. How are you?'

'Okay, I guess,' he answered, unconvincingly.

'Ross, I'm glad you're here, because I brought you something.'

The little boy's eyes lit up as Thomas fetched a plastic bag from where he had left it with his coat. He pulled out the teddy bear. Ross eyes opened wide, he smiled and cautiously reached out for it.

'Go on, take it, Ross. It's yours.'

Ross took hold of it, eyeing it uncertainly.

'What's his name?'

'Now, what do you think would be the right name for this teddy bear?'

Ross examined it more closely, thinking.

'I think his name is Twinkle!' he said finally.

'Yes. How did you know?'

'I could tell, because of his eyes. They twinkle, see?'

Thomas looked at the little glass eyes and saw that they did indeed twinkle.

'Well, there you are then. If you take good care of him, then Twinkle will take good care of you.'

'Thank you, Mr Cassidy.'

Ross bounced off to show the gift to a couple of his little friends. Most admired it, but one little boy tried to grab it away from him. A tug-of-war followed. Ross shouted, 'No, it's mine!' and started to cry.

Saoirse was on top of the situation immediately. She spoke gently but firmly. 'Jonathan, we don't do that here. Mr Cassidy gave the teddy bear to Ross for a special reason. And I'm sure that Ross will let you hold it sometime. Right, Ross?'

Ross managed a 'Yes' between his sobs, but held Twinkle tightly to his chest as he moved away.

'Now, Jonathan, how are you and Ronald doing with this puzzle? Oh, that's very good! You'll have it done in no time. Let's see how quickly you can have it finished, okay?'

'Okay, Miss Kelly.'

Thomas wondered whether he had done the right thing by giving something to one child.

'It'll be fine,' Saoirse reassured him. 'Ross is delighted; just look at him.'

Ross was sitting off to the side making his acquaintance with Twinkle, talking to it and stroking it.

'Jonathan will be fine too. He has a problem with his temper sometimes – like someone else I know,' she said, with a wry smile. 'We don't punish him for that of course. We just tell him that it is not the right way to behave here.'

Saoirse went off to a little girl who was suddenly crying.

Thomas noticed that Kyle, the boy who had sought consolation with Socrates ten days earlier, was over with the dog again. He went to join him.

'Hi Kyle. Will you introduce me to this lovely dog?'

Kyle looked up shyly.

'This is Socrates.'

'Hello, Socrates,' said Thomas, as he reached out to pat his head and give him a scratch behind the ears. Socrates wagged his tail enthusiastically, got off the floor and came to sniff at Thomas.

'Oh, aren't you a lovely dog!'

Thomas quickly returned his attention to Kyle. 'How are you, Kyle?'

'Okay.'

'Have there been soldiers back on your street, Kyle?' Thomas asked, remembering what he had been told the last time.

'No. But I still dream about the soldiers sometimes,' Kyle disclosed, with downcast eyes.

'And what are they doing, in your dream?'

'It's dark and I see them shouting at my da and waving guns at him, and he is shouting back, and he doesn't have a gun.'

'Kyle,' said Thomas after a moment, 'I met a soldier last week. He was dressed just ordinary, sort of like me, and he didn't have a gun.

He was a very nice man. I think most soldiers are very nice men, but when they wear uniforms and carry guns… well, they look frightening and are sometimes even frightened themselves.'

Kyle looked at him with big, disbelieving eyes.

'Just remember, Kyle, most soldiers are very nice people. If you believe me and remember what I just said, then you don't have to be so afraid of them.'

'Okay,' Kyle said, and went back to Socrates.

'That was perfect,' Saoirse said softly as she came by.

Thomas chatted with a couple of other children, who seemed to be comfortable with his presence.

Saoirse surprised him by asking if he would close the day by reading a fairy tale to the children.

'We do that often, as a close. The children love it. And I think it would be great if a man were to take the role.'

Thomas agreed and she gave him a book of Irish fairy tales, suggesting he read 'The Sprightly Tailor'. He scanned the text.

'All right children. To end the day, Mr Cassidy is going to read you a story. Mr Cassidy?'

Twenty-four eyes followed Thomas expectantly as he moved to a chair at the front of the room. Putting as much intonation into his voice as he could, he started to read.

'A sprightly tailor was employed by the great Macdonald, in his castle at Saddell, in order to make the laird a pair of trews, used in olden time.'

'What does "sprightly" mean?' a young girl interrupted.

'Good question. It means lively and full of energy.'

'Okay.'

Thomas carried on.

'… And Macdonald had said to the tailor, that if he would make the trews by night in the church, he would get a handsome reward.

For it was thought that the old ruined church was haunted, and that fearsome things were to be seen there at night.'

Thomas noticed that the children were listening with rapt attention, and continued. It took him about five minutes to finish the story.

'...So he held his trews tight, and let no darkness grow under his feet, until he had reached Saddell Castle. He had no sooner got inside the gate, and shut it, than the monster came up to it – and, enraged at losing his prize, struck the wall above the gate, and left there the mark of his five great fingers. Ye may see them plainly to this day, if ye'll only peer close enough. But the sprightly tailor gained his reward – for Macdonald paid him handsomely for the trews, and never discovered that a few of the stitches were somewhat long.'

The children sat in spellbound silence.
'Mr Cassidy,' a voice chirped, 'will you read us another story, please?' Saoirse came to the rescue.
'Not today, children. Only one story, remember? Thank you Mr Cassidy. Now, children, what do you think this story means?'
There was silence for a few moments. Kyle hesitatingly raised a hand.
'Yes, Kyle, what do you think?'
'I think it means that even if you're frightened, you should keep working.'
'Very good, Kyle. Anybody else?'
No one answered, but a few heads nodded their agreement with Kyle.
Time was up and parents, mostly mothers, arrived to take their children home. Thomas watched while Ross proudly showed Twinkle to his mother. When everyone had left, Saoirse told Carol it was okay for her to go too; she would stay on to finish tidying up. That left Saoirse and Thomas alone.

'That was really great, Thomas.' She winked at him when she added, 'How about coming here every day? I think the children love you. And, so do I.'

She kissed him gently. He felt himself melting into her.

'I really enjoyed myself,' he replied.

They looked into each other's eyes in silence. He once again wondered at the miracle that had allowed him to meet this amazing woman.

While they put the toys, tables and chairs away, Thomas told Saoirse about his visit to Herbert Clancy – a name she recognised – and that he thought Saoirse was doing everything that could be done perfectly.

'That's good to know.'

'Who pays for this?' Thomas asked. 'I mean, you and Carol must get paid, and then there are the paints, the paper, the puzzles, to say nothing of lighting and heating this space.'

'We get a subsidy from Belfast City Council. A couple of shops in town donate supplies, and we get donations of old toys and puzzles from families whose children have outgrown them. We get by. Now, I'd better be getting home. I called a taxi; he'll be along in a minute. I have to eat something and then get down to the pub. Are you coming in this evening?'

'No, I can't. I have a late dinner with a couple of colleagues.'

'Tomorrow?'

'I'll be there.'

Thomas spent what seemed like hours on the telephone the next morning. He managed to get the Press Secretary to the Taoiseach, the Irish Prime Minister, on the line. He requested an interview with Jack Lynch but was told that the Taoiseach was unavailable; the Press Secretary suggested trying Charles Haughey, Minister for Health and Social Welfare. Following up on this, Thomas managed to arrange a meeting for the next Wednesday morning. He called the London office and asked Henry's assistant to book him a convenient hotel in Dublin.

Thomas also called the London publisher of Maire O'Shaunnessey's book, *A Different Place*. He wanted to meet her. After many calls back and forth he eventually got the woman herself on the line. She agreed to meet him at a bookshop in Cork, late on Friday morning.

A faxed reply came in from Boston, delighting Thomas with a positive response. They would require a profile of the boy in order to find a match among the families that had indicated a willingness to host a teenage guest. Owen appeared at the appointed time. Thomas promised to visit him and his mother the next evening. Owen was delighted again, as was Thomas. He felt he was finally doing something useful instead of just writing about the problems.

As he walked through the lobby on his way to the dining room a well-dressed man in a dark suit stopped him.

'Mr Cassidy?'

'Yes?'

The man flashed a badge at him and said his name was Brannon, of the Irish Security Services. Thomas had never heard of it.

'Mr Cassidy, we are aware that you have been in contact with a lot of people. It would help us if you could tell me if you recognise any of these people.' He pulled some photographs out of his jacket.

'Mr Brannon, I'm a journalist. I can't divulge my sources without their permission.'

'Let me remind you, Mr Cassidy, that you are in a war zone. Failure to help security forces could result in trouble for you. Now please look at these photographs and just tell me if you recognise any faces.'

Later Thomas thought that he should have walked away but he felt intimidated, so he looked at the black and white photographs. Most meant nothing to him. There was one that he did recognise for sure: Dermot, Dermot McAllister, according to the name on the photograph.

'No, I don't, Mr Brannon.'

'Are you quite sure?'

'Yes, I'm sure. Now if you will excuse me, goodbye, Mr Brannon.'

'Good evening, Mr Cassidy.'

Brannon left the hotel, leaving Thomas puzzled and angry.

In the dining room he spotted Ben, sitting in his usual spot where he could watch everything that was going on. Thomas joined him, ordered a whiskey and started to calm down.

'Ever heard of the Irish Security Services?' Thomas asked.

'Nope, I haven't. What's it supposed to be?'

'I have no idea. Someone claiming to work for them just stopped me in the lobby. The man said he was looking for the fellow I met last week, the one who gave me an envelope.'

Ben scratched his chin, then leaned in towards Thomas. 'Very strange. First thing I would do is find out what this Irish Security Services is about.'

'Where would I do that?'

'Maybe the RUC would know, but for sure Special Branch. I have contact information in my room. I'll get it for you later.'

Relaxed by the conversation during the rest of dinner, Thomas left the hotel to walk to Foyle's. It was quiet, so Saoirse had time for a chat right away.

'Hey, how are you? You look a bit preoccupied.'

'Just before dinner I met a strange character.'

'Oh?'

'Some guy who said he was from the Irish Security Services asked me if I recognised a bunch of people of whom he had photographs. Have you ever heard of the Irish Security Services?'

'No, I haven't.'

She held a pint glass under a tap for him. 'Ross was as happy as can be with the teddy bear, how you related to Kyle was first class, and you read the story so well.'

A couple of other patrons came up to the bar so Saoirse moved off to help them. Thomas remembered a favourite childhood story, *Alice in Wonderland*, and wondered whether he had landed in a sort of wonderland himself, with both beautiful and scary aspects.

When she came back, he said, 'I'm going to Dublin and Cork next week.'

'That sounds very exciting. Good for you.'

'And tomorrow I have an interview with the Lord Mayor.'

'Well, you really are starting to move in high circles.'

'I'd really like to see you this weekend. Will that work for you?' he asked.

'I think I can make that work, yes.'

'Saturday after work, or would you prefer Sunday?'

'Why don't we do a bit of both?'

'Great. I'll be here Saturday evening.'

'Okay, love,' she whispered in his ear.

Thomas woke up still wondering about Mr Brannon and the so-called Irish Security Services. Was it real, and if not, who was he? It was also Friday the 13th, Thomas noted, though he was not superstitious.

After breakfast he took a taxi to the address Ben had given him for Special Branch. Security was high and it took some time before he was allowed in. Once he got inside, a man who identified himself as Special Agent Sweeney quickly came out to speak to him.

The answer was also quick: 'There is no such agency.'

Thomas explained what the mysterious 'Brannon' had requested.

Sweeney shook his head. 'Be careful. I think you spoke with someone from one of the paramilitary groups, trying to use you. The security agencies don't ask for help from journalists, certainly not foreign ones.'

'Is there anything I should do?' Thomas asked.

'Yes, I'd like you to look through some photographs to see if you can identify this "Mr Brannon".'

Sweeney led Thomas to a small office and pulled a thick file folder from a cabinet. He laid photographs in front of Thomas one by one.

After about twenty minutes of looking at sullen faces, Thomas felt quite certain that he had identified the imposter.

Sweeney thanked him and gave him a card. 'If you see this man again please call this number.'

'Should McAllister be warned, do you think?'

Sweeney replied, 'We don't know who McAllister is, but I suggest that you not let yourself get involved.'

Thomas took the taxi back to the hotel, still feeling worried, and wondering what he should do, if anything. Should he try to warn Dermot, in spite of Sweeney's words? In any case, he would leave Saoirse out of it.

In the afternoon Thomas walked the short distance to the Belfast City Hall. Security was tight there as well, with armed police outside the building entrance and in the entrance foyer. He was thoroughly checked twice before being shown to a waiting area outside the Lord Mayor's office. Fifteen minutes later a secretary appeared and said, 'The Lord Mayor will see you now, Mr Cassidy.'

He liked David Cook as a person, though he came across as totally ineffectual. 'Decades' before change might come to remove the fear? It seemed a declaration of impotence. Little wonder that so many people showed little regard for the politicians. Is this the way I want to spend my time, talking with people like him? Thomas asked himself.

Thomas dined early with Ben, and over dessert put to him his dilemma: to act or not to act on to what he feared was a veiled threat to Dermot.

'What does your gut say you should do?'

He thought for a moment.

'I think I should try to find Dermot and warn him. I think someone or some group is after him, for whatever reason. It may not help, but I think I should try. And anyway, I have a note for him from his former girlfriend.'

'Do you know where to find him?'

'He apparently used to frequent a pub called the Grange on Falls Road. It's the only place I can think of looking.'
'Hmm,' Ben mused. 'That's a dicey area up there.'
'Yes, I know.'
Ben was silent for a few moments.
'Thomas, if you like we can go up there together,' he offered. Seeing that Thomas was about to protest, he added, 'It's okay, I'd like to. If we go in sounding like two Americans out for a pint we'll be fine.'
'Okay, thanks Ben. At least we would have each other to talk to, in a natural manner and be less likely to raise immediate suspicion. But I have another call to make first. In fact I'd better hurry. See you around ten, okay?'

Thomas met with Owen and his mother, taking along all the information he had about the Irish-American Association. He was welcomed into the living room, which Margaret obviously tried to share fairly with her son, as there were posters of musicians and some prints in psychedelic colours on one wall. Margaret was dressed more brightly than most other women he had seen in Belfast, probably for the occasion, he thought.
'I still can't believe that our brief conversation almost six weeks ago has led to this. I can't tell you how thrilled I am, we both are,' Margaret said.
Thomas asked the necessary questions to complete a profile of Owen, as the Association had requested.
Mother and son were beaming from ear to ear when he left, promising to stay in close touch. They promised to apply for a passport the next week.

Thomas met Ben in the lobby at ten. The taxi driver knew where the Grange was and took them straight to it.
No light shone through the windows and there was a cage-like structure in front of the entrance, a fairly common security precaution.

A muscular, sullen man was checking out patrons before allowing them to enter. Ben took charge. 'Hi! Got room for two Americans looking for a pint?' he asked with an exaggerated American accent.

'Show me your ID,' the man demanded.

Taking care not to show their press cards, they handed over identity cards, which the man inspected carefully, though Thomas wondered whether he even knew what he was looking at.

'Okay, go on in.'

Inside it was almost as dark as outside. The walls were papered or painted a dark, dirty brown. Maybe thirty men were hanging on the long bar that stretched down the right side. Most of them looked up; strangers were probably not a nightly event. The atmosphere did not feel welcoming. Ben and Thomas moved down to the centre of the bar, where Ben wedged in and ordered two Guinnesses. Thomas scanned the patrons, trying to adjust to the unusual darkness of the place. After a few minutes Ben handed Thomas a pint, they clinked glasses and started an inane conversation about American baseball, while making sure their American accents could be clearly heard.

From time to time Thomas looked around to see if he could identify the face on the photograph. After a while he whispered to Ben, 'Wild goose chase, I think. He's not here.'

'Oh well, enjoy your pint then. You tried.'

They continued their discussion, now exchanging views on President Jimmy Carter.

Ten minutes later the door opened and two young men came in. One was Dermot. They stood at the top of the bar and placed their orders while engaging in a conversation of their own.

'Keep an eye on me, will you?' Thomas said to Ben before moving up the bar.

'Dermot?'

Dermot looked startled. 'Hello, Cassidy. What are you doing here?'

'First of all, Saoirse asked me to give you this.' He handed over the envelope.

'Thanks.'

'And there is a second reason. Yesterday a man stopped me in the lobby of my hotel. He identified himself as belonging to an outfit called the Irish Security Services which, it turns out, doesn't exist.'

Dermot and his companion made eye contact, and his companion shrugged his shoulders.

'Dermot, the point is, he was looking for you. He showed me some photographs and asked if I could identify any of them. One was of you. I denied any knowledge of course. But the point is, someone is looking for you. I wanted you to know.'

Dermot took another gulp of beer.

'Does Saoirse know about this?'

'No, she doesn't. She still cares about you, and I don't want to worry her.'

Dermot exchanged glances with his companion. Finally he said, 'Okay, well, thanks.'

'You're welcome, Dermot. I hope this helps. Take care of yourself.'

Though Dermot had been understandably cautious during their brief exchange, Thomas thought he could detect some warmth in his eyes, something that had made him attractive to Saoirse.

Ben asked, 'How did that go?'

'Fine, I think. Let's see if we can get a cab to pick us up.'

The contrast between the Grange and the upstairs bar with the Poppets could not have been greater. For once, Thomas felt more at home there than in a pub with native Northern Irish.

'Ben, I haven't seen Rupert for a while. Has he gone back to Manchester?'

Ben looked surprised. 'You haven't heard? Rupert got beaten up pretty badly a week or so ago, down in Armagh. I don't know much, but he seems to have met a bunch of people who didn't like his Oxford accent. So he's back home in Manchester. But knowing Rupert, he'll be back soon.'

That night Thomas had a dream in which Father Donald and 'Mr Brannon' seemed to merge into one and were mocking him. He woke up in the middle of the night in a sweat.

CHAPTER 14

Belfast Central railway station had seen a bombing just five days earlier. Though Thomas could see no evidence of damage as he walked through, he was glad to be rolling through the countryside half an hour later.

His thoughts drifted back to the weekend. He and Saoirse had spent another wonderful night together. One of the most wonderful aspects was waking up in the morning to find her warm body beside him.

After Saoirse left, needing to get back to her family, Thomas returned to his room to write, read up on Charles Haughey, and skim through parts of O'Shaunnessey's book again. Speaking to Haughey felt distinctly like a chore. What he had read did not make the man sound sympathetic. However, he was seen as a potential future leader of the dominant Fianna Fáil party.

The sun broke through the clouds occasionally as the train moved through the attractive green countryside on both sides of the border before arriving at Dublin's Connolly Station. Thomas checked into Buswells Hotel, a stone's throw from the Irish Parliament Building. After unpacking he went for a walk through the beautiful city park called St Stephen's Green. Dublin's busy shopping street, Grafton Street, felt more relaxed than the streets in Belfast, but he knew that IRA bombs had killed many people in Dublin in 1972 and 1974. He browsed around the Brown Thomas department store and in the jewellery department saw a little silver heart pendant on a chain. On impulse he bought it for Saoirse.

He breakfasted early, wanting to make sure he was well prepared for the interview. Between bites of toast and sips of coffee he scanned the *Irish Times*. His eyes fell on an advertisement for a play at the Abbey Theatre, a revival of Brian Friel's *The Freedom of the City*. He had heard of Friel, a friend of Seamus Heaney, and he had heard of the play. Set in Derry in 1970, it dealt with the bloody aftermath of a Civil Rights meeting; Friel had rewritten parts of the play after Bloody Sunday. He would try to get a ticket.

But business came first. He made his way to the Parliament Buildings and was guided to Haughey's spacious and comfortable office. He met a man in his early fifties, well groomed and dressed, exuding a sense of power and arrogance. Thomas did his best to suppress an instinctive dislike.

The interview turned out to be the waste of time he had feared. Haughey repeated the same political positions that Thomas had read about and deftly avoided giving direct answers to pointed questions. He was clearly a man more concerned with political power than with seeking ways to help the people of Northern Ireland.

Thomas doubted his own questioning technique with this sort of person. Should he be more confronting, he wondered. The interview made him even more doubtful that he could successfully take over Henry's role and cover the political side of the Irish question. Politicians were concerned with politics and that was what they were for. Maybe they couldn't afford the luxury of feeling involved with ordinary people.

He was overwhelmed by the play, its eloquence, occasional humour and ultimate tragedy. Although the events depicted were fictitious, he understood the impact of Bloody Sunday more than ever. He admired the emotional power of Friel's words and characterisations. Thomas didn't want to write verbal lectures to his readers, he too wanted to make his readers feel, in their hearts, what was happening in Northern Ireland, as Maire O'Shaunnessey had also done so well. Why was it, Thomas wondered, that most politicians didn't seem to 'get it', while poets, writers and playwrights could capture the agony so well? He knew for sure, now, that his mission was to write from amongst the people and their poetry, literature, drama and music. His mind was made up, and he tried not to think of the consequences.

He caught a midday train to Cork, grabbing a tasteless sandwich from the catering trolley. The trip took just over three hours, most of which he spent staring at the passing countryside. From Cork's Kent Station it was only a short walk to the Metropole Hotel. Later he spotted the bookshop where he would have his meeting the next day, but as it had started to rain he cut his walkabout short.

He was in the bookshop early and browsing the shelves when, spot on time, a woman walked in whom Thomas knew instinctively to be Maire O'Shaunnessey. In her late forties, with greying hair and dressed in a tweedy country style, she looked fit and tough, two necessary qualities if you wished to backpack or cycle solo on a shoestring through some of the most remote areas of the world.

He stepped forward to introduce himself. Her smile was immediate and welcoming as she introduced herself simply as 'Maire'.

'Now the coffee shop is next door. Shall we go?'

Maire was used to striking up conversations and he was quickly swept along. She enquired after his work and listened well. She was lively and quick with laughter. He turned to the subject of her book and how much he had enjoyed it. She responded by saying, as she had written, how much she liked nearly everyone she met in Northern Ireland.

'Do you feel you understand the Troubles now, after so many months of travelling and talking with people?'

'Not at all. I don't think that anyone truly understands. Perhaps it's a spiritual disorder that afflicts almost everybody in the North. There is an ingrained mistrust of the other side, permeating every nook and cranny of its victims' hearts and souls.'

As others had done, Maire said the only hope lay with the people themselves, dismissing the politicians as a 'bone-headed lot'. About Ivan Cooper and Sean McCann, she said, 'They are, or were, naïve idealists. They're good men and meant very well, but the march they organised was bound to end in bloodshed. They refused to acknowledge the risk and saw themselves as Irish equivalents of Martin Luther King. The disaster for most people in Northern Ireland is simply that they are not free. They are born Green or Orange and bred into captivity to the myths that sustain their own side, unable to evolve beyond the confines of the mental worlds into which they were born. But they are not evil and, as you know, I met wonderful, warm and charming people, both Orange and Green.

'Thomas, you've told me about encounters which moved you. What do your emotional responses to the stories of those people tell you about yourself?'

The question was unexpected and caused him to reflect both then and afterwards. As a first response he replied, 'I've learned that my calling, if you will, is to write about the people and to try to give voice to their hopes, their fears and their pain. Political reporting is, it turns out, not my thing at all.'

Maire smiled. 'Good for you. Maybe one thing you can try is to write a portrait of a fictional Northern Irish character, including his or her personal history. You'll be basing it on people you've met and stories you've heard, but you'll also be tapping into your own subconscious.'

They continued their enjoyable conversation until the last minute before he had to rush to the station for his return journey to Dublin and on to Belfast.

Thomas hoped it was not too early when he phoned Saoirse on Saturday morning.

'Hi, my darling, I just wanted to say I'm back and ask how you are.'

He hardly recognised the strangled voice he heard.

'Thomas, Dermot has been shot. Killed.'

'Oh my God, Saoirse!'

He was too shocked to say anything coherent.

'Where? When? By whom?'

'He was found in an alley near the Grange, on Wednesday.'

Thomas asked, 'Would you like to meet? Would you like to talk?'

'No, not yet. I'm still in shock. I need to be alone for a bit.'

'I don't think that's a good idea, Saoirse. You know how important it is to talk after painful experiences. That …'

'Don't, Thomas. Don't.'

He backed off. 'I just wish I could do something. I love you.'

'I love you too. We'll talk soon.'

'Sure, but if you want to talk, any time, just call me, okay?'

'Okay, thank you.'

'Promise?'

'I promise.'

She rang off, leaving Thomas wondering whether this had anything to do with the 'Irish Security Services' and, God forbid, whether he had inadvertently led Dermot's killers to the Grange.

Thomas was happy to find Ben, sitting alone at a table reading a newspaper, when he entered the hotel dining room for an early lunch.

'Hi Thomas. How were Dublin and Cork?'

'Yeah, they were fine. Ben, I just heard that the fellow I went to see, that we went to see, a week ago, was shot and killed on Wednesday.'

'I heard there was a shooting, but I didn't connect it with… Dermot, wasn't it?'

'Yes, Dermot McAllister. Ben, I have to find out who's behind it, if anyone knows. I need to know whether this has anything to do with that "Mr Brannon" and the so-called Irish Security Services. Did we lead the killers to Dermot when we went to that pub?'

'If we had been followed they would have nabbed him when he left after talking to you. But it was no doubt the work of one of the paramilitary groups.'

'Who? Which one? Why?'

'It's very hard to find out those things. But Edward Thompson – have you met him? – has a very good contact within the RUC. Maybe he can uncover something. I'll call his room to see if he's in.'

Thomas nodded, and Ben went off to the house phone in the lobby.

'He's in and will be down shortly.'

They waited, watching the rain pour down into big puddles on the street. 'Here he is,' Ben said after a time, pointing to a small, balding man emerging from the lift. Thomas recognised him as another journalist but they had never spoken. Ben introduced them to each other and they found a quiet place to sit.

'So,' Edward said, 'what's all this about?'

Thomas told the story, including that Dermot McAllister had been a boyfriend of a woman he knew, but over the last years had dropped out of sight and would never tell her where he had been or what he had been up to.

'So you'd like me to see whether I can get any information about this from my contact, right?' asked Edward.

'Yes, please. Anything at all. I really want to know.'

'Okay, I'll see what I can do. But it won't be until Monday.'

'Thanks very much, Edward.'

Edward warned Thomas that any information he uncovered would probably be off the record. Thomas agreed.

Thomas felt miserable. He missed Saoirse and wondered how he was going to present his decision not to accept Henry's delegation of responsibilities on covering the political angle. Should he talk to Henry, or to David? Was he throwing away his journalistic career by refusing what most would see as a golden opportunity? How long would he be able to stay in Northern Ireland? All those questions kept churning through his head, and that evening, for the first time since arriving in Belfast, he managed to get roaring drunk on the 12th floor.

The next day he woke up the worse for wear, but felt marginally better after a shower and breakfast. Back in his room, he managed to write a report based primarily on his conversation with Maire and on *The Freedom of the City*. He wrote up his interview with Charles Haughey, and what came out was polite and politic, reflecting none of his own thoughts and feelings. He also used his personal diary to try to formulate a more profound answer to Maire's challenging question: what did his experience of Northern Ireland say about him?

He met with Ben and Rupert, who, though still sporting a black eye and a bruise on his cheek, talked and acted as if nothing had happened. The conversation centred primarily on the impotence of the politicians. Maire's description of them as being 'a bone-headed lot' summarised everyone's feelings quite well, Thomas discovered. That came as a relief, and seemed to justify his decision.

Edward met Thomas and Ben for lunch on Monday. 'First, let me remind you that this off the record. The source of what I'm about to tell you cannot be revealed.'

Thomas and Ben agreed.

'Dermot McAllister was an informer. He had infiltrated the INLA, a radical offshoot of the Provisional IRA. They say he was a very courageous young man who provided several tip-offs that allowed the RUC and the British forces to foil bombing plots. The INLA is very secretive and, like all paramilitary groups, constantly on guard against informers. McAllister was exposed, though there is absolutely no telling how. He paid the price. And he was not just shot, he was tortured and mutilated before his body was dumped in the alley.'

Thomas's stomach turned when he heard that. That was a detail he would certainly spare Saoirse.

'Dumped in the alley? Does that mean he was already dead then?' he asked.

'Yes. There is no telling how long before he was found he had been picked up.'

'So it could have been right after I spoke with him.'

'It's possible, of course.'

'I'm really grateful for your information, Edward. Just one question. What can I tell McAllister's former girlfriend?'

'You can tell her that her friend died a hero, that he was an informer and was caught out. But do not mention the INLA or your source.'

'Thank you very much, Edward,' was all Thomas could manage.

An hour later and alone in his room Thomas sat down at his typewriter. His mind was a blank as he tried to think about a new article. After staring at the empty page for a few minutes, he decided to write just for himself, and he keyed out a title: 'From Outsider to Insider: Reflections of a Journalist'.

The words began to flow:

> My job is to write objective articles to inform readers about the impact of almost nine years of violence on the citizens of Northern Ireland. Others report extensively on the violent incidents themselves as well as on the futile efforts of the politicians to forge a peaceful solution.
>
> Most foreign journalists in Northern Ireland try to view the situation from the perspective of the politicians, who adopt the helicopter view: from a high vantage point they survey the strategic and political landscape and try to make wise decisions accordingly. Casualties are statistics. The man still seeking inebriated revenge four years after the death by shooting of his brother, the woman whose mind snapped after her husband was killed in a bombing, the young woman weighed down by guilt because she may have contributed to the events which led to the murder of her brother – they are not part of the picture. Yet there are thousands of people with similar experiences.
>
> A journalist is typically an outsider looking in. His or her role precludes inserting personal opinions and feelings into the dispatches they submit. That is the role to which I agreed. Though I still try to remain objective, it has become impossible for me to

remain uninvolved. I am deeply moved by the stories told to me almost every day since my arrival in Belfast. By journalistic convention, that fact does not leave a mark on my reports and leaves me feeling that my reports are cold and lifeless.

I have been hit on the head by a brick that a lad had aimed, badly, at a British soldier. A man who took exception to my being an American tried to pick a fight in a pub. I may even have been partly responsible for the brutal execution of a presumed informer by an extreme paramilitary group, after I warned him that someone was looking for him. I have come to respect, even love, many of the courageous and spirited people whom I have met. If I started out as an outsider looking in, I now feel like an insider trying to convey the drama in Northern Ireland to the outside. It is only through the insider experience that the horror of events can be accurately told.

Writers, playwrights, poets and musicians have portrayed the convulsions that continue to rack this small country with eloquent power. Most journalists, myself included, have been unable to do that.

He did not care whether the words would ever be published. Writing was cathartic, allowing him to release the turmoil and the anger he felt within. When the clock showed five pm he decided to call David. It would be noon in Boston.

'David, glad I caught you. Have you got a few minutes?'

'Yes, sure, Thomas. Good to speak with you. What's on your mind?'

Thomas took a deep breath and hoped his words would come out right.

'David, I really need to talk with you about my role, and the expanded role which Henry outlined to me. I think you know about that.'

'Yes, I do. It's a new opportunity and a challenge.'

'Yes, I agree it's a challenge. But it's not right for me. David, I have found my strength, and it's one that allows the average citizens of Northern Ireland to speak to the American readership. I think I'm good at expressing their concerns and their pain.'

'Yes, you've done a great job.'

'But I'm not good at and don't like conveying political positions. I've listened to or spoken with several politicians. I thought their positions were largely irrelevant. David, I don't want to, and therefore cannot, effectively cover the political landscape here, and in London and Dublin.'

There was a brief silence at the other end before David responded.

'Thomas, I hear you, and believe I can empathise with you. We wanted to give you this opportunity, partly because Henry wants to shift his focus and partly because we wanted to offer you a new challenge. But I'm not totally surprised by what you've just said.'

Thomas held his breath.

David continued, 'What would you like me or us to do?'

'I need to speak with you face to face. I need to review with you what my future with the *Tribune* might be, if there is a future. I have a direction in mind, but I'm not clear on next steps, whether they will be with the *Tribune* – or elsewhere.'

Again there was a pause before David responded.

'I think it's important that we talk, and I agree that it's something which cannot easily be discussed by phone. I also need some time to think about what you've just said. Look, you've been there almost two months now. You're about due for a stateside leave anyway. I don't know what commitments you have there, so pick your own date and contact Lucy to arrange travel when you're ready. Let Henry and me know what you're doing. I look forward to talking with you at greater length.'

'David, thank you very much. Oh, and by the way, before I called I was writing something that may help you to understand my thinking. It's for your eyes only. I'm going to review it tomorrow and then I'll fax it to you.'

'I look forward to receiving it. Take care of yourself there.'

He rang off, feeling relieved that he had said what he wanted to say.

CHAPTER 15

It was early in the evening when Thomas called Saoirse.
'Hi, my darling. I'm worried about you. How are you?'
'Thomas... I received a short letter from Dermot.'
'A reply to the note I passed on to him?'
'No. He wrote it many months ago. He gave it to a friend to post if anything should happen to him.' Her voice sounded weak and shaky.
'Are you able to tell me anything about what he wrote?'
'He wrote that he did still love me, and he... he felt terrible about not being in touch... he wrote that he had to break it off to protect me, and... he asked for my forgiveness.'
Thomas remained silent.
'But he doesn't explain why, he doesn't say a thing about what he was doing... I just don't understand. Why?'
'Saoirse, I can answer some of your questions. But not on the phone. I need to see you.' There was a long silence, so he added, 'I think you will want to hear what I have to tell you.'
'I need to go to bed early. But after what you've said I know I won't sleep anyway. Can you come to my place for an hour or so?'
He put on his coat and ran out of the hotel to a flower stall he had passed many times. He got there just as the flower-lady was packing things away and bought a bouquet of red roses.

He was shocked by how Saoirse looked. Her eyes were red and her face drawn and pale.
She led him up a narrow flight of stairs and through a door into her small living area. At the rear to the left was an open kitchen and

to the right a sleeping area with a narrow bed and a tiny bathroom at the back. A couple of cushions and inexpensive prints on the wall provided the only bit of colour. He removed his coat, draped it over a chair, drew Saoirse towards him and held her close. She relaxed into him and wrapped her arms around him. He inhaled the familiar scent of her neck, her hair, and had a passing fancy about carrying her off to his castle on a white charger.

'Well, it's not exactly the Europa, is it?' she said, gesturing around the room.

He reached down to where he had placed the roses. 'I hope these will cheer the place up a bit for you.'

Warmth returned to her eyes.

'Thank you, my love. Let me find something to put them in.'

After a bit of rummaging she withdrew a large empty jar from a cupboard.

'These deserve a beautiful vase, but this is all I have.'

She filled it with water, carefully inserted the roses, and placed it on a corner table beside the telephone.

'Would you like some tea, or coffee?'

'No, I'm fine. Why don't you just sit down?'

She sat down in one of the two worn armchairs. Thomas sat down opposite. She looked at him searchingly.

Looking directly into her eyes, he said, 'Though few people will ever know it, Dermot was a hero, a very brave man.'

Saoirse's eyes opened wide.

'I can't tell you how I got the information, but I trust it.'

He paused and looked down at the floor.

'Dermot was working for the security services – the legitimate ones. He had infiltrated a paramilitary group and provided information that prevented a number of attacks and probably saved many lives. He knew that this was extremely dangerous, to him and to anyone close to him. But he was found out and paid the brutal price. He deserted you because he had to, to protect you.'

She sat very still. Tears rolled down her cheeks. Her chest started to heave and then her shoulders, as she broke into heavy sobs. He got up and knelt down in front of her, taking both hands in his.

When the sobbing subsided he embraced her. She wrapped her arms around him and they stayed that way for several minutes.

Saoirse looked up. 'You look terribly uncomfortable.'

He was.

'My bed is very small, so please just lie here with me for a little while.' She placed a couple of cushions on the frayed rug and fetched a blanket from the bed.

He lay down and, with arms around each other, without talking, they stayed there for probably ten precious minutes.

He felt her shiver. She got up, picked up the telephone and called a taxi.

'I wish you could stay but… The taxi will be here soon. Thank you my love, for telling me what you found out.'

'I know it's all been a terrible shock, but I hope that what I could tell helps you.'

'I think it does. Thank you for coming.'

She gave him another embrace.

'When will I see you again?' he asked.

'How about Friday evening, for dinner?'

'Will you come to the hotel?'

'Yes, about six probably. If it's much different I'll give you a call.'

'Will you be at Foyle's this week?'

'I don't know.'

They spent a few more minutes talking about what seemed like trivia under the circumstances, until the doorbell rang announcing the taxi's arrival. At the front door they didn't say anything more, just blew kisses at each other.

He had not told her about the possibility that he had helped Dermot's killers to find him. He decided to keep that to himself forever, as well as the fact that Dermot had been tortured. He went straight to his room and spent about an hour adding to his essay, more certain than ever that he wished to report from the inside out. He dreaded telling Saoirse that he would soon be going back to the US.

The next day he faxed his essay to David and Henry, with whom he also spoke on the phone. Henry had sounded upset, or annoyed, or maybe just surprised. Thomas had undoubtedly created a problem for him. David was quick to fax back a note in which he said he understood better now why Thomas had turned down the opportunity to expand his role. He also asked for permission to print a lightly edited version in the Sunday supplement, in the column 'Letters from our Correspondents'.

On Thursday, with a heavy heart, he phoned the Boston office and asked Lucy to book him a flight back to Boston on Wednesday November 8th.

That evening he went to Foyle's, though not expecting Saoirse to be there. He spoke with Bernard, and the evening of friendly conversation did him good. The damp streets were almost deserted when he walked back to the hotel while a heavy mist swirled between the buildings.

Suddenly the sharp crack of a gunshot broke the silence, accompanied by the whine of a bullet ricocheting off a wall five or six feet away.

Instinctively he crouched down and saw several pedestrians scurry away, but there was no sign of a shooter. His shirt stuck uncomfortably to his back. His legs trembled. There was no second shot and silence enveloped the area, except for the noise of occasional passing cars. As soon as he could walk steadily he hurried over the remaining distance to the hotel. When inside and feeling protected by its relative safety he stood still in the lobby, shaking and breathing heavily. He did not feel frightened, but was in shock. As if emerging from a nightmare, he could hear someone calling his name.

'Mr Cassidy... Mr Cassidy.' The female voice came from reception. 'Someone left a message for you.' The woman handed over a plain white envelope with his name inscribed in block letters. He thanked her and sat down in a quiet corner before opening it. It contained a single sheet of paper. Also in block letters, the brief message: 'GO HOME, MR CASSIDY. GO HOME!' His head reeled as he tried to make sense of things. The shot and the note were no doubt related – both warnings. The receptionist remembered that a young boy had brought in the note around nine o'clock, while Thomas was at Foyle's. Brannon came to mind. He had lied to Brannon about not recognising Dermot's face. Could Brannon be of the INLA? Did they indeed follow him to the Grange, dispose of Dermot and were they now upset with him? It was after ten o'clock when he phoned Edward Thompson's room. He got a sleepy 'hello' but when he had identified himself and said he had been shot at and threatened and it was probably related to 'Mr Brannon', Edward said he'd be down in a minute.

'I'll call my contact at the RUC,' Edward immediately offered. 'This should be reported right away.'

He placed his call and checked whether Thomas was still up for a trip to RUC headquarters at this late hour. As he had only had a single pint, he agreed.

Inspector Carrington greeted them courteously. Carrington looked to be something over 50, and had evidently not had time to shave during the last 24 or more hours. Thomas was able to describe the spot on the street where he had been shot at, as well as the wall of a bakery where the bullet had probably ricocheted away. An officer would be sent to look for a bullet, though there was little chance of finding it and even less of being able to identify it.

Carrington wrote up his report, Thomas signed it and Carrington thanked him for taking the trouble to report the incident, reassuringly adding that not a single foreign journalist had been deliberately killed during the Troubles, so far.

Back in the hotel he offered Edward a drink, which he declined, so Thomas retired to his room, exhausted. Only with difficulty could he clear his mind enough to sleep.

As Friday afternoon wore on he was too distracted by events and the anticipation of dinner and an evening with Saoirse to do any serious work. He felt a sense of defiance grow inside him: damned if he was going to scurry out of Belfast. He did not think of himself as a hero, but neither did he want to appear a coward. At 5:30 he was waiting in the lobby, staring blankly in front of him and absorbed in thought, when he heard her familiar voice.

'Hellooo! Where are you?'

He jumped up and wrapped his arms around her. 'You're looking better, my darling, and I'm so very glad to see you.'

He led her into the bar, where they sat at a small table.

'Before we go into anything else: I have something for you.' He pulled the little box from the Brown Thomas store from his pocket and handed it to her. She opened it carefully and pulled out the heart-shaped pendant on its chain.

'Thomas! It's beautiful. Thank you.' She leaned over to give him a kiss.

'Go on, put it on.'

He helped her close the small clasp.

'I'll never go anywhere without it.'

'You'd better not. You're now wearing my heart!'

They both laughed at the idea and she planted another kiss on his lips.

When they had settled back into their chairs he asked, 'How are you now?'

'No simple answer to that. I've cried for Dermot. I've been angry with him for leaving me and putting himself in such terrible danger. I've loved him for his courage and doubted myself. Would he have done differently if I'd given him more of myself? But I'm getting it sorted out in my head, or should I say my heart. We had a pretty good year and then we both fell victim to this, this…'

She looked around and gestured helplessly.

'Thomas, I'd been thinking about it before, but I know now that, as soon as possible, I will get away from here. To Dublin. I hate Belfast.'

'You'd mentioned that that was your dream.'

She smiled a sad smile before adding, 'Is it possible to dream when you're living what seems more like a nightmare?'

She caught herself, took one of his hands and added, softly, 'You are not part of the nightmare.'

Saoirse accepted a glass of wine, and told him how the children were doing, how they had sensed that she was upset, and had been especially good. Socrates had also picked it up, in his mysterious way, and had sought her out.

'And what about you?' she asked. 'How have your days been?'

He had expected this question and had decided not to tell her about the shot and the note, yet. He pulled two folded sheets of paper from his jacket and gave them to her.

'I haven't asked you to read any of my work. But I would like you to read this. I've sent it to my bosses in London and Boston. When you've read it there is something I need to tell you.'

She accepted the pages and opened them out.

'Reflections of a Journalist', she read aloud. 'Sounds intriguing.'

Thomas excused himself to go to the men's room, but really he just wanted to give her time to read. He took his time and when he returned the papers were resting on the table in front of her.

'It's beautiful,' she said. 'This,' pointing at the essay, 'is why I love you. You are not just looking for a sensational story. You really do connect with people.'

Thomas thought for a moment before replying.

'You know, when I came here two months ago, I think I was a reporter looking for a story. But I've changed. And you've been a catalyst for that. If I hadn't met you…'

She squeezed his hand.

Thomas broke a long silence. 'Hey, didn't I invite you for dinner? How about we do that?'

'Sounds good.'

They occupied a quiet corner of the dining room, inspected the menu and ordered.

'Now, what did you want to tell me? You're looking a little stressed.'

'Saoirse, what you just read spilled out after I was asked to cover Northern Ireland from the political angle as well. But that's not what I want to do. I believe I'm good at telling the stories of the people behind the news. That might include a politician as well, if he or she is willing to speak as an individual.'

'I understand that.'

'The problem is... that by turning down the role I was offered, my assignment here will end sooner rather than later. I'll have to return to Boston.'

'How soon?'

'I'm going to fly back on Wednesday week to speak with David. After that, I don't know what I'll be doing, but it's unlikely to be a re-posting to Belfast.'

Saoirse looked down at her plate.

When she looked up, she said, 'We knew this was coming, Thomas. We – or at least I – have tried to ignore it, but we knew you weren't going to stay forever.'

'Of course. But Saoirse, I love you! How can I just leave?'

'I love you too, Thomas, you know that. Maybe...' Her voice trailed off.

'I've been thinking that I could try to find a job in Dublin.'

'No, Thomas! You know you can't do that.'

'I can't bear the thought of having three thousand miles of water between us.'

She sat up straight.

'Thomas, stop it. I hate the idea of losing you, but I will not accept responsibility for helping you to ruin your career. You have to go back to Boston. We both knew it was coming.'

'Saoirse, I...'

Her expression turned very serious and earnest.

'Thomas, listen carefully. I have thought about all of this endlessly. I love you and on the one hand would like to commit to you forever, even go to Boston with you. But…' She hesitated, and took a deep breath. 'But, though I may live to regret my decision deeply, I have to let you go. As long as my parents are alive I cannot leave Ireland. But more than that, once it becomes possible for me I have to become very selfish. My family has been dependent on me as long as I can remember. I must, finally, focus on myself. I need to study hard, earn a degree and find a job, a career. I… I do love you, Thomas, but I can't let you stand in the way of what I've decided on, and I will not stand in the way of your developing the career you're capable of.'

She stopped, looking desperately for his understanding. Thomas tried to say something, but all that came out was a faltering 'but'.

'No "but", Thomas. Now that I've said what I had to say, I'm upset and I expect you are too. We'll speak again soon, but now I have to go. If I stay I'll be blubbering in just a minute. I just hope that you will be able to understand.'

Eyes damp with tears, she pulled on her coat and headed for the exit, Thomas following, carried forward by a flood of emotions.

'Take care of yourself, dear Thomas, and remember: no matter what, I love you.' With those words she disappeared through the front entrance.

He walked back into the restaurant where he signed for the unfinished meals.

'Was everything satisfactory, sir?' the waiter enquired.

'Yes, the food was fine.'

He ordered another red wine in the bar, feeling miserable and alone.

Back in his room he switched on the television and found a vacuous movie, which did little to relieve his sense of loss, weakness and failure. That night he dreamed that he was walking a long road, no idea where, alone, and no sign of life anywhere, not a farmhouse, nothing. The road just went on straight before disappearing in the distance, and he had no choice but to follow it.

He was unsure what he would do with his Saturday when he went down for breakfast. It looked wet and miserable outside. He lingered longer than usual over breakfast and took a second and then a third cup of coffee. Back in his room he made some additions to an article he had been writing, but felt devoid of inspiration.

Towards noon the telephone rang. He thought it was probably Ben or Rupert.

'Hi, it's me.'

'Saoirse! Uh… hi.'

'My love, I feel really terrible about walking out last night. I shouldn't have done that and I'm sorry.'

'You've had a tough week. It's okay. I was sad and hurt, I won't deny that, but you had a right.'

'No, I didn't. When we told each other that we loved each other, and made love, we made a commitment about how we would treat each other. Walking out was not part of the deal. I should have stayed no matter how difficult the conversation was for both of us.'

He couldn't find any words.

'Will you come to the pub this evening, maybe around half ten or eleven? You're welcome earlier of course, but I want to talk with you after closing.'

'I'll be there.'

'Thomas, I love you.'

She rang off, leaving him feeling bewildered.

The rain stopped and the sun broke through. He went for a brisk walk through the busy Saturday streets. Children's uncomplicated laughter caught his attention. A couple of hours later he sat down behind his typewriter again, still both confused about and relieved by Saoirse's reversal. At the top of the page he typed in 'My Dreams'.

He stared at the empty page for a while and then started to write off the top of his head, recalling his essay and taking it from there. He could write a regular column called 'The People behind the News'. Human-interest stories, if not for the *Tribune*, then maybe for *The*

New Yorker. He remembered his early days at the *Tribune*, when he had covered the events around the Boston school-bussing riots in 1974 and 1975, and the furore around Indian rights and lands in the Midwest. But he had not gone behind the news at all. From now on he would. He would try his hand at fiction, perhaps starting with Maire's suggestion that he write short stories based on stories he had heard. He would enrol in a writing seminar, or master class. Maybe he could even do some teaching at a school of journalism.

He dreamed of travelling with Saoirse, sharing adventures. He would certainly cross the Atlantic as often as he could to see her. In between they would write and phone. He could not imagine there ever being another woman in his life.

Then he caught himself. What about her life? Would Saoirse wait around so that once in a while he would reappear and whisk her away for a romantic weekend? He was being ridiculous, just thinking about himself again. His dreams were self-centred. He wished her a life of happiness, satisfaction and love – love from someone in a better position than he to provide it. But just thinking of her in someone else's arms filled him with pain.

Angry with himself for getting into a fruitless loop of distressing thoughts he grabbed his coat and walked to a local cinema. The new James Bond film, *The Spy Who Loved Me*, was showing and he caught an early evening show. He had seen only two Bond films in his life and was not a great fan, but he needed the distraction. After the movie it was still early, but he went to Foyle's anyway.

Saoirse was surprised. 'You're here already! You'll not be hoisting pints all evening, will you?'

'No, I won't. In fact I'm going to have something to eat. I just wasted a couple of hours watching James Bond save the world, and I'm hungry.'

'I didn't know you were a Bond fan.'

'I'm not. Shows you how desperate I was.'

She laughed at him and pointed to the menu chalked up on a blackboard beside the bar.

'I'll get you a pint now, but drink slowly. I need you to be reasonably sober later.'

'I promise.'

He noticed the silver heart hanging around her neck.

A little later the musicians started up. Thomas was again joined by Bernard, who at one point assumed a very serious tone of voice.

'Have you been following the news, Thomas? The Pope and Ian Paisley both died yesterday.'

Thomas gave the expected response. 'No! Really?'

'Yes, and they arrived at the Pearly Gates together. Well, St Peter asked them whether they had permission to enter heaven. Paisley said…'

But he never got to finish his story because Saoirse had walked to the musicians' corner.

'Many of you have heard this before,' she announced, 'but I'm going to sing it again. I sing it for a special friend tonight. It's called "The Parting Glass". And this is my own version.'

The final verse went:

If I had money enough to spend,
And leisure time to sit awhile,
There is a fair lad in this town,
That sorely has my heart beguiled.
His winning smile and bright blue eyes,
I own he has my heart in thrall,
Then fill to me the parting glass,
Good night and joy be with you all.

It left Thomas with mixed feelings: a 'parting glass'? He wondered what Saoirse was planning to tell him later.

By eleven the guests had started to disperse and Saoirse and Colin were busy cleaning up. The musicians stowed away their instruments and left. It was just before half eleven when Saoirse said, 'Shall we go?'

Once outside Thomas flagged down a taxi.

'Are you mad, Thomas? It's only a fifteen-minute walk and it's dry. Why this?'

'I have a reason and I'll tell you, but just get in, okay?'

'So what was that about?' Saoirse asked when they were inside the hotel.

'I'll tell you. Upstairs.'

Once in the room, Saoirse looked to him again, searching for an explanation.

'Okay. Now don't get upset… Thursday evening someone shot at me as I walked back from Foyle's.'

'Say what?' Saoirse asked, with alarm in her eyes.

He told her what had happened, about the note, about his late trip to RUC headquarters. He linked it to the mysterious 'Mr Brannon' and added what he had not told her earlier, that he and a colleague had gone to the Grange and, aside from handing over her note, had warned Dermot. He ended with his own conclusion: 'Mr Brannon sent a warning.'

She sat in stunned silence. He let the news sink in as he poured two glasses of wine.

'Saoirse, I know it sounds really alarming, but that single shot was clearly not meant to kill me; if it had there would have been no need for the note. Somebody is trying to scare me away. I will not run. However, I didn't want to put you at any risk whatsoever; hence the taxi. So please try to relax.'

She remained quiet as she sipped her wine. She ended her silence explosively.

'The bastards, the fucking bastards! I hate this God-forsaken country. Fuck!'

She got up, pulled him into her arms and squeezed him tightly. After a few seconds she simply said, 'I love you, Thomas, so very much. Please be careful, please?'

He placed his hand on the back of her head and drew her towards him, meeting her lips with his.

After an extra squeeze she sat down again and took another drink from her glass, staring at the carpet.

'As I said on the phone, I apologise for walking out. I was upset, but that is no excuse. I was upset because… well, we both knew you would have to leave at some point, and I always hoped it would be later rather than sooner. But when you told me, it just became too much. Niall dead, Dermot dead, you leaving, and now you've just told me this… it just feels like all the men who were or are important to me leave. I was being childish and self-centred.'

Thomas knelt down in front of her chair and they embraced. His hands started to move over her head, her neck, through her hair and over her face.

'Calm down! I want to talk just a bit longer. I need to say something else.'

She was smiling in a teasing sort of way as she said that and he obediently moved back to his chair.

'You're flying back in ten days. But I know that we will see each other again, I just know. Now, we can choose to be sad for the next ten days, or we can make the most of them. I'd rather do that.'

She got up, took his hands and pulled him out of his chair and towards the bed. Within a minute they were under the covers.

Thomas leaned up on an elbow.

'Tell me more about your dreams, Saoirse. You said it was hard to dream while living a nightmare. But when the nightmare is over, where will you be?'

Saoirse propped herself up on an elbow as well.

She traced over his chest with a finger as she spoke. 'I will be out of this fucking country and in Dublin. I will work with children and I will study child psychology. I will qualify to enter the School of Psychology at Trinity College. That is my dream.' With a quiet passion, she added, 'I want to be *free* to live my own life, nobody depending on me but me. But I can't leave yet obviously.'

'I know that you will make that dream come true, Saoirse. You will do it, and I'll be proud of you and I'll be at your graduation. How about that?'

'I'll keep you to your word. Now, how about doing a little less talking?'

With that she threw herself on top of him.

Thomas woke up and turned his head to see her sleeping quietly beside him. He spent some time looking at Saoirse's peaceful face, strands of auburn hair draped over her forehead. After slipping into a bathrobe he boiled water, moving as silently as he could. But when he glanced back at the bed he saw she was awake, propped up with an extra pillow, and smiling.

'Good morning, my love.'

'Good morning, my darling. Tea?'

'Tea in bed sounds like a wonderful idea.'

Taking care not to spill, they sat beside each other.

'Thomas, what are your dreams?'

He looked at her sadly for a moment.

'A part of my dreams is impossible, because you – we – are a part of them. But if I can't go there now, I'll just say that I dream about writing powerfully about the people behind the stories. Maybe at some point do the same in front of a television camera, though that feels a bit scary. Maybe I'll try my hand at fiction. Maybe I'll teach. Maybe I'll travel, do my work not only in the United States. I would rather work out of Ireland but if I can't do that I want to see you as often as possible.'

She listened. When he stopped, she said, 'You used the word "maybe" four times. There are no "maybes" in dreams. You will make your dreams come true if you believe in them.'

After a pause, she asked, 'Do you think you'll ever marry?'

The question caught him totally by surprise.

'I can't imagine that really. The only person I can imagine wanting to marry is right beside me.'

'Don't look so upset, my love. We know we cannot always be together, and I want you to be happy, even when we're not. Otherwise we're not really living and we're not free. We can't tie each other down. When we see each other in a year or in five years I want to see a happy Thomas, not a miserable, lonely Thomas who is happy only because he sees me again.'

He recalled the dream of himself on a lonely road. The conversation had taken a more profound turn than he was prepared for so early in the morning. There seemed to be no opening for a return to his idea of staying in Ireland.

'You're right,' he said finally. 'I just have a lot of difficulty thinking about a relationship with someone I haven't even met. I have a hard time thinking beyond now, or the next ten days.'

'Well, you don't have to think about it too seriously,' she said. 'But we did need to talk about this, because the truth is that we will be apart for long periods of time. We have to give each other the freedom to find personal happiness.'

'Do you expect to marry, Saoirse?'

'I think I do, yes, if I find another "right" man… And guess what, if I do I want you to be my Best Man.'

'That's silly. Only the groom has a best man, at least in America.'

'Here as well. But I don't think there's a law against it.'

They both had to laugh at the thought.

'And for now, my love, you are my very best man.'

'One more question.'

'Okay: one.'

'Do you still dream of having children of your own?'

That silenced Saoirse for a moment.

'I don't know, Thomas, I really don't know.' After another pause: 'But not today. So put down your cup… '

An hour or so later there was a knock on the door, and a voice announced 'Housekeeping'.

'Could you come back in about an hour please?' Thomas asked.

'Yes, of course sir.'

'I forgot to put out the 'do not disturb' sign.'

'You were a little preoccupied last night. Now before she comes back I'll take a nice long bath.'

She disappeared into the bathroom, while he made a coffee and clicked on the television. There was nothing interesting on, so he walked into the bathroom to find her hidden, except her smiling face, under a mass of bubbles.

'Would you like to join me?'

He put down his cup, discarded the robe and carefully slid into the tub, facing her.

'See? We both fit. We don't need much room, do we?'

They laughed and giggled and blew bubbles at each other. He felt like a child, experiencing the simple joy of being alive.

Fifteen minutes later they dried each other off. It was just about an hour after the housekeeper had called that they walked towards the lift, discussing where they would go next. They decided on a nearby restaurant Saoirse knew.

It was warm, comfortable and very quiet, which suited them fine.

'What are you doing this week Thomas?'

'I'm arranging to go to a couple of schools: a Protestant school and a Catholic school. I'd like to talk with some young people – teenagers, I mean. I'm also trying to get to the Maze prison. But I'm not sure if that will work. And I would like to visit a certain child care centre again, if the lady in charge will let me.'

'I think that's more easily arranged than the Maze. But she may have you read a story again, so be warned.'

'Okay, I'll be prepared.'

'And whatever you plan, next weekend is ours. I'm taking Saturday off from the pub.'

'And what do you propose we do?'

'I want you to hire a car and I'm going to take you to a lovely little town where there is sure to be a lovely little inn.'

'Are you going to tell me more?'

'No. It'll be a surprise.'

CHAPTER 16

Thomas met six boys at the Christian Brothers school in Andersonstown. The principal was welcoming and the boys were well dressed and well behaved when they gathered in the brightly lit library after normal school hours. They were initially reluctant to open up, but after half an hour Thomas's empathic questioning and listening helped them to relax. They disclosed their fear of running into Protestant gangs on their way to and from school, their anxieties when they encountered army patrols, and talked about people they knew of who had been caught in gunfire or whose homes had been burned. Unfortunately, Thomas thought, it was a now all-too-familiar litany. Until, that is, Dean hesitantly indicated a wish to speak.

'My brother – he was ten years older than me – he was shot when he left his favourite pub about four months ago. He wasn't doing anything, he never hurt anyone. He was just murdered.'

The other boys averted their eyes while the boy spoke.

'I mean, it's sort of an IRA pub, I guess, but Aidan was never a member of anything. He was there for the fun and hated violence. So some person, a woman probably, shot him for no reason at all.'

Dean had trouble holding back his tears.

'Dean, did you say "a woman probably"?'

'That's what we heard from one of his mates. Someone saw a woman running away from the scene. But whoever it was, was never caught. There was a note pinned to Aidan's jacket saying "Greetings from Fergal". But nobody knows who Fergal is.'

A shock wave coursed through Thomas's body. His expression must have changed because all eyes were focused on him. Frantically he wondered whether he should move on to something different or tell Dean what he knew.

'Dean, I am… I'm extremely sorry about what happened to your brother. And I… I have something that I need to tell you. But just between us. Will you stay for a bit after the others have left?'

Five pairs of eyes moved quickly between Thomas and Dean. Dean looked upset and frightened.

'Please trust me, Dean. And, boys, thanks so very much for staying on this afternoon. I do really appreciate it. I just need to speak with Dean alone now.'

Puzzled, the boys filed from the room, one giving Dean an encouraging pat on the shoulder as he walked by.

'Dean, do you live far away? Might your mother be able to come here quickly?'

'I live only about ten minutes away. And I think she's at home. What's all this about, Mr Cassidy?'

Thomas tried to sound reassuring. 'It's okay, Dean. It's just something I think you and your family need to know. Let's go down to the principal's office and try to call your mother.'

Dean waited outside the office while Thomas told the principal why he needed to talk to Dean and preferably his mother. The principal understood quickly and phoned her, emphasising that Dean was not in trouble of any kind.

As they waited in the office Thomas tried to lighten the atmosphere. It turned out that Dean liked to play cricket so he asked Dean to explain to him what cricket was about and why it appealed to him. The principal fetched a Coca-Cola for both of them.

Eventually Dean's mother hurried in. The principal made the introductions and explained why Thomas had been at the school that afternoon. He then asked Thomas to take over.

Thomas took a deep breath and started.

'Mrs McMurtry, Dean told me this afternoon that his older brother Aidan, your son, had been shot four months ago. Um… first of all, please accept my sincerest condolences.'

Mrs McMurtry sat rigidly in her chair as Thomas continued.

'Dean said there was a note pinned to Aidan's jacket, a note saying "Greetings from Fergal". I have heard about that incident, Mrs McMurtry. Fergal, as I understand it, was a young man of about Aidan's age, newly married. I understand that Fergal, like Aidan, was not a member of anything and also hated violence. Fergal died at the hands of an IRA gunman in what was apparently a random killing, as was the case with Aidan, I understand.'

Dean looked bewildered.

'It is important that you know that Aidan had not killed Fergal. Fergal's widow did not know who killed her husband but she blamed the IRA. She picked out Aidan at random near that pub and shot him out of blind revenge. I know this because I spoke with her a few weeks ago.'

Dean and his mother had both gone white.

'That woman is now also dead.'

Dean couldn't hold it together any longer. Heavy sobs shook his body. His mother appeared in shock and placed an arm around Dean's shoulders. The principal sat in his chair like a statue, his face expressing sadness and disbelief. After a few moments he and Thomas made eye contact and quietly left the office.

'I don't know if I did the right thing by telling Dean and his mother what I know.'

'I think you did, Mr Cassidy. Dean and his mother are in shock now, but in the long run they'll be better off knowing.'

'Who is going to help that family now?'

The principal shook his head. 'I don't know. I just don't know.'

Ten minutes later Thomas was in a taxi again, feeling numb. Fergal, Aidan and Sarah herself: Were they indeed all innocent? Was innocence even possible here? 'How do you understand insanity,' she had asked. He remembered what Maire had said, about Greens and Oranges being trapped by their own history, stories and mythology. He wanted to help his readers make sense of what was going on at the human level in Northern Ireland, but the longer he was there the less he understood it himself. It made no sense whatsoever. Back in the hotel he started to write what became the most sombre account he had submitted.

CHAPTER 17

The next morning he put on a bathrobe, made coffee and read through the newspaper. The telephone rang unexpectedly. It was just after eight o'clock.

'It's me. I hope it's not too early to call.'

He was immediately on high alert.

'No, that's fine, I was just having coffee. What's up?'

'My father suffered a stroke last night. He's in the Royal Victoria.'

Thomas sat down on the edge of the bed.

'I called the hospital this morning. They said he was resting comfortably. They're going to run a series of tests later this morning. Then we'll know more.'

'Saoirse, I'm so very sorry.'

'Kevin came over around ten o'clock and told me to call an ambulance. Mam went with da. Kevin and I went to the hospital by taxi and spent most of the night there as well. The three of us are exhausted. I'm home now and will try to sleep a few hours. I won't be going to the children today. I…'

Her voice faded away.

'Is there anything I can do?'

'No, there isn't, not now. Just think of us.'

'Of course. Will you call me when you have further news? I'd planned to stay in the hotel today. If I'm not in my room they can find me in the coffee shop or restaurant.'

He had planned to visit the Protestant school but would cancel or postpone it.

'Yes, I'll call you as soon as I know more.'

During breakfast he thought of Saoirse and how she might feel about losing her father, after losing Niall and Dermot – and facing his own imminent departure. He wondered again whether there was any reasonable way for him to stay, but came up with nothing. He stared through the tall windows at the rain, falling in windblown sheets.

Back in his room he made some calls to see whether a visit to the Maze prison would be possible. He ran into obstacles, but was able to extract from his sources the name of a man who had spent four years inside but was now out. A first attempt to call him failed. Thomas paced around the room and finally returned to his typewriter, where he completed the article he had started the previous evening.

It was dark early because of the low, heavy clouds streaming across the late afternoon sky. He headed to the bar for an uncharacteristically early drink, stopping on the way to ask reception to look for him there if a telephone call should come in. He was happy when Rupert entered and was briefly distracted by chat about the latest news: what was buzzing in political circles, the widespread fear that the IRA was about to step up its activities again, and the protests in the Maze.

'I may have something of more direct interest to you, Thomas. I asked a local journalist who does investigative reporting and he was able to tell me that Niall Kelly had indeed been a member of an IRA cell. He was also able to say that he knew who the commander of that cell is but of course he wouldn't give me a name.'

'Thanks, Rupert. But I'm not sure I can do much with that…'

Rupert interrupted. 'But there is. Can you go to a pub called O'Flynn's in West Belfast tomorrow evening, around nine? Someone will meet you there, someone who may be willing to give you more information.'

'Does it have to be tomorrow? I can't make it. How about next Monday? Is there any way to fix that?'

'I'll pass the request through the pipeline and leave a message in your pigeon-hole at reception.'

'Thanks, Rupert. And how will I know who I'm supposed to meet?'

'Someone will know who you are, I'm sure. Here's the address.'
Rupert handed over a slip of paper.
'It's best if you go alone on this. I know it feels dodgy but you'll be okay.'
Their conversation was interrupted when the young lady from reception came in looking for him.
'There's a call for you, Mr Cassidy. You can take it beside reception.'
He excused himself and dashed for the phone.
'Saoirse?'
'It's not so good. Da is comfortable. But we spoke with a doctor, who said that though his condition is stable, it is serious. He's paralysed on the right side and unable to speak.'
'How are you all holding up?'
'We're exhausted. They're at their place and I'm at mine and I expect everyone will go to bed early. The hospital will call me if there's any change. And Kevin has said he will put in an urgent request with the telephone company to install a line at their house. Mam is stoical; she's a strong woman, and puts her faith in God. Kevin has actually been quite wonderful. This seems to have snapped him out of himself, and he's really doing his best to support mam. As for me, I just don't know. I've had to be strong too, but it feels like a charade. Sometimes I just want to cry, but I can't let myself, not now.'
'I wish I could be there with you.'
'I know, love. Thank you. But I really do need some sleep now.'
'What about tomorrow, Saoirse? I know you haven't been to the centre today; do you plan to go tomorrow?'
'I don't know. I would like to, and I really should, but it will depend on what the hospital says tomorrow morning. I'll call you around eight and let you know.'

Saoirse rang early the next morning, sounding considerably more rested. She was going to go to the centre, Kevin would go to school and their neighbour had promised to keep her mother company and to call if there was a need. Her father had spent the night comfortably; the hospital was planning on running further tests before deciding on a programme of rehabilitation.

He returned to the child care centre in mid-afternoon, and was welcomed by several of the children. Ross was there, hugging Twinkle, Kyle was bold enough to step up and say hello, and Jonathan asked whether Thomas was going to read a story again. A couple of little girls came up to say 'Hello, Mr Cassidy.' He had become a familiar figure at the centre.

When story time came around, Thomas laid aside the book of Irish tales, and said that he would tell the American story of how Brèr Rabbit fell down the well. A dozen pairs of eyes were glued on him. He took a few liberties with the story but told it much as he remembered it from when he was little.

Thomas told the children that he was going back to America, so he might not see them again. This resulted in a chorus of disappointed ah's. He assured them that he would think of them, and that he would hear about them through Miss Kelly. As they left almost all of them said 'Goodbye, Mr Cassidy.' Saoirse accompanied Thomas to the hotel.

'Dinner?'

'Yes please.'

You look absolutely drained, Saoirse,' he remarked when they were in his room to drop their coats.

'I'm worried. Something tells me da's not going to make it. His general health is poor, as you may have gathered. The stroke was severe and I don't really believe them when they talk about rehabilitation.'

'What about your mother?'

'She's doing pretty well. I think she has long known that she would probably end up a widow. I know she's worried and upset, but she's facing it all extremely bravely.'

'What will your mother do, if your father passes away?'

'We did actually talked about that once. I think she would go to stay with her sister, near Strabane, between Derry and Omagh. They've always been very close. My uncle died in 1972, my aunt lives alone in quite a large house, and her three children moved out long ago. I think it would work.'

'And Kevin?'

'Kevin seems like a changed person. The shock of it all has forced him to take responsibility for things. He would go to Strabane too, initially, but within a couple of years I expect he would return to Belfast and see if he can find a good job. I'm more confident than ever that he'll be okay. The Boston break is obviously out of the question, though.'

She laid her head on his shoulder. After a few minutes she looked up again.

'Thanks for being you and being here for me. I feel much better now. Just let me freshen up a bit before dinner.'

After they had ordered, she broached the planned weekend.

'I just don't know right now whether I can make it. I want to, very much. It's our last chance for a while.'

'I understand,' Thomas replied. 'I can always cancel the hire car. We'll just see how things go.'

'Okay. I'm also a little unsure about how to explain my absence, if we do go. I mean, normally my family doesn't question me about what I'm doing or where I'm going. But it's a bit different now. Mam doesn't know that you're more than a journalist I happen to have met. Kevin does, because I told him. He's fine with it. He in fact encouraged me to go off with you; said he'd look after mam. He even suggested making up a story about me going off to spend the weekend with an old girlfriend from school.'

Dinner arrived. They kept the conversation light. It didn't feel appropriate to bring up Sarah, Fergal, Aidan and Dean.

As dinner was ending Saoirse said, 'Much as I would like to, I'm not staying tonight, Thomas. I want to drop by Foyle's to see how Colin is getting on and to thank him for giving me evenings off. Then I'll go home, check in on mam, and try to get a good sleep.'

'Okay, Saoirse. I hadn't expected you to stay over. But I'll walk to Foyle's with you.'

Thomas visited the Protestant school the next day and was struck by how similar the boys seemed to the boys in the Catholic school. It boggled his mind to think that the two groups of boys, so similar in appearance and way of speaking, might be at each other's throats in a few years.

He had a 3 o'clock meeting with Dennis McCarthy, who had been released six or seven months earlier after serving four years in the Maze. They had agreed to meet in a café just behind City Hall.

By 3:20 Thomas was wondering if McCarthy had changed his mind when a man in his late twenties came in, wearing a worn dark brown winter coat and looking around furtively. Thomas stood up.

'Dennis McCarthy?'

'Yeah, that's me. You must be Thomas Cassidy.'

They shook hands, and Thomas invited him to take a seat.

'Thanks very much for agreeing to see me, Dennis. Would you like a coffee, or something else?'

'Just a black coffee, thanks.'

A couple of customers came in and took a table right in front of where they were seated. Thomas looked around, and suggested they move to the back where it was empty and they would be less likely to be overheard.

'Dennis, before I ask you a few questions, is there anything about me you would like to know?'

'I don't think so. You told me about yourself and your reason for being here and wanting to speak to me on the phone. And you did say that you would not use my name in anything you write, right?'

'Absolutely, Dennis. So tell me, why were you taken to the Maze?'

'I was charged with being a member of the IRA. I suppose they were right, but I never fired a gun and never planted a bomb. My worst offence was agreeing to hide several rifles. The RUC searched my home and found them.'

'So aside from being a member of the IRA, you never committed a crime.'

'No, I didn't. Well, hiding firearms is a crime, I guess.'

Dennis paused to sip his coffee before continuing. 'We were political prisoners, basically. But from some time in '76 they made us wear prison uniforms as if we were common criminals. Some guys refused, and took to wearing blankets instead.'

'Yes, I heard about that. And in March of this year things escalated further, didn't they?'

'Yeah, I was released just before that started and some prisoners started to smear shit all over their cells. I heard it stank something awful.'

'What can you tell me about what it was like to be there, Dennis?'

'It was like being in a prisoner of war camp. I saw *The Great Escape* once. Well, it was like that. We were herded around like cattle and some of the guards would have fitted well into Nazi uniforms. Sometimes it was brutal. Of course, there were a few nice guards as well, but most of them, they were, like, finding any excuse to punish us — for what? Being Irish? The food was terrible and we were only allowed occasional visitors, but they were allowed to bring in cigarettes and some food. I was lucky, but some blokes didn't have family, not nearby anyway. They had it rough. Those who did receive packages sometimes shared with those who didn't. I mean, we really had to support each other.'

'Why were you released after four years?'

'I have no idea. Maybe they needed the space for someone else. I was never formally charged with anything other than membership, and they didn't tell me why I could walk.'

Two men wearing RUC uniforms walked into the café. Dennis saw them first and, shrinking down into his seat, covered his face with the menu.

'Jesus Christ!'

Thomas turned around and saw the cause of Dennis's fear.

'Okay, Dennis, just stay calm. If you walk out now you'll attract attention. Order some lunch and we'll change the subject. It looks like they're relaxed and just having coffee.'

They both ordered a cheese and pickle sandwich.

'Hey Dennis,' said Thomas in a slightly louder voice. 'I'm thinking of taking a lady friend away into the countryside for the weekend. Where would you recommend we go?'

Dennis played along eagerly.

'Well, you know, if you don't mind the drive, you might think of taking her across the border into Donegal. I was there once. It's lovely.'

'What could we expect to find there?'

Dennis went on for a bit, recalling what he had seen in Donegal town, and along the rough coastline.

'Great pub in Donegal. Murphy's, it was. Music on weekend evenings, and good craic.'

After ten minutes, the RUC men paid for their coffee and left. Dennis breathed a sigh of relief.

'Do you have any reason to think they might be looking for you?'

'No, but they have mug shots and study them all the time. If one of those guys recognised me he would probably give me a hard time.'

'What are you doing now, Dennis? I mean, with regard to work.'

'Oh, I have a new career. I wash dishes most afternoons and evenings.'

Thomas could see the bitterness on Dennis's face.

'Are you still a member of the IRA?'

'Yes I am. But I'm keeping my head down, not getting actively involved. Yet.'

'Might you, some day?'

'Can't say for sure.'

Dennis was looking uncomfortable again, his eyes darting back and forth. Thomas remained quiet, hoping Dennis would continue.

'It's just that if I did get actively involved, chances are I'd get killed, or locked up for 25 years.'

'So it's not an easy call.'

'No, it sure isn't.'

'Dennis, what do you think the American public should know about what's going on here, and about the IRA?'

'I'll tell you what they should know. Northern Ireland is not a democracy. The rights of Catholics have been violated since forever. The British are occupying this country. The IRA seeks freedom and equality. It will fight as long as necessary to achieve that.'

'I've got one last question, Dennis. What is the INLA, compared with the IRA?'

'The INLA is a radical offshoot spouting some crazy Marxist ideology. The IRA and the INLA waste a lot of time fighting each other. They're a bunch of crazies. You don't want to mess with them.'

'Thanks very much for talking with me, Dennis. I appreciate it, and wish you well.'

'You're welcome, Thomas.'

Dennis stood up, pulled on his heavy coat, and shook Thomas's hand. As he left the café he pulled his collar up high and Thomas saw him look to the right and left before heading out onto the street.

Thomas walked back to the hotel, happy to notice that there were patches of blue in the sky. He would write up an article right away.

Around six o'clock, Saoirse called. Everything was looking okay, she said.

'But I want to check with the hospital tomorrow morning first thing. I'll be at the hotel around half ten.'

'That's great. Get a good rest.'

CHAPTER 18

The weather looked promising when Thomas opened the curtains. After picking up the car he waited impatiently while doing his best to banish the thought that this was a sort of 'last hurrah'. When 10:30 arrived so did Saoirse, looking fabulous in a sweater, jeans, knitted woolly hat and warm dark blue jacket.

'How is your father this morning?'

'He's stable, but the doctor says he probably had several minor strokes before.'

'What makes him think that?'

'It was the little things we told him about: headaches, drowsiness, clumsiness, slurring of speech. Every time da just said he was tired, or made some other excuse. But they were warning signs.'

'Are you still okay for going away?'

'Yes, I really want to. And besides, I don't know how he did it, but Kevin managed to get a telephone installed yesterday afternoon. I promised to call in once or twice and let them know where I was. And the hospital can now contact them directly.'

By 11:30 they were driving south. The farm fields looked almost ready for winter and occasional aromatic whiffs of peat smoke hung over them. He had learned to love the smell. Most of the leaves had fallen, but occasionally there was a bit of colour – just enough to remind him of New England in the autumn. He thought how he would love to show off that splendour to Saoirse one day.

He told her about his meeting with the schoolboys and with Dennis, but for the most part they exchanged comments on what they saw as they drove. The road took them straight through the centre of

Ballynahinch, which was busy with Saturday shoppers and people enjoying a rare day of sunshine.

'It's such a great name,' Thomas enthused. 'Ballynahinch! There are towns and villages all over the place with such strange and lovely names. Like Ballynamalaght or Magherafelt.'

She laughed at his attempts to pronounce the names and gently corrected him.

They found a restaurant in Dundrum with a view out over the deep blue waters of the Irish Sea, with the Mourne Mountains in the other direction. There was a light dusting of snow on the top of Slieve Donard – Northern Ireland's highest peak, Saoirse remarked.

As they waited for their meal, he stared at her warm eyes, slightly turned up nose, enchanting smile and shining hair. He pulled out his pocket camera and took a couple of photographs, before she took the camera from his hand and returned the favour.

'I'm going to take more pictures of you this weekend, Saoirse. By next weekend …'

'Hey, please don't talk about next weekend. This is this weekend. Let's stay in the present.'

They carried on towards Newcastle, just a few minutes down the road. A nice bed and breakfast would have suited them fine. But as they entered town Thomas spotted a sign pointing towards the Slieve Donard Hotel. He turned left and they drove towards a large, four-storey, redbrick Victorian building set amid spacious grounds.

'How does this look?'

'Isn't it a bit posh?'

'Does that make you uncomfortable?'

'No, but…'

'Then let's have a look.'

'Yes, sir, we have a number of rooms available,' the receptionist said, showing him a list of options.

'The Executive Double. May we have a look at it, please?'

'Of course.' The receptionist gave him a key. 'Third floor, sir.'

The room was large, richly decorated and furnished in deep reds and browns. Besides a big comfortable-looking bed there was a sitting area with a sofa and two armchairs. The view was out over the sea. He could tell from Saoirse's expression that she was as delighted as he was.

When he had registered and they had brought their bags to the room, she jumped onto the big bed.

'Oh yes, this will do just fine. Come here.'

They snuggled against each other on top of the duvet. He started to caress her face, arms, and legs, while she responded with contented sighs. But just as he thought they might stay there for the rest of the afternoon, she laughed and pulled away.

'Lots of time for that later. Let's go for a walk on the beach.'

A sandy lane beside the hotel led down to the wide beach. There was a scattering of people there, some with little children, as well as a family with a frisky black Labrador. The sea lapped gently onto the shore. What looked like a fishing boat cruised slowly several hundred yards offshore. In the distance they could see a large ship, possibly headed up the coast to Belfast. They walked down the beach hand in hand. Occasionally Saoirse bent down to pick up a small shell. She found a pretty one, undamaged, with a reddish tint to it. After brushing off the sand, she gave it to Thomas.

'For you. A souvenir.'

The walk came to an end where a stream cut through the beach, blocking their way. They went back along Main Street where a shop featuring hand-knitted sweaters caught their attention. He looked at an off-white Irish knit; she was drawn towards a sweater in a warm reddish-brown.

'Let's take them, my love. Then we'll both know that the other is keeping warm.'

She looked at the price tag.

'Thomas, isn't this a bit expensive?'

'Not today it isn't.'

She gave in easily and the sales assistant was delighted with her two late-afternoon sales. Back on the street Saoirse gave him a big hug.

'Thank you, my love.'

They approached the hotel as the sun was starting to set.

'I'm going to call my mother first. First time I will have called this number.'

She took a slip of paper from her purse and dialled.

'Hi Mam. It's me. We're in Newcastle, just back from a walk along the beach. It's lovely here. How are you, and any news on da?'

There were a number of 'uh huhs' and 'okays' while she listened.

'Well, that's good… No, Claire and I found a lovely little bed and breakfast near the centre of town. It's wonderful to spend some time with her again… Yes, she's fine.' Saoirse winked at Thomas. 'Can you put Kevin on, please, if he's there? … Hi, Kevin. Would you note down this number?'

She dictated the hotel number and the room number.

'I told mam I was at a bed and breakfast with Claire, so don't give anything away. … Okay, thanks. See you tomorrow.'

She put the phone back down.

'I'm going to take a bath, make myself look beautiful and put on this wonderful new sweater.'

'What do you mean, "make myself look beautiful"?'

'You'll see.'

She pulled off her clothes and disappeared into the bathroom with her small beauty case. Thomas stared out over the darkening sea and leafed through a hotel magazine, trying hard not to think that this sort of weekend might never again return. His only recourse was to read the magazine cover-to-cover as he listened to the bath water being drawn and, eventually, disappear down the drain.

Saoirse re-emerged.

'You look stunning.'

'I'm not done or even dressed yet.'

'Okay, I'll take a shower and see what I can do about myself.'

When he came out of the bathroom, he again couldn't stop looking at her. She did not normally use makeup, but now her grey-green eyes looked even more alluring, enhanced by a subtle application of eye shadow and mascara. Her gleaming hair fell like a waterfall over her shoulders and the new sweater, which matched the skirt below perfectly.

He dressed in his best trousers and a freshly ironed shirt under the new sweater.

'May I escort you to the bar for a drink before dinner?'

There were about a dozen people there: several couples and a group of older men. Thomas ordered a wine; after pondering the matter for a moment Saoirse said, 'I've always wanted to try a Daiquiri. It just sounds so exotic.'

They talked about their first meeting; they laughed as she admitted she had taken him for a naïve Yank, and how he had seen only an attractive barmaid. They reminisced about the times they had spent together.

Drinks emptied, they went into the elegant dining room. After carefully examining the menu, they chose the chef's special. He saw how the candle on the table reflected in Saoirse's eyes. Though they had agreed not to speak the word, this was a farewell dinner.

'So what's the first thing you're going to do when you get back to Boston?'

'First thing? Let me see... Probably write you a letter.'

'Okay. The second thing then.'

'I'll have to stock up on food and stuff. Then I'll see what I want to do. I don't know, really. Talk with David, of course, and see what the *Tribune* has for me. Maybe contact INN, get to be a television personality? That way you'd be able to watch me on the telly.'

'Well that would be nice.'

'But whatever I do, I will find a reason to come back to Belfast, or Dublin, wherever you are. I'm not going to let you go.'

'As long as you write.'

'I will, I promise.'

'You know,' he went on, 'one of those boys at the school said he didn't know when I asked them what their dreams for the future were. I thought that very sad. Now I'm being just as vague. Did it sound sad?'

She looked at him gently. 'No, my love. It just sounds as if you're searching, that's all. And that's okay, in fact it's good.'

'I guess you're right.'

'So what shall we do tomorrow? What do you think of a drive through the mountains, if the weather is still this good?'

'That would be great.'

Back in the room, he started to say something. 'Saoirse, I…'

She was stripping off her clothes, and stopped whatever he was about to say with a gesture.

'Just take off your clothes.'

She dived into the bed and lay there, smiling invitingly.

When he woke up, Saoirse was just emerging from the bathroom, freshly showered. 'Hiya, sleepy.'

'How about a proper "good morning"? Come on back into bed for a while, just a while, please?'

'How about you getting up, my love. They claim to do a smashing breakfast here. Let's not miss it.'

'Ahhh …'

'Ahhh nothing. Come on now. It's a beautiful day. Out you get.'

Realising that his pleas had been brushed aside, he got out, put his arms around her warm, naked body and gave her a long kiss while his hands did their best to entice her back to bed.

'You're so strict. Where is that coming from?'

'That's right, sometimes I am strict. Now get yourself showered and I'll make you a cup of coffee.'

She gave him a playful slap on the behind and, grumbling and smiling simultaneously, he went into the bathroom.

They were downstairs by a quarter past ten and enjoyed a full cooked breakfast while looking out into deep blue skies, broken by just a few white clouds hurrying by. Neither could think of much to say; both were still enjoying the memory of a magical night.

'Now you know, my darling, you're very good at pushing my buttons – all the right ones,' she whispered to him.

'With that smile alone you're pushing one of mine right now.'

'All right, I'll stop smiling. Finish your breakfast,' she ordered, still smiling.

An hour later they threw their bags into the back of the car and headed south along the coast. They turned right to skirt the Mourne Mountains along the southern flank and found a place to park the car that gave access to a footpath. Given the recent rains it was surprisingly dry, so they set off across the barren but beautiful mountainside. A flock of sheep stared as they walked by. They got to a point where they had a magnificent view of the sea on one side, and a long reservoir on the other. They sat down on a rocky outcrop and looked at the traces of snow further up the mountain.

'I was hoping for a snowball fight. Darn,' grinned Saoirse.

'Well then, you'll just have to visit Boston. There's often lots of snow there.'

They pointed out various highlights in the panorama in front of them.

After a few minutes she shivered. 'Brrrr. Now I'm getting cold. We'd better start down again.'

They drove a narrow, empty road through the mountains. Once back into farmland, they went on to Newry, a town that, Thomas knew, had seen its share of violence. He parked the car near a small, stout cathedral and beside a pretty little park.

A small restaurant provided hot soup and a sandwich.

After they had ordered, Saoirse, with a more serious expression and a deep breath, launched into what she had clearly planned to say.

'Thomas, this has been a wonderful weekend. I'll never ever forget it.'

He felt something coming, something inevitable.

'When we get back to the hotel, I'm going to say – well, not goodbye, but *au revoir*. This has been the perfect way to end this chapter. I don't want to spoil it by trying to engage in another goodbye tomorrow or Tuesday.'

'I understand. I'm not sure I like what you're saying, but I guess you're right.'

'We have so many wonderful shared memories now. Let's take our leave on this high note.' She reached out and took both his hands in hers, exploring his face intently. 'I love you, Thomas. Remember that.'

He nodded, suppressing his emotions. He saw that she was having a similar struggle.

'I love you. I'll never forget you and I *will* see you again,' he said.

They held each other's gaze for a long while, in silence.

They drove through Banbridge and Dromore and Lisburn. He caught a glimpse of the gloomy outline of the Maze. The light was fading when they pulled up in the hotel's parking lot.

Pulling her case out of the back he said, 'Come into the hotel, just for a few minutes. I haven't given you my address and telephone number in Boston. I have yours and I'll probably be the first to write but I want you to have them.'

'Okay, but just for a minute. Don't try to seduce me into going to your room.'

'I wish.'

He got a piece of paper and a pen from reception, wrote down his contact details and gave them to her. She put the paper into her handbag carefully.

'Now, will you let me walk you to the taxi rank?'

'Of course.'

When they got there, they exchanged quick goodbye-for-nows and a last hug. The door closed on Saoirse; the taxi moved off. He stood there until it disappeared, having caught a glimpse of the tears that she had tried so hard to hold back for the last few hours.

He wondered if he really would see her again. Or would this be like the summer romances he had heard friends talking about, romances that ended with lots of promises followed by... nothing.

The next evening he took a taxi to O'Flynn's pub, some distance from the city centre. Like the Grange, it lacked windows. The name of the pub was painted in faded letters, and a Guinness sign above the door was the only indication that it was a pub at all. The door was locked. Thomas knocked. When it opened he found himself facing two tough-looking men in their mid-thirties. Not being able to say whom he was meeting he just gave his own name, which was enough for him to be allowed to enter. It was smaller than most pubs and supplied fewer brands of beer and whiskey. The bar had room for perhaps ten men and there were four tables off to the side. The decoration was minimal but there was an Irish tricolour on the back wall. All eyes seemed to be focused on him. Thomas wondered what he had walked into this time. He ordered a pint of Guinness and stood at the bar, wondering who would come to greet him.

After a few minutes a man of about 50 walked up. He looked rugged, and as if he had not shaved in several days.

'Cassidy?'

'Yes, that's me.'

'Come over to a table.'

The man led him to the farthest corner. Thomas noticed that the other dozen or so patrons were watching carefully.

'Cassidy, I don't want you to tell anyone you were here. Clear?'

'Yes, agreed.'

'Okay, I'll accept your word. Now I understand that you know about Niall Kelly through his family, right?'

'That's right. But I'm not here for them; I'm here as a journalist trying to understand what's going on in Belfast, and the North.'

'Okay,' the man said. 'It's best if you keep your journalist hat on and not tell the family anything. I know that may be tough, but it's better for all concerned. And of course you won't mention the name of the pub or my name – which I won't tell you anyway – in anything you may write.'

'Also agreed.'

'Then here's what I'm willing and able to tell you. Kelly was with us, first of all.'

'I think his family suspect that but they don't know for sure.'

'The fewer people know, the better it is for everyone. Now, Kelly was shot by two men associated with the UVF not because he was with the IRA but because his family defied their orders to move out. But Kelly was with us so it became our business. He was a good man and we were sorry to lose him. Those two men have since been eliminated.'

Thomas nodded.

The man continued. 'You have to understand that the IRA is not only at war with the UVF and other violent Protestant groups, but also with Republicans who go their own way, like members of the INLA and individuals who step over the boundaries. The IRA depends on strong internal discipline.'

'Yes, I think I understand the need. But how is this related to...'

'I'm getting to that. Kelly told us a number of years ago that two men had terrorised his sister. Cassidy, we do not terrorise young women. What was she, 21 or 22 at the time?'

'Yes, something like that.'

'So those two men were IRA but they were renegades. Our own internal discipline unit found them and, well, let me just say they're still suffering the consequences.'

Thomas took a deep breath and swallowed a draught of his Guinness.

'That sure explains why the harassment wasn't continued. Thank you for telling me this.'

'Is that all that you came here to learn?'

'Yes, in a way it is. But now, just as a journalist, one more question.

You live in the midst of pretty extreme violence. It affects the IRA and the paramilitaries from the other side, but also thousands of people who have no direct link with any paramilitary organisation. What will it take to end this cycle of violence which just seems to go and on in Northern Ireland?'

The man smiled. 'Cassidy, I understand you've been in Belfast for two months now. You should know the answer to that question yourself. It'll end when the government, and the various Protestant groups, recognise the equal rights of Catholics when it comes to jobs, housing and political representation. It will end when Catholics are no longer the victims of the diabolical discrimination and repression inflicted by the Protestants. And not before then.'

Thomas reached out to shake his hand. 'Thank you, sir, for your time, your frankness and your openness. I appreciate it.'

'You're welcome, Cassidy.' He called out to the man behind the bar, 'Seamus, would you call a taxi for our guest here?' and got up to leave the table. Thomas finished his Guinness while waiting the ten minutes or so until his taxi was announced.

Tuesday was spent writing a final despatch and preparing for departure. He also hand-wrote a short letter to Saoirse:

My darling Saoirse,
Maybe even more quickly than you expected: a first note from me. I hope you are well and that things are looking up for your father.

I'm keeping busy, but when I think of you it's as if I were lifting off on a magic carpet, moving through time and space to Newcastle, and the many other moments we shared.

In a way I will be relieved to leave Belfast now. It's hard to be here and know that you are just a couple of miles away, literally, but also so far.

I do love you and of all my memories of Belfast, those that connect us will remain the most powerful.

Early on Wednesday morning he took the train to Dublin, memories of his last evening in Belfast at O'Flynn's still in his mind. He had certainly gained further insight into the convoluted ways things worked behind the scenes and was grateful for that. It also bothered him that so much of what he had learned – about Dermot and Niall – which directly affected Saoirse and her family had to be kept secret from them, for their own good and peace of mind.

A taxi took him to Dublin airport, where he boarded an Aer Lingus 747. Ridiculously, he thought, it flew low over Ireland to land only twenty minutes later at Shannon Airport, where passengers were invited to make use of the extensive tax-free shops. Thomas bought a Bushmills whiskey for himself and Irish chocolates for his parents, whom he planned to visit for Thanksgiving. After the 747 had lifted off again it was just over six hours to Boston's Logan Airport.

Two months in Belfast had changed his life, both personally and professionally. He remembered telling Rupert that he had come to find his journalistic style and voice. He had certainly done that and was extremely happy with this development. He had not expected that he would change as a person but he had. Father Donald rarely intruded anymore, and he had met what he could only call the love of his life, or maybe his soul mate. He would have liked to have more certainty about it, but he was confident that in one way or another Saoirse would always be a part of his life.

CHAPTER 19

He arrived in his cold apartment in Cambridge in the late afternoon. It did not feel like home anymore. For the next few days he could not think constructively about the future so he walked around familiar parts of Cambridge and Boston and met up with several old friends. But they belonged to his past and their company did little to relieve his sense of loneliness.

His body had flown back to Boston, but he had left his heart behind.

He had agreed with David that he would take a few days' leave and wrote to Saoirse almost every day. He read that the IRA had launched a bombing offensive in various cities and towns, including Belfast, injuring dozens. Two weeks later another fourteen explosions were reported, followed the next day by eleven further attacks.

Worried, he picked up his phone and called at a time when he thought Saoirse might be home.

'Hi my love,' she began, and continued before he could ask anything. 'I'm glad you called, but I have bad news. Da died of a massive stroke two days ago.' She sounded subdued but in control.

Thomas fell quiet for a moment. 'How are you bearing up?'

'I'm sort of okay, I guess. There's so much to plan and organise; the funeral is the day after tomorrow. But… I am very sad and I think, if only I had…' Her voice trailed off. 'But maybe it's a blessing. Half-paralysed and unable to speak – that was dreadful too.'

'I'll be thinking of you, my darling. And please pass my condolences on to your mother and Kevin.'

'Thank you, I will. I miss you.'

'I miss you too. Take care of yourself.'

He immediately sat down to write a letter, but after ten minutes he hurled the pen across the room in frustration at not being able to be there for her and with her. He ordered flowers to be delivered to Saoirse's mother's address before heading to the office, where he wondered what he could write about the human tragedy that had unfolded in the mass suicide in Jonestown, Guyana. It felt as if his pen had run dry.

He finished an article based on what he had discovered during his brief visit to O'Flynn's pub. He looked into the scope of the problem with Vietnam veterans suffering from PTSD and what the government was doing about it. He visited two Veterans Administration facilities in Boston and spoke with several veterans. He was not reassured by what he uncovered, in spite of the hospitals' attempts to put as positive a face as possible on their work. He wrote a strongly worded editorial, which David accepted, much to Thomas' surprise, and felt his sense of mission becoming ever stronger: he had to become a strong voice for the people. He was delighted when the VA issued a defensive statement; at least they had noticed and taken it seriously enough to say something, however inadequate, in reply.

He received a short letter from Special Agent Sweeney of Special Branch, sent care of the newspaper. Sweeney wrote that Padraig O'Shea, a commander within the INLA and the man whom Thomas had identified as 'Mr Brannon', had died in a shootout with Special Branch officers. It was probable that O'Shea had been directly involved in the killing of Dermot McAllister and the warnings directed at Thomas himself, but that could never be proven. Sweeney thanked Thomas for his assistance in the matter.

Thomas did not feel like celebrating the news; instead he poured himself a generous portion of whiskey when he got home, feeling oddly depressed, though he certainly could not mourn for this O'Shea person.

He spent Thanksgiving at his parents' home near Philadelphia. It was painful, as he had expected, because nobody spoke about anything of consequence and he felt no connection with his parents, nor could he sense any between them. He swore to himself that he would never be caught in a relationship like that, even as he remembered that Saoirse had once accused him of being as difficult to open up as a clam.

In Boston there was enough work to keep him occupied and he enrolled in a creative writing evening course, to start in January.

Saoirse wrote that her mother was indeed moving to her sister's home near Strabane, and that she had already visited Dublin to explore educational and job opportunities.

In January he received the news that Owen had arrived in the States and was staying with a family in the suburb of Brookline, about four miles south of Cambridge. The next weekend he drove down to visit.

The host family was warm and friendly. It included a boy half a year younger than Owen and a girl a year or two older. Owen looked terrific and his limp was barely noticeable. He thanked Thomas warmly for having played a role in his temporary move to Boston and said he had already registered into the senior year at high school.

'Has Owen talked about the cause of his limp at all?' Thomas asked the parents.

Kenneth, the father, replied. 'We had been told that something dramatic had happened to Owen. Robert didn't know, so one day he asked Owen about the limp. Owen told his story very openly. Robert was stunned, as were we when we first read about the beating. I think it was good that Owen was able to tell us everything; it showed that he had come to trust us. And he and Robert have already become great pals.'

'That's wonderful to know. Thank you so much for taking Owen in.'

They all agreed to stay in touch and Thomas left feeling a deeper sense of satisfaction than merely writing an article, however well received, had ever given him.

In the creative writing group he met an attractive woman called Ellen. Petite, slim, blond and blue-eyed, she pursued Thomas aggressively. They dated. Her conversation was lively and they talked a lot about the challenges of writing. She was focusing on short stories, several of which she let him read. He let Ellen read a couple of draft chapters of a novel he was working on. He told her about his two months in Belfast but said nothing about Saoirse.

A month after they met he spent the night in her apartment. While it was sexually satisfying, he felt guilty; it was as if he were betraying Saoirse as well as Ellen.

What am I doing? he asked himself again and again. He loved Saoirse, and though they had agreed to move on, it didn't feel right at all. He asked himself how he could spend a night with Ellen and the next evening write an affectionate letter to Saoirse.

The sense of double betrayal continued to haunt him. He hoped it would pass, but it didn't. He also never felt able to tell Ellen about the abuse. For that reason too there was a barrier between them. It was clear that the relationship with Ellen could go nowhere and he struggled with the question of how to end it. She had done absolutely nothing wrong, after all.

A month later Saoirse wrote:
'I just got back from two days in Dublin and I'm so very excited! I found a small apartment, two part-time jobs and an evening course in psychology. I'm moving down in two weeks. I'll be working in a kindergarten and on the children's ward at St Vincent's Hospital. I even talked with the admissions officer at Trinity. Thomas, I just can't tell you what a relief it will be to get out of Belfast and have an opportunity to build my own life at last. I'm free! I'm very happy, and hope that you are too.'

Thomas thought immediately about when he might be able to visit to see for himself. He started avoiding Ellen, and wondered how he would tell her he needed to break off the short relationship. He couldn't continue giving his heart to Saoirse while pretending to feel something for Ellen.

A few months later Saoirse wrote that she had met a young man who was doing very well in the IT industry, then starting to flourish in Ireland. She wrote that Brian was witty, charming and intelligent. Though she couldn't see him often, given her hectic schedule, when they did go out for a drink or dinner she enjoyed the breaks and had a good time.

The news upset Thomas. He had never felt jealousy so intensely. He knew he should be happy for her but he could not feel it. He did not want to lose her. He should be wishing her joy and happiness in this new relationship. Hadn't they talked about that during the Newcastle weekend? Though he wondered if he was doing the right thing, he wrote that he wanted to visit Dublin in July if she could free up a week.

To his relief and his surprise, she replied that she could, and would be delighted to see him again. But he never ceased questioning whether it was the right thing to do, for him and for her. What did it mean, that she had written with apparent enthusiasm about Brian while also welcoming news of his visit?

CHAPTER 20

Thomas arrived in Dublin on a Friday at the end of July. Kindergarten was closed, Saoirse's course was suspended for the month and she had arranged a week off from the hospital. As Saoirse's apartment contained only a single bed he had booked Buswells Hotel. Just off Kildare Street, built into a row of old townhouses, he knew it from the nights he had spent there before and after meeting Charles Haughey. The bedroom was elegant, though small compared with spacious American hotel rooms.

It was 9:30 in the evening when Saoirse walked into the small Georgian lobby. She had cut her hair, which now fell just to her shoulders. She looked terrific but tired. They held each other in a long embrace before saying anything. It had been almost eight months since they had seen each other.

'Hi, my darling. It's so wonderful to see you and to hold you again.'

'Hiya, my love,' she replied with her warm smile.

'What are you able for this evening?' he asked.

'Ah, still got some of the Irish way with words, have ye? Well, let's go out for a drink, but not for too long because I'm exhausted. I've been going non-stop since I arrived here. There are some pubs just two streets over.'

They dropped her suitcase in his room and found the Duke, which was very busy. It was too noisy for an intimate conversation so they made do with looking at each other, holding hands, and small talk. After a single drink the noise became too much and they returned to the hotel, and his room.

'Now, I have a surprise for you. You don't have to do anything. Just get undressed, lie face down and relax,' Thomas instructed.

'What are you going to do?'

'Trust me. You'll see.'

He stripped to his shorts as well.

When she had followed his instructions he opened the bottle of fragrant massage oil he had brought with him, warmed a few drops in his hands and started to knead her shoulders and the back of her neck.

'Oh, that feels so good. This is a wonderful surprise. When did you learn to do this?'

'This is my first lesson.'

He stayed around the neck and shoulders because even his untrained hands felt a lot of tightness there, confirmed by the fact that she let out a brief 'ouch' a couple of times, though he was trying to be very gentle. He worked his way slowly down her spine and back.

'How do you feel now?' he asked when he thought he had just about finished.

'Reborn,' she replied as she rolled over, eyes shining brightly again. 'Can you do that on the front as well?'

'Let's see,' he replied.

He started with the forehead, the temples, the cheekbones and the collarbones before going on to her breasts and abdomen. Saoirse had a hard time lying still and squirmed with pleasure, emitting satisfied little sighs and moans. Though focusing on providing a satisfying massage he felt himself becoming very hard.

'That's not very professional,' Saoirse commented with a laugh.

'I'm not a professional. As I said, this is only my first time doing this.'

'I'd prefer if you stayed unprofessional, then. I didn't think I'd be able for more than a quiet chat tonight, but you've just changed that.' She reached up, grabbed his buttocks and pulled Thomas down on top of her. Thomas abandoned his role as masseur and kissed her passionately. Their bodies writhed with pleasure and they made love eagerly.

Afterwards Saoirse cuddled in closely and said, 'That was the most wonderful surprise I could have imagined. I love you, I've missed you, and now I think I can sleep like a baby.'

'That'll be two sleeping babies then.'

He kissed her closed eyes and within five minutes could hear the regular breathing of sleep, just before he too drifted off.

It was almost nine o'clock when he opened his eyes again and saw Saoirse still fast asleep. Waking up to find her beside him was once again a magical moment. He was back where he belonged.

Almost half an hour later she woke up and looked at him with sleepy grey-green eyes.

They continued to lie there, side by side, looking at each other, giggling at silly comments, smiling, embracing, kissing. It was 10:30 by the time they got up, drew back the curtains, and let the sunlight into the room.

'What would you like to do today?' he asked.

'How about Bewley's Café for a late breakfast and then a stroll through the park, for starters.'

They walked the few minutes to Grafton Street and the busy landmark café.

He told her about his recent newspaper assignments, the creative writing course and his attempts to begin a novel.

'What is it going to be about? You mentioned something but didn't go into it.'

'Well, it's sort of about you.'

She looked shocked. 'You can't be serious.'

'No, I'm kidding. The setting is Derry in the middle of the Troubles and there is a woman in it who sounds and looks a lot like you. It's about people trying to make sense of their lives and in that way it's also a little bit about me.'

'Did you bring any of it with you?'

'No, I didn't.'

'Will you send me a chapter?'

'Sure...'

He reached out a hand and clasped hers.

'I have missed you so much.'

'But you don't have to miss me, not this week. Come on, finish your breakfast and we'll go walk in the sunshine.'

They walked up Grafton Street and into St Stephen's Green. The sun was warm. Flowerbeds gushed with colourful blooms, the fountains sparkled, and brightly dressed people were spread over the spacious lawns. It was an oasis in the heart of the busy city. He had been there once before, alone, but everything seemed much more alive now. They walked slowly along the paths, admiring the colours, the sounds and the people. Thomas knelt down for a close-up photograph of several ducks waddling on the path, to which one duck responded by snapping aggressively at the camera.

'Is this a Protestant duck from the North do you think?'

She laughed. 'Why Protestant? Catholic ducks are pretty aggressive too, you know.'

They quickly claimed a bench in the sunshine when another couple abandoned it.

She filled him in on what she had not told him in letters about her two jobs and the psychology course, and updated him on her mother and brother, both of whom were doing well, all things considered.

'I'm exhausted from doing so much and having to rush around the city every day by bus. But you know what's really great about being here?'

'What's that then?'

'I can do everything I want and need to do, without anyone depending on me. I feel truly free for the first time in my life.'

'Saoirse has finally found freedom, huh?'

'Yes she has and doesn't ever want to let it go. You know, when you left last November part of me wished so much that I were sitting beside you in that airplane. I really wanted to get away. But now I'm very happy to be here in Dublin.'

'Great. Have you been in touch with Colin? Do you miss Foyle's?'

'I called him a few weeks ago. He's grand, says he misses me and that clients are still asking when I'll be back. As to whether I miss it: I miss the singing, but not the work behind the bar, and certainly not Belfast.'

'Do you ever get a chance to sing now?'

'No, I don't.'

'Maybe we can find a place where you can sing for me this week.'

They continued their stroll through the park and then walked down Dawson Street towards Trinity College.

'Here is where I hope to study. Isn't it beautiful?' she said as they passed through the impressive main gate to the quiet quads.

'Will you start in September?'

She stopped, turned to face him, and with a triumphant expression announced, 'I've been admitted!'

'That's wonderful. Congratulations. But then why did you just say you "hoped" to study here?'

'I'm not sure I can afford it yet. I can get a scholarship and a loan. But even then... I can't afford to give up my two jobs. I might be able to keep the one at the hospital. I'll get there, but maybe not just yet.'

'You'll get there, I know you will.'

She led him towards the entrance to the Trinity College Library, and the Book of Kells.

"Oh Thomas, I feel so excited about coming here every day. Everything about Trinity is so beautiful.'

The next stop was a restaurant, where they discussed what they might do over the coming days.

'We could go into the Wicklow Mountains and Glendalough. I'd like to see Howth, and we could visit Maynooth and the Hill of Tara,' she suggested.

'They all sound good.' he agreed. 'I'd thought of renting a car and going west towards Galway and into County Clare. That's where my grandfather came from.'

'That would be lovely too. In Clare there's a village called Doolin, where there's always lots of wonderful traditional music.'

She finished her soup before asking, 'Are you happy, back in Boston, with your work and your course and your life?'

He was silent for a few moments.

'Yes,' he finally said, 'and no.'

'What does that mean?'

'It means that work is okay, but I have not been as excited about it as I was in Belfast. I'm not connecting with people the way I was able to do in Belfast. The assignments are too short for that. The writing course is fine, but with my novel … I'm really struggling.'

Saoirse took his hand in hers and asked, softly, 'Have you met someone else?'

'Yes, but that's over already,' he replied, looking straight back into her eyes.

She remained silent and took a bite out of her sandwich, waiting for him to go on.

'Her name was Ellen. I met her on the writing course. She was very lively and I liked her. But it's over.'

'Why?'

'She… she wasn't my type, I guess. It was fun for a while, but I couldn't see it developing into a real relationship.'

Wanting to change the subject as quickly as possible, he asked, 'How is it going with Brian?'

'It's all right I guess. But…'

She let out a sigh. She opened her mouth slightly and drew in short breaths before continuing.

'I do wonder, Thomas, whether what we're doing right now is right, for either of us. What we had and what we still have is wonderful. But we just can't build our futures on it.'

Another long silence followed until Saoirse continued.

'Seeing you now again, I know I still love you. Feeling you inside me again last night was wonderful. But… oh shit. I just don't know how to deal with this.'

He remained silent, taking her hand and looking into her eyes.

'Thomas, it's been so hard sometimes not being able to see you and talk to you, and now it's also so hard to be with you, knowing that it has to end again.'

'Does it? Does it really have to end?'

'God, Thomas! Don't be so... so... You just said you broke if off with Ellen because you couldn't see it developing into a real relationship. Don't you see that this can't either?'

Her eyes started to fill.

'We do have a real relationship, my darling. We're here, we're together, and we both love each other. That's what counts. Right now, this moment. Let's stay here and now while we can.'

She managed a smile and nodded her head. 'We can't stay gloomy for a week about what can't be. Okay.'

Threatening clouds had covered the sky. The conversation had also turned sombre.

'Where is the Savoy cinema?' he asked.

'It's a ten or fifteen minute walk up O'Connell Street. Why?'

'I saw a sign on a bus advertising the movie *Watership Down*. Let's go see it, unless you've seen it already.'

'That's a surprise, and no, I haven't. Okay, let's see if we can get there before it starts to rain.'

They arrived 45 minutes before the next showing and waited with a glass of wine in a nearby pub before going in. In the cinema they sat like two teenagers, in each other's arms, she resting her head on his shoulder for much of the time.

When they emerged the streets were wet and glistening in the sunshine that had followed the rain.

'So even in a rabbit world there is conflict and bloodshed. It reminded me a little of the North,' Saoirse reflected.

They felt more peaceful and more at ease again as they walked back south towards the Liffey. They went for another drink in an ornate pub called the Bank.

'Okay, so what will we do this week?'

'I want us to have a wonderful time. And, though I don't want to get all serious again, we both know we have to create an ending of some sorts, a closure.'

'Do you have a suggestion?'

'Yes. We rent a car tomorrow and drive west to County Clare. We see beautiful things, we listen to beautiful music and we laugh a lot. Next weekend we say loving goodbyes and let each other go.'

He couldn't prevent the pained expression flashed over his face.

'That's what we have to do, Thomas.'

'I just don't believe it has to be that way. I feel like I've come home now. I love you…'

'I love you too, Thomas,' Saoirse interrupted. 'It's because we love each other that we have to let each other go.' She held Thomas's hands in hers and looked straight into his eyes. 'But now that I've said that, it sounds so stupid.'

He felt the pressure and struggled to find the best words. He knew that she was right but found it almost impossible to accept it.

'Yes, it does sound stupid, but okay. Let's try,' he said reluctantly.

She forced a smile. 'Okay, and we won't repeat a difficult conversation we had last November. Let's go to a place where we can have a smashing dinner. Follow me.'

She led him to Il Posto, on St Stephens Green. They dined, talked and laughed again before returning to Buswells and a wonderful night in each other's arms.

It was early afternoon when they approached Galway. They turned south to the tiny village of Ballyvaughan, where they found a small hotel.

For the next couple of days they behaved much like any other vacationers, first exploring the magical limestone formations of the Burren before going on towards Doolin.

During the drive he asked, 'Will you tell me more about Brian?'

'Oh, okay,' she began, hesitatingly. 'I met him at a friend's place.

He's quite good-looking and certainly intelligent. He's witty and can be charming. He laughs easily. He's very independent. He doesn't need me in a way that makes demands of me. He leaves me free to pursue my own things.'

Thomas flinched, and gripped the steering wheel more tightly. There it was again: if he were to settle in Dublin, knowing no one, he would need her and to some extent be dependent on her.

'And do you…?' Thomas didn't know how to put his question properly.

'Do I love him?'

'Yeah, something like that.'

'Oh shit, Thomas! What do you want to hear? But honestly, if I knew for sure that I did, would I be sitting here with you now?'

'No, I guess not.'

'I like him and find him very attractive. Maybe I could love him if I opened myself up in that way to him. But… I have to really let you go first.' She looked out at the passing countryside, her expression serious, and then looked directly at him again. 'I still love you, damn it.'

Doolin's reputation had made it a popular place but they found a bed and breakfast in the lower village, beside a stream flowing into the ocean. Saoirse was delighted that Gus O'Connor's pub was just a few minutes' walk down the road.

'We've got to go there tonight,' she said, bubbling with enthusiasm. 'It's one of the most famous music pubs in Ireland.'

They were fortunate that the legendary Micho Russell, who drew magical sounds from a simple tin whistle, was performing with his friends that evening.

The next morning they took a ferry across the choppy waters at the mouth of Galway Bay to Inishmore, the largest of the Aran Islands. In the tiny fishing village of Kilronan they rented bicycles, with Saoirse showing off her best Irish, though differences in dialect restricted communication. Nevertheless, she was delighted and so was the man in the bike hire shop.

They struggled up the steep hills and made their way to a large, ancient ring fort from where there were stunning views over the sea back to the mainland.

'Who built this huge place, and what was it for?' Thomas asked.

'I don't think anyone knows. It's just another of those places in Ireland which is shrouded in mystery.'

'I count four walls in concentric half rings. They make me think of the walls people put up around themselves, to protect themselves. Like so many people I spoke with last year: adults, teenagers, some of the children at the centre…'

'And a bit like you, my love?'

That had not been a question and Thomas didn't answer, which was answer enough. They looked out over the deep blue waters, flecked with the white foam of breaking waves, in silence.

That evening they went to McDermott's pub. It was packed with a younger crowd who looked like college students on vacation. The musicians were also younger and had a repertoire of what was described as 'fusion': traditional Irish mixed with modern rhythms. During a break Saoirse approached two of them. Thomas heard her speak Irish and saw the musicians nod. When the session began again, she was introduced as a special guest and sang 'Eibhlin A Rún', which Thomas had understood as 'Aileen Aroon' so long ago in Belfast. She was in great form in spite of not having sung in many months. Later she explained that the song was about a secret love.

She consulted the musicians again. He saw them shake their heads and then nod. She announced that she was going to sing a special song for a special friend and excused herself to the audience for the fact that it was not an Irish song at all. Accompanied by a few chords from a guitar, she sang 'Help me make it through the night'. Only at the end did she look straight at Thomas. When she sat down she squeezed his hand and gave him a look which said, 'I meant what I just sang.'

'I know you did.'

Saoirse opened the windows wide to let in mild morning air.

'Okay. Something tells me this is a good day to wear jeans and an old shirt.'

'Why's that?'

She smiled at him mysteriously until he agreed.

They drove several miles south to a parking area where a sign pointed up the coastal hill towards the Cliffs of Moher. At the end of the path they were met by magnificent views over the ocean, the distant Aran Islands and the surf pounding on the rocks many hundreds of feet below. Lying flat on the grass they peered over the edge. Seabirds with nests on the cliffs swooped down and back up. A boatful of tourists moved slowly along the sea line.

An old watchtower stood on one of the highest points. 'What were people on the lookout for?' he asked.

'I have no idea The English? The Spanish? Who knows? There was always someone to be on the lookout for.'

Continuing south after lunch, just beyond the tiny hamlet of Spanish Point, they came upon a small, almost deserted beach.

'Perfect!' Saoirse cried.

They walked to the beach with a towel she had taken from their B&B, took off their shoes and felt the sand between their toes.

'Do you remember that Sunday at the beginning of October? At Helen's Bay?' she asked?

'Sure.'

'Do you remember what I asked you?'

'You mean something about going in deep with you?'

'Good. You remember.'

They walked down the beach towards a place where the sand was broken by large rocks. She led him very gradually into the water. It sloshed around their ankles, their calves and then their knees. At first it felt cold but as they got used to it, it was refreshing. She bent down and splashed a little water up at his face.

She took his hand and stepped boldly out from shore a couple of paces, Thomas following. They were up to their thighs in the water. Her slim jeans, glistening from the water, stuck against her skin.

'You look damn sexy, know that?'

Saoirse laughed.

'I never did this when I was a child. I had to wear bathing trunks to go into the water,' he confessed.

'That doesn't surprise me a bit. And how does it feel?'

'Silly, stupid, and fun.'

'I like it when you allow yourself to be silly.'

She flung her arms around him and pulled him close. The little waves folded around them. Her lips found his. They drew apart, smiling at each other with growing desire.

'Do you think it's possible to make love while standing in the surf?' he asked.

'Sure we'd probably be fallin' down and getting drownded,' she answered with an exaggerated accent. 'But now you're getting into the spirit of things.'

He glanced up and down the beach. He couldn't see anybody taking any notice, in fact the closest people were several hundred yards away.

'But you still don't want someone to see you like this, do you?' she teased.

She led him to a flat black rock that little wavelets washed over occasionally.

'Let's sit here and enjoy the waves, the sea, the beach, the sun, the moment.'

They did, and he wondered whether, if she tucked her legs up under her, she might look like the Little Mermaid in Copenhagen.

They sat quietly, arms around each other, occasionally pointing out a small fish or a crab, while seagulls swooped overhead. Aside from their calls and the gentle sound of the ripples on the water they were wrapped in a blissful silence.

The water had drawn up into his T-shirt and Thomas shivered involuntarily.

'We'd better see about warming up,' she said. 'Come on.'

They waded back onto the dry sand and towards the long, soft grass behind the beach. They lay down on the towel. The sun warmed them while the grass waved lazily in the light breeze. He closed his eyes and might easily have drifted off, but then remembered something she had once said, also at Helen's Bay, something she had wanted to do sometime.

Her eyes were closed. He undid the top button of her jeans, slowly pulled the zipper down, and gently slid his hand underneath. She opened her eyes with a surprised smile.

'What are you doing?'

'You told me once there was something you'd like to do someday...'

'Yes, but I never expected you to take me up on that.'

'Neither did I.'

'I do love you this way, Thomas.'

Her hand went to his buttons and after wiggling out of their wet jeans they lay in each other's arms. They rolled towards each other, onto each other, into each other.

The screeching gulls overhead took no notice.

Half an hour later they looked around at blue and yellow flowers and a pretty dark brown and red butterfly. In the distance they heard children's voices and laughter and quickly struggled into their wet clothes.

'Whatever happened to the shy, easily embarrassed man I met at Foyle's?'

'He's been replaced.'

'Good!'

Thomas turned the car heating to high as they drove to the bustling county town, Ennis, and on to Quin and a B&B, where they were happy to get out of their damp clothes. The evening was spent at a lively medieval banquet in Knappogue Castle.

The next morning they visited the ruins of Quin Abbey, almost opposite their B&B. 'Ireland is just crammed with ruins – they're all over the place. They make me wonder whether conflict has always been a feature of this country and leave me amazed at how cheerful and friendly most people manage to be.'

She laughed. 'Even if you spent your whole life trying to understand Ireland and the Irish, you wouldn't. Except maybe that we're usually extremely good at enjoying the moment. So we'll take our example from that.'

The Folk Park beside Bunratty Castle provided impressions of rural Ireland in centuries gone by. He photographed her pretending to pound grains of wheat with a stone pestle on the floor of a small round hovel.

'Must have been a wonderfully simple life back then,' he said.

'Don't you believe it; it was backbreaking.'

For the name alone they couldn't resist dropping in to Durty Nelly's pub, in the shadow of the castle. The sign on the yellow-stuccoed wall described it as 'The Village Inn, Established 1620'. The enthusiastic man who served them lunch told the tale of Durty Nelly.

'She was famous around here, you know. She made the finest poitín in the land. People came from miles around for it.'

'What's poteen?' Thomas asked.

'Now we'd call it whiskey, but miracle cures were reported after people drank a glass of her brew.'

'Do you still serve it?'

'No, it's been outlawed these many years now.'

Ireland, thought Thomas. Mythology keeps this country afloat.

In the village of Adare they dropped their bags in a charming old-fashioned room with a four-poster bed in the Dunraven Arms Hotel and went out to explore. The many interesting little shops drew their attention: shops selling handicrafts, locally woven and knitted clothing, and speciality foods. For dinner they chose a small restaurant in a thatched cottage.

It was still quite early when they arrived back at the hotel and selected a quiet corner in the bar, where they sat looking at each other, as if hoping to catch a glimpse of what was going on under the surface.

'What are you thinking, Thomas?'

'I think you know… This our last evening together… and…'

'Yes it is, for the time being.'

He looked at her silently, desperately, pleadingly.

'Thomas, you will always be a part of my life. I know that.'

'You will always be a part of my life too.'

'Then be happy, my love, with what we have and will always continue to have.'

Thomas let out a deep sigh.

'Please don't be so sad.'

She drew a small package out of her purse and handed it to him. He undid the wrapping carefully and opened the small box. Inside was a silver ring with strange designs that he could not decipher, except for a heart.

'It's a Claddagh ring. Very Irish; it's a token of love. I want you to wear it. Here, it's usually worn on this finger.'

She drew his right hand towards her and slipped the ring onto his middle finger, making sure that the heart pointed towards the fingertip. It fitted perfectly.

'Good. I guessed right.'

'But when did you buy this?'

'This afternoon, in that little handicrafts shop, when you weren't looking.'

'I don't know what to say. Thank you.'

'You can look at it every day and know that I do cherish you, so be happy, please.'

He raised his glass. 'To us, then.'

She raised hers and returned the toast before setting it down and kissing him on the lips. 'Let's go upstairs.'

Without further words they got under the duvet and, in spite of the melancholy gripping them both they made love with great tenderness.

Saoirse fell asleep first, leaving Thomas staring into the darkness. Sleep eventually overtook him. He dreamed. They were at a beach together, in the water. A strong current was pulling him out to sea. As he was drawn further and further away from the shore he tried to call out, but no sounds came from his mouth. He waved an arm above the waves. A small, disappearing figure waved back.

When he opened his eyes he saw her, supporting her head with a hand, smiling down at him.

'Good morning, my love,' she said softly.

He mumbled something that sounded like 'uhmmm'. As the fog of sleep lifted he realised what day it was and what that meant.

'Smile. We still have today.'

She leaned over and kissed him lightly.

Over breakfast Saoirse appeared light-hearted, determined not to let the day be spoiled by sadness and regret.

Roadworks slowed their return to Dublin. But hurrying to get back was the least of their priorities. Navigating with the map on her lap, Saoirse suggested that they detour so they would approach Dublin from the south, through the Wicklow Mountains.

They found their way to Glendalough, with its famous round tower.

After lunch they followed the road over the mountains towards Dublin. It was overcast, but the high clouds did not obstruct the views over the city.

'What will you do first next week, when you're back in Boston?'

'Haven't given it much thought yet. Probably print and frame one of the photographs of you. Of course I'll be thinking of you, and writing to you. And I'll look forward to reading your letters.'

As they entered the southern outskirts of Dublin he asked, 'Shall I drop you off at your place? I'd really like to see it.'

'No, there's nothing to see and I'm not going to let you get lost in Dublin. I'll help you get the car back.'

'Are you sure?'

'Yes, I'm very sure. Now just follow this road. I'll tell you when to turn right.'

It was almost six o'clock when they stopped in front of the car hire agency. They retrieved their cases and stood facing each other on the forecourt.

'Well, this is it for now. I'm going to catch a bus.'

She gave him a long hug. She took his hand and held it. The sunlight caught the ring.

'Remember what this symbolises, Thomas. Be happy. I will write, I promise.'

She smiled, gave him a quick kiss on the lips and picked up her case. She walked down the street without looking back.

His eyes followed her until she turned a corner. He looked down at the ring.

A voice interrupted his thoughts.

'Are you returning the car, sir?'

CHAPTER 21

1983

Four years after his previous lonely return from Dublin, Thomas once again landed at Boston's Logan Airport. This time, however, he was buoyed and excited by the prospect of Briana joining him in just a few weeks. He also kept wondering where Saoirse was, what she was doing and how she was feeling. He still had difficulty dealing with thoughts of her and Brian sharing honeymoon bliss in some luxurious Tuscan hideaway. He was infatuated with Briana and delighted that she had suddenly entered his life, but he still loved Saoirse – he thought. Or was he weirdly disturbed in some way? He couldn't understand his own cocktail of feelings so he did his best to ignore them. To force his thoughts in a more positive direction, he sat down at his typewriter and wrote an enthusiastic letter to Briana, setting out some more activities and places for them to visit. He put away the new shirt and jeans, intending to save them for when she arrived. He was smiling widely when he sat down in his comfortable armchair with a glass of Bushmills, imagining Briana walking around his apartment, circling him as she stripped off one article of clothing after another before pouncing on him like a playful tigress. What a contrast with the day four years before, when he had felt totally unmotivated to do anything at all, except maybe fill a glass with whiskey. The aim then had been to drown his sorrows. It had taken him a week to recover the motivation to move forward.

He had eventually entered into talks with INN. He had also entered into another relationship, with an attractive brunette he met at INN, but that self-destructed after several months. Saoirse had written regularly, first announcing that she had been able to start her degree course at Trinity, then that she had resumed her relationship with Brian. Thomas had dropped out of the creative writing class and suspended work on his novel.

His best journalistic writing had covered the return of the Iran hostages, writing about the impact of the ordeal on the victims and their families. Once again, after obligatory debriefings, and the initial fanfare and welcome-home celebrations, there was only minimal follow-up. He had not even tried to keep a sense of outrage out of these articles.

Some months later Saoirse had written that she had moved into Brian's apartment, which had enabled her to save enough money to buy a small car. He had threatened to sink into a self-pitying funk. The 'what ifs' and 'if onlys' had raged through his mind. They returned in early 1982, when she wrote that she and Brian had become engaged, though the wedding would not take place until after her graduation. In June of 1983 she had announced the wedding date for September 3rd and made it clear that she expected Thomas to be there – as her 'best man'. 'I know that only grooms are supposed to have a best man, but I don't care. I want you there,' she had written. Around that time she had also reported graduating *cum laude*, and that she had found a job with a child welfare agency in South Dublin. He had read her joy and happiness clearly between the lines, and had tried to respond in an equally upbeat manner, but he had always felt a deep ache in his heart when he thought of her.

But now he felt so different. Maybe, just maybe, Briana would fill up the emptiness in his life and allow him to leave Saoirse behind. He was therefore delighted when, a week after his return to Boston, he received a letter from her. She wrote enthusiastically about her planned trip: she had booked a flight to arrive on a Saturday early in October. She asked about probable weather conditions and what clothing she should bring. But that was not all she wrote about.

Well, dear Thomas, what are you wearing right now? The new slim-fits? I imagine you wearing those and my hand moving up your legs and between your thighs, feeling a growing, warm bulge.

What do you think of when you go to bed by yourself? I think of you and, as I have a good imagination, can sometimes see you and even feel you beside me. That turns me on! But of course you're not really there, so I've had to take the matter into my own hands a couple of times. It's second best, but will do for now!

Am I embarrassing you? Probably, but I don't care. Ha ha! It's just between us after all. Enjoy me, as I enjoy you, even while we're apart. You can dress me up any way you like – or undress me. The thought of you satisfying yourself while thinking of me really warms me up, so do, and write to tell me how it feels!

He wrote back immediately, trying with limited success to mirror Briana's uninhibited style.

A week later there was a message on his answering machine. It was Saoirse.

'Thomas. Hi. Please call me back as soon as you can.'

Her voice sounded strained. She must just have returned from their honeymoon. It was too late in Ireland to call back, so he left it until the following day. He slept restlessly. She wouldn't have called him like that unless it was important.

He called early the next afternoon; it would be early evening in Dublin.

'Hello, this is Brian.'

'Hello Brian. Thomas here. Saoirse called me yesterday. May I speak with her?'

'Yes, of course. Just a minute.'

He heard some background muttering.

'Hi, Thomas.'

'Hi, Saoirse. What's up?'

'Thomas, I have terrible news.' He could hear that she was

having difficulty getting the words out. 'Briana... was in a... road accident.'

He sat in stunned silence.

'Thomas, she is dead... Are you still there?'

All he could manage was a choked up 'yes'.

'I am so terribly sorry, Thomas. I know that there was something developing between you.'

With difficulty he managed, 'Thank you, Saoirse.'

'I know you're having difficulty talking right now. Do you want me to stay on the line, or would you rather call back or have me call you back?'

'I'll call you back.'

'Okay. Any time. I mean it.'

'Okay. Bye.'

He sat in an armchair for at least an hour, staring straight ahead, while tears rolled down his cheeks.

He left his apartment and walked towards downtown Boston. He wanted to be around people but not talk to anyone. He thought of how he had planned to walk these streets with Briana and imagined the delight she would have experienced with everything.

It was late afternoon when he opened the door to his apartment again. There were two calls on his answering machine, one from Saoirse.

'Thomas, me again. I know you said you'd call back, but it's been hours and I am very worried about you. Please call as soon as you can.'

He glanced at this watch and decided that ten o'clock Irish time would probably not be too late to call.

'Thank goodness you called back. I haven't been able to stop thinking about you and about Briana. It's so unreal that she's gone, she was so full of life.'

'She was supposed to arrive here in Boston in just a few days.'

'I know... she was so happy, she left a message on our answering machine while we were still away. She couldn't wait to tell me, she was so excited.'

'When did it happen?'

'Just over a week ago. I heard when we got back from Italy so we weren't even able to go to her funeral.'

'Where? How?'

'She was driving down to Wexford to visit her brother and his family. She lost control on a bad road and smashed into a tree. She was killed instantly.'

Thomas remained silent, trying to digest the news, trying to imagine Briana's last terrifying seconds. He recalled that she had used the word 'reckless' to describe herself.

'Thomas, I don't know what else to say. I've been in shock too. Try not to spend a lot of time alone. Is there someone you can talk with?'

'I don't know.'

'Well, try to get out. I'm thinking of you, just remember that. And will you call me again within a couple of days, or at any time if it would help? I need to know that you're alright.'

'Okay, Saoirse. You've lost one of your best friends too. I'm so very sorry for you.'

'I know. Take care of yourself, Thomas. Talk soon. Bye for now.'

He poured himself another large Bushmills and relived every minute he had spent with Briana. He put on the jeans she had insisted he buy and imagined her hands on his body. She had wondered what they would look like soaking wet. Inebriated, sad and aroused at the same time he staggered into the bathroom and turned on the shower. He watched the jeans turn an even darker blue. His hands massaged the glistening wet jeans between his thighs as he tried to imagine her standing behind him, using her hands. He almost lost his balance when he came violently. Crumpled down on his knees, sobbing uncontrollably, he called out Briana's name repeatedly. Suddenly he heard himself calling out for Saoirse as his memory flashed back to the afternoon on the beach near Spanish Point.

In the morning he couldn't remember drying himself off and getting into bed. After a late breakfast he pitched the jeans into the bin before wandering around Harvard Square and then across the river into the Soldiers Field Athletics Area and the nearby park. He couldn't get out of his mind how his drunken cries to Briana had suddenly been directed towards Saoirse. Had Briana, however attractive she had been, been no more than a substitute for Saoirse, a way of breaking out of the close bond he still felt with her? That evening he acknowledged to himself that that must indeed have been the dynamic in his sodden mind and, to his chagrin, recognised that he had, in a way, been 'using' Briana. It shocked him to realise how little he understood himself.

CHAPTER 22

1983—1994

Thomas threw himself into his work – it was the only thing that stopped the memories and regrets from crowding in. He tried to raise awareness about the millions of ordinary people, worldwide, who had become the victims of war, violence, government action or inaction, or corporate greed. In December he travelled to London after an IRA car bomb killed six people and injured ninety outside Harrods department store. His first article was rejected because the editor disapproved of its virulent anti-IRA tone. He asked Thomas to revise it, be more objective and avoid revealing his own feelings about the situation.

In regular letters Saoirse wrote that she had started work and that Brian was on a fast upward track in his career, becoming a respected IT consultant in the banking and insurance sectors. He was frequently away on assignment or at international conferences.

In 1984 Thomas joined INN part time and covered urban crime and drugs, interviewing users, petty criminals and victims. As always, he went beyond the statistics to reveal the human faces behind the stories. In June he travelled to India after some two thousand people were killed during the storming of the Sikh shrine in Amritsar. He was fascinated by the culture and the people he met and stayed in India for nearly a month, reporting on the impact of sectarian tensions on the people of the subcontinent. Later he made two highly-praised television documentaries, relying on people he had met in India to do the local reporting. It was his work on India that brought him the renewed attention of INN management.

He joined the INN news team full time in early 1985, usually working from a Boston affiliate station when not travelling, but sometimes having to work from INN Center in New York.

Saoirse wrote that she was very happy and very pregnant. In July she reported that the delivery had gone well, that it was a boy, and they had named him Eoin Tomás O'Donnell.

'We both had a great laugh when we realised we were now the proud parents of E.T. I wanted his middle name to be Tomás, thinking of you. Shhh! Brian doesn't realise that, I don't think.'

Several months later Thomas had reason to visit Dublin. Brian and Saoirse invited him over for dinner. She looked wonderful as a young mother and Brian was witty and charming, as she had described him way back in 1979. But he did not feel comfortable, and spent more time than was probably appropriate looking at Saoirse. Twice he thought he caught signals from her that all was not as it seemed, but decided that he must have been imagining things.

He became a key personality on INN, travelling the world as well as the United States, remaining focused on 'the people behind the news'. He had neither the time nor the interest to form a new relationship.

Saoirse continued to write regularly; she had assumed more organisational responsibility although she was working only part-time. Eoin was in a day-care centre three days a week.

In early 1987 she wrote that was pregnant again; eight months later she gave birth to a daughter, whom she named Briana. This time, she said, she had been very upfront with Brian about the source of the name, that it was not only him but also her former friend. She wrote that her mother would be moving from Strabane to Dublin; they had found an apartment near where she and Brian would soon be living, in a 'fantastic' house near Herbert Park in the upmarket Ballsbridge area. Her mother would help to look after the children. She wrote little about Brian, other than to say he had accepted a senior position at Irish Allied Bank, in charge of IT at the vice-presidential level.

Thomas remembered how he had reacted to Brian's father and

that character Reilly, and wondered if Brian was indeed becoming like his father. It worried him that Saoirse rarely wrote anything about him and nothing at all about their relationship.

The futile thought kept coming back to him that he should have been the father of her children, that he should have stayed in Dublin no matter what she had said. Occasionally his thoughts depressed him, but he was very happy with the ongoing correspondence between them, and the years flew by. In 1990 he was once again in Dublin; this time she joined him for dinner in a restaurant near his hotel. Though she was bright and cheerful, especially when talking about her work and the children, Thomas again got the feeling that she was not as happy as she pretended to be. He desperately wanted to know how she really was, but didn't pry.

Had he made a terrible mistake by not pursuing Saoirse with greater determination? Had she made a mistake by following her head rather than her heart when she moved to Dublin? Why did they see each other so rarely when, as Thomas mused occasionally during his melancholic moods, they were true soul mates? He laughed at himself too, because he wasn't even sure if he believed in the idea. But he had no other words to describe the extraordinary connection he felt with her. Nevertheless, the bitter fact was that there were 3000 miles of ocean separating them.

CHAPTER 23

On a chilly February morning in 1994 in New York, a senior INN executive offered him what he had been hoping for, but it came as a surprise nonetheless.

'Thomas, we would like you to go to London to be our deputy bureau chief there. You'll be working with Bob Winters and probably replacing him in a year or so, as he wishes to return to the US. I'd like you to go to London next week to spend a few days with Bob. If all goes as we hope, you'll be in place there by May.

'We know you'll have things to arrange, but one reason we thought of you is that you have no family to tie you down. And most of all, of course, we really appreciate the work you've done. Congratulations!'

He wrote a quick letter to Saoirse that evening, sharing his delight at the fact that he would now be only a short flight away from Dublin. He hoped he would see her and the children soon. Only after he had sealed the letter did he realise he had neither mentioned nor asked about Brian.

Thomas and Bob had met before and got on very well. He was given a tour of the office and studio space, met everyone, and they discussed current and upcoming events, as far as those could be foreseen. They agreed a division of responsibilities.

He was taken to see various rental properties by an estate agent. He chose a bright, furnished two-bedroom apartment in South Kensington, in an elegant white five-storey Georgian house, one of a long row stretching the length of the street. He was very excited.

Ten days later, back in Boston, he received Saoirse's reply.

Dearest Thomas,

I am so happy for you. Congratulations! And I do hope to see you soon.

The children are doing very well. My mother is getting old and frail. Minding the children is not something she is able for anymore. But with the children both at school, there is less need, and we have someone who picks them up and looks after them after school.

Brian is doing very well at IAB, but I see less and less of him. He works very hard and there always seem to be special events and dinners he has to go to. I worry that the children see so little of their father. But: when he does have time he's very good with them, and even tends to spoil them. If I say something about that he tells me to 'cut the child psychology crap', which hurts sometimes. I don't think he means it quite the way it sounds.

I have my own big news too. I have been given a wonderful position in the Department of Education and Science, helping to create policy and mechanisms to better help disadvantaged and troubled children and youth. I've been at that for two weeks now. It's going to be very challenging and I will get to meet and work with many interesting people. The only disadvantage is, the only children I get to relate to directly are my own. But I believe I can make a contribution.

You hold a very special place in my heart, Thomas. Let me know your new address and phone number in London.

With warm affection, as always
Saoirse

The impression he continued to get about Saoirse's married life disturbed him. He determined that he would fly to Dublin as soon as possible, whether as part of a journalistic trip or privately.

He spent Easter with his aging parents before flying to London a few days later.

'How are you, my dear?' his mother asked, in that same tone of voice he had heard so often when she ritualistically greeted her 'friends'.

'How do you find London?' his father asked, as if more concerned about the state of the city than the state of his son.

He found the visit depressing, as usual, but with the experience of years he survived the ordeal and left wondering if he would ever see his parents again.

In London, a taxi took him to the estate agent, who drove him to 43 Stanhope Gardens and explained how everything worked. He got himself unpacked and organised and wrote a quick note to Saoirse. He scouted the neighbourhood, noting shops, pubs, and restaurants and found he was only a five-minute walk from Gloucester Road tube station. It was an ideal location.

The next morning he took the tube to Holborn, near INN's UK offices and studios. He was interested first and foremost in developments in Ireland. The previous months had seen extensive consultations and complicated announcements from all sides. London and Dublin were heavily engaged in the process, with even President Clinton weighing in on some issues, as when he dropped a long-standing ban on the IRA's political leader, Gerry Adams, entering the United States.

He planned a visit to Belfast and Dublin, wanting to learn what those directly involved thought of the peace process, which was repeatedly marred by violence from both Unionist and Republican sides. Fortunately his office had a very efficient organiser, a woman who knew her way around. If she was not able to fix interviews then probably nobody could. He left it to her to make appointments and book travel, but insisted he wanted to spend a weekend in Dublin for personal reasons.

Three weeks later he arrived in Dublin and stayed in the Westbury Hotel, just off Grafton Street. He met with two government officials for what turned out to be informative talks. They gave him more insight into the tricky road that Prime Minister Reynolds's government was trying to navigate. There was optimism, however, that there would be an agreed ceasefire soon and the people of Northern Ireland could rest easy again after 25 years of violence.

Shortly before four o'clock he took a seat in the hotel lobby to wait for Saoirse, who had promised to meet him after work. It was now almost 11 years since the wedding. He wondered how much she had changed. She was now 43, after all, and he was 50.

He did not have to wonder for long. She was smartly dressed in dark grey business wear. Her hair was the same colour, her figure had not changed and he could still see the attractive woman he had met in Foyle's bar almost sixteen years before. His heart pounded more than he had expected. She walked over to him quickly, wearing her familiar wide smile. They gave each other a long hug and kisses on the cheek.

When Thomas had poured the tea, Saoirse looked at him carefully.

'You haven't put on any extra weight, the way so many men do at your age. There is grey in your hair, but you still have it all. In fact, you look great. It's wonderful to see you, Thomas.' She spoke the last sentence with warmth.

'You look almost the same as you did when we first met, do you know that? How are you, Saoirse, and how are the kids?'

'They're doing very well. Eoin is almost nine and Briana is six and a half. They're active and high-spirited. Quite a handful sometimes, but a lot of fun. You must meet them. In fact I have a plan for that.'

She told him about some of the initiatives her department was working on to better meet the needs of various groups of children and young people. This included special needs education, psychological services, and working with parents, particularly in dysfunctional families. Most of her work took place in and around meetings throughout the country. These were tiring but also exciting, because of the many committed and wonderful people involved. She said she felt she was making a significant contribution.

'Terrific. I'm delighted to hear all this. It's amazing to think you are now working in a government department. I can still remember when you announced you were starting at Trinity. You've come such a long way since then.'

'Now what about you?' she began. 'Tell me all about your new job in London.'

Thomas told his story, about how he was still trying to tell stories from the people's perspective, even if he had to speak to politicians and their deputies once in a while. But he was getting used to that. He enjoyed working in television.

Time flew by and at 5:30 Saoirse said she had to leave.

'Now, about seeing the children: I'd like to take them to the Phoenix Park zoo tomorrow. Will you join us?'

'Great. I was there once by myself, the day before your wedding, as a matter of fact, and it's lovely.'

'After that I will take the children home, but I can arrange for a baby-sitter and come back into town for dinner. How does that sound?'

'Wonderful. And Brian?'

'No, he has something else, I don't know exactly what. He's tied up all of tomorrow. Business meeting and dinner or something.'

Thomas noticed that as she spoke these brief sentences about Brian her expression changed.

'How do you commute? Do you drive?'

'No, I usually take the bus. There's a good service out to Ballsbridge. Tomorrow I'll drive, though. Shall we pick you up?'

'No, I'll take the bus. I even still remember which number to catch. I'll meet you there, in the Tea House. What time?'

'How about 11?'

'Great.'

As she started to walk towards the stairway that led down to the exit, she turned.

'Will you book a table for half seven tomorrow? Il Posto is nearby; remember it?'

'I'll have the concierge book a table. Bye.'

He went out for a walk, eventually sitting down for a dinner in one of the many restaurants in the Temple Bar area. Back in the hotel he made some notes based on the day's interviews. He fell asleep thinking of – and worrying about – Saoirse.

She entered the Tea House on time, two children in tow.

He was introduced as 'Uncle Thomas'.

Eoin shook his hand politely and formally. Briana bounced towards him with a bright smile and a twinkle in her eye. 'Hiya, Uncle Thomas.'

'What can I get you all, before we visit the animals?'

'Tea for me please and some juice for the children would be fine.'

When everything was on the table, Eoin took the initiative.

'Are you American?'

'Yes, I am.'

'I could tell from the way you talk.'

Thomas and Saoirse laughed.

'Mam said you met a long time ago in Belfast.'

'Yes, that's right.'

'Are you really on TV? Mam said you were.'

'Yes, I am, sometimes.'

'Are you an actor?'

'No, I'm a journalist. I talk with people and sometimes that gets on TV.'

'Oh, okay,' but it sounded as if Eoin meant 'boring'.

Briana stared at him without inhibition, smiling whenever she caught his eye.

Tea and juice consumed, they headed towards the door.

'I wanna see the giraffes,' Briana called out.

'I want to see the lions,' said Eoin.

'We'll see them all, don't worry,' Saoirse reassured them.

Once they were in the zoo she was kept busy keeping track of them as they rushed from one viewing point to another. 'Oh look!' they kept exclaiming. Two tiger cubs playing like kittens thrilled Briana. The snakes in the reptile house fascinated Eoin, but Briana found them scary.

Saoirse and Thomas followed the children's lead. He almost took her hand. Though it seemed such a natural gesture, he controlled the impulse.

'Eoin and Briana are delightful. Eoin seems like a perfect little gentleman and Briana… well, she reminds me a lot of her namesake, even though she has your colour hair.'

'Yes, I've often thought that too. If Briana had still been alive I'm sure I would have asked her to be Briana's godmother.'

'Did I ever tell you that Briana once described herself to me as impulsive, spontaneous and reckless?'

'No, I don't think so. But those words are pretty accurate descriptions of both of them, though I hope my little Briana doesn't become too reckless.'

After almost two hours, Briana announced that she was tired and hungry.

'How about you, Eoin? Would you like something to eat as well?'

He nodded and the four of them walked to the Phoenix Café. Saoirse had to negotiate with the children before they could agree on what to eat.

During lunch the children dominated the conversation, exchanging opinions on their favourite animals.

He enjoyed watching Saoirse in the role of mother. She seemed to know exactly what she was doing, which was no surprise of course. It was a perfect family outing and he felt pure joy at being a part of it.

After lunch she dropped him off at St Stephen's Green. He was pleased to hear two voices calling out 'Goodbye, Uncle Thomas'.

She reminded him, 'Il Posto, half seven,' before driving off.

He was there early, of course, and remembered the modern and distinctly Italian décor. At the same time he felt as nervous as a schoolboy on a first date as he awaited Saoirse's arrival.

She entered on time, wearing an elegant deep purple dress.

'I thought you should know, the children approve of you.'

'Well, that's a relief. I enjoyed today and was delighted to meet them at last. Being a mother suits you.'

'Most of the time,' she replied with a laugh.

He raised his glass. 'Here's to us.'

'To us,' she replied, smiling radiantly.

As they finished their entrée, Thomas posed the question he had wanted to ask all along.

'Saoirse, how are you, really? I don't mean your job, I don't mean your children. How are you? Though I hope I'm wrong, I've sensed something in your last letters.'

He saw her expression tighten, and there was a considerable pause before she replied.

'No, I'm not great, Thomas.'

She paused again. He stretched out his hand to take hers.

'We agreed long ago we would always be there for each other. Well, I'm here for you now.'

'Oh, where should I begin? I guess I don't recognise the man I thought I'd married. He's away so much, like today and this evening. He seems only to think of business and money. He's doing very well in that regard. We have a grand house and three cars. But he's not really there for me or the children anymore.'

She averted her eyes and took a short breath.

'I've suggested couples therapy but he won't hear of it. So I don't know how to move forward. Besides, though I have no real evidence, I think that some of his evenings away are not business at all, but…'

'But?'

'I think he has another relationship.'

She dabbed at her eyes with the napkin. As she recovered her composure, the main course arrived. It deflected the conversation to the delicious food.

She turned attention away from herself when they resumed talking.

'What about you? How are you? Nobody special in your life?'

'No, there isn't. Nobody special. I've immersed myself in my work and find that to be exciting and satisfying. I expect it will stay that way. I'm fine.'

'You're such a wonderful man. You don't deserve to be alone.'

'I'm not alone. I'm here with you. That's good enough for me.'

It was her turn again to reach out a hand.

'That doesn't sound good enough to me.'

It was his turn to change the subject.

'I'm going to Belfast tomorrow. I have a cameraman flying in from London, and I'm going to interview a couple of key individuals. But while I'm there, there are other people I'd like to speak with. Can you give me Kevin's phone number? Is Colin still at Foyle's? And I also want to try to find that boy who hit me with the brick back in '78, and maybe his mother.'

'Yes, I'll write Kevin's number down for you and Colin is still at Foyle's, though he works less and is looking to sell the place. He's getting on.'

As they were stirring their coffees, he directed the focus back to Saoirse.

'What are you going to do now?'

She paused before replying.

'I don't know. In this country divorce is illegal.'

'You've got to be joking. Illegal?'

'Yes. There's a lot of activity to try to get it legalised, but… it's still Holy Catholic Ireland."

Thomas shook his head in disbelief.

Saoirse continued. 'Legal separation? Maybe. But for that I'll certainly need a lawyer. Brian and his family have tons of money and I know they will fight any attempt to claim the house, or even the children.'

'But you can't just do nothing, can you?'

'No, I can't. And I will do something.'

'Saoirse, I have no advice to offer you. But I want you to remember that I will always be there for you.'

'I know.'

'Also, and I don't know if I should say this, but I still love you.'

She looked straight at him when she said, 'I know that too. Thank you.'

After a few moments of silence, Thomas asked, 'What are you going to do tomorrow?'

'I'll go to mass with my mother. She really appreciates that now. Then she'll come back with me for Sunday dinner with the children, whom she adores. I don't know whether Brian will be there. To be honest, I don't care, though the children look forward to seeing him.'

'Does Brian know I'm here?'

'Yes, I had to tell him because I was going to bring the children to see you. He knows you're here for your work and that we were going to the zoo. As for tonight, he thinks I'm having dinner with a colleague. Or maybe he thinks I'm having an affair. Wouldn't that be funny?'

She laughed a humourless laugh. Thomas paid and they left.

'Thank you so much for everything today. We'll see each other very soon again, I hope.'

'So do I. And remember what I said. Call or write, any time.'

They embraced and Saoirse aimed a kiss full on his lips, before quickly breaking away.

She picked up a taxi in front of the Shelbourne Hotel and he walked back to the Westbury. Dimming his joy at seeing her again and meeting the children was his concern for her. He couldn't suppress the recurrent feeling that he belonged here in Dublin, with her, and she with him.

He caught a morning train to Belfast and was settled into the Europa Hotel by early afternoon. There was evidence of considerable renovation, but it was recognisably the same place that had been home for two months years before. He called Kevin, married now with three children and sounding very confident. Kevin knew from Saoirse that Thomas would be in Belfast and had been expecting the call. He agreed to meet at the Crown Bar, opposite the hotel, the next evening.

Thomas set off in the direction of the house where Anne and Ryan had lived back in 1978. He found it easily, unchanged except there was no rubble on the street anymore. He rang the bell and waited. A tired-looking man in his sixties opened the door.

'How do you do. My name is Thomas Cassidy. I was a journalist posted to Belfast in 1978 and Anne McEwan offered me tea and kind hospitality back then. Does she still live here?'

'Yes, she does. Just a minute. I'll fetch her.'

The door closed.

A few moments later the door opened again. Anne, like her husband, looked tired and of course older.

'Why, Mr Cassidy, Thomas. What a lovely surprise.'

After a moment's hesitation, she said, 'Will you come in for a cup of tea? It's wonderful to see you again and to know that you haven't forgotten us. Please.'

He was shown into the sitting room, which looked just as it had so many years earlier.

'William, this is the American journalist I spoke to you about so many years ago, the one who came by to talk with me and Ryan after he was hit by something which Ryan or one of his friends had thrown at the British troops.'

'Oh yes, I remember vaguely now. You're very welcome, Mr Cassidy.'

'Thomas, please.'

Anne went off to the kitchen to boil water for tea.

'What brings you back to Belfast, Thomas?' William asked.

'I'm here to speak with a few of today's leaders, now that there seems to be some sort of peace agreement in the making. And I also want to speak with a few people I met in '78, to learn how they have fared since then and how they look at their future in Northern Ireland.'

'Well, if you want my opinion, there will be no cease-fire and all this will drag on for another 25 years. The politicians all say they care about the people, but what they really care about is power. They're just playing silly-bugger games with each other.' William spoke with tired resignation.

Anne came in with a tray and set it down.

'I heard what you said, William. We have to hope. It's the only thing we can do. There was some talk about an IRA cease-fire a few weeks back, but then there were four more killings. So when we read about peace talks now, we don't know what to believe.'

'How, if at all, has life changed for you both since September of 1978?'

'Not so much, really. We see fewer troops on the streets, but the bombings and shootings have been going on, maybe not so many or so random – it's as if they're targeting people and places more carefully. It is safer to go shopping. But William has never been able to find a steady job, so life has been difficult.'

'You had two daughters in addition to Ryan. How are they doing?'

'The girls are both married and doing well.'

'And Ryan? He wanted to study medicine.'

William muttered something and looked down at the floor. Anne sighed.

'No, Ryan never did get to study medicine. A couple of years after you were here he got caught up in some form of IRA activity. I don't think he ever handled a weapon, but he did steal a car that a group used for a getaway. He was picked up and sent to the Maze prison for three years.'

'I am very sorry to hear that, Anne.'

'William was terribly angry. He's still upset. It's been ten years now since Ryan got out. At first William wouldn't let Ryan back in the house.'

'What is Ryan doing?'

'We don't know what he was doing for the first years after he got out. But then he pulled himself together and went into training as a paramedic. He works in an ambulance crew. But William will still hardly speak to him.'

'Do you know where he lives?'

'Yes, I have an address and a telephone number. He lives with his girlfriend.'

'Do you think he would agree to see me?'

'I don't know why not. Here, let me write down the details for you.' She picked up a small note-pad and a pencil.

They chatted on for another twenty minutes, Anne telling him how her daughters were doing, and showing him some photographs.

Thanking them for their time and the tea and wishing them well, Thomas left. While walking back to the hotel, he wondered how many other families there were in Belfast who had had to endure so many years of hardship and heartache.

All attempts to meet with major political players personally had failed, but Thomas's assistant had managed to obtain interviews with key associates of SDLP leader John Hume, Sinn Féin leader Gerry Adams and Ulster Unionist MP James Molyneaux, spread over Monday and Tuesday morning.

To all of them he asked the same question: 'What is your message to the people of Northern Ireland today, the people who have suffered so much over the past 25 years?'

From all he got basically the same answer. All emphasised their commitment to peace and that talks at all levels had been proceeding for some time, including many secret talks. There was slow progress. For the rest, their responses consisted of platitudes about efforts made and the determination shown by 'their' side. When questioned about exactly what these efforts consisted of, Thomas got the same political statements he could read in the newspapers.

Ryan agreed to meet at Foyle's on Tuesday evening. Thomas also tried to contact Owen and learned from his mother that he was married, had joined the RUC, was doing well and living in Armagh. Margaret gave him a telephone number that he called from his room.

'Hello Owen. This is Thomas Cassidy. Do you remem…'

'Thomas! Hey, it's great to hear from you. Where are you?'

They spoke for about half an hour. Owen repeated his gratitude for what Thomas had done for him in 1978, and said that those six months in Brookline had meant a new start. Unfortunately it was not going to be possible to meet up, but Thomas promised that he would do his best to meet on his next trip to Northern Ireland.

'You're a Catholic, Owen. What's it like for you to be in the largely Protestant RUC?'

'It's not so bad. In some districts, like here, they're really making an effort to change the culture, and I'm happy to be a part of that.'

Thomas was delighted that Owen sounded so positive, and that he had been able to arrange that trip to Boston for the angry and fearful young man in 1978 gave him great satisfaction.

At 8 o'clock on Monday evening he entered the Crown Bar, with its mosaic floor, beautifully painted ceiling and long red granite-topped bar. It was very quiet, but Kevin was already there.

He smiled broadly and extended his hand. 'Welcome to Belfast again, Thomas. It's very good to see you. Let me get you a pint – Guinness?'

He suggested they sit in one of the ten snugs. Thomas remembered the withdrawn 16-year-old. The change he had seen at Saoirse's wedding had continued.

'Kevin, you look as if life has been treating you well. You look terrific.'

'I can't complain. Got a good job – I'm general manager now, you know – and the wife and kids are marvellous.'

He talked a bit about his work, the family and the situation in general.

'Do you think the violence will really end?' Thomas asked.

'No. Not yet. I expect we'll be in for more. And it may never end entirely, because the guys carrying guns and bombs will probably carry on for some time, but as criminal gangs. They're into drugs, extortion and whatever. People who have been fighting all their lives don't know anything else.'

'Kevin, what caused you to change from the frightened, withdrawn teenager to, well, what you are now?'

Kevin thought about it. 'There were a few years when I saw myself and everyone around me as just victims, you know? Nothing I could do would make the slightest difference to anything or anyone. I drifted along in my own little world, watching telly a lot. Then my da went into hospital and later died and I felt needed again. I think that's what did it.'

'Well, it's wonderful to see how you've changed, Kevin.'

'Thanks,' he replied, looking slightly embarrassed before continuing, 'You saw Saoirse while you were in Dublin. How is she?'

'She looked really well, she loves her new job and I met the kids of course. They're delightful.'

'Good, but how is she in herself? Did you get any sense of that?'

Thomas hesitated, not sure how open he should be about her, but then she was his sister after all.

'Not great.'

'Though she never speaks openly about anything, that's the impression I get as well. Something is not right between her and Brian.'

'No. It saddens me.'

'You and Saoirse were quite close, back in '78 and later, weren't you?'

'Yes, we were, in fact in a way we still are.'

'I probably shouldn't be saying this, but I sometimes wish that you and she had gone on to build something together.'

'Well, that didn't happen.'

Conversation turned to Kevin's family.

'The children have fortunately not been confronted directly with significant violence, but they do ask why it's happening. It's not easy to explain in a way which makes any sense to them, or to anyone else for that matter, as you know.'

They conversed for another hour or so. It was very relaxed and enjoyable. Saoirse was not mentioned again.

On Tuesday evening Thomas went to Foyle's, which looked unchanged. There were new people behind the bar, of course, and when he enquired he was told Colin might come in later. He ordered a pint and engaged someone in a brief conversation. When he asked how people looked at Northern Ireland's future, he got a short response.

'If only those fuckin' politicians would stop fuckin' around, we'd be fine. They just keep repeating the same useless dance around the same fuckin' issues. Hopeless, the whole fuckin' lot of 'em.'

The man had obviously already had a couple of pints so Thomas didn't pursue the matter further.

A little later Ryan walked in. He was a good-looking young man now, still with a dishevelled mop of dark hair.

'Hello, Mr Cassidy. How are you?'

'Hello, Ryan. Thanks for coming by. And just Thomas, please. Let me get you a drink, if you're not on duty.'

'Half a Harp, thanks. What brings you back here then after all these years?'

'Work. To talk with a few of the "fuckin' politicians" as your man over there calls them. And to a few other people, like yourself and your mother. I met her and your dad on Sunday.'

'Did you?'

'Your mother told me that you got into some trouble not so long after we met, but that you're doing well now. Ambulance paramedic, I understand.'

'Yes, and I really enjoy that. It's very satisfying when you can save someone's life.'

'I remember years ago you said you wanted to become a doctor, and hoped not to get involved with the IRA. But you did. What happened to draw you in?'

'There was a lot of pressure on all of us to help the cause, to fight for freedom and justice and all that crap. I said I wasn't going to go around shooting and bombing, so this guy said I could help by "borrowing" a car and bringing it around to a specified location. I agreed. It was stupid.'

'What happened?'

'I stole a car and drove it to a pub. Next thing I knew I heard a couple of shots and two guys got in, telling me to drive, and fast. I did, but the RUC was onto us and we were cut off. The three of us were arrested and I was sent down without trial.'

'To the Maze.'

'Yeah, that's right. That is one rough place. I mean, there were people like me in there who hadn't really done much, but there were also hard-core sons of bitches who sort of ran the place. Tougher than the prison guards, they were.'

'Were you interrogated?'

'Yeah, for a couple of days they came on pretty strong. Wanted names and places and everything I knew. But I didn't know anything, not even the names of the other guys in the car, so there wasn't much I could tell them. In the end they gave up and told me to enjoy my stay. Well, I was in for three years and never formally charged. Then one day I was released, also without explanation.'

'What did you do then?'

'I had nowhere to go. My da wouldn't speak to me, didn't want me in the house. So I stayed at a friend's house and did some odd jobs for a while. Finally, when I had gotten used to being out, I applied for paramedic training. Found myself a girlfriend. We live together now.'

'Do you think we'll see an end to the Troubles, at long last?'

'I don't know. We all hope, but all this has gotten into the blood of Catholics and Protestants alike. It's not going to be easy to get it out of the system. Medical problems are easier. Antibiotics or blood transfusions can save individuals, but not a society.'

'Ryan, if you were talking to a young lad today who said he was thinking of joining one of the paramilitary groups, what would you say to him?'

'I'd say, don't be a fuckin' eejit. Get yourself a life.'

Thomas bought another round.

'Ryan, have you ever heard of Daly's pub? I don't have time now to go there, but it's a Protestant pub I visited a couple of times back in '78.'

'Daly's? Yeah, and even if you had the time you wouldn't find it. It got bombed by the IRA back around 1982 I think. Three people were killed in that blast.'

Thomas's face must have betrayed something because Ryan asked, 'Did you know anyone there?'

'Yes, a couple of folks. I just hope they weren't hurt.'

When Ryan said he had to go and Colin had not yet appeared, Thomas asked the bar attendant to pass on his best wishes.

CHAPTER 24

During the next couple of busy months Thomas looked forward to receiving the periodic letters from Saoirse, in which she wrote positively about her work and the children. Brian was never mentioned. He also had a very enjoyable dinner with Rupert, who was still with the Manchester *Guardian*, writing mainly about British politics and therefore frequently in London. They continued the amiable debate they had had years before about whether journalists should focus on politicians and other opinion leaders, or on average citizens.

An unexpected telephone call interrupted a quiet evening with a book.

'Hello, Thomas. It's me. Am I calling at a bad moment?'

Saoirse's voice sounded shaky.

'Hi, Saoirse. No, it's fine. What's going on?'

'I probably shouldn't be calling you, but…' A silence followed.

'Saoirse, you called and I'm here for you. Please, what's happened?'

'Thanks, I know, and I really wanted to talk to you. I hope I'm not disturbing anything.'

'I told you, not at all.'

'Okay, well, Brian and I had a real fight a few days ago, not with fists but it may have been close to that.' Her voice sounded as if it was about to break. 'I told him I was fed up with him being away without saying what he was doing or for how long. He got angry and told me to stop trying to control his life. We yelled at each other. Briana came into the room and said something, and he yelled at her. She burst into tears. I told him if he wasn't prepared to be a father and a husband he might as well stay away. He picked up a vase and threw it against a wall, cursing at me. I told him to get out. Thomas, I feel dreadful. Brian's been back in the house a couple of times, sleeping in the guest room. If we see each other we don't speak a word. It's terrible.'

He could hear her crying at the other end of the line.

'God, Saoirse, I wish I were nearby, I just want to hold you right now.'

'I know. I needed to hear that. Thank you,' she replied, with a voice barely more than a whisper.

'Would you like me to fly over? I can manage that.'

'No, not now. For now it's enough for me to know that you're thinking of me. I, I...'

'What are you going to do?' Thomas asked.

'I don't know yet.'

'Okay. Please, Saoirse, stay in touch. I'll be in London for the next week or two, anyway. May I call you?'

'No, don't call. I never know when Brian might be here. But thank you... Hey, I hear Briana crying. I'd better see what's going on.'

She hung up. He poured a glass of wine and paced around his apartment, feeling helpless, and watching the rain pelt down into puddles on the street.

The next week a letter arrived.

Two days after we spoke I went to a lawyer. I want him banned from the house and I want a legal separation. It's not going to be easy to get all that in place, but my lawyer is as good as they get. I have confidence that she will do everything possible. We may even hire a private investigator to establish whether or not he is really having an affair.

Thank you for listening and for thinking of me. I can feel that. And I'll be okay.

Thomas once again welcomed the distractions offered by his work; without that he knew he would be thinking about her and the children continually. He learned that Yasser Arafat had returned from exile to lead the Palestinian National Authority and that he, Yitzhak Rabin and Shimon Peres had established some form of contact, mediated by the United States. Bob and Thomas decided to send a team to Israel and the Palestinian territories to, as usual, speak to people on the ground.

Thomas tried to track down Reginald Adderley. That proved to be very difficult. It was not hard, though, to find out that Adderley had been in and out of jail a couple of times. After a series of phone calls he got a 'last known address', in a rundown area of Slough.

He took a train out and hired a cab to stay with him for as long as required. The driver took him to the address he had been given, a shabby rooming house. The landlady looked at him suspiciously before saying that he wasn't in, but might be at a pub called the Bald Pheasant, just half a mile or so down the road.

The pub looked about as unattractive as a bald pheasant might. Inside he saw what might best be described as a motley crew. Most of the men were unshaven and looked as if they had not enjoyed a haircut for many months, if not longer. Their clothing looked as if it had been picked up from a second-hand store – ten years earlier. Nevertheless, there was laughter. It felt like a clubhouse for the down-and-out, at least for those with enough money to pay for a pint.

Not for the first time in a pub, Thomas felt uncomfortable as he peered through the smoke. It had been almost twenty years since he had seen Adderley, after all.

Sitting in a corner with a companion was, he was quite sure, the person he was looking for. He walked over.

'Reginald? Reginald Adderley?'

The man looked up with vacant eyes. 'Yeah? What've I done now?'

'Nothing, Reginald. I'm Thomas Cassidy. We spoke back in 1978, when you told me about your experiences during Bloody Sunday. Do you remember?'

Adderley smiled, revealing a big toothless gap in his mouth. "Yeah, I remember ye. Ye was one of the officers, weren't ye? Well fuck ye.'

'No Reginald, I'm a journalist and I spoke with you in the Holiday Inn at Heathrow.'

'Journalist? Nah, don't remember no fuckin' journalist. So bugger off.'

Thomas excused himself for the intrusion and left. Once outside he muttered to himself in anger and frustration, drawing worried looks from a couple of passers-by. 'Jesus Christ! Fucking bloody hell!'

He walked back to the waiting taxi.

'Back to the station, sir?'

'No. Stanhope Gardens, South Kensington.'

'Yes, sir!' the driver said with enthusiasm. It was probably the biggest fare he had had in months.

The next day he pondered once again how he could make a hard-hitting programme on the abysmal lack of attention veterans on both sides of the Atlantic were receiving to help them deal with their traumas. Adderley had sacrificed his life for his country, and his country had then sat by and let him go to ruin.

Meanwhile he looked for a plausible reason to visit Dublin again. A ceasefire, to be observed by both the IRA and the Loyalist forces, appeared imminent.

In early August Saoirse phoned. She sounded in control of herself and the situation. Thomas heard a new toughness in her voice, particularly when referring to the situation with Brian.

'The lawyer is terrific, very supportive and also optimistic. There is a private investigator on the case. Brian knows it's a legal battle now, and I hardly see him. But…'

Her voice faltered again before she went on.

'But what's hardest is the children. They know something's not right and even with my professional knowledge I don't always know what to tell them and what not. It's heartbreaking, sometimes.'

'Saoirse, is there anything, anything at all, that I can do to help?'

'No, just… just be there for me and… and well, if there's a chance, I would like to see you again… I'm sorry, Thomas… I…'

Emotions threatened to overwhelm her again.

'You don't have to be sorry, not to me. I'm planning a trip to Dublin and Belfast within two weeks and I'll be free for a weekend. I'll let you know, but call me any time in between if you want, okay?'

'Thank you, my dearest.'

They rang off. He wished he could have flown over right away.

Ten days later he flew to Dublin on a Friday afternoon and checked in again at the Westbury Hotel, where Saoirse met him as before. She looked tired and stressed. She put her arms around him and squeezed him to her tightly without saying a word. Only after a minute or so did she release him, look into his face, manage a wan smile and say, 'Hi! Thank you for being here.'

'I'm just sorry I couldn't come sooner.'

They sat down on a sofa, Thomas looking at her, waiting for her to begin.

He held out a hand, which Saoirse grasped firmly in both of hers. She wiped her eyes and managed a thin smile.

'It's been a nightmare. I'm coping. I have to.'

He reached out for her face, drew it close and gave her a light kiss on the lips before ordering tea. When they had taken their first sips she went on.

'Brian and I communicate via our lawyers. The private investigator discovered where Brian has been staying and with whom. He has been temporarily banned from the house and is very angry. He has the right to see the children every other weekend. So far he hasn't bothered. I have told the children that their da is not coming home again, but that they can see him sometimes. I don't think Eoin will even want to; he's very upset and angry.'

She sounded and looked tough as she spoke, but it came across as a mask.

'My lawyer is terrific. Thank God I have her on my side.'

'And you've got me too. Hey, when you've finished your tea would you like a glass of wine?'

'Yes. Let's see if there is a spot on a terrace somewhere. It's lovely out.'

They were lucky to find a table in the late afternoon sun, at the Duke again. When their glasses had arrived, Thomas raised his and said, 'Here's to you, and that you may find happiness again. What's that blessing we saw on the wall at Durty Nelly's? Something like, May the road rise up to meet you. May the wind be always at your back…'

She continued. 'May the sun shine warm on your face, the rains fall soft upon your fields and until we meet again, may God hold you in the palm of his hand.'

They both laughed, recalling the fond memories.

'Talking about "until we meet again",' Thomas started, 'how much time can you make this weekend?'

'Kevin is coming down. I can be back in the hotel around three tomorrow.'

The sparkle was starting to return to her eyes and Thomas felt a familiar surge of affection and longing to be near her again.

'I'll be waiting for you.'

'Unfortunately, now I do have to get back. I'll see you tomorrow.'

'Say hello to Kevin and the children for me.'

'I will. Don't be getting into any trouble tonight.'

They laughed, and he walked her to the bus stop.

It was about half past three when Saoirse rushed into the hotel looking distraught again.

'Sorry I'm late. Brian showed up all of a sudden this morning and wanted to take the children out. I said their uncle was driving down from Belfast to see them, so we had a row about that. Oh, shit, it's just so hard sometimes.'

She collapsed into his arms again and he held her close, happy to be with her and frustrated with not being able to do anything practical.

'Anyway, Brian left, angry as usual. Kevin arrived, and I'm here.

Kevin sends his greetings. I told the children that I was going into town to see Uncle Thomas and they asked if they could see you too. How about that?'

'I'd love to, if there's time.'

'That can be arranged if you're free tomorrow, but how about a walk now?'

They walked towards St. Patrick's Cathedral and wandered about inside for a few minutes until she said, urgently, 'I'd like to leave now.'

Once outside, Thomas looked at her with questioning eyes. 'What was that all about?'

'I married Brian in a church, before God. Now that same church will not allow me to divorce him. Jesus Christ, His fucking church screws up so many lives.'

She calmed down and looked at him with the same warmth and tenderness he had seen many years before in County Clare, as well as a deep sadness.

'I made a terrible mistake, Thomas,' she began. 'Brian is just like his father, who I never warmed to. Brian is a corporate executive and all he cares about is career and money. I'm as important to him as his flashy Mercedes coupé: a status symbol or something. He doesn't need me. And to think that that was what once attracted me to him. He doesn't depend on me for anything except for being a good housewife and mother, and that's why…' She stopped mid-sentence again.

'I still love you, Saoirse,' he said quietly into her ear.

'I know you do, and that's why it's so good to have you near me again.'

She pulled herself together and said, in a brighter voice, 'I know just where we'll go next.'

She led him down the road until they stood in front of the Brazen Head, which announced itself as 'Ireland's Oldest Pub, Established 1198'.

Over drinks they examined the pictures and posters on the walls. He recognised portraits of James Joyce, Brendan Behan and Jonathan

Swift on the rough stone and brick walls and asked the barman if they had all been in the Brazen Head.

'Aye, they have indeed. As have Irish patriots and revolutionaries like Robert Emmet, Wolfe Tone, Daniel O'Connell and Michael Collins.'

He pointed to another row of portraits.

After finishing their drinks they walked back along the Liffey. He asked whether she knew the Boxty House restaurant in the Temple Bar area. She had heard of it but never been there. It was his turn to lead her by the hand and without too much difficulty he found it.

'What time do you have to be back, Saoirse?'

'No time pressure. Kevin knows how to put children to bed. In fact, do you know what he said? He said to stay away as long as I liked, but to be sure to be back by three tomorrow because that's when he has to head back to Belfast.'

She smiled and he wondered what was going through her mind. She answered his unexpressed question.

'I know what he meant. Part of me would love to stay the night.'

'The other part says?'

'It's too soon. I'm not ready yet. And besides, just as I put a private investigator on Brian's trail, for all I know he's done the same to me. I just don't want to risk throwing a spanner into the legal works at this point.'

'It's entirely up to you, Saoirse. What the first part of you says means a lot to me. But I understand your concern.'

She looked at him with a sad smile.

'Another time… I hope.'

The traditional boxty pancakes were delicious and they did their best to keep their conversation light. Their eyes carried on a different conversation, though.

When they emerged dusk had almost fallen and the streets were crowded and lively. They walked back slowly and had a last drink just short of the taxi stand at the bottom of Grafton Street.

'Would you like to come to Dun Laoghaire tomorrow? I'd like to take the children, mother and Kevin there for lunch. Eoin loves to look at the boats.'

'Sure. Where shall we meet?'

'The easiest place to find is the Marine Hotel. On the terrace, if it's warm enough. At about 11?'

'I'll find it and be there by 11.'

'It's been a wonderful afternoon and evening. Thank you!'

She hesitated briefly before stepping into a taxi. There was a sad smile on her face as she was driven off.

He took a seat on the Marine Hotel's terrace and looked out over the marina, the bay and the families gathering for a Sunday outing. Sun was breaking through the clouds and the morning light sparkled on the water. He felt envious of those happy families. Shortly after 11 a group of five came his way. When they spotted him, Eoin and Briana ran towards him, shouting, 'Uncle Thomas!'

He hugged them both, greeted Saoirse's mother, then Kevin and Saoirse.

'How are you doing, Mrs Kelly? It's so nice to see you here today.'

'Oh, Thomas, I'm getting old. But the little ones do their best to keep me young. It's lovely to see you again.'

The children dominated the conversation, pointing out sailboats setting out from the marina and then a ferry heading out to sea.

After lunch they walked along the pier while Eoin pointed out the boats and yachts that had caught his eye. Saoirse and Kevin kept warning the children not to get too close to the edge. Thomas chatted with her mother.

When she had a chance to speak to him Saoirse said, 'Kevin gave me hell for coming home last night. Maybe he understands me better than I do myself.'

'He's a wonderful guy. But it's your life and you have to move forward in your own way, in your own time.'

'I sometimes wonder what "my" way and "my own time" really mean.'

'You'll stop wondering and know when the time is right.'
'Eoin, be careful!' she called out when Eoin leaned over the edge of the ten-foot drop to the rocks below.
Kevin pulled him back from the edge.
'It really helps not being the only one to have to keep an eye on them.'

While walking back towards where Kevin had parked his car, she found another moment to speak to him.
'Kevin is so sweet. You know what he said this morning?'
'No, but I think you're about to tell me.'
She smiled and went on in a low voice, so as not to be overheard.
'He said if I ever want to go to London for a weekend, he is prepared to come to Dublin with his whole family to mind the children.'
'He's amazing.'
'Yes, for sure. He says it would do me good to get away for a couple of days. But I think he means it would do me good to spend a couple of days with you.'
'Do you think it would do you good?'
She paused before answering.
'Yes. But give me a little more time, will you?'
They reached the car and everyone said goodbye. Thomas and Saoirse did their best to appear casually friendly.

The next day he had a couple of useful interviews in Dublin and took an evening train to Belfast. While he was there, he phoned Kevin and thanked him for coming down to Dublin.
'It was my pleasure. And if you ask me – which you won't because it's none of my bloody business – you two need some time together.'
'Thanks, Kevin.'

A couple of weeks later, he got a call from Saoirse during which she said she was set up to use email. They started to use the medium almost every day. Her frustrating legal battle continued, but there was some sort of end in sight.

'Are you getting any rest at all, Saoirse?'

'No, not much. And my mother is not well – a thrombosis. She has seen a doctor and is taking medication, but she may have to go to the hospital if the drugs don't work.'

'You have too much on your plate.'

'I do, but there's not much I can do about it now.'

'Do your best to stay in touch, even if you only have time for brief messages.'

'I'll do my best, I promise.'

In November Yitzhak Rabin, Shimon Peres and Yasser Arafat were announced as joint winners of the Nobel peace prize for their efforts to bring peace to the Middle East. INN had wanted a permanent presence in Israel and the Palestinian territories for some time, and decided the time was right. Thomas travelled to Jerusalem, Tel Aviv and Ramallah with Helen Richardson, who would establish the permanent presence. They talked with Israelis and Palestinians, and encountered hope as well as a great deal of mistrust – in that way it felt strangely similar to Northern Ireland.

Saoirse reported that she and Brian had finally agreed to sell the house. She had put in an offer on a four-bedroom house in Sandymount, counting on the likelihood that her mother would also move in. Conveyancing was planned for early February.

He called a week before Christmas and thought she sounded at the end of her tether, with the pressure of Christmas adding to the burden.

Two days later he got a call from Kevin.

'Hello, Kevin. What a surprise. How did you get my number?'

'Saoirse gave it to me. I told her I had some information for you about the situation in the North. I don't, but I want to talk to you about her.'

'Is she all right?'

'I don't think so. She's extremely stressed and I'm worried. So is Mother.'

'Is there anything I can do, Kevin?'

'Well, I may be out of line but here's what I have in mind. I'd like to send her to London right after Christmas for a few days or even a week. Margaret, the children and I will go to Dublin to look after things there. To put it plainly, I would like you to do your best to look after Saoirse and make sure she gets some rest.'

'Of course. But will she agree?'

'Don't know, but I wanted to ask you first.'

'I don't plan to go anywhere between Christmas and New Year. So if you can persuade her, that's terrific.'

'I'll be in touch soon.'

Two days later Kevin called back. Saoirse had agreed and would fly to London on the 27th.

During the next couple of days Thomas busied himself cleaning and tidying the apartment and even bought a few Christmas decorations.

Saoirse complained about the plot that he and Kevin had hatched, but also said how much she was looking forward to the break.

When December 27th arrived, Thomas was filled with happy anticipation, as well as concern. He took the Gatwick Express from Victoria Station, was at the airport in good time and waited outside Arrivals impatiently. Finally she appeared, dragging a small suitcase behind her.

'You look absolutely exhausted, Saoirse.'

'I am, I really am, but also delighted to be here.'

They looked into each other's eyes and gave each other a light kiss on the lips.

'My job is to make sure you get some rest. So give me your bag.'

She followed obediently as he led her to the platform. It was just after four when the taxi pulled up in front of the 19th-century townhouse.

'Impressive.'

'This is only the outside. Come in quickly. It's warmer there.'

Thomas led her up one flight of stairs, through another door and into his London home.

'It's lovely, Thomas.'

She handed him her coat and collapsed on the sofa.

'God, I don't remember when I have felt so tired. Maybe that's because I can finally let go of everything for a few days.'

'You don't have to do anything now. In fact, I forbid it.'

He lit a few candles and drew the curtains.

'What may I offer you? Or would you like to take a nap first?'

'No, no nap. But I will go to bed early. So how about a glass of white wine, if you have it.'

While he fetched two glasses, she wandered around the living room, inspecting. She paused in front of a photograph of herself.

'Hey, that was in Ballyvaughan, wasn't it?'

'It was. I love that photograph.'

They sat down next to each other and raised their glasses. They looked deep into each other's eyes for what seemed like a long time.

'Welcome, Saoirse. You're so very welcome. It's good to have you here at last.'

'I'm very happy to be here. Thanks to you and Kevin.'

Thomas had determined not to question her about the situation back in Dublin. She would talk about that when she was ready to.

'You know, I don't even know how long you want to stay.'

'If you're good to me and if you'll have me, I'll stay until the second. That's when my return flight is booked for.'

'Oh, I'll have you, all right. And I'll knock myself out to be good to you.'

'In fact, Kevin said I wouldn't be welcome back earlier.'

'Well then, let me show you the rest of the apartment.'

Thomas showed her the kitchen, the bathroom, the main bedroom and then the guest room, where the bed was neatly made and towels laid out.

'Expecting someone else?'
'No, I just didn't know...'
She interrupted him. 'You didn't know what?'
'Well, in Dublin you said that your head...'
'Oh, I left that behind.'
Thomas closed the guestroom door and kissed her. She replied, her tongue seeking out the corners of his mouth.
'But don't expect too much of me tonight,' she whispered
'Just having you beside me is enough... for now anyway.'

He warmed up a seafood stew, cooked some rice and set the table with two tall white candles while she called Dublin to say she had arrived safely and to check on how things were there.
'I'm not a great cook, so this is store-bought, readymade. But it's from a good fishmonger.'
'It smells delicious.'
After dinner, she apologised for the fact that she just had to get some sleep, promising to be better company tomorrow. When she was under the covers, he kissed her goodnight, saying he was going to tidy up and would join her shortly. But he could hardly finish what he was saying before her eyes closed.

She was still sleeping when he woke up. He got out from under the duvet quietly, put on his dressing gown, turned up the heating and put on fresh coffee. Some light snow had fallen overnight, settling on branches and the tops of cars.
As he was setting the table for breakfast he heard noises from the bedroom. She emerged fully dressed, but with sleep still in her eyes.
'Good morning.'
'Good morning, my darling. How did you sleep?'
'I don't know, I don't remember a thing.'
'That's a good sign. Would you like a cup of coffee while I get dressed?'

'So what would you like to do while you're here, my darling?'

'I just want to spend time with you, walk around, sleep in, look into shops, enjoy nice meals and relish not having to run after things and people. I want to enjoy my freedom for a couple of days.'

'And what about a West End musical if I can get tickets?'

'Well, that would be absolutely fabulous!'

He made a call to the office and they used their influence to book two box seats for *Cats* the following evening. Saoirse was thrilled.

They spent the afternoon wandering around shops in Knightsbridge, still decked out in Christmas finery while sales were on everywhere. She bought small toys for the children. It was cold and when he asked where she might like to have dinner, she quickly said, 'Let's eat in again.' They bought tapas-style snacks in the Harrods food hall and took a taxi back to Kensington.

He lit the candles and opened a bottle of his best wine before sitting down on the sofa next to her. He sensed that something was weighing on her mind.

'Anything you want to talk about?'

There was a slight note of irritation in her response.

'No, it's nothing. But I've been in overdrive for so many months now. Don't expect me to drop everything just because I'm here. So yes, I am thinking of the children and about legal proceedings, wondering how that's going to work out and then there's the move in less than two months. I'm not even thinking about work, fortunately.'

'Okay, I understand that. But please, if there's anything you want to talk about, then say so. I'd rather do that than watch you stew over all kinds of things.'

'Thanks. And sorry if I sounded bitchy just then.'

'You're allowed.'

After dinner, at her insistence, he slid a videotape into the player and showed her a couple of his recent television appearances. She laughed at his 'television presenter' persona.

He refilled the glasses and put his arm around her. She snuggled in close. A few minutes later he was surprised and taken aback when he felt her chest starting to heave, just before heart-rending sobs burst forth.

He pulled her up against him even more firmly and let her sob. He was relieved that the emotional pressures that she had kept a lid on for so long, were now escaping. After a few minutes she settled down. He offered a clean handkerchief. She dried her eyes and sat up straight.

'I'm sorry.'

'No need for sorries.'

When she opened her mouth again she almost yelled.

'I fucked up, fucked up!'

He tried to think of something to say, but given the strength of her emotions he held himself back and let her go on. Much as it hurt him to see her so deeply upset he also realised that he was probably the only person in the world with whom she could let herself go like this.

'Fifteen years ago I made a choice. I loved you, Thomas. But I refused to listen to my heart and followed my head instead. I decided to be selfish and independent and… look where it's got me.'

'You do have a wonderful career and two lovely children.'

She interrupted. 'Yes, but look where it's left *me*. I'm exhausted most of the time and angry much of it. Yes, my career gives me a lot of satisfaction, and Eoin and Briana are delightful. But, but… and I hate to say this, it sounds so maudlin and self-pitying, but happy I'm not. I feel like I gave away the right to be happy.'

She started to cry again, while Thomas kept quiet, stroking her hair gently.

After a couple of minutes Saoirse continued.

'And… well, Eoin and Briana. They don't have a father anymore, and sometimes I think I'm so fucking busy creating policies and plans to help other children that I ignore my own. Should I even be here, leaving them in the hands of their aunt and uncle?'

He countered, 'They love the children, and Kevin insisted that he would take care of them so you could get a break. Don't do this to yourself.'

She looked him directly in the eyes.

'I made one huge mistake. When I moved to Dublin I wanted my freedom; I didn't want anyone to be dependent on me. I wanted out of the trap which I had felt myself to be in for so long in Belfast.'

'I remember you talked about that.'

'Brian seemed ideal because he didn't need me.'

'And you thought that I would.'

'No,' she corrected him. 'I *knew* that you would.

She continued to look directly at him, her eyes sadder than ever.

'I've finally realised that when two people truly love each other, they also need each other. Not in a clingy way, but…'

He wrapped an arm around her again.

'Thomas, I loved you, but I was just, well, afraid. I was afraid to commit to you. I love you, Thomas. And I need you.'

She rested her head on his shoulder as a few quiet tears rolled down her cheeks. His own eyes filled as well.

She looked exhausted after this catharsis so he gently urged her to get up, move to the bedroom and go to bed. Obediently, she followed his instructions. He tucked her in and gave her a kiss.

'I love you, Saoirse. I'll be with you in a few minutes. If you're up for it, I'll give you a massage.'

She smiled, but by the time he slid under the duvet beside her she was fast asleep again. He pulled her head up onto his chest, put an arm around her, and spent at least an hour thinking about everything she had said before he too fell asleep.

This time when Thomas woke up, he found Saoirse looking at him.

'Thank you.'

'Good morning. For what?'

'For letting me ventilate last night.'

'Do you feel better for it?'

'Yes. And if the offer of a massage still stands tonight I'll try to stay awake for it. But now, may I use your bath?'

'As hot and as long as you like. There is some bubble stuff I bought specially for you. Enjoy.'

Thomas wondered whether he should raise the memory, and at breakfast did so.

'Saoirse, there was one moment during the reception which I will never forget. We had just finished our dance. A tear almost rolled down your cheek. Do you remember that?'

She hesitated before saying, 'Yes.'

Her expression regained its cheerfulness and she said, 'Now let's plan to do something fun today. It's raining and looks pretty cold and miserable but we'll not let that stop us.'

The next couple of days they ducked in and out of the Tube and, sheltered by an umbrella, visited Oxford Street, the Tate Gallery and restaurants, as well as, of course, the musical *Cats*. On New Year's Eve they stayed indoors. Neither wanted to get caught up in a lot of public festivities.

He cooked a meal of salmon steaks with mashed potatoes and asparagus tips, complemented by a bottle of Chardonnay. She phoned home to wish everyone a Happy New Year and they watched a silly but entertaining show on television while lounging in each other's arms.

'Thomas, you mentioned that tear. Well... I don't know exactly how to put this, but it surprised me as much as it probably surprised you. There I was, just married, and I... I saw you slipping out of my life. It was so strange. I didn't know what to make of it.'

'What can I say to that, my darling? Except that you never did slip out of my life. We're together again and, well, I'll not slip out of your life, ever. I promise."

At the stroke of midnight, Thomas uncorked a bottle of champagne and filled two glasses to overflowing. They clinked glasses and Saoirse moved in very close. She kissed him deeply.

'Thomas, I want to make love to you tonight as I have never done before. Happy New Year!'

Half an hour later they went to bed. He allowed her to take all the initiatives. Her hands stroked him: his head, his torso, his legs. He let waves of sensation wash over him, as she caressed his body all over. He took some initiatives and she moaned softly. Lips and tongues joined in on the exploration.

'Thomas, take me. I want you inside me.'

She guided him inside her and before long fireworks only they were aware of rang in the New Year.

He woke up, put his head back on the pillow, and waited. A half hour later she stirred.

'Happy New Year, my darling.'

'Happy New Year. It sure got off on the right foot,' she replied.

'With a bang, I'd say.'

They put their arms around each other and lay there another half hour.

'How about going down to Brighton,' she suggested enthusiastically.

'Brighton?'

'Yes, Brighton. Ever been there?'

'No. Okay, let's do it.'

Dressed warmly, they set off for Victoria Station after breakfast.

A brisk walk south from Brighton station took them to an area of narrow streets with many shops, pubs and restaurants known as The Lanes.

They stopped in front of a jewellery shop. He pointed to an emerald ring.

'Isn't that ring beautiful. Look.'

'It's magnificent! You know, emerald is my favourite stone.'

He took her by the hand and pulled her into the shop.

The woman behind the counter greeted them. 'Good morning. Can I help you?'

'Yes. We'd like to see an emerald ring which you have in your window.'

'Thomas, what are you doing?'

'Hush now.'

The woman pulled out a tray, which included three emerald rings. Thomas pointed out the one that had caught his eye and she plucked it from the tray.

'Saoirse, show us your finger… No, not that way. Don't be rude.'

The ring was a little too small.

'I can size it for you,' the woman said. She measured Saoirse's finger. 'It will take me half an hour.'

They exchanged glances.

'It is beautiful Thomas, but …'

'We'll take it. We'll be back after lunch.'

They found a table by the window in English's Seafood Restaurant. Raising his glass, he said, 'Once again, Happy New Year, Saoirse.'

'Happy New Year. And thank you. I'm overwhelmed!'

'Now we're even. See? I always wear the Claddagh ring you gave me. This is so you won't forget me, or how we celebrated the New Year.'

'As if I would ever forget either.'

He lifted her hand and gave it a kiss.

'That's where the new ring will be shortly. Through it and this one,' he said as he held up the Claddagh ring, 'we will always be together. Will you wear it always?'

'No, of course not.'

He looked surprised and hurt, and she laughed at him.

'Thomas, emerald is a soft and fragile stone. I'll not be wearing it when I'm scrubbing floors or working in the garden. I'll protect it carefully, and wear it whenever I can. Okay?'

'I just learned something new.'

They walked down to the sea and to the end of Brighton Pier. People were out on the beach, enjoying the fine weather. To the west lay the Grand Hotel.

'Hard to believe that the IRA blew the face off that hotel ten years ago, isn't it?' he said.

As it began to get dark they headed back to the station.
Back at the apartment, Thomas lit the candles and put on some soft music.
'Thomas, let's dance.'
'Like ten years ago?'
'Forget that, and remember this.'
They danced cheek to cheek for about fifteen minutes.
He smiled at her. 'No tears?'
'No tears.'
They made love slowly and intensely, aware that this was their last opportunity for some time.

They were up early in order to get Saoirse to a mid-morning flight.
They didn't say much after they got to Gatwick; it was if everything that needed saying had been said.

CHAPTER 25

Saoirse moved to her new Sandymount home at the end of February. She and Thomas remained in regular touch and looked for opportunities to spend a day or a night and occasionally a weekend together. This worked out every month or so but those moments always felt rushed and unsatisfactory.

He visited Belfast in April amidst difficult negotiations, and went to Sarajevo in June. The siege there had been lifted the previous year.

In 1996 the IRA showed its teeth again with heavy bomb attacks in the London Docklands and in Manchester. In July 1997 the Provisional IRA renewed its ceasefire and shortly thereafter signed the so-called Mitchell Principles, allowing multi-party talks to resume. Thomas and INN covered these developments carefully, always exploring the hopes, fears and feelings of the average citizens.

During May of 1998 the Belfast Agreement was signed and many people hoped that the Troubles were finally coming to an end. The agreement was supported by an overwhelming majority of citizens in both Northern Ireland and the Republic.

Newsworthy events in the world allowed Thomas to focus his attention on other things, at least for some of the time. Saoirse's post-Christmas visit had only confirmed for him that they needed to be together. But they weren't, and whenever he slowed down enough to reflect, he experienced recurrent loneliness and frustration. She had admitted that she, too, was dependent on him and confessed to bouts of loneliness, in spite of her wonderful colleagues, her children, and her mother. Why were they so caught up in the lives they had created for themselves while each continuing to accept their own — and the other's — personal loneliness as inevitable 'facts of life'?

Saoirse's mother died after a mercifully short illness. Thomas flew over for the funeral but there was no time during the brief visit for just the two of them. The fact that he could only be with her for such a short time during a period of grief just underscored what he felt was an impoverished existence.

He phoned a week after the funeral to ask how they were all getting on.

'It's hard getting used to the fact that she's not here anymore. Same goes for the kids; they really loved her and mam doted on them. It's been busy at work but I seem to have less energy; even a few of my colleagues have remarked on it.'

'Saoirse, I think it's time for you to take a major break, to recharge.'

'I wish,' she replied.

'I'm serious. I've been thinking that you and I could travel to the northwest sometime soon. I've never yet visited Yeats Country. How would that sound, for a week?'

'It sounds lovely, but the kids?'

'Well, I overheard Eoin say he would love to visit his uncle in Belfast; I'm sure they would welcome him. As for Briana, wouldn't Amy's parents welcome her for a week?' Amy was Briana's best friend.

Saoirse sounded dubious.

'I don't know, Thomas, I…'

'I know you're tired now and organising everything is just more stuff to do. But will you think about it seriously?'

She hesitated before answering. 'Okay, I'll think about it seriously. Maybe later in the summer.'

'You know, we could even visit Omagh and you could show me where you grew up. I'd really like that.'

'I'll think about it, I promise.'

She finally accepted the suggestion and they pencilled a week into their diaries. He flew to Dublin on a Saturday in early August and stayed in a hotel near Sandymount. He phoned Saoirse when he had settled in.

'Everything okay with you?'

'Hi, yes I'm fine.' She sounded her normal self again. 'I put Eoin on a train to Belfast this morning. He was all excited about making his first solo train journey. But I can't drop Briana off at Amy's until the morning so I'm going to have to leave you by yourself tonight.'

'It'll be a night like many others then: just thinking about you.'

'But don't think of me all night. Get some sleep too. I'll be there around half ten.'

Saoirse's hair, fairly short but smartly styled, now showed some streaks of grey, but the features that had so attracted him twenty years earlier were still unmistakably present. He knew that he too had changed; he had turned 53 four weeks earlier. His hair was shorter and definitely greying, and his face showed the years. People had told him he looked 'distinguished' when he appeared on television. He wasn't sure whether he appreciated that adjective.

'Well, they're right. I think you look very distinguished, too,' she said when he told her. 'It's a compliment, so live with it!'

It was late afternoon when they arrived at the Sligo Park Hotel; after that they planned to use B&Bs. As soon as they had dropped their cases, she placed her arms around his waist, drew back her head, and looked at him with the familiar smile.

She simply said, 'Hiya.'

'Hiya. Are you the beautiful woman I fell in love with twenty years ago?'

'Aye, the very same. Well, not quite the same, after twenty years. And are you the same man who bowled me over in Foyle's?'

'Same answer as yours. Yes, but not totally the same.'

'You look good enough to me.'

He pulled her close and kissed her lips.

'You know, you look quite different from the you I now see on the telly once in a while. Less distinguished, softer, more real, more cuddlable, if that's even a word.'

'When you smile like that you're still the most cuddlable woman in the world.'

'Okay. Let's see if they'll serve us a drink.'

They went down to the terrace adjoining the lounge, where warm sunlight filtered through the trees. The stress Saoirse had been carrying seemed to flow out of her and she became younger in front of his eyes.

'A whole week together again, at long last. This is wonderful,' she said as she stretched out and relaxed all the muscles in her body.

'Saoirse, I have something very serious to tell you.'

She looked alarmed for a moment, but saw from his expression that he was having her on. She looked back at him in mock seriousness, and said,

'What's that then?'

'I love you, very much.'

'Now that is serious. What are we going to do about it?'

'There's nothing can be done about it, I'm afraid. It's incurable.'

'In that case, finish your drink and we'll… take a walk through the gardens.'

She laughed at his expression on hearing her suggestion, which clearly wasn't what he expected.

They admired the flowering plants, the trees, and the hills in the background. On their way back to the room she picked up a couple of folders and a tourist map of the area.

She kicked off her shoes and lay down on the bed to study them while Thomas lay down beside.

She whispered conspiratorially in his ear.

'I have a secret. Will you promise not to tell anyone?'

'Sure.'

'I think – but I'm not a hundred percent sure yet – that I still love you.'

'Then why the hell aren't we together all the time?'

'Good question. I… have some other important news. The divorce came through at last! Divorce was legalised last year and, well, I'm a free woman again. Only I can't be married by the Church again – as if I would want to.'

He took her is his arms and they lay side by side for about half an hour.

After dinner they went under the duvet, cuddling and kissing. Gradually all restraints were released and he felt as if the 26-year-old Saoirse was with him again. They fell asleep with satisfied smiles.

The next morning they drove straight through Sligo town and on to Drumcliff and W.B. Yeats's grave in the small churchyard, well tended and quiet, in the shadow of Ben Bulben, the table mountain that Yeats had loved so much.

'Would you like to be buried in a lovely place like this?' she asked unexpectedly.

He laughed. 'Well, I don't expect that to come up for a long time yet. But no, I would want to be cremated, now that you ask, and perhaps have my ashes scattered on top of a mountain like that one,' as he pointed towards Ben Bulben.

'Just wondering. And I don't want it to come up for a long time either.'

As they sat on a wall of the graveyard he pulled a thin volume of Yeats's poetry from his pocket. He read 'The Lake Isle of Innisfree'.

'That was my first and favourite Yeats poem.'

'Does it refer to a real place?'

'No, they say not.'

'Well, it's lovely.'

'If it were real, would you join me there in a "small cabin of clay and wattles made"?'

'Sure, but I don't think "nine bean rows" would keep us fed.'

'I guess you're right.'

During the next days they toured the countryside at their leisure, much as they had done in Clare so many years before. It was never boring and, rain or shine, they enjoyed everything they did and laughed a great deal. During one of the first evenings, Thomas gave her a wrapped parcel.

'I brought something for you, Saoirse.'

'Oooh, what is it?'

She felt the parcel and immediately knew.

'It's a book.'

She unwrapped it.

'*Beyond the Shamrock*, by Tomás Kenny. Who's that?'

He smiled at her.

'It's you!'

'Aye, the very same indeed.'

'You haven't mentioned this for so many years. Congratulations. Wow! But why "Tomás Kenny"?'

'I didn't mention it because it was such a struggle and I was never sure it could ever get published. It finally was, just after Christmas and I wanted to surprise you. As for "Tomás Kenny": INN agreed that to use my real name might confuse people. This is fiction. So I used my grandfather's first name and my mother's maiden name.'

'Thank you. What a surprise. Now I'll be reading all night.'

'Oh no! Then I'll have to take it back because I have different plans. But just open it and read what I wrote on the inside cover.'

She opened it, and read, 'For Saoirse, my inspiration and my only true love.'

'Shall I try to give you a little more inspiration tonight then?'

'That sounds more like what I had in mind.'

Two days later she read the book for a couple of hours while it rained outside.

'I'm enjoying it. You really write well. But…'

'Thank you.'

'…but the two main characters, Michael and Carol: I sort of feel that I know them.'

'I'm not surprised.'

'Oh?'

'I have to confess, there are autobiographical elements in the character of Michael and in developing Carol's character, well, I used aspects of you as my model.'

'But Michael is such an eejit sometimes.'

'Well, that's pretty accurate then, isn't it?'

'But there's something else, Thomas,' she continued. 'Michael is sometimes a very sad character. He is often painfully lonely. Is that also a reflection of you?'

He held her eyes but didn't answer with words.

Her eyes suddenly looked sad. 'Of course it is. For almost twenty years I've hoped that you would find an ideal woman to share your life with and you never did…' She stopped, realising they were moving into an extremely sensitive area.

Very softly he said, 'I did find an ideal woman, Saoirse. Twenty years ago. There could never be anyone else.'

A tear trickled down her cheek.

'Thomas, my love, my dear, dear Thomas.' She put down the book and moved up against his body. He folded his arms around her.

When she spoke again it was just above a whisper.

'And I pushed you away. I wanted my freedom. And… what did it get me? A loveless relationship, feeling trapped by it, and often feeling very, very lonely myself.'

He kissed her forehead and her eyes gently, before saying, 'We can always try to start from the beginning again, my darling.'

She shot him a look that seemed to say, 'You're crazy,' so he quickly added, 'We can't go back to 1978 nor erase what's happened in our lives. I mean, we can decide that from now on we start again, you and I, on a new beginning.'

'I hope we can.'

They continued to lie in each other's arms, trying to come to terms with what that might involve, until she said, 'Make love to me, Thomas.'

When they had finished they lay with eyes locked onto each

other's. The next morning they argued briefly about whose eyes had closed first.

On Saturday they visited Omagh. Saoirse showed him where she had completed her A-levels at Omagh Academy and took him by the small, tidy house with an overgrown front yard where she and her family had lived. He listened as she lost herself in memories of those days, which had been happy ones. Not once did she mention the Troubles, which started shortly before she left school and the family moved to Belfast, where her father was looking for work.

They walked up the busy main street, where Saoirse remembered some shops and reminisced about others she had known that had since disappeared. There were one or two premises that were boarded up, but no other outward signs of the Troubles. She went into several shops to savour memories rather than with any intention of buying anything, while he followed along, smiling with shared pleasure. Market Street turned to High Street and they continued towards the grey courthouse with its four Grecian columns and a heraldic lion and unicorn protecting a crown on the top.

Two RUC vehicles appeared and officers calmly moved people away from the courthouse, citing routine security measures. The pair obediently moved along towards the Sacred Heart Church and its impressive twin spires. Following the road to the right of the church they came across McElroy's, which Saoirse also remembered from long ago, and went in for lunch. On the outside it looked like a cute cottage, but inside it was spacious. Two more police vehicles drove by at a high speed.

While they ate she continued to share memories of her teenage years in Omagh.

Suddenly a heavy boom rattled the windows.

'Jesus Christ, that was a big one,' a man called out. Two men dashed for the door, obviously intent on finding out more. Saoirse grew pale and put down her fork.

'Oh God.'

They sat in silence waiting for more news. After a few minutes one of the men returned, out of breath.

'Near the bottom of Market Street… black smoke… screams …'

They heard the wail of distant sirens.

Saoirse sat absolutely still. Silence had fallen on the restaurant. Some sat stone-faced, some with tears streaming from their eyes. Shocked silence eventually gave way to sporadic tumultuous conversation.

Saoirse and Thomas waited.

The second man came running in and announced, breathlessly, 'Ran down as far as I could. It's all cordoned off. There are bodies all over the place. Fires. Stores shattered.'

More sirens could be heard converging on the scene.

Saoirse raised a fisted hand to her ashen face and stared straight in front of her, while other people continued to sit in shocked silence or talked wildly with each other.

'I should go down and see, I…'

In a pleading voice she said, 'Thomas, please don't.'

He stopped short and looked at Saoirse's face. Tears were streaming down her cheeks. He reached over and held her hands.

'There could be another bomb and I… Please stay. I need you with me, Thomas.'

He pulled his chair around to sit beside her and drew her towards him.

'I'm here, I'll stay. I'm sorry.'

After a few minutes she looked at him with pain in her eyes and said, 'I want to go, now, and get away as far as possible from here.'

He put enough money on the table to cover their bill, pulled her out of the chair and made for the door.

She led him a long way around back to the car, staying as far as possible away from Market Street. Everywhere people were running around with shock and disbelief etched on their faces.

Once they got to the car, he said, 'Give me the keys.'

She slid into the passenger's seat, staring straight ahead. Many cars were leaving and emergency vehicles were everywhere. It took a while before Thomas found the highway heading south. A police checkpoint halted their progress briefly.

After half an hour he stopped the car in a lay-by, reached over, and put his arms around her.

'Omagh, my hometown. Why? Why? It was supposed to be over. Will this madness never stop?'

He had no answers, but held her tightly and after a few minutes said, 'I'm sorry, Saoirse, that I even thought about leaving you there alone.'

She looked at him again. 'I need you, Thomas. I needed you then, and I need you now.'

He had never heard anyone say these words to him so plaintively before. 'I know that now.'

Some cows stared curiously at the car from just over a fence. Swallows swooped down over the field. Few cars came by, and it was an incongruously quiet, pastoral scene.

'Let's go on. I want to get back to Dublin.'

He concentrated on driving, and both were lost in their own thoughts. As they approached the city she took over the driving again. 'I'm okay now. I know the way.' She navigated to his hotel.

'Stay with me tonight, Saoirse. No need to go home yet.'

'Yes, please,' she replied, with a weak smile.

A bellhop helped unnecessarily with the luggage. 'Have you heard about Omagh, sir?' he asked.

'Yes, we were there,' Thomas replied, while giving the man a look which said, 'And we won't discuss it further.'

She flopped down onto the bed and stared at the ceiling. He lay down beside her. She turned and put her arms around him and they lay there in silence. Occasionally he could feel her body heaving with grief.

'Shall I order something from room service?'

'Yes, please,' she replied softly.

Two salads and a bottle of chilled white wine were brought in. He poured two glasses. She walked over to the television and turned it on.

News of the bombing was non-stop. Real IRA – 29 reported dead — several hundred wounded — images of carnage — hospitals reporting floods of victims. Hysteria – pain – suffering – shock – anger — speculation about the impact on the peace process — political statements — outrage.

She turned it off and sat down heavily in an armchair.

'What a God-forsaken, fucking country! I never want to go back to the north. Never!' Saoirse's anger showed itself again, almost to Thomas's relief.

'And I don't want you ever to go back there either. "The Troubles", people call it. Well, those fucking troubles cost me Niall, Dermot, almost lost me Kevin and were for sure partly responsible for the loss of my da. I won't have them costing me you as well.'

'They won't, my darling.'

She pulled his head towards her and kissed him fiercely.

'I love you, Thomas, dammit. I love you, and I need you.'

They picked at their salads and had another glass of wine. When they went to bed she clutched him tightly. His arms held her as close as possible until he felt her relax and heard the gentle breathing of sleep. He lay awake for what felt like hours. It had taken a horrendous tragedy, an unspeakable act of terror, but he felt he was finally where he had belonged for so many years: with Saoirse, in deep, loving need of each other.

The next morning she was still subdued but, rested, also able to smile again. They went around the corner to Roly's Bistro for breakfast and walked around Herbert Park, while the sun broke through the clouds occasionally. The fields were full of young people playing football or hockey and the tennis courts were busy. It was a normal Sunday. Omagh seemed far away. They sat by a pond hand in hand and watched the fish and the ducks, choosing silence most of the time.

'Will I see you more often now?' she finally asked.

'Just as often as I can make it and as you have time for. I promise.'

'That's not enough anymore.'

'No, it isn't. I will do my very, very best to change that, and finally move to Dublin.'

She kissed him, smiled, and said, 'Thank you, my love.'

'But I have to say something you may not like. I will want to return to Omagh within a week or two.'

She gave him a disapproving look.

'I will not go to witness and report on violence. I will go only if I am sure that things have settled down, and just to speak to people there. I really feel I have to do that.'

Saoirse shook her head and examined the gravel beneath the bench. She sighed and then replied, 'I know you want to and maybe have to. I don't like the idea, but I can't keep you from doing your work.'

'Thanks for understanding, my love.'

In the early afternoon they picked up Briana, who was delighted to see 'Uncle Thomas' there as well. She gave him a big hug.

'Did you have a good time?' she asked brightly.

'Yes, we did. It was lovely. And how about you, what did you and Amy get up to?'

Briana told about her week in lengthy and enthusiastic detail as they drove into the city to pick up Eoin at the station. He also had lots to tell about his week in Belfast with his cousins.

The four of them had a simple dinner near Sandymount before Saoirse dropped him back at the hotel.

'Me here, you in your house… it's not right anymore.'

'No, it isn't.'

CHAPTER 26

Thomas continued to work from his London office, coordinating correspondents in Rwanda, Islamabad, Jordan, Brussels and other international focal points. He visited Omagh with a cameraman for two days, travelling via Belfast, and stimulated INN to create a new series of reports focusing on the victims of man-made – and natural – disasters worldwide. They needed more than water, food, medicine and temporary shelter. They needed qualified help in order to deal with the traumas they had suffered. The INN campaign mobilised some significant action, but of course far from enough.

He and Saoirse spoke and emailed frequently but their intention to see each other often didn't work out as they had hoped. One reason, which he did not disclose to Saoirse, was that he sometimes felt unwell. He was unusually tired and had frequent and persistent headaches. A doctor told him he had high blood pressure and a high cholesterol count, prescribed medication and offered dietary advice.

It was early December before Thomas travelled to Dublin again. He stayed at the Herbert Park hotel and interviewed several people before meeting Saoirse late on a Friday afternoon.

'It's been too long again,' she began. 'We promised not to let so much time elapse between moments of seeing each other. Why can't we change that?' She sounded desperate and even a little angry.

'I know.'

'Well, we need to look for an answer. I'm ready for a glass of wine, and I booked the Lobster Pot for seven o'clock. It's just around the corner.'

She continued, 'I know your work is in London and mine is here, but…' She threw up her arms in a gesture of despair.

'Not a week goes by that I don't think about what I can do to arrange my life and work differently. And I'm working on a plan. I'd like to spend alternate weeks in Dublin and London if I'm not travelling somewhere. I'm the Bureau Chief in London and can't just pick up and leave. But I've been in touch with New York. I said I wanted more time for myself, even at the cost of some salary. I've asked them to consider appointing Conrad Armstrong as my deputy, to take charge of things when I'm not there. He's experienced enough.'

She brightened up at the news. 'That sounds promising. How soon do you think you can get it sorted?'

'I've even looked into apartment rentals in Dublin. There's a wide choice and some of the prices seem reasonable.'

'Now I'm getting excited, but that bit about apartment rentals is pretty dumb. Let's talk more over dinner.'

When they had made their selections from the extensive seafood menu, she picked up where they had left off.

'There are some good rental apartments for sure. But, my love, why are you thinking of that? You know that I have a house, I have a double bed, and I have a room which could be converted to be your office.'

Thomas looked into her eyes and smiled.

'I would just like to have you beside me at night' she continued. 'I'd like you to sit at our table, laugh with us, watch the telly with us, be with us. It just sounds so silly that you might be in an apartment nearby. I'd be bumping into you at Tesco's and you'd be cooking up your own dinner less than a mile from Sandymount. We'd still end up feeling lonely.'

'That is silly, isn't it?'

'What are you doing for Christmas?' she asked suddenly.

'I have no plans.'

'Would you like to spend it with us? The children would love it. Eoin even suggested it and Briana agreed.'

'That sounds a lot better than anything else I might have been able to arrange. I'd be delighted.'

'Just one thing. I may have to put you in the spare bedroom. I don't know that I'm ready yet to share my bed with you with the children around.'

'I understand. That's fine.'

'Hey, couldn't you protest at least a little?' she laughed.

On Saturday they went with the children into Dublin city centre, where the Christmas lights and decorations dispelled the gloom of a dark and drizzly December day. On Sunday they went to a cinema in the large shopping centre in suburban Dundrum for an afternoon movie before he caught an evening flight back to London.

He returned to Dublin for five days over Christmas and was delighted to be able to experience the day with enthusiastic children. Some snow fell on Christmas night, and on St Stephen's Day they drove up into the Dublin Mountains, where more snow had fallen. The children made a snowman and Thomas joined them in a snowball fight.

Saoirse had changed her mind and, after a conversation with the children, told him he could share her bed after all.

During one evening when the children were in bed she spoke to him seriously.

'I haven't said anything yet, but sometimes you don't look well. Is anything wrong?'

Thomas tried to laugh it off. 'The doctor said my cholesterol count and my blood pressure are on the high side. But I've got medication and I'm fine.'

'Well, you don't always look fine. Like now, in the evenings especially. And you should have told me.'

'I'll be fine, please don't worry. I should try to get a bit more exercise, though, and I'll watch my diet.'

'Well, you'd better – and no secrets, okay?'

In January Saoirse spent a long weekend in London. They had high tea at the Ritz, took in a show, and spent hours wandering the shopping streets. Above all, they laughed a lot and made the most of two nights together.

Saoirse again expressed concern about his health.

'I'm serious. You're not looking well. You should see a specialist.'

'Hey, I'm not 40 anymore. I'm fine. But I'll think about your advice and discuss it with my doctor.'

'Don't think about it, just do it. Promise?'

'Yes, as soon as I can.'

With more than a hint of exasperation she exclaimed, 'Shit, Thomas. Don't keep putting it off.'

When he visited Dublin again in February she had made an appointment for him. The specialist advised him to undergo a series of tests as soon as possible.

They continued to see each other regularly but Thomas encountered opposition from INN on his plan to divide his time between two cities.

Tests showed there were constrictions of two major arteries around his heart and he was placed on stronger medication.

Thomas spent lonely evenings fighting his growing frustration. He had the successful career he could only have dreamed about years earlier. He was admired and respected by his colleagues, but he was still lonely a great deal of the time. Now, finally, the way out of that feeling seemed so close; all he had to do was go to Dublin and be with Saoirse. He felt trapped by his own success, and also felt that he was letting her down.

It all seemed so glaringly obvious. Twenty years earlier he had begged her to let him move to Dublin, to build his career there as a journalist, writer, teacher. What was stopping him now? Why not simply resign from INN, do freelance work and offer his services to

RTE, the Irish state broadcaster? But back then he was 34. Now he was 55. He was afraid of taking a radical step. He had become addicted to his work and to his success.

He had found a high degree of journalistic freedom at INN, but felt imprisoned in his role. Saoirse had sought freedom in Dublin and now also told of feeling imprisoned in the aftermath of a disastrous marriage.

They did manage to see each other more frequently; those brief days were like moments spent inhaling deeply of life-giving emotional oxygen before once again diving into the maelstrom of their everyday lives.

The next Christmas rolled around quickly. This time he spent ten days with Saoirse and the children, enough for both of them to leave their everyday lives behind them.

During one relaxed evening he said, 'At last we can spend wonderful quiet evenings together. It feels like heaven.'

'It only took us 21 years to get there,' Saoirse replied ruefully. 'And we're still not where we would like to be.'

In June 2000 he told her that he and a cameraman would be going to Portadown.

'What would you be wanting to go to Portadown for?' she asked, frowning.

'Because the annual trouble is expected there. I'd like to understand why.'

'There's always trouble there. And I thought you promised never to go into the North again.' She looked and sounded upset.

'I'll be very careful, I promise.'

'I really wish you wouldn't, Thomas. I can't tell you where you can and can't go for your work and I guess there are more dangerous places in the world than Portadown. But I still wish you wouldn't.'

He gently cupped his hands around her face and kissed her. 'Don't worry, please, Saoirse.'

Thomas and cameraman Gary Levitt arrived in Portadown on Friday 30 June. They were shocked by the sight of an eight-foot high wall, the so-called 'peace line', separating Loyalist and Nationalist areas. Thomas had seen the same thing in Belfast years before, but in such a small town it looked even more grotesque. They interviewed an Orangeman who called for all-out war against the Irish, and a Catholic who expressed his virulent hatred of Loyalists and especially the Orange Order and the RUC, which, he said, had long lost all credibility as Northern Ireland's impartial policing organisation. But, he said, the IRA was too weak in Portadown to deal effectively with Loyalist 'gangs and thugs'.

From the hotel in Armagh Thomas phoned Owen on the number he had kept from many years earlier. Owen answered and they quickly arranged to meet at the hotel the next evening.

It was a delightful meeting. Owen again thanked Thomas profusely for his help back in '78. He was now a sergeant, had three children, and was extremely happy with his life.

'Do you still listen to The Undertones?'

'Yes, occasionally. Did your nephew like the record, by the way?'

'I have no nephew,' Thomas answered sheepishly. Owen laughed and they ordered another round.

'So why are you here?' Owen asked.

'My cameraman and I are here to report on the annual trouble in Portadown.'

'Well, you'd better be careful. It gets pretty violent there sometimes. In fact I'll probably be there myself over the coming days.'

'I'll be careful,' Thomas replied.

Thomas and Gary visited Drumcree Church, which had a long history of being associated with the Orange Order. Marches to and from the church had always gone through Catholic/Nationalist parts of town, and every year that led to renewed conflict.

On Tuesday 4 July Thomas remembered to call Eoin on his birthday. Saoirse said she had been following the news of the summer violence across Northern Ireland, much of it triggered by the annual unrest in Portadown. She begged him again to be especially careful.

Having heard rumours of another imminent confrontation at the Drumcree barricade, meant to prevent Loyalists from marching through Catholic areas, Thomas and Gary took their camera there. They witnessed a tense stand-off between rock- and abuse-throwing protesters and security forces. Thomas was vaguely aware of an uncomfortable pressure in his chest. He broke out in a cold sweat but shrugged it off. He tried to get in among the protesters in an attempt to get someone to explain to the viewers what it was all about. It was impossible, however, to obtain a coherent statement, given the noise and the volatility of the situation. The crowd surged towards the police barricade and Thomas and Gary were pushed and shoved in various directions.

They saw a large vehicle moving through the police lines. 'Water cannon!' a few voices called out. Thomas and Gary decided it was time to get away and did their best to elbow their way out of the crowd, some of which was still moving forward to taunt the water cannon. Thomas suddenly felt a sharp pain in his chest. His knees buckled and he fell to the ground, losing consciousness.

A bystander shouted, 'The bastards have shot this old guy!' but Gary saw immediately that there was no bullet wound. While trying to protect his bulky camera he knelt down beside Thomas and confirmed that he was still breathing. Calling for help, he found a couple of demonstrators willing to lift him out of the crush to the side of the road, where he was carefully laid down on the grass.

Thomas regained partial consciousness. 'It's my heart, I think. Call Saoirse...' He and Gary had shared personal contact numbers as a precaution.

Less than fifteen minutes later an ambulance appeared. The paramedics worked swiftly and told Gary they would take Thomas to Craigavon Area Hospital, just a few miles away. Within a few minutes the ambulance was driving off at speed, while Gary stayed behind to retrieve their hire car. He tried to call Saoirse but got no response.

By the time Gary got to the hospital Thomas was on a heart monitor. He was conscious but could hardly talk, groggy from medication and uncomfortable with an oxygen mask in front of his mouth. The nurse said that an ECG and blood tests had been taken, that he was stable, but they were as yet unable to discount the possibility of serious damage. The small hospital would be unable to do more and a transfer to the Royal Victoria in Belfast was imminent.

Gary tried to call Saoirse again. It was late and he got a sleepy voice, but when he had identified himself and said it was about Thomas her voice became alert immediately. He explained what had happened and that Thomas would be moved to Belfast. Saoirse phoned Kevin and asked him to check on Thomas in the morning and to keep her informed. Worried and angry, she didn't sleep the rest of the night.

Kevin got to the hospital before nine o'clock. He learned that doctors had performed an angioplasty and that Thomas's condition was stable. They expressed concern, however, and the need for surgery could not be ruled out. They would keep him under observation for a couple of days, meaning he would probably be discharged on Saturday. Kevin called Saoirse with the update. She said that she would drive up from Dublin to fetch him. She did not want him to return to his solitary apartment in London and would prepare the guest room for him.

On Friday Owen appeared at his bedside, in full uniform.

'Come to take a statement, sergeant?'

'No, if I had I'd have to book you for ignoring police warnings. How are you?'

'I guess I've been better, but I feel okay now. How did you find out about me?'

'We hear just about everything on police radio. When I heard that an American journalist was down it wasn't difficult to put two and two together.'

'Thanks very much for coming Owen. And how did things end in Portadown?'

'As well as can be expected. No serious injuries and after a while the police got things under control.'

'Owen, it means a great deal to me that you showed up here.'

'That's okay. Anything less would have been dereliction of moral duty. Thank you, Mr Cassidy... er, Thomas.'

They shook hands firmly.

Saoirse arrived at the hospital shortly after noon. Kevin had arrived half an hour earlier to ensure that Thomas be ready to travel. He was advised to make an appointment with a cardiologist in two weeks' time; they referred him to the cardiovascular unit at Dublin's Mater Hospital, assuming he would still be there, and advised him not to return to work for the time being.

When they were finally settled in her car, she looked at him gravely.

'You frightened the hell out of me. When Gary phoned I thought I had again lost someone to the Troubles. How do you feel now?'

'Just tired. But it's wonderful to see you and I'm really grateful for all the trouble you've gone to. Thank you for that, my darling, and for inviting me to convalesce in your home for a few days.'

'Not a few days. Two weeks at least. I want you where I can keep an eye on you, as you don't seem to be able to take care of yourself. I'll lock you in a room if I think I can't trust you not to run off on some new crazy adventure. I'm still angry that you went, you know.'

'I should have listened to you. I'm sorry.'

'What do you remember happening last Tuesday?'

Thomas told her what he could remember, and then about Owen's visit. 'You know, that was one of the most loveliest moments, for me, in my whole involvement with Northern Ireland – aside from you, of course.'

'You deserve no less. You're just a great person, if incredibly stubborn sometimes. But — and I want you to promise this — you must never go back to Northern Ireland to cover any form of trouble or violence. I mean it.'

'Okay, I promise.'

She looked at him sceptically.

'No really, I mean it.'

During the drive to Dublin, he dozed while she focused on driving, once in a while reaching out a hand to touch him and shoot a quick smile his way.

'Hey, I prepared the guest room for you, but if you prefer you can sleep with me. That way I can keep an eye on you even better. Whatever you like and are comfortable with.'

'I'd rather be with you, as long as you don't expect much of me for a while. Sex is forbidden for now, they told me.'

Saoirse laughed.

'I think I can live with that… for a while.'

The next two weeks were extraordinarily happy ones for Thomas. Saoirse went to work and the children to school, leaving him free to read and go for short walks and visit nearby shops or pubs when the weather was fine. He also put together an account of what he had seen and heard in Portadown. The office told him to take all the time he needed before even thinking about returning to work.

He learned to play a couple of games with the children and helped out in the kitchen. Saoirse took him to several shops to buy the clothes he needed. He felt wonderfully comfortable; it was as if they were married, something which she also remarked on one evening. At night they enjoyed the warmth of each other's company, but restricted themselves to cuddling. As his strength came back so did his desire, but he followed doctor's orders and she made sure he did.

Two weeks after he had arrived in Dublin, Saoirse took him to the Mater Hospital and stayed for the day.

'I want to hear what the doctors say. I can't count on you to tell me everything, can I?'

'It's almost embarrassing to be looked after like this.'

'Get used to it. You're bloody useless at looking after yourself.'

The cardiologist ordered a range of tests and returned in the afternoon. There continued to be cause for concern, double by-pass surgery might be necessary, but they preferred to wait until the tests had been redone in another two weeks. Would he still be in Dublin then, or should his records be sent to the London Chest Hospital, St Bartholomew's?

Saoirse didn't give Thomas time to reply.

'He will stay in Dublin, doctor.'

She looked at Thomas with an expression that indicated she would countenance no argument. Once he had acquiesced she gave him a long, affectionate kiss.

'Careful! Isn't that against doctors' orders?'

'Fuck the doctors. Oh, excuse me, doctor! I didn't mean that personally.'

The doctor laughed.

He looked and felt better and stronger every day. The medication was doing its work, but the uncertainty about his condition continued to weigh on them both. She took a few afternoons off work. Sometimes with the children, sometimes without, they visited the Dublin Mountains, Wicklow and Glendalough, avoiding the hectic city centre.

Rupert had heard about what happened in Portadown and during a visit to Dublin came to the Sandymount home for a relaxed and friendly dinner.

In late August Thomas successfully underwent surgery. Following a week in hospital he again convalesced under Saoirse's care, aided for the first week by a home nurse while Saoirse was at work.

He resigned from his bureau chief position at INN but agreed to write and, using Irish television's RTE studios, to appear on occasional INN programmes. Together with Saoirse he went to London in November to clear his belongings from the Kensington apartment. Sandymount was now home.

Thomas read a great deal and started to write a new novel, tentatively titled *In Search of Freedom*. Into it he tried to weave the theme of misguided life choices and regret for time irretrievably lost. His protagonist came to realise that a sought-for 'freedom' could result in isolation and loneliness and could only ever be truly found within a loving, committed relationship. He shared some of his writing with Saoirse, who sometimes listened with tear-filled eyes. He realised that he was writing about them and about himself, and struggled to move from autobiographical writing to true fiction.

Eventually Thomas and Saoirse were able to resume their sexual relationship and found themselves leading a life of loving harmony. He felt loved, cared for, and protected as never before. He realised how much he had missed in his life and sometimes, when he was alone, this moved him to silent tears. What he had now was worth more than all his professional success. He started to understand what the concept of 'home' meant, or should mean. In Philadelphia he had not had that. Now he did his very best to play his part in providing a caring home for Eoin and Briana – though it was sometimes challenging, given their adolescence and increasing sense of personal identity. Eoin was fifteen, Briana thirteen. Eoin was turning into a serious young lad, while Briana continued to show the same spirit that had made the 'other' Briana so attractive to him: spontaneous, sometimes impulsive, and very open.

They went on occasional holidays, including a week with the children in a rented cottage near Doolin. Briana told him the legend of Tír na nÓg, the Otherworld. From the heights of the Cliffs of Moher they all stared into the west, wondering how far they would have to travel to reach Tír na nÓg.

In early 2003 Thomas was deeply shocked by news of Ben Anderson's brutal murder in Pakistan. He had been taken hostage while reporting from the country's tribal regions in the northwest of the country, focusing on the plight of women and girls. There were indeed more dangerous places in the world than Portadown or Belfast. Outraged at the murder, Thomas worked overtime to put together a programme in Ben's honour, using video links with INN journalists all over the globe and with the full co-operation of the people managing the facilities at RTE, as well as of course the *Washington Post*.

In 2004 he wrote several lengthy articles relating to the child sexual abuse scandal in the Irish Catholic Church. The public outcry was increasing amid reports that both the Church and the Gardaí had ignored or suppressed accounts of abuse. News of these reports generated a great deal of interest in the United States, vindicating his efforts. The stories also touched him personally, and he managed several challenging and occasionally heated interviews with prelates. Saoirse reported that the organisations she worked so hard for frequently encountered suspected or even probable victims but were also constantly frustrated in their attempts to get to the truth about what had happened. There were even unconfirmed reports that some instances of abuse had taken place inside the Pro Cathedral.

'You'll never catch me entering that place again,' was Saoirse's angry response. 'I wonder whether the fucking priest who married me was guilty.'

She very rarely used the f-word any more.

Most evenings he was at home, where Saoirse also preferred him to be. However, in March 2004 he travelled to Kosovo in the aftermath of violent unrest that left 28 dead. A year later he travelled to Beirut to cover a huge demonstration a month after the assassination of former Prime Minister Rafik Hariri. He always had to argue his case for travel, though, and Saoirse held her breath until he returned safely. He was never caught in the middle of violence and once he was home he was able to say, 'See? You don't need to worry so much.' He enjoyed the opportunity to undertake these trips and they boosted his sense of professional self-confidence. The children were impressed by the exotic destinations he visited.

On 24 February 2006 the newspapers and television news announced that permission had been granted for a demonstration and march in Dublin by a Unionist organisation called 'Love Ulster'. Included among the planned marchers would be members of the anti-Catholic Orange Order. While sanctioned by mainstream parties in Dublin, the march was opposed by a radical splinter group calling itself the Republican Sinn Féin. Some trouble was expected but the Gardaí expressed confidence that they could keep everything under control. Thomas was fascinated by this strange phenomenon – a Unionist group marching in Dublin, and resolved to go to O'Connell Street the next morning.

Saoirse was upset. 'Thomas, why? Isn't it time you left this kind of work to younger people?'

'I'm here, it's in Dublin, covering this sort of march is part of my work and besides, the Gardaí will make sure everything is kept under control. I'll be fine.'

'That's what you said before you went to Portadown. Isn't it time to put me first? Don't you care how much I will worry about you? Stick to interviews, writing and television appearances.'

'What will I write or talk about if I don't cover some events first-hand? I can't just wait until I see what's on the evening news. This is Dublin, not Belfast or Portadown. It'll be peaceful.'

'Dublin has not always been peaceful, as you should know. And there's no precedent for this: a Unionist march including the Orange Order in the centre of Dublin for God's sake. You don't know that it will be peaceful.'

'I'll be very careful, I promise. Don't worry.'

'Yes, that's just what you said six years ago. You're being pig-headed and stubborn.'

'Saoirse, I am going and I'm sorry that you're so upset about it.'
'Well fuck. Just don't count on me to fetch you from a hospital again.'
With that she stomped out of the room.

Saoirse had gone to work when he got up. He took a bus into the city centre, bringing along a small high-definition video camera. He felt bad about the previous evening's argument; they rarely had words. But Saoirse had been unreasonable.

It quickly became clear, however, that the Gardaí were not able to maintain control of a counter demonstration. He managed to ask a couple of demonstrators what they represented. One identified himself as being of the Irish Republican Socialist Party, which had opposed the march from the start. A youth answered that he represented nobody in particular but just wanted to let those Ulster Unionist bastards know they weren't welcome.

Everything got seriously out of hand in front of the General Post Office, which still bore scars of the 1916 uprising. He saw a petrol bomb as well as rocks and bricks being thrown at the police, and a shop window shattered. Several people were randomly attacked, including a pregnant woman. While he was filming that incident several youths attacked him. He was kicked and punched repeatedly and his camera smashed. He caught a glimpse of a youth swinging a hurley at him. A blow to the back of the head sent him crashing to the ground.

'Saoirse!' was his last thought before blacking out.

A bystander saw blood oozing from the back of his head into a dark red puddle and yelled for a garda. An ambulance arrived but it was too late. Thomas was pronounced dead at the scene.

OBITUARY

By Rupert Williams, the *Guardian* (March 7, 2006)

Ten days ago, an outstanding American journalist was brutally killed on the streets of Dublin. Thomas Cassidy had been a personal friend and colleague since his days in Belfast 27 years ago.

Thomas Cassidy (1944 – 2006) began covering the Troubles in Belfast for the *Boston Tribune* in 1978. Later, as INN Bureau Chief in London, he frequently returned to Belfast and Dublin to pursue his deep interest in the human consequences of the ongoing conflict. He was tireless in his pursuit of the stories of normal citizens wherever he went. He went into semi-retirement in late 2000 and had lived in Dublin since.

On 24 February he went into the city centre to cover a march organised by a Loyalist organisation. The Gardaí failed to maintain control, and violent rioting broke out. Cassidy was savagely beaten after filming a pregnant woman being set upon. He died at the scene.

The perpetrator was quickly apprehended. He was a 23-year-old tourist from Europe who, high on drugs and alcohol, had joined in a street-fight the causes of which he did not understand and could not have cared less about. Cassidy died a tragic and indirect victim of the Troubles that he had spent so many years covering.

The funeral took place in Christ Church, Sandymount, Dublin. There to mourn were his partner, Saoirse O'Donnell, whom he had met in Belfast shortly after arriving there, her two children and her brother from Belfast, accompanied by his entire family. There was a large number of Dublin friends and neighbours. A dozen journalists represented the press corps, from INN London and various newspapers in Ireland and the UK, while two television crews sought broadcast material.

One surprising guest was a PSNI sergeant from Armagh, who asked that his identity not be revealed. He told me that Cassidy had been instrumental in creating an opportunity for him, then a teenager, to spend six months in the Boston area with an American family. During those months he had been able to regain his balance, following his traumatic adolescence in Belfast.

The service was a solemn but simple occasion. Following moving words from Saoirse O'Donnell's brother and her son, and a wonderful rendition of 'O'Connell's Lamentation' played on the guitar by her brother, Saoirse managed these words through her tears, speaking to a large portrait photograph of Cassidy but in a voice which was clearly meant for all present to hear:

Thomas, my love, we finally had five wonderful years together. Had we both had the courage to follow our feelings from the start we might have had 27.

I wish you had listened to me, and had not put yourself in harm's way once again. But you were dedicated to your profession, and to the people whose suffering you covered with such warmth and humanity.

I have loved you for more than 27 years, as you have loved me. It was so difficult for us, for so long, to deal with that.

Now you will always live in my heart. You will not be forgotten.

I don't know where you are now, but I hope you are at peace and thinking of me.

Thank you, my love, for being the wonderful person who you were.

A reception followed in a nearby hotel. In true Irish fashion, what started as a subdued gathering turned into a celebration of the life of someone who had been important to so many. Accompanied by her brother, Saoirse sang what she said was Cassidy's favourite Gaelic song, 'Eibhlin a Rún'.

Saoirse confided that his ashes would be scattered in the Dublin Mountains, as he would have wished.

ACKNOWLEDGEMENTS

I owe a debt of gratitude first of all to Lucy McCarraher, Managing Editor of Rethink Press, for her support and encouragement over a period of almost two years. Verity Ridgman, my editor at Rethink, did a wonderful job, offering many helpful comments as well as doing a meticulous final edit. Jane Dixon-Smith designed a brilliant cover.

Throughout the sometimes painful process of writing initial chapters, members of the Amsterdam Writers Group gave critical, sometimes confronting but always constructive feedback. Special mention goes to John Donnelly and Brian Christopher, who both read the whole book at earlier stages.

Finally, I am grateful to Linda Gunther, Karen Walters and Erik Boers for taking the time to read and comment on the entire work at different points in its development.

Writing is mostly a solitary endeavour but the encouragement, support and critical eye of others is, at least for me, indispensible.

THE AUTHOR

Nico Swaan is a retired Dutch-Canadian who has lived in The Netherlands for the greater portion of his life.

He spent his professional life helping individuals, throughout many countries around the world, to increase their personal awareness and enhance their interpersonal skills, through training programmes and personal coaching. He is co-author of *Making Connections*, published by Bookshaker in 2012. His keen interest in human behaviour and the complexities of human relationships forms one of the foundations for his current fiction writing.

For over forty years Nico has been extremely interested in the Irish nation, its people and its culture. He was struck by the apparent contradictions between the relaxed, friendly and fun loving world he found during his many visits, and the country's conflict-ridden and often bloody history. In particular, he was moved and mystified by that bitter, decades-long conflict in Northern Ireland known as 'The Troubles'.

Printed in Great Britain
by Amazon.co.uk, Ltd.,
Marston Gate.